WARMAGE: UNRESTRAINED

WARMAGE: UNRESTRAINED

THE NEVER ENDING WAR™ BOOK TWO

MARTHA CARR

MICHAEL ANDERLE

LMBPN

DISRUPTIVE IMAGINATION®

LMBPN Publishing
PMB 196, 2540 South Maryland Pkwy
Las Vegas, NV 89109

First US edition, March 2020
Version 1.01, April 2020
ebook ISBN: 978-1-64202-817-1
Print ISBN: 978-1-64202-821-8

THE WARMAGE: UNRESTRAINED TEAM

Thanks to our Beta Team:
James Caplan, John Ashmore, Larry Omans

Thanks to our JIT Readers

Diane L. Smith
Dave Hicks
Dorothy Lloyd
Debi Sateren
Peter Manis
Veronica Stephan-Miller
Jeff Goode
Deb Mader
Paul Westman

Editor

SkyHunter Editing Team

CHAPTER ONE

C onnor Alby finished writing the last letter and folded the parchment paper with a heavy sigh. He poured melted wax onto the flap from the green candle at his desk before he stamped it with the Alby family seal—a large, intricately scrolling A. Finally, he picked up the letter he'd received, read it once more, and tossed it into the fire.

The letter that started this whole damn mess. You can never be too careful.

Quickly, he stood from his desk and hurried through the small house toward his bedroom, where he retrieved a small traveling satchel and jerked it open. Into it, he thrust a few changes of clothes, a half-full coin purse, and a few premade potions. Everything else was flung aside as he whirled through his belongings in search of what he needed. Satisfied, he hoisted the strap of the satchel over his shoulder and ran a hand over what was left of his graying hair.

My granddaughter finding her own path and my magic

MARTHA CARR & MICHAEL ANDERLE

returned. I had a feeling things might come to this. I merely hoped I'd have more time.

The floorboards creaked beneath him as he stormed through the house toward Raven's room. The sight of her beneath the blankets, completely oblivious and innocent in sleep, made him clutch his chest in sudden indecision. *She can handle it, old man. She'll have to.*

Connor lunged across the room and grasped his granddaughter's shoulders to shake her awake. "Raven. Wake up."

The girl groaned and tried to roll over, and her red hair spilled across the pillow. "I'm not…more sleep…"

"Right now, girl." He shook her a little harder. "Raven Alby, for your mother's sake, get up."

When she uttered another groan and a loud snore, he jerked the covers off her body and dropped them on the floor. Her eyes snapped open. "What—"

"Listen to me, granddaughter."

"What's wrong? Did I oversleep?" She moved her hands sluggishly to her mussed hair, and she blinked before her gaze settled into a vague stare around her bedroom. The space was lit softly by the fire crackling in the main room. "I never oversleep."

"No, it's a few hours before that time. But I can't leave without saying goodbye to you."

"Goodbye?" Raven pushed quickly to a seated position in the bed and rubbed the sleep out of her eyes. "You look like you've seen a ghost."

"Maybe I have. But I won't know until I've finished what I need to do." Connor cupped her cheek and his eyes glinted with a few tears beneath a pained brow. "I love you, Raven. You're strong and capable and fierce, exactly like—"

"My mother. I know." She frowned. "I love you too, but you're not acting like Connor Alby right now. Am I still dreaming?"

"If only it were that simple." He stooped to press a kiss to his granddaughter's forehead, blinked the tears away, and nodded. "Whatever you set your mind to, Raven, you can do it. Don't forget that."

Before she could respond, he whirled and strode out of her bedroom, his traveling boots thudding on the floor.

Raven froze for a moment. *Oh, hell no.* She launched herself from her bed and her bare feet slid across the wooden floor as she raced after her grandfather. "You forgot the part where you tell me what's happening and where you're going." She glanced out the window at the pitch-black night. "And why you're leaving hours before we're supposed to be up."

"If I could tell you, granddaughter, I would." He snatched his cloak off the peg at the door and draped it over his back, satchel and all. "But it's too dangerous. I wish I could say I'll send word when I get there, but I don't know if that's even possible."

Her mouth worked open and closed a few times. "Oh, I get it. This is a joke, right? Some kind of test? I know I'm going to Fowler Academy as a mage in—to be a mage—and I know bonding with a dragon as my familiar is a big step beyond that too. But I won't drop my chores. You don't have to leave to see if I can run the ranch on my own. I have that down."

"It's not about the ranch, Raven." Connor strode across the living room again and retrieved the thick stack of letters from the desk beside the crackling fire. "And it's not a joke or a test. Creative thinking, but no."

"But you don't ever leave the ranch!" She stared at him with wide eyes while her brain attempted to push through the last foggy traces of sleep. *This has to be a dream.* "You took a big first step when you came to watch Leander and me win the competition before the trials, but this is—you can't simply pick up and leave."

"I can, I need to, and I have to. I'm sorry I can't tell you more than that." He stepped toward her and handed her one of the letters clutched in his hands. "Take this to Headmaster Flynn when you get to Fowler today."

"Headmaster Flynn knows where you're going?"

"No. But he'll know what to do once I'm gone." The front door stuck a little before he jerked it open and stepped into the cold, brisk air. *I have to go. If leaving Raven doesn't kill me first.*

"Grandpa, wait!" Raven lurched after him and ignored the whip of cold air through her pajamas and the freezing, dew-studded grass and hard dirt beneath her bare feet. "When will you come back?"

Connor paused and spun to face her again. He tried to smile but didn't quite manage it.

There's that far-off look again.

"I don't know, Raven. I don't know enough to be certain of much at all other than that I have to go."

She rushed across the short distance between them and almost knocked him over when she threw her arms around him. "Whatever it is, be careful."

He chuckled and ran his hand over her wavy red hair.

"I'm a careful man—frugal goat-rancher and grandfather to one incredible mage in training."

"Yeah, well, you used to be a dragon rider too, so I wouldn't say your track record of being careful is completely clean." Raven laughed, but her grandfather's sad smile made her stop.

"Exactly like you."

"Except I don't run off in the middle of the night and hand out mysterious letters."

"But you'll do what has to be done too, won't you?" Connor glanced at the night sky studded with stars before the glow of dawn and nodded. "I have to go. I love you and I trust you to do the right thing when it's most important, Raven. Whatever and whenever that is."

"I love you more, Grandpa."

He pulled her in for another tight hug, kissed her cheek, and stepped away. "If you really, really need me, you can always find me with a calling potion."

"Ha. Right." *As long as I don't call him from the sky.*

"Be good, girl." With another nod, Connor Alby turned abruptly and strode away from their home and across the Alby Ranch. The hem of his cloak fluttered around his ankles.

Raven watched him until the darkness swallowed him. She shivered and rubbed her arms as she glanced at her bare feet.

He won't be gone that long. That satchel was small and only half-full. Test or not, I can keep things running around here, no problem.

She scurried into the house, closed the door behind her, and stepped toward the fire with a sigh. For a few seconds, she stood with her hands outstretched for the flames to warm them before she lowered them again.

"Yeah, it's too quiet in here. No way will I go to sleep again."

Once she'd accepted the inevitability of wakefulness, she hurried to her room and changed into her clothes for the day, snatched up her jacket with her mother's silver and red pin, and slipped into her work boots. Unperturbed by the darkness, she headed across the Alby Ranch toward the empty land away from the goat pen and the ranch hands' cabins.

A fire inside is nice but manipulating it out in the open is even better.

Raven started the large fire where Connor had first taught her the spell, stepped back, and nodded. "*Sequantur flamma.*" She pulled a streak of fire from the blaze and directed it with ease toward the closest unlit torch. It burst to life and cast a flickering ring of light onto the dew-covered grass. *It's a heck of a way to clear the mind, too. And while Leander's still at Moss Ranch, playing with fire is the closest I can get to him from here.*

She lit the next few torches as easily and stared into the flames as one arc after another moved with no hesitation at her command. With a deep breath, she released the stunned urgency of Connor's flight from the ranch to filter into the darkness.

Yeah. Leander would like this part too.

CHAPTER TWO

When Raven finished lighting the torches, the stars were a little dimmer in the sky although the sun hadn't come up yet. She wandered toward the goat pen and the barn, now fully awake although her fingers were a little cold from the chill.

I can't believe I've been awake this long already.

The dwarf goats bleated and jumped toward her when she brought the sack of feed and fresh hay closer. "Okay, you greedy little gremlins. Okay, it's coming."

One of them uttered a loud, cut-off cry, which made the others leap away. "Cody! Get off Jezabele's back, will you?" She swatted at the young goat who'd almost grown out of being a kid altogether. "She's not a crate or a bale of hay."

Cody's less than graceful leap thrust him into a larger animal beside him. They both bleated at the collision before they focused on their breakfast.

She shook her head and dragged the empty sack into the barn. "Those animals. They give the best milk and cheese in Brighton and they still don't know what's good for 'em."

As she always did, she double-checked the latched gate on the pens and made sure the animals had everything they needed for the day. Satisfied, she returned to the house to change out of her boots, grab her satchel, and head to school.

Exactly like I do every day. Only Grandpa's gone off some-where and left me with a letter for someone else.

Raven picked the letter up and stared at it for a few moments, then shook her head and stuffed it into her backpack. *I'm curious, all right, but not curious enough to break his trust.*

Despite the early start, she'd dawdled somewhat and now had to run across the Alby Ranch, past the goat pen and the fence posts, the barn, and the other small cottages where the ranch hands lived and worked on Connor Alby's land. When she reached the front gate and the huge sign with the ornately curling A branded into it, Henry Derks was there waiting for her. She yawned, covered her mouth, and shook her head.

"What happened to you, Alby? Did you just wake up?"

"And have my ass handed to me by a whole pen of dwarf goats gone hangry? I don't think so."

He slapped the top of the gatepost and turned to walk with her down the long dirt road into town. "Then why do you look like you didn't sleep at all? It's been a week since you and Leander killed at that competition out in Nadine. I know you had to be good to win, but don't tell me the adrenaline's still keeping you up."

"You know what, Derks? I slept like a baby that night.

Nothing's keeping me up, only waking me up way earlier than anyone should be awake, even a rancher."

"Did one of the goats get out and cry to get in again?"

"No. They slept later than I did." Raven lifted her hair off her back and drew it over her shoulder to braid it with quick, experienced fingers. "My grandpa woke me a few hours early."

Henry snorted. "Did he have extra special chores for you today?"

"Yeah. The kind where he picks up and leaves in the middle of the night without telling me a damn thing about it."

"What? Connor Alby doesn't leave the ranch. Okay, maybe once last week, but that was a big deal. He crawled out of his shell to watch you and your dragon fly into first place—woah!" He lurched forward to catch his toad familiar—who had leapt from his shoulder bag—before he could land in a nice muddy puddle. The young mage splashed across it instead and carefully deposited Maxwell where he belonged. "Which was awesome, by the way. Now you guys are exempt from the trials, right?"

"Yep. Leander is officially a trained dragon and a mage's familiar."

"Familiar in training, though, right?"

Raven gave her friend a playful punch and rolled her eyes. "That's pushin' it, Derks."

Grinning, he darted away from her and splashed through a few more puddles in the road.

"You know, I see more and more every day why you chose a toad as your familiar."

"Thanks." He shook a few extra beads of muddy water

off his boot and patted his bag where it rested against his hip. "Now if I can only figure out how to snatch food the way Maxwell does, I might die happy." He jerked his head forward and stuck his tongue out, and his eyes bulged.

She laughed. "Careful what you wish for, Derks. I know a few people who'd punch your lights out before they let you lick their food, especially when you make that face. I might be one of them."

"Naw, you wouldn't hit me, Alby. I'm your best friend."

"No, maybe I'd sic Leander on you. Those rolls from Mrs. Whittaker can be hot but burning your mouth on dragon fire is a whole different level."

He stopped short on the road, his eyes still wide and his mouth open but in a very different reaction.

"Henry, I'm kidding." She laughed and shoved him again before she adjusted the strap of her satchel. "Of course I'm kidding. Come on. I would never do that."

Her friend uttered a small, wary chuckle and caught up to her again as they moved quickly down the road. "Leander might, though."

"Not if I didn't want him to." She gave him a sidelong glance, and he pointed at her and shook his head.

"Fool me once, shame on you. Fool me twice, I need to get myself a new best friend."

Raven rolled her eyes and grinned at the tree branches hanging over the road that had begun to sprout new, leafy buds. "You mean like Jenny?"

"Like—no, I don't mean like Jenny. That's completely—" He stopped and ran a hand through his hair.

"Completely what, Derks?"

"Different. It's different. We're not talking about Jenny

and you changed the subject." Henry spread his arms, glanced down, and pressed Maxwell's head gently under the flap of his shoulder bag again. "You were talking about your grandpa."

"Right." She sighed. "I'll tell you as much as he told me. He had to leave, couldn't tell me why or when he'd be back, and I was to always do the right thing when it counted."

"Well, that's not very exciting."

"Yeah, tell me about it." *Not that anyone else thinks Connor Alby's a very exciting wizard these days. But I know the truth about that one.* "So I'm gonna keep doin' my thing until he gets back."

"I wouldn't expect anything else from you, Alby. So who's, like…uh, running the ranch while you're at school?"

"Besides all the ranch hands we have working the property?" She frowned playfully at him.

"Oh, yeah. 'Cause your grandpa sat around all day and watched other people work for him. Not."

"I don't know." Raven shrugged and tossed her red braid over her shoulder. "But I didn't even think about how I'll explain to everyone that he's gone and some of the guys are gonna have to pick up the extra slack. I'll still handle my chores, no problem. You're right, though. Someone's gotta be around to make decisions if both of us are gone for most of the day."

"Oh, sure. Someone will know what to do."

"Yeah, that's exactly what my grandpa said about Headmaster Flynn."

They walked on in silence for a few more steps before the first rows of buildings and the fences around the center of town came into view at the end of the road. "Uh…

Raven. You can't say something like that and drop the conversation."

"What? Oh." She blinked her thoughts away and gave Henry a half-smile. "Sorry. I guess I assume you can read my mind sometimes."

"Ha. That is one ability I'd say no thank you to in a heartbeat."

"What?" She laughed. "Why?"

"Hey, if we open that can of worms, there's a chance you'd be able to read my mind too. I love you, Alby, but not that much."

Raven shivered at the thought, nodded, and pointed at her friend's head. "Yeah, let's keep your thoughts in your head. They're easy enough to read anyway. Food. Food. Lay low but not really. Food. Jenny."

"Hey, I'm just sayin'." In response, His stomach emitted a loud growl and he slapped it. "I think you forgot one more 'food' in there. But seriously, what did he say about Headmaster Flynn?"

She nodded at Mrs. Whittaker as they moved up to the stall and the scent of freshly baked rolls wafted over the morning air still clinging to an early-spring chill. "Morning, Mrs. Whittaker."

Henry groaned and rubbed his hands down his cheeks. "She's never gonna tell me."

Ignoring him for the moment, she withdrew a few coins from her pocket, grinned, and set them on the counter. "Three, please."

"Raven Alby, if you keep buying this Derks boy's breakfast for him, he'll never leave you alone." The baker laughed and handed the young mage three warm, steaming rolls in a strip of parchment paper.

"I won't leave her alone even if she stops buying me breakfast." He saluted the woman and leaned toward his friend as she handed him one of the rolls and muttered, "Thanks. Do I tell you that enough?"

"Probably." She bit into her roll and closed her eyes. They suddenly felt way too heavy. *Well, that was not a great start to the day—not enough sleep and no clue what Grandpa got himself into.* "He gave me a letter and said it had to get to Headmaster Flynn."

"A letter? Please tell me you read it." Henry all but inhaled the roll, but his stomach grumbled again. "Maybe I should start buying my own breakfast."

"I couldn't read it." Raven swallowed her mouthful. "He sealed it and everything."

"Woah. A secret letter from Connor Alby, who left his ranch to go on a mysterious journey, to the Headmaster of Fowler Academy." He gave her a wide-eyed look of complete disbelief. "And you still didn't read it?"

"Trust me, it definitely crossed my mind."

"See, that right there is one of my favorite things about you, Alby." Henry laughed and shook his head. "You won't open a sealed letter that would drive anyone with an ounce of curiosity out of their mind, but you go against all tradition and choose a dragon as your mage's familiar."

"Yeah, well, one of those is about trust and the other's about choosing my own destiny. There's a big difference."

"Uh-huh. That dragon."

CHAPTER THREE

They reached the fountain at the center of the town square where Murphy waited for them. The girl's eyes lit up when she saw her friends approach, and she bounded from the edge of the low wall to join them. Her barn cat familiar Fitz pounced far more gracefully off the fountain and wove through Murphy's legs before he padded silently at the girl's side.

"Morning, Murphy." Raven grinned and held out the last roll to her friend.

"Hey, thanks."

"Careful, Murphy. If you keep letting her buy your breakfast for you, she'll never leave you alone."

The girl frowned, and Henry darted away with a laugh when Raven swatted at him. "Ignore him. He got called out by Mrs. Whittaker."

With a shrug, the dark-haired young mage bit into her roll and made an appreciative hum. "These are still so good. Did you guys get in good practice with your familiars? Professor Worley said we had stepped up a notch with learning how to keep them under control."

"Maxwell's been a little jumpy lately," Henry said and fumbled again to pry the toad gently off the edge of his shoulder bag to tuck his familiar safely away. "Like he can't sit still. Isn't the phrase, 'Like a toad on a log,' supposed to mean something?"

Raven smirked and nudged his shoulder again. "You're setting an excellent example for not being jumpy."

"Hey, that's because someone's always trying to push me—oh." Henry opened the flap of his shoulder bag to give Maxwell a sympathetic nod. "I get it, Maxwell. We'll work on that too."

"What about you, Raven?" Murphy watched her friend with wide eyes as she took small, nibbling bites of the steaming roll.

"Okay, yeah, I see Leander every day. We do more flying than actual familiar training, though."

"It must be hard when you can't have him with you all the time." The girl glanced at Fitz who moved close to her heel. The barn cat's tail flicked continuously as the young mages strolled to the front gates of Fowler Academy.

"A little." Raven shrugged. "I can't take him home and make him a bed in my room, though."

Henry snorted.

They passed the bulletin board in the town square, and Raven paused to look at it. "They're really changing things on this board—"

"Oh, boy. Not this again." Henry tugged her sleeve and gestured ahead of them down the road. "Remember what happened the last time we stopped to investigate?"

"We were so late," Murphy muttered.

He ducked as he searched the house on the other side of the road from the bulletin board. "Quick. Let's get outta here before Mrs. Easton arrives for another round of Spin the Conspiracy Theory."

Murphy laughed. "I remember you being really into her beetle familiar, though."

"Hey, I like bugs. And toads and getting dirty. You know, normal stuff."

"So they took down all the flyers for missing people and posted...what? These warnings don't even make sense." Raven strode directly to the bulletin board, leaned forward, and squinted a little to study the notices.

"What's so hard to understand, Alby?" Henry darted another nervous glance toward Mrs. Easton's front door. "'Beware of Raiders.' That's been there a while. Besides, it's not like anyone wouldn't beware. 'All citizens are advised to lock their property gates securely and reinforce security measures wherever possible.' Okay, that one's a little more specific, but they put something like that up every year before the spring rains. It's not like we need a warning about that, either—"

"But those other warnings didn't have this." Raven pointed to a large seal stamped in red ink at the bottom right corner of the flyer in the center—a thick circle around a staff tilted across a sword with a thick tower in the background.

Murphy joined her to study the seal. "I've never seen that before."

"Those things are sent in from all over the kingdom. I bet half don't even apply to us out here." When neither of the girls responded, Henry leaned forward and tugged Raven's sleeve again. "Okay, war mage. I didn't know weapons stamped on parchment paper got you goin' like this."

"No, Derks." She sent him a sidelong glance with a tiny smile. "You're the one who can't wait to be Brighton's number-one warrior by laying low. Hey, did you get any practice in with a bow yet? It runs in the family, right?"

"Yeah, and right out of it again. My parents have some kind of surveillance spell on my brother and me. Like, they know every time we're about to have a little fun and they storm out to stop us with more chores." He chuckled and folded his arms, his wariness at the possibility that Mrs. Easton would find them again completely forgotten. "They weren't fast enough to keep me from launching a stone into the middle of Norman's forehead, though. It looks like he's growing a third eye now. Or maybe it's only a bad zit. It's too soon to tell."

Murphy turned and wrinkled her nose at him. "That's so gross."

"Hey, it's the truth. Be glad you don't have to wake up to it every morning."

Raven turned away from the bulletin with one final glance at the odd seal. *I'll find out where that's from.* She nodded at Henry. "You know, I'm constantly amazed by how different you and your brother are."

"Because I'm ridiculously good-looking?" He grinned.

"More like you eat literally everything in sight and probably won't ever be half Norman's size." They headed down the road again. "And I'm reasonably sure he didn't get the ancestral-archer gene."

"Nope." Henry puffed his chest out. "He took all the clumsy from our dad, and I got everything else."

"Which is…"

"Alby, how many times do I have to say ridiculously good-looking for you guys to get it?"

Raven rolled her eyes playfully and shifted her satchel on her shoulder again.

"Well, I get it," Murphy muttered. Both her friends turned to look at her with wide eyes, and the girl's cheeks colored a little. She blinked furiously and stared at the road beneath their feet as Fowler Academy's front gates loomed into view.

"Uh…thanks." Henry smacked a hand on Raven's back. "See? Murphy knows how it works. You build confidence up by agreeing with the little white lies your friends tell themselves."

"Oh, okay. I won't say anything the next time you tell me you've handled a levitation spell and end up dropping another rock on your foot."

"White lie, Alby. That means it doesn't hurt anyone."

They reached the entrance to the academy and the open courtyard at the front where it swept out in front of the smaller outbuildings of the school and the towers that rose in the back. The other students were already milling around, using what time they had before their first class to talk and joke with each other on the grounds.

"Oh, hey!" Henry nodded at some of his friends, then muttered to Raven, "Thomas told me before the week's end that he'd get his sheepdog familiar to stand on her head by today. I gotta see this. Be right back."

He hurried away and gave a few high-fives to the other

guys crowded around Thomas' familiar, all of them waiting for a good show.

Raven smiled at Murphy, whose face had only become redder since they'd stepped onto the grounds. "Are you okay?"

"I don't know why I said that." The girl looked at her friend with wide eyes. "Why did I say that?"

"Don't worry about it." She patted her shoulder. "He didn't even notice. Half the things I tell him go in one ear and right out the other. Or they never go in at all." *And that's exactly what Henry wants everyone else to think. White lies, right?*

Murphy shook her head as Fitz rubbed against her leg. "I can't believe this—"

"Hey, Raven!" Thomas waved at her and nodded a greeting, and his black-and-white sheepdog familiar stood at his side and wagged her tail with her tongue lolling out of her mouth. "Hey, hold on. I have a question for you."

"What? Seriously?" Henry spread his arms wide. "You were about to—yeah, okay. Way to avoid what matters."

Thomas and his friends moved toward Raven before she'd covered more than a few yards past the school's entrance, and he followed while he continued to mutter about his expectations not being met.

"Hey, so we all heard about you winning that dragon competition last week." Thomas grinned and leaned toward her. "But...you know, none of us were there and you haven't said anything about it."

Raven shrugged. "There's not that much else to say. And it wasn't only me. Leander did most of the work. We won."

"Yeah, yeah. Right. Both of you." The boy glanced at his

own familiar and laughed a little hesitantly. "What's it like, though? Riding an actual dragon?"

"Probably exactly like you imagine." Raven leaned away from him a little. "You don't have to get so close. I can hear you."

"Sorry. I only...really wanna know."

"It's awesome. That's basically it."

"Huh. Awesome." The kid's eyes widened and he glanced at one of his friends before he slapped another boy's shoulder. "Do you think you could ride a dragon, Dawson?"

"Totally."

"Yeah, before you woke up and realized your familiar is a parakeet."

Raven stepped away from the group of boys who poked fun at each other and joked about who was the least likely to be a dragon rider. Murphy simply shook her head and walked beside her. Henry came up behind them, squeezed between the girls, and draped his arms over both their shoulders. "Can you believe those guys? They can't even focus on one thing. Can't stick to the plan or finish a single..."

"Sentence?" Raven gave him an amused frown. "Yeah, that must be frustra—"

"Hi, Raven."

She turned away from Henry to where Daniel Smith stood in front of them with a lazy half-smile. The upperclassman studied her face and raised his eyebrows.

"Hi..."

"It's Daniel."

"Right. I've heard your name." *I didn't think he knew mine but I guess everyone does now.*

"Cool." He didn't break her gaze as he stepped aside and nudged Henry's arm absently from around her shoulder. "Can I talk to you for a second?"

Henry gave a derisive snort, and Murphy blushed even more during the split second his arm was around only her shoulders before he folded them to stare at Daniel.

"Sure." She glanced at her friends with a little shrug and stopped only a few feet away when the older student touched her arm. "What's up?" She looked at his hand and frowned.

"I want you to know that I think it's seriously awesome."

When she looked up again, Daniel grinned at her and his head lowered a little more than normal for someone who'd never spoken to her before. "Well, thanks. I'm not sure what you're talking about—"

"The dragon. It takes guts to announce that as your familiar and it takes even more to make it happen. Some of the other students here..." He looked up and skimmed the crowd that milled around before class officially started. "Well, they can think whatever they want. I think you're great. I mean, having a dragon as your familiar is great. And the fact that you both won that competition and got to skip the dragon trials altogether. Really, really great."

Raven pressed her lips together and tried not to laugh. *It must be because he's nervous, right?* "Just to double-check, you think it's great, right?"

Daniel laughed and shrugged in a somewhat awkward way, and his bright eyes flashed in the morning sun. "Yeah, something like that. If you ever wanna…you know, hang out and talk about it, that'd be cool."

"Okay." She grinned at him and nodded. "Thanks for letting me know."

"Totally. I only—"

"Hey, Alby." Behind them, Henry shouted a little louder than he had to and gave an overly enthusiastic wave. "Do you know who else thinks you're really great? Me and Murphy. Right, Murph?" He elbowed the girl beside him, and she laughed in surprise before she flushed a little.

"You have some…cool friends," Daniel said and leaned toward Raven again.

"Yeah. They are. I think everything's moving into the great hall now, so I'll see you around."

"See you around, Raven Alby." With a wink, he turned away and joined the flow of students who now walked inside, laughing and joking with his friends like nothing had happened.

"You believe me now, don't you?" Henry stepped alongside Raven and nudged her in the ribs with his elbow. "That guy won't stop talking about you. Now, he probably won't stop talking to you. I'm not even sure what happened."

"Me." She wrinkled her nose with a confused smile and didn't expect to see Daniel turn around again and flash her another wide grin over the sea of students' heads. "You know, I can't tell if people are excited about talking to me now because of Leander or because of me."

"Both, probably," Murphy said.

"Right again, Murphy." Henry scratched his head vigorously and shrugged as the students streamed into the great hall. "I'm not sure about that floating-beanbag guy, though."

"It seems like he wants something," Raven muttered.

"Oh, he wants something, all right. It's kinda pointless to even ask why—oh, hey! Rory! Did Thomas show you the trick with his dog?" Henry patted Raven on the back and moved toward Rory Davidian and the boy's owl familiar that perched on his shoulder.

She laughed and Murphy leaned toward her to ask, "Is it that simple with all guys?"

"I'm sure it is. Or, at least, they're all pretending. You know what? I have no idea." She shook her head as she and Murphy followed the other first-year students before they separated into their various classes. *I wonder who else is gonna come out of the woodwork now that the whole school knows about Leander.*

A few heads away from where Henry broke into raucous laughter with Rory and Thomas and a few other guys, Bella Chase stood with her firedrake familiar on her shoulder. The dark-haired girl met her gaze, raised an eyebrow, and turned to say something to her friends.

At least I already know what to expect from her.

CHAPTER FOUR

T he first-year students had assembled for their last class of the day. Familiar training with Professor Worley took place in the open arena of the barn and the huge, burly man with a deep, booming voice stepped into the center of the dirt that comprised the floor.

"Today, you'll work on something I honestly don't enjoy, but it's necessary."

A few mutters issued from the students. Raven glanced at Henry, who stood beside Rory Davidian and Thomas Anders, his hands clamped gently around a still and silent Maxwell. He met her gaze and swallowed.

"Now, you've all chosen your familiar," the professor continued. "You've bonded with them and you've each discovered at least a little of what makes them uniquely suited as your familiars and what makes them uniquely powerful when bonded with you. You're learning about their strengths. Today, however, we'll focus on their weaknesses."

Tessa Hambridge raised her hand and didn't wait for

acknowledgment before she launched into her question. "Professor, I don't see how paying attention to our familiar's weaknesses will make them stronger. My Aunt Mable says we are what we think. I don't want Ellie to lose progress."

"Right." Bennett Cotton snickered. "'Cause your butterfly has so much to lose."

Professor Worley turned toward the boy and his chuckling friends and merely raised an eyebrow. It took two seconds for the boys to shut up and pay attention again.

"Miss Hambridge, your Aunt Mable is a smart woman. Yes, I would say we manifest our thought patterns, perhaps especially when we work with our familiars and learn to stretch them to their limits. But we also learn how to stretch ourselves."

"By focusing on weaknesses instead of strengths?" At the other end of the line of students, Bella Chase folded her arms and frowned. "What if our familiar doesn't have any weaknesses?"

Professor Worley chuckled and scratched his bearded chin. "Then you don't know your familiar as well as you think you do, Miss Chase."

Another round of chuckles came from a few other groups of students. Bella turned to look at her firedrake Wesley perched on her shoulder. The small reptile snorted a thin plume of smoke.

"We all have weaknesses and strengths. That's how we grow and that's why you're here. But let's all keep Aunt Mable's advice in mind, hmm?" Professor Worley stepped toward the other side of the barn's arena and lifted a small latch set a foot above the floor. A thin, narrow slat in the barn raised another foot when he pulled it, then he hooked the latch over a nail and gave the open door a satisfied glance.

"It looks like the cat door I built for Fritz," Murphy muttered. The barn cat sat at her feet and his tail flicked idly in the dust.

"Now, when I say focus on your familiar's weaknesses, I'm not talking about calling them out, noticing them, and brushing them aside. They are, after all, animals. Some of them are wild and others are domesticated, but they have instincts and natural inclinations that we as witches and wizards have evolved to overcome. A strong bond with your familiar is essential for any mage and yes, our familiars help to strengthen our magic. We work together. But true control and the true power of that bond comes from training our familiars to overcome their instincts."

A soft whisper rose from the other side of the arena.

Henry gulped. "Oh, man."

A few mutters of confusion and trepidation rose from the students and one girl in the back screamed. "A snake! Professor, there's a snake in the barn!"

Some of the students backed against the far wall. Others glanced with wide eyes from Professor Worley to the huge albino boa constrictor that slithered through the open slat on the other side of the arena.

"Great," Mike Jeder muttered and tucked his squirrel closer to his chest. "That monster just found the ultimate buffet."

Professor Worley didn't even turn to look. "There is much to be learned from this exercise. I urge you all to focus on the benefits of what this type of control and bond of trust with your familiars will achieve. The intention here is to identify the instincts that may be the most detrimental to you and your familiar—should they act on these instincts instead of following your guidance—and to work together to overcome such…distractions."

The snake slithered across the dirt, stopped beside the giant of a professor, and curled the end of its tail around the heel of his boot. Worley glanced at it and nodded. "Like I said, I don't particularly enjoy or approve of this exercise on principle, but I also know the absolute necessity. This is Vastra." The reptile raised her head slightly and her long, forked tongue flicked in and out. "One of my familiars."

Raven and Murphy shared a wide-eyed glance of surprise. "Didn't someone say Professor Worley had three familiars?" Murphy whispered.

"Well, at least we know he has more than one." *I didn't think it was even possible.* Raven grinned and turned to study Vastra's long, lithe body settled in the dirt. "She's beautiful."

"She's big enough to eat any of us and our familiars." At the other girl's feet, Fitz uttered a warning hiss.

"But she won't," her friend pointed out. "That's the point."

"Now, before I pull names out of a hat, would anyone like to volunteer for a demonstration with Vastra and me?" Professor Worley gazed at the line of students—some clearly terrified, some gazing in awe at the huge boa constrictor, and others who smirked with confidence.

No one said a word. The giant professor released a booming laugh. "I assure you, Vastra and I have been together for a very long time. There's nothing to be afraid of. The first part of this lesson, I suppose, is to learn to trust what we know and brush the rest of it aside."

A loud croak broke the uneasy silence before Henry lurched forward between two students in front of him and thrust them aside. "Maxwell, get back here," he whispered harshly. He swiped to catch the toad, who leapt away from his outstretched hands and hopped about the barn to flurry sprays of dust from wherever he landed.

"It looks like your familiar has volunteered you both, Mr. Derks."

The boy froze in mid-swipe and turned slowly to look at the massive snake that lay motionless beside the man. "Maxwell doesn't know what he's doing."

"That's precisely the point." With his lips together, Worley waved him forward. "Collect your familiar, Mr. Derks, and stand here beside me."

Maxwell had finally settled and now faced the other side of the barn while Henry crept up behind him. The young wizard scooped him up with both hands and turned him to gaze into his familiar's eyes. "I don't think we have a choice."

He stepped rigidly toward the professor in the center of the arena, and Worley gave him a reassuring nod. "This is the exercise. Controlling your familiar against his natural instinct. In this case, I believe that would be in the inclination to flee."

"Yeah, that's kind of my inclination right now too," he muttered. A few subdued, nervous chuckles rose from the other students.

Raven grinned. "You got this Derks. He's your familiar for a reason, remember."

"Yeah, but a toad can't help anyone heal if it's already been eaten."

She turned to glare at Bennett, whose smile faded when he saw her before he shrugged.

"You can joke about it all you want, but each of you will work with your familiars in uncomfortable situations today. There are a few weaknesses to overcome. Instinct is one. It comes in many forms with these animals. Your job is to bond enough with your familiar that their only true instinct is to anticipate your thoughts and your intentions and to brush everything else aside like I've said. All right, Mr. Derks. Set your familiar on the ground, please."

"Are you serious?" Henry drew Maxwell toward his chest.

"I hardly think I would have been given this job as a Fowler Academy professor if I didn't say exactly what I meant." Professor Worley clapped a thick hand on his shoulder and made the young wizard stumble sideways under the weight. "On the ground. And use your connection with your familiar to keep him there and to ignore his natural instinct to run from predators."

With another heavy swallow, Henry bent to set Maxwell in the dirt again and muttered, "I should've picked a familiar with wings. Or claws."

The toad crouched in the dirt and remained there, his huge eyes wide while his flat, broad chest heaved quickly in and out.

"Good." Professor Worley took a step back and tugged on Henry's shoulder. "Move away with me, now. Keep the connection, Mr. Derks, but don't interfere."

With a grimace, Henry stepped back slowly. Vastra's

tongue flicked in and out again and tasted the air. Maxwell's sides swelled and compressed even faster.

The albino boa constrictor began to move and slithered away from Maxwell before she veered toward the toad again. The young man glanced at the professor. "She looks hungry. What's she doing?"

"Focus."

Vastra turned to inch slowly toward the terrified creature.

Raven clenched her fists at her sides. *You got this, Henry. Jeeze, they both look terrified.*

When Professor Worley's familiar reached Henry's, her forked tongue darted out again and barely brushed the top of Maxwell's head. Both familiar and young wizard flinched but the toad remained where he was.

"Very good," Professor Worley rumbled. He stared at the familiars playing food-chain roulette and nodded. Vastra opened her mouth slowly, wider and wider, and Maxwell twitched again.

"Holy crap!" Rory shouted. "Look at the size of that mouth!"

Vastra's wide, strong jaws snapped shut.

Henry lurched forward as Maxwell leapt away from Vastra in a panicked display of amphibian acrobatics. The creature's limbs were fully outstretched as he smacked against the boy's face, and he stumbled forward across the dirt to catch his flopping familiar with both hands.

A few laughs echoed, and he clutched Maxwell to his chest while he gasped short, heavy breaths and puffed his cheeks. "Yeah, keep laughing. Let's see who else is gonna volunteer."

"You didn't volunteer, Derks."

"But I didn't say no, Percy," Henry shouted in response. "What about you?" Completely pale now, he lifted Maxwell to his face and whispered, "Don't worry, buddy. If there's a round two, we're callin' it quits."

CHAPTER FIVE

"All right, settle down." Worley raised his hands and sent irritated looks at the boys who pushed each other forward in an attempt to volunteer someone else next. "Mr. Derks, that was a fine job. You showed more control than I expected, actually."

Henry turned toward him with raised eyebrows. "Yeah, me too."

The professor placed a much gentler hand on his student's shoulder and leaned in to add in a softer voice, "You were clearly more concerned for your familiar's well-being than your own. I think the trick now is to overcome your fear to help Maxwell do the same. Remember, the goal is to make your intention his number-one instinct. When you trust each other enough, he won't feel you worrying about him."

"It's easy for you to say. Your familiar's at the top of the food chain."

Worley chuckled and nodded toward the other students. "Go on."

He moved quickly toward the edge of the arena but instead of joining Rory and Thomas, he slipped into the line on the other side of Raven and stared at her, his eyes huge.

"You did great." She nodded with a reassuring smile. "Both of you. You weren't even a little jumpy except right there at the end."

"I thought I was gonna have to wrestle a boa constrictor into coughing its lunch up." He glanced at Maxwell. "That was awful."

"It makes sense why Professor Worley doesn't like this exercise," Murphy added. She scooped Fritz into her arms and rubbed behind the barn cat's ears, then looked at Henry. "You guys did well."

His panicked expression faded into an unsure half-smile. "Thanks. I think."

"As Mr. Derks demonstrated very well for us," Worley continued and his voice boomed throughout the barn again, "there's considerable ground to cover with both your own emotions and intentions and your own familiar's instincts. We want to always respond, never react. Having seen that, it might help some of you to know that, on my instruction, Vastra has not gone out this morning to hunt for her next meal despite the last being four days ago. This is another instinct to be wary of with predatory familiars. Hunger is a powerful distraction but Vastra trusts me and our bond enough to listen to what I asked of her and knows she does and will have everything she needs."

Without any prompting from the professor, his boa constrictor familiar slid across the dirt in a wide path and moved along the front line of students without pausing, even when she passed the smaller familiars huddled against their mage's legs. A few students picked theirs up to get them out of the way before the snake turned and slithered toward the open slat in the wall. In only a few seconds, she was gone.

Professor Worley went to close the tiny door and latch it again, then clapped briskly. "Now, everyone spread out. You'll work one-on-one with your familiars but I will make rounds and stop with each one of you to help you pinpoint specifically which instincts to work on subduing within your familiars. That will then teach them to trust you and not the call of nature."

The students fanned out across the arena and talked in low voices. A few of them cast wary glances at the closed trap door in the wall.

Murphy stroked Fitz in her arms and shrugged at Raven. "Unless Professor Worley pulls a handful of mice from his pocket, I'm not sure what we're supposed to work on."

"I bet he'll find something." She gave her friend a reassuring nod. "You guys will be fine." A short, high-pitched shriek of laughter came from behind her and she turned to Bella and the firedrake on her shoulder.

"I know Wesley and I already trust each other. From what I heard about that competition, Raven, it sounds like you think you have the same kind of bond with your dragon."

"Of course I do. That's how we won." She smiled and studied the other girl's face. *That sounded like a compliment.*

"Too bad your familiar's so far away, though." Bella shrugged and Wesley stretched his wings with a little growl. "There isn't much for you to learn when you stand here all on your own."

"Well, Leander and I have enough time together and we've already learned a lot."

"Right. But not approved by the Fowler Academy curriculum. If I were you, Raven, I'd be worried that it would affect my final grades at the end. You don't want to be held back a year because you couldn't advance with your familiar."

Henry tilted his head a little cheekily. "If you were Raven, you would've had your head bitten off by a dragon months ago."

Raven pressed her lips together to keep from laughing.

"No. I'm smart enough to stay away from dragons in the first place. I don't simply trust luck. I make sure I know what I'm doing first." Bella stared at Henry, then glanced at Raven again with a pert, inauthentic smile. "I'd hate to see good competition drop out at the end of the year. It makes it harder for me to leave an impression."

"Thanks for your concern, Bella." Raven folded her arms. "Trust me, I'm not going anywhere."

"If you say so." Without a backward glance, Bella Chase stalked away to take her place among the students scattered in the arena. Her firedrake turned on her shoulder to look at Raven and her friends, then launched himself with a screech.

Henry snorted. "Bella Chase is wearing passive-aggressive now, huh?"

"Raven, it almost sounded like she was trying to compliment you," Murphy added. "Until she didn't."

"I noticed that too." With a shrug, she smiled at her

friends. "It's not like it matters. Leander and I have enough under our belt. I'm not worried."

"Yeah, I wouldn't be either." Henry glanced at Maxwell and sighed regretfully. "Dragons don't have serious confidence issues with boa constrictors."

"True."

"Miss Alby," Professor Worley called from across the arena and gestured for her to step forward. "Over here with me, please."

Henry nudged her in the arm. "Do you think you'd be able to keep Leander from breaking out again for a rescue if Worley set that giant snake on you?"

She laughed. "Why would I want to? And no professor will attack anyone with their familiar, Derks, but thanks for the concern."

"But just in case," he called after her. "He'd show up for it, right?"

Shaking her head, she moved through the students toward Professor Worley at the other end of the arena.

The man grinned at her through his thick beard and mustache, then rubbed his hands together. "Miss Alby. The mage in training who chose a dragon as her familiar. Although, as I understand it, you haven't yet managed to get that familiar onto school grounds like the rest of your peers."

"I'll think of something," she replied quickly. "Whatever I have to do to make sure I pass this class, Professor, I'll do it—"

"Oh, hold on." He chuckled and glanced around the arena as students chatted and familiars darted through the air and across the dirt floor. "This isn't a punishment, Miss

Alby. That dragon has been your familiar for a week, and from what I saw the day it was made official, the two of you have a strong enough bond. I can work around the circumstances if you can."

"Absolutely." She nodded. *Bella's trying to unravel me and that is not gonna happen.* "So...why did you call me over here?"

"To be my assistant. If you won't train in class with your familiar, you'll train in a different way." Worley's eyebrows drew together and he scratched his chin again. "There's quite a difference between keeping your own familiar at bay and knowingly and willingly putting someone else and theirs in...uncomfortable situations. You might learn something from having to do what's necessary, even if it makes you squirm."

"Oh. Great." Raven glanced quickly at the students. "We won't hurt anyone, right?"

"Not physically. And nothing that won't make them stronger because of it. I hope." He gestured for her to walk with him and strode toward the closest student.

Raven set her jaw firmly and followed him. *No wonder he said he didn't like this part. It turns us both into the bad guy simply to teach a lesson.*

"Now, Miss Knowles." Worley clapped briskly. "It looks like that wombat of yours has a problem keeping her nose out of the dirt."

The girl looked at Raven with wide eyes, then glanced at their looming professor with a grimace. "I guess."

"Well, then. Let's get to work."

CHAPTER SIX

R aven was among the first students out the barn
  door once Professor Worley dismissed them for the
day. A few of the others gave her disapproving looks. Rory
Davidian slowed at her side and frowned. "Ignore everyone
else. Worley asked you to help and that's all you did."

"I know." She sighed. "I can't help but feel a little guilty,
though."

"Hey, it's not like you shoved those mice down Ernie's
throat. I'm not sure what trying to make him keep down a
handful of owl pellets was supposed to do, but he got
through it." Rory glanced at his shirt and brushed it off
with a grimace. "Mostly."

"Well, thanks, Rory."

The kid walked away, still brushing his hand across his
clothes. His owl familiar tucked into himself on his shoulder, apparently asleep.

"Wow. That was intense to watch." Henry came up
beside her and bumped her with his shoulder. "Did you see

how Percy's robin couldn't keep herself together when Worley began to fling worms everywhere?"

"I sure did," Raven muttered, still smiling when he jumped in front of her with wide eyes. "I was right there for all of Worley's little tests."

"Hey, lemme tell ya, there are a few people I wouldn't mind making uncomfortable. Like Bennett when his jackal wouldn't stop sniffing at everyone else's familiar. Oh, and Bella."

"You don't have to remind me, Derks. Class literally just finished."

"Yeah, but her face when that firedrake leapt off her shoulder to snatch…what'd he call it again?"

Raven offered the other students a small, sympathetic smile as they filtered out of the barn with their tired familiars. "Dragon jerky. It's only dried lizard, but I guess it gets to firedrakes too."

"Man, he couldn't keep his little snapping jaws off the stuff. I thought he was gonna bite Worley's hand off."

She caught a glimpse of Bella Chase who stalked across the grounds away from the barn. The girl scowled furiously while her firedrake fluttered behind her. Raven readjusted the strap of her satchel and sighed. "I think Bella and her familiar both know that eating teachers definitely crosses the line."

Henry chuckled and spun again. "Woah. Murphy. He hit you guys kinda hard, huh?"

The girl hurried toward them, her shoulders hunched and her face flushed. She tucked her hair behind her ear and glanced at Raven. "That was rough."

"I bet." She rubbed her friend's back as Fritz slunk behind his bonded witch and looked equally as dejected. His fur was still drenched and clung to his body while drops of water left a trail behind him across the grass. With every other step, he shook a front paw and stepped a little more lightly than usual. "Murphy, I honestly didn't know what that spell was supposed to do. Worley gave it to me and told me to cast it."

"I know. He made you his assistant. I don't blame you but I'm sure I have a few more scratches than I wanted."

Raven leaned closer to look at Murphy's forearms. "Ouch. Hey, I know a tiny healing spell. It might help a little."

The girl shook her head. "That's okay. You probably shouldn't, anyway, unless you want everyone else to come begging for a healing spell."

All three of them glanced at Elizabeth Kinsley, who walked away from the barn alone, a long gash on her temple visible beneath the dark bangs that almost fell over her eyes. She cradled her bat familiar in her arms and didn't look at anyone.

"What did they have to do?" Murphy asked and winced at the sight.

"Besides the bat being awake and active during the day?" Raven sighed sympathetically. "She had to keep him from roosting for three minutes and then, he couldn't hang upside-down from anything."

"Weird training, if you ask me." Henry deposited Maxwell safely into his shoulder bag and gave it a little pat. "On the bright side, Maxwell and I didn't get eaten."

"I didn't know being a guinea pig would put you in such a good mood, Derks."

"Hey, it's simply good to know I'm not the only one who hasn't discovered all my familiar's tricks. Or weaknesses. Worley didn't look too happy about it."

"No." Raven turned as Professor Worley closed the doors to the barn. The man didn't look at anyone and headed across the grounds behind the others, his huge hands thrust into the pockets of his trousers. "I totally understand why. Trust me, I didn't like it either."

Murphy scowled and automatically skirted a puddle in the path through the grass. Fritz gave it a wide berth too. "I can't imagine what Worley would have to do to help you test Leander."

"Maybe you'll have to keep your dragon from burning the whole school down next time you bring him on the grounds." Henry snorted and clapped before he spread his hands wide. "Then you'll be good to go. Passed with flying colors."

Raven gave him a warning glance. "Dragons aren't like that. Leander doesn't merely set everything on fire for no reason. The others don't either. I'm sure the Moss Ranch wouldn't have lasted this long if that were the case."

"Well, whatever his weakness is, you'll find it." They stepped beneath the stone archway and inside the main courtyard of Fowler Academy. Henry glanced at the tall towers and looked both nervous and disgruntled. "Hopefully it's not anywhere near as hard as it was for the rest of us today."

"Actually, I think we've already been through that part,"

Raven said. "I'm not sure a dragon's first instinct is to let a mage throw a saddle on their back and climb aboard." She rubbed her shoulder absently, although it didn't hurt as much anymore. "And I had the bruises to prove it."

"You always kill two traditions with one dragon, don't you, Alby?"

"Maybe." She tried to hide a proud smile at that. "More like bend tradition, though. I'm not trying to tear anything down." They headed across the main courtyard toward the front entrance, but Raven stopped. "Oh, I almost forgot. I have to find Headmaster Flynn."

"Oh, yeah. Mystery letter time."

Murphy looked from one to the other in bewilderment. "What?"

"My grandpa wrote Flynn a letter, I guess. Before he left this morning."

With wide eyes, the girl glanced at where Fritz stalked toward the road off the Fowler Academy grounds before she leaned toward Raven. "He left?"

"Yep. It's kind of a longer short story. Do you wanna come with me? I'll tell you all about it on the way."

"Uh...no, that's okay." The girl pointed at her familiar, who had now circled on the road and sat on his haunches to stare at his witch with his ears flattened against his head. "I'm gonna go home and dry Fritz. I'll maybe give him a bowl of milk or something. I feel so bad."

"Sure. See you tomorrow, then." Raven waved goodbye as Murphy wandered away. The girl turned once to give Henry a questioning glance, but he paid no attention.

"Derks." Raven slapped his shoulder with the back of

her hand. "Are you gonna let Murphy walk to the town center alone?"

"What? Uh…" Henry stared across the main courtyard on the grounds and his mouth fell open a little.

"Earth to Derks!"

"Hey, you don't have to yell it in my face." He stuck a finger in his ear and wiggled it, then looked away again. "I was actually, uh…Jenny asked me to help her with a combat spell she's having trouble getting down… You know, to improve her aim."

"Really?" She laughed and wrinkled her nose at him before she looked away and waved across the courtyard. "Hey, Jenny!"

The girl waved in response, a little unsure, but didn't say anything.

"Jenny Connors asked you to tutor her with a combat spell?"

"Right?" He shrugged. "I couldn't say no."

"Of course you couldn't. It's a good thing perfect aim was one of the first things you pinned down."

"My thoughts exactly, Alby. She chose the right wizard for this one. So, I'm gonna…" He walked backward across the paved area and stuck his thumb over his shoulder toward Jenny. "Hey, I wanna hear about that letter and what Flynn has to say about it, okay? Don't forget."

"That'll be hard. Have fun carrying Jenny's books on the walk home."

Henry gave an exaggerated laugh before he turned and shoved his hands in his pockets.

Raven watched him and Jenny talking, his head lowered as he watched the girl with a wide grin. When they left the courtyard together and disappeared, Raven pivoted to look at the tall tower in the center of Fowler Academy. *It's time to play messenger.*

The school had thinned out quickly as the students headed off either to their homes in town or toward the dormitories. Raven passed a few second-year students inside the stone walls of the main building before she almost skipped up the wide, winding staircase to the top of the tower and Headmaster Flynn's office. *Wherever Grandpa went, it has to be in this letter.*

The wide, thick oak door was closed when she reached the top of the staircase, so she gave it a few quick, hard knocks.

A muffled laugh came from inside and Headmaster Flynn called, "Come in."

She pulled on the iron loop of the door handle and had to step down the last step to open it before she entered the massive circular room.

Headmaster Flynn stood in front of his desk, still smiling and nodding at Professor Fellows and Professor Gilliam beside him. He glanced at Raven in the doorway and raised his eyebrows. "Ah. Miss Alby. How can I help you?"

"My grandfather gave me something to bring to you." She took a quick look at his two companions, who both smiled with equal curiosity. *I'm not sure if anyone else is supposed to know about this.*

"Excellent. Please, come in. If Connor Alby has something for me, I most certainly won't say no."

Raven walked across the room toward the desk in the center and glanced at the tightly packed bookshelves lining the walls and the huge round stained glass window set high in the tower wall at the back. Green, blue, yellow, and red light streamed through the office. She slipped her satchel off her shoulder and balanced it on her knee to remove the letter.

"I heard you had the chance to assist Professor Worley today during familiar training." Professor Fellows smiled even wider and leaned forward a little like they shared a secret.

With the letter in her hand, she swung her satchel over her shoulder and focused on the professor. "Yeah. How did you hear about it so quickly?"

"I overheard a few students talking about it. It's a rough part of the training, but Professor Worley's one of the best for that kind of thing."

"It can't be much rougher than weapons training with you, though, right?" She held Fellows' gaze as she crossed the room toward Headmaster Flynn.

He shrugged. "It depends on the day, I suppose. It takes considerable strength and willpower to test other people's limits too, Miss Alby."

"Yep. That was my biggest takeaway." She looked at Headmaster Flynn and slowly extended the letter stamped with the Alby family seal.

"Oh." The man stroked his graying beard and inclined his head as he took the folded parchment paper. "A letter."

Professor Gilliam uttered a small sigh and shook her head. "Connor Alby still won't leave his ranch and instead, has a message delivered."

"Not exactly." Raven's attention slid away from Gilliam

when the headmaster walked quickly around his desk to open a drawer.

"As far as I'm concerned, the man's earned his right to do as he pleases." The headmaster rummaged in his drawer. "Where did I put that magnifying glass?"

Raven couldn't help laughing. "What do you need a magnifying glass for?"

Headmaster Flynn looked quickly at her and raised an eyebrow. "Have you ever tried to read your grandfather's handwriting? Oh, well, I'm sure you haven't come anywhere close to having eyesight problems. Embrace and cherish your youth, Miss Alby. It'll slip through your fingers before you know it."

"Yes, Headmaster." Professor Gilliam folded her arms with a little smirk. "That's exactly the kind of thing we want to drill into our students' heads."

Flynn hummed with satisfaction when he finally retrieved the magnifying glass, broke the seal on the letter, and unfolded the parchment paper.

Professor Fellows cleared his throat with a little smirk. "Don't tell me you never seized the day in your youth, Eleanor."

Gilliam glanced quickly at Raven, then raised an eyebrow at the weapons professor. "That's Professor Gilliam if you don't mind. And for the record, I firmly believe I spent my youth adequately and with as much of an eye on the future as I had on the present. Thank you very much. That's how I've been so fortunate to have taught at this mage academy for the last twenty years."

"Hmm. You must have grown up awfully fast then, huh?

Did you start teaching right after graduation?" Beneath her glacial stare, he laughed and tried to hide it with a cough.

"If I didn't know better, Professor Fellows, I'd say you were trying to hide one insult by wrapping it in a compliment I'm not so certain either one of us believes."

Fellows eyebrows raised sharply and he turned a wide-eyed look of surprise toward Raven. The young mage in training merely hitched her satchel to a more comfortable position and smiled politely. *Even Professors have their class clowns and overachievers. I wonder if Gilliam ever shot a few arrows at her competition.*

"Miss Alby." The advanced spells professor turned her back on Professor Fellows to settle an intent, scrutinizing gaze on the student in the room. "I don't believe I've had the chance yet to congratulate you on the competition in Nadine."

"Oh. Thank you." Raven glanced at Headmaster Flynn, who had placed her grandfather's letter on the desk and moved his hand rhythmically to scan it with the gigantic magnifying glass. "Leander worked hard for it."

"Hmm. I'd venture to say you both put in a fair amount of—"

"Professors." Headmaster Flynn's voice cut through her words. Everyone turned to look at him, but he stared at the floor on the other side of his desk. "Would you kindly give Miss Alby and me the room?"

"Absolutely." When the man still didn't look at anyone, Professor Gilliam sent Professor Fellows another warning glance before she brushed past both him and Raven toward the open door.

Fellows coughed over another laugh and tipped his head at the girl on his way out. "The trick is finding balance. Exactly like the edge of a blade, Miss Alby. Don't let your youth run away with you but don't let it limit you either."

"I'll keep that in mind." She chuckled as the weapons professor gave her a thumbs-up and headed out of the office.

"Professor Fellows." Headmaster Flynn finally looked up from the floor. "Please close the door behind you if you don't mind."

The man nodded and turned on the top step to shove the heavy wooden door into place. It shut with a thud that echoed through the huge circular office.

Raven turned to face the headmaster. He stroked his beard a few times and set the magnifying glass carefully on the desk but wouldn't look at her.

That's the same look Grandpa had when he stood over my bed this morning. "Headmaster?"

"One moment, Miss Alby." He lifted Connor's letter in one hand, snapped his fingers with the other, and muttered, "*Incendium.*"

The parchment paper burst into flames and he released it. In seconds, the entire letter was reduced to a loose pile of curled, charred ribbons and a melted puddle of green wax.

Her mouth dropped open. "Why did you do that?"

"I assume that's a question asked out of surprise and not because you can't imagine the answer." Headmaster Flynn cupped his hand over his mouth and drew it down to tug on his long gray-white beard again.

"Headmaster, I stayed so I could see what my grandfather wrote in that letter."

"And it's a good thing you did, Miss Alby. I wouldn't have enjoyed trying to locate you before you left the grounds for the day." The desk drawer jerked open again, and he slid the magnifying glass inside with a thump. "Because you and I have a few things to discuss."

CHAPTER SEVEN

Raven stared at the pile of ash on the desk. *I should've read that letter when I had the chance.* "What did it say?"

Headmaster Flynn blinked at her and pressed both hands flat on the top of his desk. "Not much, to be perfectly honest."

"No one burns a letter when there's not much in it." When he looked quickly at her with a stern frown, she shook her head. "I'm sorry. I only wanted to know... He didn't tell me anything before he left, only that he had to go and couldn't tell me anything. I thought the letter would have a few more answers."

"A few, yes, but not for you."

Raven took a deep breath and stared at the man as he rummaged through his desk drawers again. "Okay. Well, what can you tell me?"

He placed a few blank leaves of parchment paper on the desk and drew the inkpot toward him, then nodded and finally looked her in the eye. "Well, Miss Alby, I believe your grandfather will be gone much longer than any of us can anticipate. And I think it's best that we move you onto the school grounds for the foreseeable future until he returns."

"What?"

Headmaster Flynn continued to search in the drawer again before he whipped out a feathered quill and frowned at it. "That's unfortunate." He blew on the mangled pleats of the feather a few times and fluffed them with his fingers, then gave up and set the quill on top of the parchment paper.

"Headmaster, I can't simply pack and move onto the grounds. I have the ranch—my grandfather's ranch—and chores every morning before anyone else wakes up. We have help, obviously, but I don't think any of them will jump at the chance to pick up extra work I leave behind. That's not how it works."

"I understand, Miss Alby. And I see that you're frustrated by this."

Ya think? She released a wry laugh but kept her mouth shut.

"It seems Connor has already planned and provided for the details of redistributing the workload on the Alby Ranch so there's no need to worry about the goats." Headmaster Flynn lowered his head and regarded her with a restrained smile. "I wouldn't suggest this if it endangered your father's ranch or the livelihoods of anyone on it, goat or otherwise."

"I still can't leave the ranch." Raven shook her head and gazed at the dimming streams of colored light that poured through the stained-glass window. "It's much closer to

Moss Ranch than Fowler Academy. I'm out there every day with Leander. And I don't want to be—"

"Farther away from your familiar than absolutely necessary. Believe me, I understand the sentiment completely." A gentle scratching came from the other side of the closed office door. The headmaster flicked a finger across his office and muttered, "*Recludo.*"

The door creaked open and his familiar Rider padded in. It shut as quickly behind the giant gray wolf who walked swiftly and silently across the floor. He stopped at the end of Flynn's desk and sat as one ear flicked back and he stared at Raven.

Headmaster Flynn glanced at his familiar with a little smirk. "Well, that was well-timed."

She stepped toward the desk and gazed at the man until he finally focused on her. "Please, Headmaster. I can't move here and be farther from Leander. It cuts down on the time I get to spend with him, and I already have to go through all my classes here without him. I can handle the ranch. However long my grandfather's gone, I can handle it."

"I have no doubt in your ability to juggle so many of these things at one time, Miss Alby." He gave her a slow, sympathetic smile. "This is more a matter of safety. Your safety. Connor…was a powerful mage and he has more experience than he might openly be willing to share. Now he's gone away and I can tell you that letter said nothing about when he'll return. But it's my responsibility as head-master here to ensure that all our students are safe and provided for and that they have the opportunity to put their studies first."

"Please don't tell me I have to make a choice." *I'd choose*

Leander every time but then I'd be a goat-rancher with a dragon familiar. That's not in my blood.

Flynn studied her for a few seconds before he chuckled. "I wouldn't dream of it. And I have no doubt you'd choose that dragon over this school and find your own path to becoming a mage—a path much less controlled and far more dangerous, which goes against everything this academy believes in. No, Miss Alby, a mage in training does, in fact, need her familiar with her for her studies. It's about time we made that happen."

"Wait—you're saying you want me to bring Leander here?"

"Precisely."

"I…" Raven gave Rider a confused smile and shook her head. "He definitely won't be in the dorm with me. Even if I asked."

"It's a good thing you won't have to ask. We'll set a pen up for your dragon on the school grounds near the barns. He may stay there while you stay here with the other students living in the dormitories. We'll find answers for everything else when your grandfather returns."

"That was honestly the last thing I expected." A bark of a laugh escaped her, and she shut her mouth to swallow it hastily before she grinned at the headmaster. "Thank you."

"Thank me by going home, packing your bags, and returning with your familiar before the sun sets." Headmaster Flynn dipped the quill into the inkpot and filled his office with the sound of words scratched into parchment paper.

I could hug him but I won't. Raven looked at Rider again, and the massive wolf lowered himself to the floor to rest his huge, regal head upon his paws and lick his snout. *I definitely won't hug him, either.*

"I'd get started on that soon, Miss Alby." Flynn raised an eyebrow.

"Right. Yeah, we'll be here later tonight, then." She turned to walk across the circular office, then stopped. "Thank you, Headmaster. For trusting us enough to bring Leander here."

"You and that dragon have already demonstrated remarkable potential, Raven. I expect to not be proven wrong in that regard."

"Never." With a broad grin, Raven hurried to the office door and pushed it open. She stopped abruptly before she raced away and shut the door hastily, then took the winding staircase down the tower two steps at a time. *Staying in the dorm will be a piece of cake with Leander here. I love you, Grandpa, but this is turning out to be better than I imagined.*

She reached the hallway at the bottom of the stone tower and almost barreled into Professor Bixby, who waddled past with an armful of huge parchment paper rolls.

"Oh!" The squat, round professor jolted in surprise and a few of the larger rolls tumbled from the pile. "Miss Alby. What are you doing racing through the school like that?"

"I'm so sorry." Raven stopped to gather the wayward scrolls and stacked them gingerly on top of Bixby's load. She had to stoop a little to not drop them on the vertically challenged professor. "I'm excited."

"Well, I hope that excitement stems from something

school-related." Bixby blew a few strands of frizzy copper hair off her forehead.

"Definitely. I'm breaking tradition!" She wiggled her eyebrows and whirled away to walk quickly across the main hall toward the building's exit.

A few students lingered in the courtyard, most of them upperclassmen. Three girls stood near the stone archway into the field in front of the barns. One of them waved her wand and muttered a spell, and the girls stood back to leave enough room for the horse-shaped fountain made entirely out of water. Another group of boys just inside the front gates of Fowler Academy tossed the beanbag using spells and every part of their bodies but their hands.

"Hey, Raven." Daniel Smith turned out of the circle to flash her a wide grin. The fist-sized beanbag streaked past his chest but stopped in midair when he muttered, *"Supervolo."*

"Hey, Daniel." She spared him a quick glance and a hurried smile but continued to walk toward the road.

He snatched the beanbag from the air and headed after her. The circle of boys around him groaned. "I didn't think I'd see you hanging around the grounds this long after classes."

"Yeah, it happens. I'll be back. See you around." Raven gave him a quick wave and stepped out onto the road toward the center of Brighton.

"Come on, Dan!" another second-year shouted. "Get your head in the game or get outta the game, huh? I'm trying to break that fifty-year-old record."

"Yeah." Daniel stared after her a little longer, her red

braid swinging from side to side against her back as she sprinted down the road. *What is she up to now?*

"Daniel!"

"Okay, okay." With a lazy smile, he turned and threw the beanbag into the circle. "Jeeze, Marcus. I didn't think breaking some old guy's record was such a big deal."

"Yeah, well, I'm hoping Bixby will give me good marks on that History in the Present report she assigned. If I beat this record, I make my point."

"And what's that?" He chuckled as his friends kicked and kneed and magicked the beanbag around the circle.

"That the present is better than the past, man. We shouldn't waste our time learning history because we make it. Right now."

The group burst into snickering laughter while all of them focused on the beanbag as it launched from one side of the circle to the other.

"And yeah, it wouldn't hurt to get rid of History of Magic as a class altogether." Marcus grinned. "I'll make my case in that report too."

CHAPTER EIGHT

Raven's pace had slowed by the time she reached Brighton's town center. She wiped the thin layer of sweat from her forehead, stopped beside the bulletin board, and frowned. Across the fountain courtyard, Zeke set an empty wooden crate outside the door of his tavern and raised a hand in greeting. "Hey, Raven."

"Hi, Zeke." *I bet Headmaster Flynn knows whose seal that is.* She turned away from the board and glanced at the houses that lined the street. Mrs. Easton's wide eyes peered through the window as she passed before the woman stepped away and jerked the curtain aside. At the next house over, Raven paused and studied the empty stoop.

"It's a heck of a warm day out, huh?" the tavern owner called. "Bright and clear. And it's warming up, too. I had to start puttin' more than your grandfather's goat milk in the cellar, I tell you what."

"Yeah. Spring's coming." Raven dropped her satchel to shrug out of her jacket, which she folded over her arm. Her mom's silver and red pin glinted under the sun. "Hey, have you seen Peter around lately?"

"Peter?" Zeke scratched his receding hairline as she walked across the fountain courtyard toward the front door of his shop.

"The veteran next to Mrs. Easton with the big green hat."

"Oh. Huh. You know, Raven, I can't rightly say. He's been talkin' his crazy for at least a decade, now. Who knows where the man heads off to when there's no one around to listen?"

Raven sent the man a disbelieving frown. "I wouldn't say he's crazy. A little eccentric, maybe."

"Well, whatever he is, he takes off from time to time. I can always tell." Zeke nodded and jerked a thumb over his shoulder into the doorway of his business. "My patrons arrive early, stay longer, and leave later when they're not trying to avoid a cr—an eccentric lecture on their way here."

"But he comes back, right?" *I bet he'd be able to answer a few questions if he doesn't start yelling at me again.*

"As far as I know, sure." The man dusted his hands off and shrugged. "Trust me, when he turns up again, we'll all know."

"Right. Thanks, Zeke. Have a good one."

"You too, girl. See you in the morning on delivery. Just in time, too."

She turned as she passed the fountain on her way to the road leading out into the open fields around Brighton. "You'll see Deacon, not me this time."

"Well, okay. Enjoy the sunshine before it goes into hiding for another two weeks."

She waved goodbye and hurried down the road. *Where'd that veteran run off to? I bet he and Grandpa knew each other once from somewhere.*

By the time she reached the gates of the Alby Ranch, Raven had to wipe the sweat off her forehead again. She glanced at the blue, cloudless sky. "Boy, it got warm fast. It's a really good day to fly, though."

She grinned, increased her pace again, and quickly passed the ranch hands spread out across the fields and working the harvesters. Patrick raised a hand in greeting as he hefted the last of the fence posts he'd replaced around the property. She returned the wave but they were too far apart for conversation.

The goats kicked up a storm of bleating and jumping and knocking each other aside when they saw her step up the road toward the house. "Okay, you goons. I have to pack and I know you're not starving. As soon as they are done replacing the fence, you'll have a little more freedom. I'll fill that trough before I leave, don't worry."

On her side of the pen, the fence thumped and groaned when one of the young adults butted his head against it. He uttered another loud bleat, and she pointed at him. "Don't make me come in there."

She burst through the cabin door and took a deep breath to call, "Guess what I—" As she shook her head, she chuckled at herself and gazed around the empty ranch house. "Wow. It sure feels empty."

A frown settled on her face as she stared at the counter that separated the small kitchen from the rest of the main room on the way to her bedroom. *For the first time in my life, Grandpa won't put a plate of food up there at the end of the day. I'll be fine and he'll be back before I know it.*

The satchel fell onto her bed with a muffled thump and made the bed frame squeak. "Okay. I need to cover all the bases. Clothes, shoes, all my textbooks..." Raven stopped and inclined her head in thought. "The school has soap, right? Maybe I should've asked about the details."

Irritated at herself, she went to her dresser and opened all the drawers to dig through and pull out the clothes she knew she'd need and a few extras for a surprise change in the weather. The pile on her bed grew quickly and she knelt beside her bed and felt under it for the larger canvas shoulder bag she knew was under there. She brushed the dust bunnies off and shook it before she placed it on her bed. *That bag was much bigger in my mind. It's not nearly big enough.*

After a moment's thought, she moved quickly across the hall to her grandfather's bedroom. *He only packed a small satchel. There's gotta be something bigger in there.* The door was still open a little, and when she'd pushed it wide, she stopped. "Woah. You were really in a hurry, weren't you, Grandpa?"

She stepped carefully over the pile of discarded clothing beside the door. The bed hadn't been made, more clothing lay everywhere, and all the dresser drawers were open. She navigated her way through the mess, knelt beside Connor's bed, and felt beneath it. The thick oilskin fabric at her fingertips was unmistakable. "Gotcha."

The huge, barrel-shaped bag slid neatly toward her across the floor and she hefted it into her arms and headed to the door. Raven paused once to give the mess an appraising glance, then shook her head. *Headmaster Flynn said I had to be back before dark. And Grandpa's the one who taught me to clean up after myself anyway.*

His huge bag had more than enough room for all her things and even a little extra to spare. After she'd dragged her borrowed luggage and her satchel into the main room, Raven went through the small house one more time to make sure she hadn't missed anything. A few more necessities went into the bag before she stopped when her gaze fell on the huge metal trunk Connor had hauled from the cellar. It called to her from beside the empty hearth, and she glanced over her shoulder before she shook herself out of her momentary distraction.

Before she could second-guess herself, she knelt in front of the trunk and the hinges groaned as she lifted the heavy lid and propped it against the wall. There, right on top, was Connor's dragon-rider patch beside the two old journals. Raven scooped them up and ran a hand over the triangular patch with a dragon in mid-flight embroidered across the surface. *It's still hard to believe this was real and it feels kinda wrong to bring Mom's patch and not Grandpa's.*

Next, she turned her attention to the two faded leather journals with the dusty, yellowed leaves of parchment paper inside. *He said these don't leave the house, but if I'm not living here for who knows how long, I won't have the chance to read them. They'll be back in the trunk before he returns and what he doesn't know won't make him angry, right?*

With a shrug, she grasped the edge of the hearth to push to her feet and glanced at the cold ash left from the fire that morning. A trace of red ink on a charred fragment of parchment paper caught her eye. "What?"

She brushed aside as much ash as she could without touching the unburned fragment, picked it up carefully, and turned to hold it under the light streaming through the window. *That's the same seal from those new flyers. Is this where he went?*

Raven tucked her discovery into her front pocket and sifted through the rest of the scattered ashes. *At least I found something in here. Headmaster Flynn might not be the right person to ask after all.*

Once she'd tucked the journals and Connor's old patch into the oilskin bag, she buckled the straps quickly and slung all her important belongings plus her school satchel over her shoulder. With a grunt, she stepped toward the door and readjusted the bags to free her hand. *Now I get why he traveled so light.*

When she shut the door behind her, the goats burst into loud, excited cries again. "Now hold on. I didn't forget about you."

"Well, I didn't even know you were here."

She almost dropped both bags when Deacon stepped around the corner of the far pen, dragging a new hay bale behind him. "Deacon?"

"I didn't expect you to be back anytime soon, girl." He gave her a lopsided smile and hauled the bale over the fence before he dropped it into the trough. The goats rushed to their fresh meal and jostled each other before he had a chance to break the bale up a little, and he jerked his hands back and laughed. "Woah. You weren't kidding about these guys, were you?"

"Nope. Once that new fence is finished and they get out to graze a little, they'll settle. I hope."

"That is very reassuring, Raven. Thank you." He lifted his wide-brimmed hat to scratch his head and chuckled as he stepped around the pen toward her. He noticed the bulging oilskin bag slung over her shoulder and nodded. "It looks heavy."

"A little. I got it." She inclined her head and regarded him with a confused smile. "Why are you here feeding the goats?"

"I guess you wouldn't buy it if I said I wanted to try it, huh?"

"Not really."

"Connor came past my cabin at the most ridiculous time this morning—or last night. I'm not exactly sure. He handed me a letter, shook my hand, and said he appreci-ated what I was doing and hoped to see me still here when he returned."

Raven stepped toward him. "Did he say when he'll come back?"

"Nope."

"What about where he's going?"

"Sorry, girl. I don't have those kinds of answers. But apparently, he was handin' out letters left and right to the other ranch hands, doling your chores out to the rest of us."

Wrinkling her nose, Raven released a sigh and tried to shrug beneath the weight of Connor's old bag. "That's what Flynn meant by 'taken care of.'"

"Say what, now?"

"Headmaster Flynn. Grandpa wrote him a letter too,

and whatever was in it convinced the man that I need to be on the school grounds instead of staying in the house by myself. So…" She jiggled the bag slung over her shoulder. "I'm moving to Fowler Academy."

"Oh…wow." Deacon swiped at the loose straw clinging to his tunic and chuckled. "That's a big move."

"I know. Hey, I'm sorry that you and the rest of the guys have to take over my work. My grandpa should've talked to me about it first. And I tried to tell Headmaster Flynn that I'd have no problem staying here to keep doing what I've done for the last few months anyway—"

"Woah, hey. Slow down, girl." Deacon patted her over-loaded shoulder with another low laugh. "Connor didn't drop a whole list of extra duties on us without making it worth our while."

"He didn't?"

"Of course not. Hell, you could stay here in your own house and sleep in every morning, and none of us would say a damn thing after the kinda raise your grandfather offered. And everyone knows Connor Alby's a man of his word."

"He gave you all a raise?"

The man nodded and stuck his thumbs through his belt loops. "Yeah, I was a little surprised about that too. Not that I have anything against your grandfather, girl. He's a good man—"

"But he doesn't throw money around. I know." Raven stared at the goats that continued to shove each other aside to get to the hay. "I guess he really did think of everything."

"At least on our end, yeah." He shrugged with a little laugh. "It looks like you're off the hook."

"Only until he gets back. I don't know when that is, but I'm not running away from my chores here."

Her determined frown made him chuckle again. "No one will blame you for heading off the ranch for a little while. Trust me. Times are good, like Connor's word, and the rest of us can handle things around here no problem. Plus, you have more important things to think about. If I were you, feeding these goats wouldn't even be on my top-five-priorities list."

She licked her lips and couldn't help but laugh at the spectacle the dwarf goats created when they crashed into the trough, the hay, the wall of the pen, and each other. "Keep an eye on that chap with the one black ear. He likes to butt heads. Literally. And the one with the gray down his back will bolt the second he thinks you're not watching."

"Oh, I'll be watching." Deacon pointed at the offending animal, who ignored him completely and munched contentedly on the hay.

"Thanks, Deacon." Raven nodded at him and took a deep breath. "I'd say I owe you one, but I guess my grandpa already took care of that too."

"Uh-huh." He lifted his hat again and swiped across his brow before he returned it. "You know, that bag still looks heavy. Let me hitch Presley and we'll drive you to Fowler Academy. You might not get there before dark otherwise."

Raven turned down the worn path that cut across the Alby Ranch from her house. "I'm not going straight to Fowler, though."

"Oh, sure. Wherever you need to stop, we can take you. I have to pop into town to drop my other pair of boots with Finnegan Ofstad. The damn sole fell off in the middle of mucking out Presley's stall. It's amazing what bad timing that was." Deacon followed her down the path and the sound of bleating goats faded steadily behind them.

"I'm stopping at the Moss Ranch before I head to the school."

The man cleared his throat and shot her a sidelong glance. "Of course you are. Well. We'll take you as far as the turn-off, but you'll have to carry that bag yourself the rest of the way. You saw how much trouble Presley had with a bad storm. Dragons are even worse."

"I can't blame her for that. But a ride would be great. Thanks."

"You betcha. All right. Now, hand that bag over, girl. I can see you shrinking by the second under it."

Raven almost told him she'd considered a levitation spell in her head and would have used that for the walk to Moss Ranch. Deacon was so eager to help, however, that he took the heavy oilskin bag off her shoulder to sling it over his and she didn't stop him. *Magic still has a price and I might need it for something more important in the future like everyone keeps telling me.*

She rolled her shoulders and settled her satchel more comfortably, her neck already sore from carrying everything she had to take with her to her new temporary home at Fowler Academy.

CHAPTER NINE

Deacon tugged on the reins and Presley stopped obediently. The wagon rolled to a bumpy stop on the main road into Brighton, and its driver turned to tip his hat toward Raven.

"It's time to get back to riding dragons and studying as a mage in training." He laughed and shook his head. "Hoo, boy. I never thought I'd say both those things in the same sentence. That'll take some getting used to."

"Don't worry. It gets easier after a while." Raven scrambled from the seat of the wagon and grinned.

"I can't imagine it's any easier when you're the one doing both those things at the same time. You have a great thing inside you, girl. No matter what anyone tells you otherwise."

"Thanks, Deacon." Raven dragged the oilskin bag from the back of the wagon and hefted it over her shoulder again. "I'm not worried about what anyone says. I know I have it in me. War mages and dragon riders run in the family, so bringing them together into one person was bound to happen sooner or later, right?"

He laughed again. "If anyone can handle all that at once, it's Raven Alby. Go enjoy yourself, girl. Maybe I'll see you in town."

"I'm not leaving forever." She laughed. "Thanks for the ride."

The wind blew across the fields skirting the Moss Ranch property and tickled the sweat on her face and the back of her neck. Presley stomped a hoof on the road and snorted.

"Yeah, I think I can smell those dragons too. We're goin', Presley. I hear you." Deacon flicked the reins, the wagon bumped down the road again, and Raven wiggled her fingers beneath the straps of her bags when the driver turned to wave over his shoulder.

When she reached the stables and pens of Moss Ranch in front of the massive open field where most of the trained dragons roamed freely, she squinted against the sun. It almost touched the first peaks of the Mountains of Jared. *We still have enough time.*

"Raven." William stepped out of the stables and wiped the sweat off his face with a rag before he dropped it on the ground. "What happened?"

She laughed and lowered the oilskin bag and her satchel into the dirt. "You'll have to be a little more specific with that."

"You've been here every day at the same time after classes for months. And now it's only a few hours before sundown."

"William Moss, are you trying to say you were worried about me?"

He chuckled and ran a hand through his sweat-dampened hair. "Generally, I'm confident that you can handle whatever you're doing. But yeah, it was a little weird that you didn't come when you usually do."

"I'm sorry to worry you."

"I didn't say—"

"It's okay. I get it." Raven brushed her braid over her shoulder and grinned at him as she turned toward the lone pen on the other side of the stables. "I got a little held up."

William glanced at her luggage with a raised eyebrow before he walked after her. "What's in the bag?"

"Everything. Well, everything important, at least. Almost."

"For what?"

"I'm moving out."

"You're what?"

She turned to smile at him over her shoulder. "Only temporarily. My grandpa up and left this morning and wouldn't tell me where he was going. But his letter to Headmaster Flynn apparently made it super-obvious that I couldn't stay in my own house anymore or keep working on the ranch while Connor Alby's not where Connor Alby's supposed to be. So I packed and I'm here for the most important part."

He stopped, clenched his eyes shut, and shook his head. "That went way over my head, Raven. Can you start over and tell me again like I'm a person who has no idea what's going on right now?"

"I did." She looked across the open field of trained

dragons who lay in the warm sun, wandered about with their clans, or jumped into the air for a few playful wing-beats before a graceful landing. "Where is he?"

"Leander?" William rubbed the back of his neck. "When you didn't show up like you usually do, I think he got a little...frustrated."

She spun away from the field and raised an eyebrow. "We talked about this. Today was the day we intended to let him out and give him a little freedom with the others."

"I tried, Raven. You weren't here and Leander didn't want anything to do with me or a lead, even when I told him where I was taking him. It's like he reverted to a dragon who never felt a saddle or a rider on his back."

Her eyes widened. "So you left him in that pen?"

A nervous chuckle escaped him. "Can you blame me?"

With a sigh, Raven headed toward the stables and the single-dragon pen attached to the back. "I want to, but no. I can't blame you at all. So when you say 'frustrated,' do you mean like normal stubborn Leander who swats aside young mages trying to saddle him, or is he—"

The metal walls of the pen clanged ominously as she approached, followed by a menacing snort. A cloud of dirt sprayed seconds before a pillar of fire erupted after it.

"The kind of frustrated that almost burned my hair off." William pointed to his head and shrugged. "He doesn't listen to anyone but you, Raven. It's not a surprise but I did try to get him out of there."

"I believe you. This is my fault for taking so long to get here. He's come to expect me at the same time every day. I should've come here first instead." Another column of fire burst from the ring of the pen and she stopped to unhook the gate latch.

"I'll be right here if you need anything," he said and frowned at the thick gray smoke and dirt that billowed.

"Thanks, but I got this." Raven opened the door, slipped into the pen Leander had called home for most of his life, and shut the door quickly behind her.

William stepped onto the platform beside the wall to peer over the top of the enclosure. *I hope this didn't set them back. They worked so hard to get where they are.*

Raven stood inside the wall and watched as Leander snorted and pawed at the dirt. He turned in tight, jerky circles while his wings twitched and spread only halfway. "What's going on in here?"

Either he didn't hear her or he simply didn't care. The dragon's glimmering red scales flashed in the late-afternoon sunlight as he worried a huge divot in the middle of the pen. A piercing screech rose from somewhere out in the dragon field, and Leander raised his massive head on his long neck to respond with an echoing cry.

It was so much louder than the other shrieks she'd heard from him that she had to clamp her hands over her ears until he had finished. He snorted and blew a cloud of thick gray smoke. "Leander."

She said it loudly enough to get his attention in the silence. The dragon whirled to face her and his tail whipped through the dirt. When he saw her, he pawed the earth once again, his flanks heaving, but at least he'd stopped moving.

"I'm so sorry." She took a step toward him, her hand outstretched toward his snout. He didn't back away but the stream of hot air that escaped from his nose was enough to make her pause for a second. "I know you're upset—"

"I should be out there right now," Leander rumbled and his great yellow eyes locked onto his mage.

"I know. I really should have come here first and if you're angry with me, I can't tell you that you don't have the right. But I'm here now."

"You left the animal trainer to take me out on his own." Leander lowered his head until it was level with her chest as she approached. "I don't respond to commands. No leash, remember?"

"Oh, I remember. I think William's the one who forgot for a second."

"Hey, I'm only working with what I got here." William leaned a little forward over the top of the pen. "I only wanted to help you, Leander. To keep my word when I said I thought you were ready to head out there with the others."

"Your opinion means nothing to me, flyboy."

He looked a little startled at that but remained calm. "Yeah, but I thought the open field and a little more freedom might."

The dragon pawed the ground again and snorted. William lifted both his hands in surrender and shook his head. "I'm done."

"Hey, come here." Raven extended her hand to stroke the dragon's smooth, scaly snout. He lowered his head even more so she could hold him with both hands. "Okay. Everything's fine, huh? I know I arrived late and I know what we planned to do today. I am sorry. This whole day's been a little—"

"Off." The dragon stared at her and lowered himself to his belly on the ground, although his wings still twitched a few times in agitation. "I felt it."

"Really?" She smiled and drew her hand up the ridged scales between his eyes. "I know you can tell when I'm in trouble, but that's not what happened today."

"It doesn't matter. I felt it anyway. Your sadness and your excitement." Leander's tail whipped in the dirt before he curled it around his forepaws. "And then you didn't come."

"Oh…" *This giant flamethrower is simply a big softy.* "Did you…did you think I left?"

"I can't read your mind, little girl. Only feel it."

"Wow." Raven patted the back of the dragon's neck behind his head and nodded. "Okay. New lesson learned today. I promise you right now that I won't keep you waiting if something happens. This one's on me."

A low growl rumbled through the dragon's belly. "I know."

At the pen wall, William snorted a laugh and shook his head.

"So we're on the same page with that. Good." She glanced at the sky that now took on the orange and pink of sunset. "Because I have good news for you too. I'd call that the excitement you felt."

"It's only good news if it includes releasing me from this cage. The trainer broke his word."

William shook his head again and blew out a frustrated sigh. *Raven and that dragon have a connection, all right—the same levels of stubborn until it hurts.*

"Well then, it's good news for both of us." Raven

grinned at her dragon and leaned closer to his scaly hide warmed by the abnormally warm spring sunshine. "You get to leave this pen. For good."

"What?" William jerked a hand over the edge of the pen but immediately clamped it down again to stop himself from wobbling off the platform. "He's not ready for that on his own, Raven. You're not here all the time and there aren't enough William Mosses to handle the workload around here and keep an eye on Leander. If he wouldn't listen to me today, I won't be able to control him out there when something goes wrong."

"Nothing will go wrong." She gave her friend a reassuring nod. "And you won't have to keep an eye on Leander because he's coming with me."

The dragon uttered another low rumble. "Only if you want your goats to die of a heart attack. It makes an easy meal for me."

"Yeah, and no meals after that for a goat rancher." William bit his bottom lip. "I know you want him with you, Raven, but the Alby Ranch doesn't have the right setup for a dragon. Even a bonded dragon. Okay, yeah, even a familiar."

"We aren't going to the Alby Ranch. My grandfather left this morning on a secret errand no one wants to tell me about, and if I want to keep training as a mage at Fowler, I have to live in the dorms."

He turned partially to eye her oilskin bag and satchel lying in the dirt. *Now that makes sense.* "Raven, I don't think—"

"So." She gave him a bright grin that in no way apologized for cutting him off. "I'll grab the saddle. You and I will take off, Leander. Headmaster Flynn's building a place for you near the barns as we speak. Ready?"

"Woah, woah, woah," he shouted. "No."

Leander exhaled a burst of smoke and pushed to his feet with remarkable speed and a spray of dirt. "No barn."

"What?" Raven glanced at William, who hung over the pen and chewed on his bottom lip. He shook his head a little and she looked at her dragon again as Leander lifted his long neck to stare at her. "Oh, come on. We'll be fine. Leander, you'll be right there with me on the grounds every day. No waiting for me to show up late—"

"You promised you would not."

"Yeah, that was hypothetical." She patted the side of his neck and chuckled. "I know. A promise is a promise, and we keep our word to each other."

Leander lowered his head and tilted it to study her with his yellow eyes. "A school is not freedom, Raven."

He hit close to home with that one. "True. But it's one step closer. I know neither one of us cares what anyone else thinks about it, but you're officially my familiar now. I know I'd rather have you closer to me all the time instead of only when I can make it to this ranch. Don't you think that's an upgrade?"

"To be closer to you, yes. I have no desire to be ogled by all the other children who think they know what it takes to be a mage."

William snorted and Raven smirked but managed to restrain her laughter. "Hey, at the very least, they'll get to see how a mage and her dragon familiar get the job done."

"Mage in training, little girl." The dragon nudged her with his snout.

"Oh, come on. You too?" She sent him a playful frown, then stroked his broad muzzle affectionately. "Let's go. We need to be there before dark and I hoped we'd have extra time to fly before we have to land."

Without waiting for an answer, she turned and headed toward the pen's gate. William remained where he was and stared at the red dragon, who didn't move a muscle. She turned and gestured for Leander to follow. "Are you ready?"

"This is what you want?"

Oh, boy. He's not ready. Taking a deep breath, she nodded. "Yes. This is what I want. I want to be a dragon rider and I want to graduate from Fowler Academy as one of the best mages in the kingdom. Maybe the best. Who knows? I won't lie to you about that. But I will say that if you really don't want to leave this pen for the school grounds, I won't make you."

A hiss of air escaped the dragon's nose when his chest rumbled again. "You couldn't."

"I know that too." She grinned and brushed away a few drops of sweat with the back of her hand. "Look, Headmaster Flynn and my grandfather are the ones who gave us an ultimatum, essentially. Flynn knows I won't go to school there if I have to move into the dorm and you can't come with me. He told me you could come before I even had a chance to ask. So yes, I want both and I believe it's possible to do what we're doing, Leander. What no one else has done before. But if you don't go, I won't go. It's as simple as that."

She folded her arms and held Leander's gaze while she

waited for him to make his mind up. *At least he's considering it. The best I can do is tell the truth and hope it's enough.*

The dragon took a few slow breaths before he stretched his wings almost to their full span until their leathery tips brushed against the walls of the pen. "Get your saddle, dragon rider."

CHAPTER TEN

With Connor Alby's old saddle fastened securely on Leander's back, Raven double-checked the straps beneath the dragon's belly, patted his flank, and headed toward the gate. "Trust me. This'll be a big improvement. I'll sleep in the next building over."

"And I doubt I'll sleep at all," he mused.

She turned and grinned. "You might be surprised. Thank you for at least being willing to try."

"It's what you want, Raven." The dragon's snort of warm air brushed the back of her shoulders. "It becomes more difficult every day to separate that from what I want."

Her gaze met William's before he jumped off the platform as she opened the gate. "I understand that completely. It works both ways, Leander. I want what's best for you too."

"I know."

When she stood aside, the magnificent red dragon shouldered through the open gate. The minute Leander was free from his pen, he stretched his wings wide to their fullest extent and shot a short burst of fire into the sky. *And if me being a few hours late today made him that distressed, bringing him to Fowler with me might be the best thing for both of us.*

William stepped behind the dragon to close the pen gate by habit, then circled toward her. "I'm still not convinced this is the best idea."

"I convinced Leander to at least give it a try." Raven shrugged and looked up at her friend's dubious frown. "Setting your mind at ease can't be that much harder, right?"

"Still…" He rubbed a hand over his mouth and focused on the orange and pink sunset that spilled light through Leander's translucent outstretched wings. "How will that school keep Leander there on the grounds without the same kind of containment spell we have at the ranch?"

"The same containment spell Leander burst through to come to find me at Fowler?" She smirked.

"Hey, it's kept hundreds of dragons right here, safe and sound, since my grandfather ran Moss Ranch. Probably even since before that."

"I don't think we'll need any kind of extra security. I'll be there with him the whole time."

William raised an eyebrow. "Except for when you're in class."

"Hey, if Headmaster Flynn was willing to build Leander a new pen on the school grounds so I can have him there with me every day, I don't think it's out of the question to change things up a little and bring my classes to him."

"I'm not going to school, little girl," Leander added and shook his massive head before he stretched to his full length. His tail thumped into the dirt with a puff of dust. "Your classes don't interest me."

"The familiar training might, though." Raven turned to move past the stables for her packed bags.

"And what about the rest of Brighton?" William asked as he followed her before he realized what he'd done. He darted a hasty glance over his shoulder at Leander, who swayed from side to side with his eyes closed as he soaked in his newfound freedom and the last of the sun's warmth. *What am I thinking, turning my back on an uncontained dragon with no halter or lead?*

"What about them?" she called in response.

He hurried toward her again. She reached her bags and hauled them over her shoulder, completely at ease with having left Leander where he stood. *These two really have it down.* "Fowler Academy is much closer to the center of town than Moss Ranch. People are gonna flip when they hear there's a dragon on the grounds."

Raven blew a few strands of loose red hair out of her eyes and returned to Leander with all the determination William had seen in her since they were young children. "Well, we'll have to show them that Leander and I trust each other. Everyone else will have to trust that."

"Right." He scratched the back of his head in his nervous habit and followed the mage in training toward her dragon familiar. *Anyone who can't see how confident she is about this is an idiot.* "Okay. But if anything happens—if there's an issue and Headmaster Flynn or the other professors change their mind—"

"That won't happen."

"There's so much about this we can't predict, Raven. It's

rare because it's a dragon trainer's job to make sure it doesn't happen, but if a dragon causes problems, that reflects on Moss Ranch as a—"

Leander snorted so forcefully that he had to turn away from the blast of hot breath thick with the meaty scent of dragon feed. "The only problem with dragons is your insistence on training us like animals. My decisions are my own, flyboy. No dragon trainer can take credit for any of them."

"Yeah, I'm well aware of that." He raised his hands in surrender and took a small, slow step back. "I didn't call you a problem, Leander."

"No. Merely a potential mark on your reputation."

Pressing his lips together, the dragon trainer turned to Raven and gave her a knowing look.

"I'm not worried, William." She set her bags in the dirt beside Leander. "You shouldn't be either and besides, you're not even the one who trained him."

He uttered a wry chuckle. "I'm well aware of that too."

"So, no problems and no potential problems. I'm glad we're on the same page." She turned toward her dragon and grinned. "Are you ready to fly?"

"Always."

"I'm right there with you. Oh, I almost forgot. Headmaster Flynn's old saddle is still in the stables with the other tack, right?"

William glanced at the stables. "I think so."

With a nod, she put her hands on her hips and surveyed her bags. "Leander, this is kind of a first. Is it gonna be a problem to fly with me and two packed bags and a saddle?"

The dragon's wings flicked out before they curled in

again against his back. A jerking hiss escaped him. "If I were left on my own to roam free, little girl, I'd fly with a cow in my belly and a fat sheep in each paw."

She snorted. "Noted. And to be clear, we won't go after cattle or sheep tonight or any night."

Leander's tail curled around his hind leg. "Pity."

After a playful frown at the dragon, Raven turned toward the stables. "We can bring Headmaster Flynn his old saddle while we're at it. Grandpa's sits like it was made for me anyway. Leander, I'll be right back. Don't go anywhere."

"I'm not even remotely tempted to tour the facilities."

"I'll take that as a 'Sure, Raven. You can count on me.'"

William followed her into the stables and retrieved Teo's riding tack from the wall as she located the worn black saddle with silver stitching.

"What are you doing?"

"Coming with you." He smirked and threw the saddle over his shoulder. "You're not the only one who likes long dragon flights at sunset. And someone who knows what they're doing around a dragon needs to check that new pen at Fowler and make sure Leander has everything he needs. After that, the rest is up to you."

"I can't argue with that logic."

"Excellent."

Once Teo was fully saddled and ready to head out, William climbed on his back and slipped his boots firmly into the stirrups. He ran a hand up and down the silver dragon's long neck and patted it. "It's a nice evening for cloud-surfing, huh?"

"Indeed."

With a grin, Raven waited for Leander to lower his belly to the dirt before she stepped up into the stirrup and swung her other leg over the saddle. The reins hung loosely from her hands to remind her that she'd had to use them less and less as her connection with him strengthened. She settled the straps of her satchel over both shoulders. *Grandpa had the right idea. There's a trick to traveling light.* "The sun's only up for a little while longer. Let's fly!"

Leander stamped a front paw on the oilskin bag in front of him. She grimaced a little at the thought of Connor Alby's journals crushed to a pulp. When the great red dragon beat his wings and rose swiftly and steadily into the air, however, the bag dangled safely from his razor-sharp claws. "Wait, we forgot the—"

Teo's beating wings lifted him onto his hind legs before he scooped Headmaster Flynn's old dragon saddle up and launched gracefully into the sky after Leander and his rider. Raven laughed and gave herself over to the flight. *They are so much more than fire-breathing beasts. I wish more people knew that.*

The wind whistled above and below Leander's mighty wings and the looser membranes along their sides ruffled in the airstream as he soared across the sky and leveled out far above Moss Ranch and the open dragon field below. The buffeting current brought tears to her eyes, and she uttered a loud whoop and glanced at the reins on the saddle horn before she spread her arms wide.

"Hey, look! No hands!" William shouted from Teo's back and laughed when she lowered her arms and looked at him in surprise. "I wouldn't make that a habit, though."

"Thanks for the advice." She laughed at herself too and

picked the reins up gently to hold them slackly in her hands. *But if I did make it a habit, it wouldn't matter. Our connection's strong enough that I probably don't even need the saddle.*

To test that thought, she looped the reins over the saddle horn again and leaned forward to stroke Leander's long, scaled neck. *Go ahead and take the wheel. Wherever you wanna go for a little while before we head to the school.* She patted the red, glistening scales once and Leander responded with a bellowed roar.

His wing dipped, and they banked to the right and slightly downward.

"What?" William tugged Teo's reins gently toward the right, and they angled after Leander and Raven before they leveled beside them. "Did you lose your sense of direction in the sky, war mage? Fowler Academy's the other way."

Raven grinned at him and shrugged, her hands clearly not closed around the reins. "I'm not making him go from one pen to another without a little fun first. We still have time."

With another laugh, William lifted Teo's reins enough to make sure she saw the gesture while he held his dragon steady beside Leander.

She cupped one hand around her ear and turned her head. "What was that? Sorry. The wind's too loud. I can't hear you."

Leander's wings beat with a furious thump against the rushing wind and his muscles rose and fell beneath her. He took them higher toward the thin wisps of clouds against the orange and pink sky. She whooped again, and William watched the silhouette of dragon and rider climb above him and Teo.

Not bothering to rush after them, Teo bent his long neck enough to catch his rider's gaze. "Those two are playing with fire up there."

He chuckled. "That's what they do, isn't it? Mage and dragon?"

"You know I spoke metaphorically."

"Yeah, I know, Teo." *It merely happens to be literal too.* "You get philosophical, don't you?"

"Only in the sky." The dragon turned his head away and beat his wings to catch another current.

William nodded and looked at the wheeling black shadow of the most untrainable dragon to step foot on Moss Ranch. *Only in the sky. It's the best place to be.*

CHAPTER ELEVEN

They soared over the grounds of Fowler Academy and approached from the southwest side across the open grounds moments before the last sliver of the setting sun faded behind the Mountains of Jared. William and Teo had pulled back slightly behind Raven and Leander, and her thick red braid streamed out behind her. *At least she didn't take him over the center of town. She knows what she's doing, even if she's not aware of it. Remember that.*

Leander slowed when they reached the barn and descended gracefully. Raven patted his neck and focused on the dark shapes that moved around the side of the stables beside the huge domed barn. "Do you see that? It's for you."

"Do any of them know what they're doing?"

"Actually, yes." The shapes of Fowler Academy professors grew larger and easier to distinguish as they approached at a sedate speed. "Headmaster Flynn was a dragon rider in the Great War. Even if he's the only one who knows about dragons, that's good enough for me."

"He fought with Connor Alby."

She swallowed and glanced at the worn saddle horn in front of her. Her fingers moved instinctively to touch her mother's pin on her jacket. "Yes. He did." *And maybe even with my mom.*

"Then I have expectations of him."

She laughed. "Many people do, I think."

The people on the ground at the edge of the stables paused what they were doing and turned to watch the quickly descending dragons. A few of them stepped back when Leander pulled up and beat his wings to settle himself sinuously into the grass. Raven's oilskin bag thumped down in front of them and William and Teo landed a few yards away.

"Good work." She rubbed the dragon's red scales again before he lowered his belly so she could dismount. His only reply was to incline his head and turn to look at her with one glowing yellow eye.

"Miss Alby." Headmaster Flynn was the first to approach and his long gray beard fluttered against his chest with his quick pace.

To Raven's surprise, the headmaster stopped a few yards in front of Leander and held the dragon's gaze as he lowered his head in a small bow. She slid onto the grass, and her dragon's head dipped ever so slightly toward Headmaster Flynn in return. *Yep. Flynn knows dragons, all right. Even after fifty years without his.*

That thought made her set her hand gently against Leander's muscular shoulder, which reassured them both. His head curved toward her enough to fix her with one eye, but he said nothing.

"So that's his new home, huh?" She nodded past the headmaster toward Professors Fellows, Gilliam, and Ambrose, all of whom stared at the two dragons.

Flynn turned to look at the other professors and raised his voice a little more than necessary. "We're almost finished but are still working on the last few details."

Professor Fellows chuckled and turned toward the mostly built pen. He raised his hands toward their project to cast a few more pieces into place. The other professors jolted out of their fascination and returned to their task.

"Huh." William walked toward the headmaster and stroked his chin as he watched the professor mages complete their work. "If we had mages around to do repairs, things would be much easier at the ranch. And more expensive."

Flynn smiled knowingly at the dragon trainer. "I believe you've pinned that down very well." He glanced quickly at Teo and gave the silver dragon a nod as well before he focused on Raven. "Miss Alby, I was under the impression that we would accommodate only one dragon at this school."

"Oh, William and Teo came to see us off and make sure Leander gets settled in."

"I don't want to stay out long past dark, anyway." William tried to restrain a chuckle. "Don't worry, Head-master. I'm definitely not trying to build a dragon ranch at Fowler Academy."

The man's smile widened and he leaned a little closer to them. "I might say that's a good thing, Mr. Moss, but I would speak only for my staff and no doubt quite a few students' parents. There's a great deal to learn from spending time around dragons." He straightened again and studied Leander with appreciation. "A great deal."

"We agree on that." William nodded toward the new pen, where the professors' spells finished tacking the posts and latched a wide gate into place. "Do you mind if I take a look before Teo and I head back?"

"Be my guest." Headmaster Flynn gestured for him to follow, then turned to lead the way.

William caught Teo's reins and led his dragon gently toward the stables. Raven gave Leander a questioning look.

He hadn't moved from where he'd lowered himself to let her dismount and now actually looked quite comfortable. "I'll stay here."

"Okay." She caught up to William and walked beside him. "Any thoughts so far?"

"Yeah. So far, it looks like they've gotten the basic shape right."

She smiled and shook her head. "Headmaster Flynn's overseeing the whole thing. I think he knows what he's doing."

"Maybe." His frown remained in place as he leaned toward her and lowered his voice. "Still, keep an eye out and be careful with Leander on the grounds. I'm not saying you wouldn't be already, but dragons aren't built for academia."

Raven laughed in response, then pressed her lips together when he didn't seem to think it was very funny.

"What I'm saying is that dragons are either with their clans or in a pen like Leander's. They aren't part of a menagerie or a school playground."

"I hear you." She nudged his arm with her elbow. "And I

have total faith that Leander will be absolutely fine—maybe even better than waiting for me at the ranch every day. It might take a little adjustment, but that's nothing new for us."

Finally, his frown softened and he gave her a crooked smile. "No, it's definitely not."

They reached the pen as the professors finished lifting everything into place. The glow of their spells faded, and Professor Fellows stepped back with a nod. "I think that's everything."

"Thank you." Headmaster Flynn nodded and studied the large pen with a satisfied nod.

"Wow." William glanced at Teo but the regal silver dragon beside him said nothing. "That's a big pen."

"It's perfect." Raven glanced at the eaves of the stables hanging out over one side of the structure. "It's open to the sky and has a little shelter. And it's almost twice the size of the pen on Moss Ranch. That's a ton of extra space."

"Yeah, enough to build considerable momentum if he makes his mind up to try to charge through these walls." William squinted at the new pen, handed Teo's reins to Raven, and leapt up the stairs onto the platform beside the gate. He peered over the top and gestured inside. "Do you have feed to fill that trough?"

Headmaster Flynn gazed at the dragon trainer without raising his head. "And a basin Miss Alby can fill with water as needed."

"Right." He jumped off the platform and nodded toward the stables. "Do you have space for extra dragon tack in there?"

"It's sufficient."

"What about the other animals? Keeping any sheep or goats nearby might be more of a problem than you might think."

Flynn clasped his hands behind his back and lowered his chin to stare at William from beneath his bushy eyebrows. "This isn't my first time around a dragon, young Mr. Moss."

"I know. But it's your first time around a dragon at a school full of mages in training." Clearing his throat, William turned and made another sweeping glance of the pen and the adjoining stables. "I have to ask about containment, Headmaster. Moss Ranch uses a—"

"Mr. Moss, I'm sure it won't surprise you to hear that none of the staff at Fowler Academy have a dragon trainer's experience, nor are they equipped to handle any... containment issues, should they arise."

"They won't," Raven added and handed Teo's reins to William.

"Yes, Miss Alby. I'm inclined to agree with you. Otherwise, I wouldn't have suggested this arrangement. But I will say that we've built something of an alarm system into this pen should anything happen."

"It won't."

"Yes, Miss Alby. Thank you."

Raven bit her lower lip and shared an amused glance with William but fought not to laugh.

"Both myself and these staff members here will be alerted—as will you, Miss Alby. In addition, I'm sure you'll be pleased to know that the wards around your dragon's pen have been specifically bound to your access rune alone, Miss Alby."

She touched her forearm beneath the sleeve of her jacket and glanced at the gate. "Only mine?"

"That is the only key, yes. I sincerely hope the mages in training attending this school have more than enough sense to keep well away from a dragon enclosure, but I understand the follies of youth all too well."

"What about you?' she asked.

"What about me, Miss Alby?"

"Can you open that gate?"

"I have absolutely no reason to want to try in the first place." The corners of the headmaster's mouth twitched in amusement. "Neither do your other professors."

"That is a...remarkable understatement, Headmaster Flynn." Ambrose stared at Teo with wide eyes and licked her lips.

"Headmaster." Raven waited for him to turn toward her. "Thank you. For making this happen and building this for Leander. And for trusting me with..." She chuckled and patted her forearm. "The key."

"As I mentioned this afternoon, Miss Alby, I expect great things from outstanding potential. And I believe that potential is impossible to reach from the end of a very short leash."

CHAPTER TWELVE

With a broad grin, she nodded and looked at William again. "So, it's a good deal, huh?"

The dragon trainer laughed despite his reservations and ran his hand through his hair. "Yeah. I'd say most of my concerns at this point are probably instinctual."

"Which means you're doing your job, Mr. Moss." The headmaster nodded and turned toward the other professors. "I believe we're finished for the evening—unless there's anything you may wish to add."

"No," Ambrose muttered and her voice squeaked a little as she shook her head. "Goodnight." The woman turned on her heel and hurried across the open field toward the main cluster of Fowler Academy's buildings.

Gilliam gave Raven a polite smile. "Get your familiar settled, Miss Alby. I'll wait for you in the girls' dormitory when you're finished. You have settling in of your own to do today."

"Thanks, Professor."

As the woman turned away, Professor Fellows grinned

at Teo, then peered around Raven for another look at Leander. The red dragon's head rested on his front paws, his eyes seemingly closed.

She didn't have to turn to check. *He's listening to everything.*

"It's incredible," Fellows said and shook his head in amazement. "Having that dragon around might put an extra bounce in Worley's step, huh? Well done, Miss Alby. I'll see you in class." The weapons professor turned and left those gathered around the pen.

"Why didn't Professor Worley come out tonight to help?" Raven asked the headmaster. "I thought he'd be almost as excited as you to have a dragon around."

"Oh, I'm sure he is." Flynn smiled at her again but it suddenly made him look tired and sad. "Professor Worley turned in early for the evening." The headmaster looked at the sky and the brightest stars already visible before twilight faded into black. "And I'm not that far behind him. If you need anything else, Miss Alby, you know where to find me. Mr. Moss. Goodnight."

"'Night," William replied with a nod.

"Thank you, Headmaster."

Flynn raised a hand in reply but didn't turn as he headed back toward the school's main buildings.

"Who's Professor Worley?"

"He handles familiar training." Raven stared after the fading shapes of her professors. "And he has at least two familiars. Probably more."

"Two?" William scoffed and shook his head. "Mages."

"I heard that." Raven smiled at the sight of Leander,

who still lay motionless with his head on his paws. "It's time to show my familiar his new temporary home."

"All right. It's almost dark." William nodded at Teo. "We should get back too."

"I agree." The silver dragon raised his head to gaze at the rapidly darkening sky.

"Keep an eye on him, okay?" The dragon trainer leaned his head toward Raven and lowered his voice as if they were still surrounded by all her professors. "You're the only familiar thing he has here, so try not to mix things up too much."

"Like today. I know. Dragons and consistency."

"And consider taking him out on a lead, at least while you're here. There are other animals in the stables, students everywhere...that's many more distractions than on the ranch where he grew up."

"It can't be any more distracting than all the other dragons and trainers packed together in Nadine." Raven folded her arms and bit her lip to keep from laughing. "Leander passed with flying colors on that one."

"You both did. But Nadine didn't have a horde of hormonal teenagers running around while they try to get a grasp on their mage abilities. Plus whatever else goes on here."

"What is that supposed to mean?"

William laughed and stepped closer to Teo when she fixed him with a mock frown. "Hey, how am I supposed to know? I've never been to magic school."

"Okay, well, for the most part, it's like any other kind of school—except for the occasional explosion and a few familiars temporarily running around as hybrid animals. And a dragon."

"Yep. Only regular, everyday stuff for non-mages too. Totally."

Raven folded her arms, still feigning insult. "Watch it, flyboy."

"Woah. Do you hear that, Teo?" With a chuckle, William stepped into the stirrup and swung into his dragon's saddle. "Now I'm starting to wonder if it's the dragon training the rider."

Teo stared at him, then turned his head on his long neck and bared his teeth in a dragon's grin. "You mean to say you never considered the possibility?"

"Okay, buddy. Don't get any ideas." He settled into the saddle and turned to call, "'Night, Leander."

The red dragon didn't open his eyes. "Not yet."

"Thanks for the help. And the tips." Raven thumped her foot idly against her satchel and grinned. "Try not to worry about us, okay? We got this. You showed us how and we'll be fine."

"I know, war mage. Don't be a stranger while you're livin' the life at magic school."

"It's a fifteen-minute flight, William. If we take our time."

"Uh-huh. Good luck."

Teo inclined his head toward her as his wings stretched fully. "Raven."

"Bye, Teo."

The silver dragon launched high and a few blades of broken grass flurried in the slipstream before the thick flap of his powerful wings receded into the night.

Raven watched them until they vanished in the darkness. *It's still an awesome thing to watch a dragon land and take off. I prefer being the rider, though.* She walked toward Leander, who made no effort to move even when she stopped a few feet in front of him. "Are you ready to break your new home in?"

"I've grown fond of this patch of grass."

"I think you'll grow even fonder of a much bigger pen and far more privacy. Unless, of course, you look forward to being woken by a horde of ogling…what was that again?" She smirked when Leander opened one eye and settled his gaze on her.

The massive red dragon snorted but he pushed to his feet like she knew he would. "Children."

"Oh, that's right." She stretched beneath his belly to unfasten the straps of the saddle, pulled it off carefully, and placed it on the grass. "If you're not an early riser, I can't promise the children won't wake you."

"I rise before the sun, Raven. Exactly like you."

She didn't voice her surprise but instead, pressed her hand against his shoulder as they walked toward his new home. *Can he really feel it when I wake up?*

When they reached the gate, she removed her jacket despite the returned chill after sundown and tossed it over her shoulder. She raised the underside of her forearm toward it and exposed the access rune put there on her first day of school. It glowed with a dim orange light before the barrier did the same. A bolt slid out of the pen wall and the gate opened. "No handle, huh? At least that'll stop people from trying to open this on their own."

"It wouldn't have stopped you from trying." He nudged her shoulder with his snout.

Raven laughed and stepped through the open gate into his new pen. "That's a good point. It's not the same here, though. Everyone knows you're my familiar and there's nothing to try to save you from now."

"Not even the threat of clipped wings." He passed gracefully through the open gate, which left far more room for his broad shoulders than the pen at Moss Ranch.

That one was way too small. He'll be happier here. "That's right. Not even the threat." She walked backward across the enclosure and glanced at the stairs before she gestured around her. "It's seriously roomy in here, right?'

"Maybe for you." He stopped in the center in front of her and spread his wings as far as they would go. A low rumble rose from his chest. "Maybe for me."

"Look at that. There are a few extra feet on either side. No more wing cramps, either."

The massive, translucent wings folded over his back and he turned in a few slow, lumbering circles before he settled and curled into himself. "It might benefit you to study more dragon anatomy, little girl."

Chuckling, she stepped toward him. The dragon's forelegs shifted apart to give her space to step as close as she could to his huge, regal head. "Really? What did I miss?"

"I don't get cramps."

"Oh, okay." She laughed and with both hands, stroked his large, ridged muzzle. "But you gotta admit the extra room to stretch is a big improvement."

Leander closed his eyes as she ran her hand from the

top of his nose to the middle of his broad forehead. "I appreciate the grass."

"I'm glad. This will be good for us, Leander. I know it. Do you need anything before I go find out where I'll sleep?"

"Which building?" His voice was quieter now, almost soft.

Raven turned and could barely see the top of the girls' dormitory where it peeked above the edge of the pen. "It's the wide rectangular building on this side of the towers. I bet I'll be able to see you from my window." *I hope.*

"I'll be waiting for you." The dragon pressed his snout against her side and with another small laugh, she wound her arms around her familiar's warm, scaled head.

"I won't be late."

CHAPTER THIRTEEN

With the saddles stored in the stable and her dragon turned in for the night, Raven stopped at the entrance to the girls' dormitory and looked at the multiple stories. She sighed and grimaced as the oilskin bag cut into her shoulder. *I hope I'm not all the way at the top.*

The door opened and Gilliam poked her head out. "Follow me, Miss Alby. You're in time for lights-out and I suggest you turn in." The woman's mouth widened in an enormous yawn that ended with a little hiccup. "Excuse me. Obviously, I'll do the same very soon."

"I hope I didn't make you wait too long."

"No, no. It's fine." The woman gestured for her to enter and waited for her to comply before she pulled the door shut again. "One can't rush a dragon, I suppose."

She stifled a laugh. "Very true."

"All right, Miss Alby. This is the common room. It's open for use whenever you wish, but we do expect the students living on academy grounds to abide by lights-out. The last time I was woken in the middle of the night by a backfiring invisibility spell, that student had detention for a month."

"Woah. That sounds kind of harsh, doesn't it?"

Gilliam looked over her shoulder with a highly amused little smirk. "Not compared to the alternative. Professor Fellows wanted to help the boy perfect the spell, then make him attend weapons classes for a week where none of the others could see him."

Yeah, being invisible wouldn't be good around all those weapons. "Fair enough."

Professor Gilliam led her across the common room filled with couches, armchairs, low tables, and a few desks. At the far end of the room, a large staircase rose before it separated to the left and the right. "Those take you to the east and west wings. You'll be on the west, although they connect again on each floor. Oh, let me help you with your bag."

"I got it, thanks."

"Don't be silly." The woman slid her hand around the strap of the oilskin bag and her eyes bulged when she tried to lift it from her shoulder.

"Really, Professor Gilliam. I'm fine."

"Yes." The woman grimaced and shook her head. "I'm sure you can handle it."

She smiled and waited for the professor to lead her up the staircase. *The benefits of being a goat rancher.*

They went up two flights of steps and stopped on the third floor of the four-story dormitory. Her guide turned to make sure she was still there, then gestured down the hall. "We're almost there."

"Great." She puffed a sigh and hiked her luggage a little

higher on her shoulder. The straps dug into her even worse than before. *It feels like I've carried this all day.*

At the end of the hall, the woman stopped and knocked on the second-to-last closed door on the left. A muffled shuffle and a squeak came from the room before the handle turned and the door opened slowly. "Ah. Miss Kinsley. You finally have a roommate."

Elizabeth Kinsley opened the door a little farther and returned to her bed without a word. Her bat familiar flapped a few times on top of the comforter as the young mage climbed onto the mattress and crossed her legs. She didn't look up from her book when Raven stepped into the doorway.

"I'm sure if you have any questions, Miss Kinsley can answer them for you. Lights-out is in five, Miss Alby. That doesn't apply to your room, of course, but the rest of the building is expected to be empty, dark, and quiet for the rest of the night."

"Thank you, Professor." Raven nodded and Gilliam glanced at Elizabeth once more before she smiled wearily.

"Goodnight." With that, the woman wandered down the hall again toward the stairwell.

The oilskin bag dropped with a muffled thud. "Hey, Elizabeth."

The girl didn't look up from her book and merely tossed her dark bangs aside before they swooped over one eye again.

Before she could step into her new room, the door on their left squeaked a little. Teresa Reynolds pushed it open as far as it would go and folded her arms as she leaned against the doorframe. "Raven Alby. I thought it was you."

"It's good to know I can't be confused with anyone else."

Teresa studied her dismissively and raised an eyebrow. "Do you have any idea how long we'll be neighbors?"

"Not really." Raven smiled and shoved the oilskin bag into her new dorm room with her foot. "But I'll let you know when I find out. Goodnight."

Once she dragged her belongings inside, she shut the door quietly behind her and sighed. A moment later, she heard the sound of Teresa's door clicking shut too. She hauled her bag toward the twin bed on the opposite side of the room and nodded at Elizabeth. "Hey, thanks for sharing a room with me. I know you're probably used to having this whole space to yourself."

The girl merely shrugged, shook her bangs aside to no effect, and turned the page of her book.

I'm gonna take that as indifference. It's better than resentment. Finally, she manhandled her luggage to where she wanted it and released it beside the bed. Her satchel followed before she rummaged through the oilskin bag for her pajamas. When her fingers brushed against the old leather of Connor Alby's journals, she paused.

"Hey, do you mind if I do a little…personalized spell?"

Apparently, that was interesting enough to make Elizabeth look up from her book. Raven nodded at the wall they shared with Teresa and whoever her roommate was, and the girl turned her head slowly to stare at the wall. "Sure."

"Thanks." She crossed the room and stood just inside the door and facing their neighbors. Raising both hands, she flipped through the spells her grandfather had already taught her and pulled to mind the one she wanted. *"Incigo silentium,"* she whispered.

A copper light bloomed from her palms and spread across the entire wall. She focused on the moving spell until it covered all four walls, the ceiling, the floor, and the door. When it reached completion, she lowered her hands with a little sigh.

The room she shared with Elizabeth Kinsley was suddenly blissfully quiet. Her roommate gazed around her and her bat familiar cocked his head in very much the same way. "Wow. That's so much better."

"I'm glad you think so." She dusted her hands off and returned to her side of the room.

"Reading is the only thing that drowns out all the conversation. It's not like the walls are super-thin, but I have a hard time focusing if I can hear other people."

Seated on the edge of the bed, she grinned and couldn't help a small chuckle. *That's the most I've ever heard her say.* "Well, I guess it works out for both of us, huh?"

A small, closed-lipped smile spread across the girl's mouth. "Yeah. Peace and quiet for me and Iggy. And I assume you don't want to listen to one of Bella Chase's best friends talking all night either, huh?"

Raven shook her pajamas out and laid them on the bed with a shrug before she pulled her boots off. "It's more like making a safe space for myself—and you too. I didn't know I'd have to sleep right next door to Teresa, but I'm not gonna worry about a slipped word here or there. If no one can hear us outside this room, I won't waste time wondering who might've heard me say what."

Elizabeth snorted. "It probably wouldn't have been that big of a deal anyway. No offense, Raven, but I'm not really into staying up late and swapping secrets."

Her boots clunked on the floor and she looked at her new roommate and laughed. "Me neither."

"Cool. Welcome to the dorms." The other girl returned to her book and didn't say anything else.

Okay. I think this whole dorm thing might work out better than I expected.

Once she'd slipped out of her clothes, she pulled her pajamas on and tried to tidy everything. *I can unpack tomorrow.* With the dirty clothes roughly folded in a pile at the foot of her bed, she headed toward the wide window in the middle of the back wall.

She brushed the thin curtains aside and peered into the darkness. Even from there, she could make out the large dome of the barn and the stables beside it. They only looked a little larger with the new extension, but at least she could see the pen from there. "This is perfect."

Elizabeth closed her book and set it on the nightstand. "Can you see him?"

"You mean Leander?"

"If that's your dragon's name, then yeah."

Raven took one more glance out the window and nodded. "Well, his pen, at least. I bet I'll see him stretching over the walls in the morning."

She wandered to her bed and turned the covers down. "So does the whole school already know that I finally brought my familiar to Fowler? 'Cause I only found out after classes let out today."

"Professor Gilliam came to tell me after you got here, I guess." The girl slipped under her covers. "I have no idea who else knows, but I'm sure everyone expected you to bring your dragon with you soon anyway."

"Yeah. The circumstances were kind of weird but I know everything will work out. And I'm sure everyone will know tomorrow by the time class starts for the day."

"Probably." Elizabeth snuggled under her blanket and didn't move at all when her bat familiar scrambled onto the pillow and buried himself in her dark hair. "I'm gonna sleep like a baby tonight."

With a quiet laugh, she slid into bed, pulled the covers up over her shoulder, and pointed at the large lantern hanging from the ceiling. *"Nullen lucidis."*

The magical light snuffed out and from where she lay, she could see the stars and the end sliver of a waxing moon through the window. *Hopefully, Leander's sleeping like a baby dragon, too.*

CHAPTER FOURTEEN

Despite the little sleep she'd had the night before, Raven woke on instinct a little over an hour before dawn. She reached sleepily toward her nightstand on the right, but her fingers cracked against the wall of her dorm room instead. "Ow."

Whoops. She glanced at Elizabeth's dark, curled form in the bed across the room and sighed. *I hope lights-out doesn't apply to waking early. I won't go back to sleep.*

As quietly as she could, she slipped out of bed and crouched beside the oilskin bag. *"Circum inlustro,"* she whispered. A small, soft white glow formed and hovered over her bag while she rifled through her things for new clothes. She dressed quickly, located her boots, and was out of the room without Elizabeth stirring even a little. The glowing light bobbed along behind her, giving her enough to see by but hopefully not enough to wake any of the other girls still sleeping behind their doors.

The girls' dormitory was quiet, but she caught a few snores and voices muttered in sleep as she moved down the hall to the bathroom. *That silence charm is a good one. Thanks, Grandpa.*

A short while later, she reached the common room and finally stopped to put her boots on before she eased outside into the cold air. Fowler Academy looked completely different beneath all the stars and the moon on the other side of the sky. She took a deep breath through her nose and tilted her head as she considered the odd feeling within. "Huh. I never thought I'd miss the smell of goats and hay in the morning."

The muted light of her spell hovered over her head as she hurried through the curved archway and into the field. The grass whispered beneath her boots, everything perfectly quiet in the hour when everyone but the kingdom's hard-working ranchers was still asleep.

Before she reached the closest side of the stables, Leander snorted. His steaming breath rose in plumes above the top of the pen. She grinned and increased the pace but tried not to disturb any of the other animals that slept in the stables. Quickly, she slid her left arm out of her jacket to hold her access rune to the gate, which unlocked as quickly as it had the night before. The barrier squeaked a little when she opened it and she stepped inside and shut it again.

Raven turned hastily and came face to face with shimmering scales and glowing yellow eyes only a foot away from her face. "Woah. Are you trying to sneak up on me?"

"As much as you were trying to sneak up on me." Leander pressed his muzzle against her shoulder and she laughed quietly and slid both hands up the sides of his face.

"I wasn't trying to sneak up on you, only trying not to

wake anyone else. I didn't even hear you move across the pen."

"I heard you halfway across the field."

She patted the top of his nose below the brilliant yellow eyes. "I guess I'll have to work on my stealth, then."

"Why? You have me." He pulled away from her and as he circled the pen, his tail cut a thick, snakelike path through the grass.

"Huh. Actually, that's a really good point."

"I know." The red dragon looked at the dark sky and stretched his long neck as far as it would go. A forepaw scratched the grass and damp earth beneath him as he sniffed the air.

"So. How was your first night at Hotel Fowler?"

Another snort escaped him. "Uneventful."

"Hey, that's a start."

"Raven." Leander lowered his head and hunkered in the grass again, although he didn't curl or rest his head on his paws.

He looks like he's about to pounce. "What's wrong?"

"Something feels…not quite right."

With a frown, she walked toward him and scanned his long neck, broad shoulder, and the massive wings tucked closely against his back. "Does something hurt? You look fine to me."

"Not me. Something in the air—or the earth. Perhaps both."

"Hmm." She bit the inside of her lower lip, stepped toward him, and trailed her hand from the top of his head all the way down his back. "Is there any chance you could be a little more specific?"

"If there were, little girl, I would have been more specific."

"Right. You know, it was weird for me to wake up here too." When he turned his head toward her and curled his tail in the same direction, she sat on the grass to lean against his rough, leathery side. "I've spent every night, for as long as I can remember, waking up at home on Alby Ranch. I almost broke my fingers thinking I was still there in my bed. We'll get used to being here. Like I said, though, it might take a little time."

His head curved closer toward her on his long neck until he rested it on the ground beside her. "That's not what I meant."

"It's not?"

"I already enjoy this pen much more. You're closer, it's quiet, and I look forward to not hearing trainers bark commands at dragons all day."

Raven laughed. "William doesn't bark."

"No. I suppose it's more like a squawk."

She buried her face in her hands and laughed again. *We're gonna wake every animal in those stables.* "Well, I'm really glad to hear you're already settling in. I knew you'd like it."

"Like is a strong word, little girl."

"Oh, sorry. How about tolerate?"

A low rumble vibrated through his chest against her back but it cut off quickly. "Yes. Even still…"

"Something feels not quite right, huh?"

The dragon's large yellow eye facing her closed slowly as he released a long sigh. Steam rose from his nostrils. "Something, yes, and I can't say what."

"Okay. For now, let's chalk it up to the strangeness of being in a new place, huh? Which doesn't mean we sweep it under the rug. I can't say there's nothing going on or nothing to be worried about, but until you can be a little more specific, there's not much we can do about it, right? I wish there were."

Leander opened his eyes again and studied her face. "You're learning, little girl. Months ago, I think you would have told me to either explain this…feeling or deal with it."

Raven chuckled again. "Yeah, you've taught me a thing or two about patience, haven't you?"

"I trust you, Raven. You've taught me that in return."

With a sigh, she smiled and rested her head against his side to gaze at the stars. "You know, I think I could live with this new routine. I could skip feeding the goats altogether and spend the first few hours of my day hanging out with a dragon."

"There are no goats and I'm the only dragon here. You don't have much of a choice." He uttered another low rumble and hissed a little through rows of sharp teeth.

"Ha, ha. I meant hanging out with you, specifically." She stroked the top of his huge head beside her. "I like not having to wait until after school to see you."

"The pen on the grounds is as far as I go. I hope you don't expect me to step into your classes with the other familiars."

"Nope. No one expects that. But I'm happy with the tradeoff. Sure, the other students have their familiars with them almost every second of every day, but I'm the one who gets to fly."

"Hmm. The conversation's not horrible either."

She snorted and settled comfortably into the warm pocket of her drackan's leathery hide behind her and his head beneath her hand so his warm breath blew against her legs. *Maybe this is where we're supposed to be for now. And if there is something going on, we'll find out what it is.*

Utterly contented, she stayed with him until the black sky lightened to the blue-gray before dawn. "*Nullen lucidis.*" The glowing light hovering above her head winked out. "Are you hungry?"

"I will be eventually."

"Well, yeah." She scrambled to her feet and stroked his side again before she stepped across the pen toward the gate. "I guess I'm still feeding someone early in the morning, huh? I'll be right back."

Leander's wings twitched where he lay but he didn't say a word.

Yeah, I could probably have fallen asleep again like that too. Raven pushed the gate open and headed quickly to the stable entrance. Already, a few of the horses and less dorm-friendly familiars stirred in their stalls. The crate of dragon-feed in burlap sacks wasn't that hard to find stacked with the other animals' food, and she bent at the knees with a little grunt before she threw the sack over her shoulder and carried it outside again.

Even in that short space of time, the darkness had lifted significantly. She almost dropped the bag of feed when she saw the gate wide open. *Come on, Raven. Remember where you are.* She quickened her pace and turned halfway toward the dark shapes of Fowler Academy's buildings against the lightening sky. "Leander?"

He looked at her with a drowsy surprise when she stepped into the pen. "Were you expecting someone else?"

"Um…" She exhaled a sigh of relief and shook her head as she headed to the empty trough beneath the stables' awning. "No. But apparently, I've forgotten the importance of closing gates behind me." The sack of feed thumped into the grass and she stooped to slide her fingers along the inside of her boot. The dagger slid free quickly and she cut a hole in the top of the sack and returned the blade before she heaved the burlap over the edge of the trough. Dragon feed spilled into the long metal container with a metallic ping, and she wrinkled her nose. *It smells like pickled sausage and…maybe I don't wanna think about it.*

Leander sniffed the air but didn't move. "You seem overly worried about an open gate. I told you I wouldn't leave."

"You did. And I know you keep your word. It's everyone else I'm worried about." *And the earful I'd get from almost everyone if someone wiggled their way into a dragon pen. Including the dragon.*

"I thought these mages in training had to be smart to attend this school."

Raven snorted and turned to smirk at him as she folded the empty bag over her arm. "They do. And there's the part about magic being a requirement. Hey, if I were anyone else, I might take insult to that. You know, because I'm smart and I didn't stay away from dragons."

"You are different, Raven Alby. We both know that."

She sighed again, nodded, and crossed the pen. "You're different too, Leander. I guess that's what makes us such a good team."

The dragon rose to his feet and turned to face her as his tail whispered through the grass. "That basin's still empty."

"What—oh." She pointed at him and gave him a playful frown. "I know you agree with me, by the way. Nice job trying to deflect."

He responded with another gentle rumble as she strode through the gate again to find a big enough bucket to fill the basin with well water. This time, she made sure to close it again behind her. *I have manipulating fire under my belt, no problem. Water manipulation would be nice right about now. Grandpa's gone, so I guess I'll have to look for it on my own.*

CHAPTER FIFTEEN

R aven left her dragon familiar with a full trough, a mostly full water basin, and a promise to be back as soon as her last class finished, if not sooner. The animals in the stables sounded hungrier than he did as she crossed the field on her way to the main buildings. *Worley takes care of those guys. He has it covered.*

Her stomach grumbled noisily as she entered through the curved archway into the school's main courtyard. She gave the stone a pat in passing and frowned at the buildings. *No hot rolls on the walk through Brighton and no Henry Derks first thing in the morning, either. It's gonna take some getting used to.*

She was about to return to the girls' dormitory for her satchel but stopped a few feet into the busy common room. "Woah."

A long table against the left wall held a huge bowl of fruit, assorted pastries, blocks of cheese and sausage, a smaller bowl of hardboiled eggs, and crocks of butter and honey. The girls living on the Fowler Academy grounds milled around the common room, talking, practicing spells, studying, and lining up along the table for breakfast. *No one said a thing about meals.*

Without hesitation, she joined the back of the line that moved quickly down the long table and snatched an apple. When she reached the tray of pastries, she couldn't help but laugh. "Yes!"

With three steaming hot rolls stacked in her hand, she moved farther and peered into the ceramic pitcher at the end. She leaned forward to take a quick sniff. *It smells like goat milk. It'd better be Alby goat milk.*

As she tore a huge chunk of roll off between her teeth, she scanned the tables in the common room and peered around the other girls who moved between the service table and their chosen seats. Elizabeth sat at one of the tables and nibbled on a hunk of cheese as she stared at the book on the table. With the other hand, she fed her bat familiar one ripe blueberry at a time.

Raven moved to the table and pulled out the chair with her foot before she plopped into it. "Morning."

The girl nodded but her gaze lingered on the page until she finished reading and turned it. She finally looked at her new roommate. "Oh. Hey, Raven. When did you get up?"

"At my normal time." She bit into the roll again and shrugged. "A couple of hours ago."

"Wow. Did you go out for a dragon visit?"

"Yeah. He's doing well out there so far." *Except for something 'not quite right.' We'll keep our eyes open on that one.* "Hey, how great is this, huh?"

Elizabeth only frowned when Raven lifted the hot rolls and her apple. "You've…never had an apple before?"

She laughed. "I had no idea they served breakfast here. Okay, I guess I never thought about it before when the dorms weren't part of my day. Seriously, I think this might be the first time I have three rolls in my hand and the chance to actually eat all of them."

That only confused her companion more, so the girl shrugged and glanced at her book. Her dark bangs swooped across one eye again but she didn't bother to push them aside. "Welcome to living at Fowler."

"It's kind of better than I thought." She leaned back in the chair and ate the second roll in under a minute. Elizabeth didn't look at her once. "Okay. I'll leave you to your book. See you in class."

The girl nodded without looking up from the page and fed another berry to her bat.

Raven passed a few more girls in the stairwell on her way to the third floor. Many of them were upperclassmen but all of them either said hello or gave the newest resident a warm smile. *Yeah, this is okay. There isn't as much personal space as there was at home, but I'll get enough of that with Leander later.*

When she reached her room almost at the end of the hall, the rolls were finished and the apple halfway eaten. She tried to open the door and almost smacked her face against the wood when the doorknob didn't turn.

"What?" She glanced around the empty hallway and jiggled the doorknob again. "Okay, there's no keyhole, so... oh!" With a grimace, she shrugged her arm out of her jacket again and held her forearm to the doorknob. The access rune glowed orange, as did the doorknob, and after a soft click, she was able to finally open the door. *Headmaster Flynn had it right. Actual keys.*

She hurried to her bed and retrieved her satchel from the floor, then opened it to make sure she had everything she needed. "And then some."

A few extra textbooks thumped onto her bedspread and she hefted the satchel over her shoulder and grinned. *Yeah, I'm packing light.*

Before she left, the thin curtains over the window caught her attention again. Smiling, she pulled them aside and gazed at the perfect view she'd been given. The new dragon pen was more visible in the morning light, and the tips of two huge wings flashed a bright crimson in the sun where they peeked over the top of the pen wall before they vanished again. *I think he's enjoying himself.*

Raven joined the other students gathered outside the stone archway into the field. Professor Fellows had already set up a few sectioned-off sparring rings with lines of thick rope laid in the grass. Beside the outer wall surrounding Fowler Academy's main buildings, two wheelbarrows overflowed with various training weapons. Raven couldn't help but glance at the barn across the field, but so far, Leander was lying low.

"Hey, Alby! What the hell?" Henry shoved around the last stream of students gathering for their first class, his eyes wide and his brown hair protruding in every direction. He ran a hand through it and only made the disheveled look worse.

"Morning." She grinned as he finally squeezed through to her side. "What happened to you, Derks?"

"What happened to me? What happened to you? I

waited for half an hour for you at the gate this morning and you never showed! Then I had to run all the way here so I wouldn't walk into a class half an hour late."

"We've been late to class before, remember?" She nudged him with her shoulder. "And I'm fairly sure it wasn't that big a deal."

"Yeah, that was you, me, and Murphy. It's much easier to keep a low profile when I'm not the only person to catch everyone's attention." He spun on the grass and searched through the other students engaged in their conversations for the next few minutes. "Speaking of Murphy, I have no idea where she is either. She wasn't at the fountain when I got there because you weren't at the gate!"

"Okay. Slow down, killer." Raven gave his back a few quick, heavy pats. "I didn't know that would freak you out so much. Sorry."

"I'm not freaked out." He looked at her with wide eyes and they both laughed. "Seriously, Alby, I thought something happened. After all that weirdness about your grandpa up and leaving, you decide to change up our morning routine without any kinda warning."

Raven caught sight of Murphy as the girl stepped through the archway and waved. Fritz crouched in the tall grass behind her before he pounced on a bug. "Much more than that got changed up, Henry. It wasn't my plan or my first choice, but I think it's working out all right."

He stared at her and tucked Maxwell's head absently into the top of his shoulder bag without looking. "Define 'much more.' And tell me why I'm only hearing about this now."

"Hey, I would've told you everything yesterday after I

gave Headmaster Flynn that letter." She smirked at him and raised an eyebrow. "But you had a date with Jenny."

Henry blinked. "It wasn't a date."

"It's totally cool, Derks. I get it. And I'm not gonna hold it against you or anything. She's into you."

"I was tutoring her on that spell—"

"Okay. We can call it that." She laughed when his nose wrinkled in frustration. "But I wasn't at the gate this morning because I was already here."

A sharp laugh burst from him, and a few other students turned to regard him with curious amusement. From the corner of her eye, she saw Bella Chase turn with a smirk of superiority aimed at Henry Derks before the dark-haired girl settled her gaze on her.

"Why the hell would you wanna be here that early?" he asked.

"Hey, guys." Murphy shuffled between the other students until she stopped on the other side of Henry. "Is everything okay?"

Raven laughed and shook her head. "You too, Murphy?"

"Um…well, I didn't see either of you at the fountain this morning, so I was worried."

Henry stepped back to point at the girl before he nodded vigorously at Raven with wide eyes. "See?"

"I'm fine. And I'm sorry I made you guys worry by changing up the routine." *I guess that's on the list of things to avoid with dragons and mage friends.* "I moved into the girls' dorm last night."

Her friends both fixed her with incredulous looks. Leaning forward, Henry whispered, "Are you trying to make my head explode?"

"What? No, Derks. When I brought Flynn that letter yesterday, he said—"

"Okay, first-years! Settle down." Professor Fellows clapped and stalked across the grass beside the wall toward the wheelbarrows full of weapons. "Tongues in your mouths, eyes on me."

"No problem," Murphy whispered and tilted her head to watch their weapons professor with a dreamy haze in her eyes. Henry took another step back and frowned at the girl. Raven chuckled.

"Magic is a powerful tool." Fellows' voice lifted across the gathered students and his long gray hair fluttered around his shoulders in the breeze. "You're learning how it can become even more powerful when strengthened by the bond between you and your familiar."

"Have you had any progress with that one, Alby?" Henry muttered.

"Oh, yeah."

"What?"

She darted him a sideways glance and nodded at Professor Fellows. "I'll tell you later. Promise."

He puffed out a sigh and stuck his hands in his pockets.

"Almost as strong but no less important than your connection with your familiar," Fellows continued, "is the bond formed with those fighting beside you. No mage works entirely alone, and let's hope we never see the day when that becomes a necessity."

"Oh, boy," Henry muttered. "Team battles."

Professor Fellows gestured toward the wheelbarrows beside him with a smirk. "In a moment, each of you will choose a training weapon from our selection. After that, I will assign partners and each team will be matched for two-on-two sparring. Get moving. We have much to cover."

The students filed toward the wheelbarrows and formed some semblance of a line as each of the first-years selected their training weapon. Raven pulled a long, dull-edged sword out and swung it a few times. The air whistled around it but it was poorly balanced and would deliver more bruises than anything else. *If I even get a hit in. Grandpa's sword is a hell of a lot better.*

"Uh, Professor?" Henry tucked his toad familiar's head into his satchel again as he stepped aside to lower his voice. "What if we brought our own weapon?"

"No daggers, Mr. Derks. Not today."

"Nope. No daggers." He chuckled nervously and watched Bennett remove a long wooden staff with a ball at the end instead of a spear's sharp point. "Only a slingshot. It's kinda my go-to. Not for battles or anything, but my aim's fairly decent."

Fellows licked his lips, folded his arms, and fought back a laugh. "And you want to improve your battle skills with a slingshot this morning?"

"Not unless you have any bows in there and...non-lethal arrows."

This time, the professor laughed. "Not today, Mr. Derks. But if you think you can offer your partner something of value with a slingshot over any of these other weapons, by all means, sling away."

"Right." Henry frowned at the man, then nodded quickly and bypassed the wheelbarrows altogether. "Thanks."

The weapons professor chuckled and called, "I thought I said hurry, people. This class will be halfway over by the time you've all chosen your weapons if you shuffle around like a class full of old men too deep in their cups."

"You'd think comparing student mages to a group of drunks would be one of those frowned-upon things at a school like this, right?" Henry lifted the strap of his shoulder bag over his head and set it on the ground. Maxwell hopped out and sat completely still in the grass at his mage's feet.

Raven shrugged. "Probably. I don't think he cares. He called Professor Gilliam by her first name yesterday."

"Oh, the horror." He snickered.

"And that was right before Headmaster Flynn asked them to step out of his office so they wouldn't see him burn my grandpa's letter."

"What?"

With raised eyebrows, she nodded. "We have so much to catch up on, Derks."

Murphy joined them as the students spread out across the grass again. The girl hefted a comically large ax with both hands. The head was dented and so dull, it was almost rounded along the blade.

Raven chuckled. "I can't wait to hear your reasoning for choosing that one, Murphy."

"Uh...well, it was either this or a wooden dagger." She glanced at her barn cat familiar and shrugged. "I'm not sure I like the odds of a battle royale with a blunt piece of wood."

Henry eyed the weapon with an unsure smile. "Can you even lift that above your shoulders?"

Their friend took a step back and swung it with both hands like she wanted to fell a whole tree in one chop. With a yelp of surprise, he leapt back and burst out laughing. Murphy's cheeks flushed again but at least this time, she smiled. "That felt like a good start."

"Okay, people." With his hands clasped behind his back, Professor Fellows paced slowly in front of his students. "I call your names, and each group takes their place in one of these sparring circles. Remember, this is only one day. You didn't form a connection with your familiars in one day, and I hardly expect you to get to know each other in the span of an hour while fighting someone else trying to do the same. The importance of this is that you try and you learn, and there will be a prize for the team with the most wins. Mr. Derks and Miss Aberdeen will face Mr. Cotton and Miss Knowles."

"All right." Henry grinned, wiggled his slingshot in front of Raven, and pulled a huge handful of stones out of his pocket. "It's a good thing I've already bonded with this little beauty here."

"They'll never see it coming." Raven grinned and gave him a thumbs-up as he and Julia took their places on the far end of the first sparring ring.

"Then I want Miss Alby and…oh, yes. Miss Chase. Pair up, please. You'll spar with Miss Reynolds and Miss Murphy this morning. Take your places."

Murphy's eyes widened as she watched Professor Fellows move down the line of students and call out one team after another. She met Raven's gaze and went a little pale. "You and Bella are gonna win that prize for sure. It's kind of an unfair advantage there. No offense."

"I'm not offended at all," she said as Bella Chase gave her a haughty smile before the girl tossed her hair over her shoulder and headed toward them. "We might have more of a disadvantage too."

"The two witches at this school with the best handle on their magic and a long line of powerful mages running through the family? That doesn't sound like a disadvantage."

"No. But I'm not sure Bella will play fair on a team at all." Raven lifted the dull practice sword in front of her and tested its weight. "Not with me, anyway."

"Not against me either, I bet." Murphy swallowed.

"Come on." She nodded toward their sparring ring set up in the grass, where Bella and Teresa were already in the middle of a conversation. Leaning toward Murphy, she muttered, "Don't be afraid to really swing with that thing, huh? Don't hold back."

The girl glanced at her friend's dull weapon and grimaced. "I wish I could say the same about that sword."

CHAPTER SIXTEEN

"The goal is to balance both offensive and defensive techniques. To balance using magic with using your weapons. And, of course, to find balance in fighting with your partner and your familiar to defeat your opponents." Professor Fellows frowned a little, but more than anything, he looked highly amused.

Bella darted Raven a sidelong glance and sighed. "I heard your dragon finally made an appearance at Fowler Academy."

"Not only an appearance." Raven glanced across the field toward the stables and the new dragon pen attached to the end of the building. "Leander's here to stay now. And so am I."

"But you're still not one hundred percent qualified for these lessons without your familiar at your side, are you?" Bella struck the butt of the bo staff she'd selected into the grass and dirt with a thud.

She shook her head and lifted her practice sword in readiness. "I'm completely qualified, Bella. That's why I'm

MARTHA CARR & MICHAEL ANDERLE

here." *Maybe even overqualified with a dragon as my familiar.* "You're smart. You'll figure it out soon enough."

"Figure what out?"

Across their sparring ring, Murphy and Fritz took their places. The ax seemed particularly huge in the girl's hands. Beside her, Teresa and her ferret familiar looked a little worried—probably not at the prospect of fighting with Murphy but to fight against Bella. *And maybe me, even without my familiar.*

She crouched into a fighting stance and gave Bella a determined smirk. "You'll hopefully see that I learn what I need to learn one way or the other. My familiar might not be sparring with me but he's close enough now to make a difference."

Bella's pert smile faded for a second as she glanced at the stables across the fields.

"Any foot that steps beyond the ropes of the sparring arena forfeits the match," Professor Fellows called. "I want to see you working together. On my mark!"

Bella recovered from her surprise, twirled the bo staff a few times, and assumed a ready stance beside her team-mate. Teresa laughed nervously as she swung her practice sword, and Raven met Murphy's gaze. *She looks terrified.* "Don't hold back," she muttered and gave her friend a reassuring nod.

"Don't worry, I won't," Bella said. "Wesley and I won't have any problem picking up your slack."

She pressed her lips together and swung the practice sword at her side to test its weight again. "I wasn't talking to you."

"Begin!" Fellows shouted.

The field filled instantly with the clash of wood and steel sparring weapons against each other. A few students shouted warnings to their impromptu partners and familiars darted in and out between weapons and opponents. A few spells were cast.

Bella didn't hesitate and surged toward Teresa with the bo staff raised. Her firedrake launched himself off her shoulder and darted in front of the girl's face to distract her. His mage attacked with the bo staff and swung it against her friend's dull metal sword.

Raven shook her head, stepped toward Murphy, and lifted her sword. "Let's go."

The girl laughed and circled the edge of the sparring ring. When she hefted the giant ax and swung, her opponent barely managed to deflect it with her weapon. Both were surprised by the strength of the attack, then Raven grinned. "That's what I'm talking about!"

Before she could respond with her attack, the firedrake darted between the two girls, flapped around Fritz, and raked aggressively with his tiny, sharp claws.

"Hey!" Murphy shouted. "We're not trying to fight our familiars—woah!" She ducked when Bella's twirling bo staff whistled. It would have struck her shoulder if she hadn't been fast enough.

"*Adsulto protentia,*" Teresa shouted. A shimmering burst of translucent light launched from her hand toward Bella and Raven and slid them back across the grass.

Raven looked at the girl in astonishment. *I need to ask about that spell.* Teresa swung her practice sword at her but she blocked it easily enough. Bella raced forward to attack Murphy with the bo staff again. The girl was able to swing the ax in time to defend herself, but that was the limit.

"Hey, watch out!" Raven slipped between the other two girls a moment before Teresa's practice sword swung into Bella Chase's back. The blow when the weapon connected with her sent a jolt up her arm, but she moved quickly and swiped her blade at their opponent.

The only thanks she received was a sneer from Bella, who wasn't about to let her take the credit for defending her or for fighting off their sparring opponents. Her bo staff lashed out at Teresa, who barely managed to block the attack. The move forced Raven back a few steps to avoid being knocked over and her partner stretched her hand out and shouted, "*Pareo telum*!" A yellow light flared around the head of Murphy's ax and jerked it sideways. The girl held on tightly.

Bella advanced and her firedrake familiar flapped around the sparring ring while it uttered tiny shrieks. Teresa slipped around her to swing her sword in an aggressive arc toward Raven again.

"Woah!"

Their weapons met with a jarring impact and she spun aside and prepared to deliver a retaliatory strike against Teresa. Before she could, however, Bella stepped between them again and delivered a strike with the bo staff. The other girl deflected it and in the next moment, Bella Chase fought the two other students on her own and drove them across the sparring ring.

She didn't even try to defend me.

"Bella, we're supposed to be a team!"

"It's fine." The girl spun away from Murphy's whistling

ax and cracked the staff against the other girl's calf before she jerked the opposite end up and jabbed at Teresa. "You can pay me back later."

Not for this.

With a grunt of frustration, Raven hurried to where Murphy and Teresa did everything they could to defend against their attacker's wildly spinning bo staff. The cat darted between Bella's legs, and the fierce mage in training cried out in surprise when she almost tripped over him. Teresa took the chance to swing her blade toward Bella's hip but Raven was there to block with her dull sword. Her partner looked at her in surprise, and she shoved the blade away before she prepared to attack again. "I think I paid you back."

Her uncooperative partner growled and stepped sideways to shove her out of the way with her shoulder and hip. "I got this. Stop getting in my way."

The bo staff arced toward Murphy's head. The other witch ducked aside and lifted her ax. It was too heavy to do exactly what the girl wanted and only glanced off the staff and Bella launched into a rapid series of strikes that Teresa almost couldn't deflect.

"Hey, there's no I in team!" Raven shouted.

"Nope. But there is a me." Bella leapt away from their opponents before she could reach her side again and almost knocked her down. "Wesley!"

The firedrake gave a piercing shriek—not anywhere near as loud as a dragon's—before he dove toward their adversaries. The glow of fire built in the firedrake's open mouth and Raven shoved her practice sword into her other hand. *She can't attack them with fire like that. It's way too dangerous.*

Murphy swung her weapon again and didn't see the pillar of fire that streaked from the firedrake's mouth toward her.

Raven thrust her hand out and shouted, "*Sequantur flamma!*"

The fiery attack stopped in midair and Murphy looked up with wide eyes that reflected the glowing orange. Raven pulled her hand away and tossed the churning fire into the sky. It sailed harmlessly behind the sparring students and over the field before it finally petered out. A few distracted students stopped their mock battles to watch it soar above them.

"What the hell are you doing?" Bella shouted and whirled toward her. "That's crossing the line."

"No." With a frown, Raven returned the practice sword to her right hand and straightened to glare at the girl. "Attacking Murphy and Teresa with your firedrake's abilities when they only have crappy weapons to defend themselves is crossing a line. You could have seriously hurt them, Bella. And we're supposed to fight together."

"What you did directly undermined my attack. If you're so worried about being a team, you should've used that as an opportunity to win."

"I'm not trying to seriously hurt anyone else simply to win a sparring prize." Raven shook her head. "That can't be all that matters to you."

"Well, I'm fairly sure Professor Fellows isn't trying to teach us how to save our enemies and turn against our partners." Bella raised her staff and swung sideways toward Raven's ribs.

She deflected the blow with ease and positioned to defend herself with the dull edge of the practice sword. "Hey, I didn't attack you."

The girl thumped the end of her bo staff into the grass again and glared at the other mage in training. "Stick to your dragon, Alby. I'm the only one who gets to control my familiar and his abilities." Her firedrake responded with another shriek and swooped to land on her shoulder.

Raven scoffed. "Not if you're trying to fry other students to a crisp."

"Isn't that what dragons do?"

By now, the closest students had forgotten their sparring altogether to watch their altercation.

She gritted her teeth and stood her ground. "Yeah. On command. But I'm not trying to hurt anyone and I'd never tell Leander to attack anyone else like that."

Right on cue, a much louder shriek than Wesley's rose from the other side of the stables across the field. Many of the students jumped in surprise, and although Bella didn't react physically, her gaze darted toward Leander's new pen. Raven didn't turn to look.

"Holy crap, you were right," Bennett shouted and smacked one of the other boy's shoulders. "She did bring a dragon to Fowler."

"That's a dragon?"

"Did you see it blow fire?"

"That's only smoke, Rory."

"Enough." Professor Fellows stormed across the grass toward the young mages in training who confronted one another. He darted one fleeting look at the stables, then stepped into their sparring ring and folded his arms. "Did you two forget the object of this exercise?"

"No, Professor." Raven shook her head but wouldn't look away from Bella's burning gaze. "Only one of us did."

When the weapons professor stepped toward them and leaned forward to get their attention, Murphy drew in a sharp breath. Her ax thumped into the grass, but he ignored her. "My reason for pairing you two together wasn't arbitrary. I want you both to understand that. If you can't come to some kind of an arrangement that doesn't endanger other students or disrupt my class, we'll have to look at very different alternatives I don't think either one of you is willing to explore."

Raven forced herself to look up at him and nodded. "I understand." *And I'm not worried about it. I know I did the right thing.*

"Miss Chase?" Fellows raised an eyebrow at Bella, who sighed with exaggerated patience and finally looked at him. "You said there was a prize. I'm only trying to win it."

"Yes, you've made that perfectly clear. But what I said, Miss Chase, is that the object of this lesson was to find balance and to learn to fight together as a team. And don't try to use 'I didn't hear that part,' as an excuse. We both know you're too smart and too driven for that."

Her nostrils flared, but she didn't say anything else.

"I want both of you to return your weapons and wait at the wheelbarrows for me. We'll rotate Miss Murphy and Miss Reynolds through a few other matches until the end of class. Go on."

Bella glared at her partner again and hefted the bo staff

in her hand before she turned swiftly and stormed out of the sparring ring. Raven headed after her. She caught Murphy's gaze and whispered as she passed, "You should practice with an ax more, Murph. I think you got somethin' there."

The girl giggled nervously before she realized she'd dropped her practice weapon.

Professor Fellows instructed the other students to resume sparring again, while Raven joined Bella beside the wall around Fowler Academy's main buildings. She tossed the practice sword into the wheelbarrow and turned to wait for their professor. The other girl folded her arms and fumed.

"Hey, I'm not trying to cut you down," Raven told her. "I know you want to win, but these aren't real battles, Bella. You know that."

Her partner uttered a derisive snort and tossed her hair behind her shoulders. "If it was a real battle, I definitely would have won."

She scrunched her nose and couldn't help but laugh a little. "And I wouldn't have stopped you or your familiar with that fire blast."

Bella's gaze darted from the field of sparring students toward her, and she tilted her chin. A tiny smirk flickered across her mouth although her glare remained. "I won't pull back from my potential because you tried to give me a compliment."

Raven shook her head and watched Professor Fellows move quickly toward them. "I don't expect you to."

"Good." The girl gave her a sidelong glance and licked

her lips. Her familiar stretched his wings wide from his perch on her shoulder. "I don't expect you to either."

With a small nod, Raven turned her attention to the approaching professor, but her mind had taken off again. *Did we make some kind of pact? It's progress, I guess. Now, I only need to find a way to get Leander involved as my familiar and we'll pass this first year with flying colors.* She laughed inwardly at herself. *Or maybe only flying.*

CHAPTER SEVENTEEN

At the end of their last class for the day, the entire student body of Fowler Academy was told to meet again in the main courtyard of the grounds inside the entrance gates. While the professors stood outside the front doors into the main hall, waiting for all the students to gather together at the end of a long day of learning, Henry slipped through the jostling, laughing, joking students in the crowd toward Raven.

"Okay, Alby. Time to spill it." He nudged her shoulder and rolled his shoulder to ease the weight of the bag he carried.

"Spill what?"

"You were in the middle of telling me about your new living arrangements." He glanced toward the outer wall that separated the main campus from the fields, barn, and stables beyond. He couldn't see all the way to Leander's pen, but she got the point.

"Right. That letter I gave Flynn apparently made him think my grandpa will be gone for a long time. And everyone seems to think I'll be safer living on the grounds in the dormitory than staying in the same house I've lived in my whole life."

"What about the goats?"

Laughing, she turned to face him and gave him a playful frown. "Really? That's the first question you have?"

"Wasn't it yours?"

"I guess. Tied with, 'What about Leander?'"

"Yeah, the dragon's definitely out of the bag now." Henry glanced around them and nodded at Murphy and Fritz who tried to squeeze through the press of students to reach them. "You're not worried about keeping a dragon at Fowler Academy?"

She grinned. "Do I look worried, Derks?"

He studied her for a long moment, then snorted. "Not even a little. And it's weird that I'm not surprised by that."

"It's not weird. It's much better this way. He told me this morning he prefers this new pen to the one at Moss Ranch. Honestly, I can't blame him."

"You brought your dragon?" Murphy asked as she reached them and dived into the conversation. "That was actually approved?"

"It was Headmaster Flynn's idea in the first place, so yeah."

"And you're not, you know...worried that something might happen?"

Raven wrinkled her nose and regarded her friends with a playful frown. "Why does everyone keep asking that? We're fine. Leander's doing great, I have my familiar with me, and yeah, it's weird to be away from the ranch all the time like this. But it looks like Connor Alby covered all his bases before he left so there's nothing to worry about."

"Except for some idiot breaking into that pen when he thinks no one's looking," Henry muttered.

"Except for a dragon looking at him and saying, 'Thanks for bringing me lunch.'" Raven burst out laughing when her friends looked more terrified of that than she'd expected. "Hey, I'm kidding. No one can open that gate. I'm the only one with a key." She patted her forearm and the rust-brown rune tattooed there on their orientation.

"Wow." Murphy's eyes widened. "Private access?"

"I'm not sure anyone else would even want access, Murphy."

Maxwell croaked loudly from Henry's bag, and he stroked the toad's head before he tucked him inside again. "I don't know, Alby. I heard Mike daring Thomas to go up to the pen and have a closer look."

"Seriously?"

"Yeah. Thomas refused and said he wasn't an idiot, so we can give him points for that." He looked at the gathered students and shook his head. "There's bound to be at least one person who's dumb enough to think they're brave."

"I sure hope not." Raven scanned the faces now too. "You know, William was hesitant enough to even let me see Leander the first time. If a dragon trainer feels the need to stay away, I don't think Leander will have a problem scaring the stupid out of anyone who tries something."

"Or fry it out of them," he muttered.

"That's not gonna happen."

"Attention, please!" Professor Gilliam called at the front of the gathered crowd. She pressed the tip of her wand against her throat and muttered, "*Magis clamabat.*" The next time she spoke, her voice boomed over the central courtyard. "Everyone, quiet down. We're here to make an announcement, not to supervise your shenanigans. I'm talking to you, Mr. Jeder."

The spell for manipulating wind that Mike had cast on himself and his friends around him ended abruptly. Their flapping tunics and ruffling hair settled and the boy cleared his throat as his friends jostled and teased him for being called out.

"Thank you," Gilliam continued. "Now, as I'm sure you've noticed, we're officially out of winter and making our way quickly into spring. It's the start of the planting season, the growth of new things, and the return of some much-needed sunshine and warmth after the coldest months. And, as I hope you all are well aware, a reminder that the second semester of the school year is underway and will be over before you know it. For you first-years, that means extensive exams before the end of the year and hope and determination that you'll pass and enter one more year here at Fowler Academy. Don't forget to study."

Henry rolled his eyes and groaned quietly. "We're not even halfway through the semester and already, she's going on about exams."

Raven nudged him with her elbow. "I bet you'll be completely prepared after all that time spent tutoring Jenny."

He gave her a scathing glance and folded his arms. "It's only one spell."

Murphy looked nervous and focused on Fritz, who had curled around her foot.

"But don't get me wrong," Professor Fellows added with a little chuckle. "We also know that all work and no play makes for angry and volatile mages in training."

Professor Gilliam frowned at him, her entire demeanor unamused, and he merely laughed again. "What Professor Fellows means by this is that we'll hold a little event at the school at the end of next week. It will be a chance to give your brains a rest from so much studying and an opportunity to simply have fun."

Henry pumped a fist at his side and grinned. "Getting rid of all exams forever."

"We'll host a spring gala here on the grounds, and all of you are expected to at least make an appearance."

With a sigh, he lowered his fist and rolled his eyes. "Way to build up for too much disappointment."

"What's a gala?" one of the first-years shouted, followed by a round of laughter and a few jokes at his expense.

"A dance, Mr. Alderman." Professor Gilliam looked entirely unamused. "And feel free to find yourselves a date."

Most of the first-year boys either groaned or exchanged disappointed glances. A good number of girls seemed excited and whispered to each other while they cast hopeful glances at the boys who barely paid them any attention. The upperclassmen didn't jump up and down in excitement, but they smiled and jostled each other, knowing exactly what to expect.

They've all been through this before.

On the other side of Professor Gilliam, Headmaster Flynn cleared his throat. "Anyone interested in joining your professors on the planning committee for this event, please speak to Professor Gilliam at the end of these announcements. It's not required, of course, but it's an excellent skill to have in one's repertoire."

Henry snorted. "Yep. Powerful mages who can decorate to a theme are in popular demand throughout the kingdom."

Raven laughed, and Murphy leaned past her to raise her eyebrows at Henry. "It sounds kind of fun. I bet they'll teach us a few extra illusion spells. Remember all the colored lights at the ceremony when we announced our familiars?"

"The lights?" He frowned.

"Murphy, I'm fairly sure he was more focused on the food."

"Well, I might check it out anyway." The other girl faced the professors again, her pursed lips drawn to the side in consideration.

"Go for it." She smiled at her friend as Headmaster Flynn clapped to quiet the students once again.

"A last word, please. I want to make it perfectly clear that you are all still expected to attend classes, to pay attention, and to learn. Even with this upcoming gala. This is a formal event, so if you don't have anything to wear that couldn't be confused for something other than formal attire, I suggest you use the next week and a half to find something. Thank you all for your time." With that, he turned away from the gathered students and disappeared inside the main building.

A few of the other professors followed, and Professor Gilliam remained in her place outside the doors and watched the students' reactions for a moment longer before she joined her peers inside the main hall.

"This could be fun," Raven said with a shrug. "Except for the fact that I have no idea where I'll find formal attire."

"Fun? How is worrying about fancy clothes and finding a date to this supposed to be fun?" Henry shook his head. "I can hit a target with my slingshot from at least six yards away, but I'll tell you right now, Alby, Maxwell's a better dancer than I am."

"What about finding a date?" Murphy asked, her eyes wide and her cheeks faintly pink again.

Raven bit her lip to stop herself from saying anything. *She's getting better at hiding it, at least.*

"Yeah, I don't know, Murph." He ruffled his hair and turned in a slow, distracted circle to scan the students around them. "I'm not sure that's gonna happen."

"Oh." Murphy looked away quickly before he caught her watching him.

"Yeah, I'm not so sure about the whole date thing, either," Raven added and hoped that would make both her friends a little less tense. "I don't mind the dancing part, though."

"Well, as long as there's food, I'll be there." Henry grinned and his stomach gurgled obnoxiously. He slapped it with both hands. "Someone should form a planning committee for after-school snacks. I'm not the only one who could use something to munch on right about now."

"For all the growing boys, huh?" Raven folded her arms and smirked at her friend as the students filtered away from the gathering to either head home or stay on the grounds where they lived.

"You've been paying attention, Alby." He pointed at her with both hands. "Nothing gets past you, does it?"

"Hey, Raven." Daniel Smith stood so close behind her, his voice made her jump before she turned slowly. "Sorry. I didn't mean to startle you."

"I'm not startled." Raven gave Henry a disapproving glance—her friend merely grinned—before she raised both hands and took a step away from Daniel. "I'm simply not used to having people in my bubble like that."

"Sure." His blue eyes crinkled at the edges as he grinned at her and completely ignored both her friends. "I heard you moved into the girls' dormitory last night."

Great. Everyone's talking about it now. "I sure did."

"And that you brought your dragon familiar with you." The upperclassman raised his eyebrows and stared relentlessly at her.

Raven glanced quickly at Murphy, who merely gazed at him with the same dreamy look she wore around Professor Fellows. "Yup," she told him. "I finally have my familiar on school grounds with me. It makes training with him much easier, too."

"I bet. That's so cool." Daniel ran a hand through his dark hair and took another step toward her.

Raven leaned back a little. *This guy doesn't get the hint about personal space, does he?*

"So, do you have a date for the spring gala yet?"

She couldn't help but laugh. "Not yet. I know it's a little surprising, seeing as we only found out about it two minutes ago."

"Cool. Wanna go with me?"

"Uh…" *Wow. Daniel Smith's not wasting any time.* "I don't know, Daniel. I wasn't planning on having a date at all, so—"

"Well, think about it. We'd have fun together."

"Yeah, I'll think about it. Thanks." She nodded and raised her eyebrows, but the guy simply stood there and grinned at her.

"Cool. See you around, Raven Alby," he said finally when she made no further effort at conversation.

"Yep."

Daniel tossed his dark hair out of his eyes and wandered away toward the group of upperclassman who watched him and mumbled whatever jokes they were about to fling at him.

"Cool," Henry muttered and nodded. "Cool. He doesn't have much of a vocabulary, does he?"

"You know, I heard that happens when guys get nervous." Raven couldn't help but laugh when he rolled his eyes.

"He doesn't look nervous to me. He looks—"

"Dreamy." Murphy sighed, still focused on Daniel as he reached his group of friends.

"Uh...that wasn't really what I was goin' for, Murph, but okay." Henry snorted. "I thought more like overly confident. Puffed up."

"Like a toad?"

"What? No, not like a toad. I'll have you know, Alby, toads are majestic creatures. And there's much more goin' on inside Maxwell's head than dances and dates and— Maxwell!" His familiar uttered another loud croak and leapt from the shoulder bag. Henry's fingers were too slow to catch the toad's legs, but they knocked Maxwell's leap off-kilter and the creature flopped clumsily at his feet.

"So majestic. The most." Raven laughed as he lunged toward his familiar and caught him in one swipe.

"Hey, no one's perfect. Even majesty takes time." He tried to look offended but smiled as he tucked Maxwell away again. "Are you gonna go with him to the gala?"

"I have no idea." She shook her head.

"I would," Murphy said and the color rose in her cheeks again.

"Well, it's not exactly the most important thing on my mind right now."

Henry's stomach growled. "I'm right there with you. Duty calls." He spun toward the entrance gates to Fowler Academy. "Are you comin', Murphy? I'm much faster walking home than I am walking to school."

"'Cause there's a plate of food waiting for you at the other end," Raven called after him.

"You know me so well."

"Yeah, I'm coming." The girl leaned toward Raven and grinned. "You should totally go with Daniel to the gala. He might not ask again, you know."

"Okay, I'll think about it." She hugged her friend good-bye. "See you tomorrow."

"Yep."

"Later, Alby!" Henry called and gestured impatiently for Murphy to catch up. "It's gonna be weird not beating you in a race home anymore."

"You never beat me."

"I would have."

She waved in response and turned away from the front gates before her friends had even reached them. *I'll miss that walk a little too. But I definitely won't miss the walk to Moss Ranch.*

With a deep breath, she hurried toward the stone archway in the wall leading to the fields and wished she could fly to her dragon.

CHAPTER EIGHTEEN

Leander was waiting for her when she reached the pen and snorted at the sound of the latch releasing to her access rune. Raven stepped inside and smiled to see him curled in the grass, watching her.

"You look comfy."

The dragon raised his huge head as she approached. "It's the grass. And I enjoy not having to wait so long to see you."

Raven stroked his long snout and nodded. "I like that part too. So, tell me about your first day at Fowler Academy."

Leander maintained his stare but didn't say a word.

"Okay, maybe I'm playing it up a little, huh?"

"An understatement I'm willing to ignore." He stood to his full height and stretched his wings before he tucked them in again. "Your mock battle this morning was amusing."

"Amusing? Huh." She patted his thick, scaled shoulder

and swiped a few strands of hair out of her eyes. "I don't know if I'd call it amusing."

"Perhaps not for you."

"Could you see it from all the way out here?"

He released a low rumble and took a few slow steps sideways before he settled onto a fresh patch of grass. "A dragon sees with more than their eyes. I heard it. You were frustrated."

"That's an understatement I'm willing to ignore." With a chuckle, she joined him on the grass, sat in front of his huge forepaws, and crossed her legs beneath her. "You're here, Leander. On the school grounds with me, and I want to be able to train with my familiar the way everyone else does. We'll find a solution for that."

"Nothing you do is what everyone else does." The red dragon's wings twitched against his back and he snorted a hot breath of air, not quite at her but not away from her either. Its warmth was close enough to heat her cheek and neck.

She smiled at him and enjoyed the way the early-afternoon sun danced along his glistening scales. *He could be made of fire right now.* "No, I don't. Neither do you."

"We are what we are, Raven Alby." He pressed his snout into her outstretched hand, then lowered his head onto his paws again. "I would very much enjoy a chance to train the way we do."

"Me too. The last thing I want is to make you feel as cooped up here as you did at the ranch." Raven drew a long, deep breath, looked into the bright sky with very few clouds, and sighed. "I didn't have the time to ask about taking you flying. The last two days have really shaken things up, huh?"

"Some things. Not all."

"Do you mind waiting to fly until after I ask about…you know, when's the best time?"

Another snort from Leander's nostrils ruffled the tips of the grass in front of his head. "We don't need permission."

"I know. But I want to make sure I don't do anything that risks you being here with me. It's safer to ask, I think."

"No, I do not mind. I can wait for another day."

"Good, and I'm sure there won't be an issue. I'm very good at negotiating when I want something."

Leander hissed between his rows of razor-sharp teeth and lifted scaled lips a little to reveal them. "I hope your negotiating skills are better with full-grown mages than they were with me."

"Very funny." Raven stroked affectionately between his eyes again. "I learned my lesson on that one. It's not always about me." The dragon said nothing more but closed his eyes beneath her touch. They sat there like that for a few minutes before she pressed a hand to her stomach. *I guess the day built up my appetite too.* "Are you hungry? I can open another bag of feed again before I go. I hope the dorms serve dinner too."

"I'll be fine until the morning."

She stood and moved to check the trough. "You barely ate half of it, Leander. Is everything okay?"

"My appetite will return."

With a frown of concern, she turned to study him. The

red dragon glistened in the sun and seemed healthy enough. He didn't move and he'd now closed his eyes to soak in the warmth. "Do you still feel like something's not quite right?"

"Yes. And no, I still do not know why."

"Hmm. You know what? I'll try to get us out tomorrow. We'll fly and take a breath of real fresh air. And I'll work to find a way to get you out of this pen to at least do familiar training with Professor Worley. I'm not sure how much he knows about dragons but he has at least two familiars. He'll have something for us to work on."

"If you say so." Leander's voice was much quieter now.

He's actually falling asleep. That would be a little hard if his not-right feeling was getting stronger.

"Okay. I'll talk to Headmaster Flynn tonight and I'll be back in the morning. Try to eat a little more between now and then, okay?"

The dragon gave no reply or indication that he'd heard her. With a small laugh, she waved in defeat and walked through the gate. When she'd latched it firmly behind her, she turned toward the stables and narrowed her eyes. *There's another way to find out if something's wrong, even if it won't tell me what that is.*

Raven walked down the long wall of the stables and stepped through the front gate at the far end. One of the horses whickered at her and stepped toward the end of its stall. The young mage smiled. "I'm only passing through to check a few things. You have nothing to worry about."

The horse shook its head and the long brown mane flicked against the side of the stall. When she reached the back and the tack hooks, she found Headmaster Flynn's old saddle easily enough. The little bag she'd tied to the side was still there too, and she detached it before she withdrew the white orb Connor had given her.

It's not white anymore. At all. Only a thin streak of pale pink was visible at the top of the glass ball that fit snugly in one hand. The red had also darkened a little since the last time she'd checked it. *Whatever trouble this thing picks up is getting worse. Or closer.*

She slid her satchel off her shoulders to tuck the orb inside, strapped her school bag on, and glanced around the stables. *If the animals are this calm, there's still enough time to find out exactly what that trouble is.*

With the sphere safely stowed, she left the stables and strolled across the field toward the school's main building. Her satchel felt a little heavier with the orb inside, but her stomach grumbled anyway.

"Dinner first." She nodded and increased her pace.

The common room had begun to clear by the time Raven stepped into the girls' dormitory. The table had, in fact, been laid with a huge array of food for dinner, although there wasn't much left to choose from. She took a few slices of buttered bread and cheese and added the roast beef left on the platter. Seated at the closest empty table, she stared at her plate, shrugged, and stacked all the food together to take a bite of everything at once.

This is the way to eat. Someone should come up with a name for it.

Another girl passed, eyed the stack of dinner between the slices of bread, and frowned. She grinned at her. "It's efficient, right?" She shrugged and took another bite as the girl walked away. *At least there was food left.*

She wolfed the rest of her meal and swiped a few crumbs into her hand before she strode across the main grounds again. A few students stood in small groups, studying and practicing their spells. One circle of girls burst into a fit of giggles as they clutched textbooks to their chests and darted glances at four upperclassmen who played with the floating beanbag again.

Raven shook her head, then noticed Daniel Smith in the circle, watching her move toward the doors into the main hall. The girls giggled again when she passed them, thinking Daniel was looking at one of them. Before he could say anything, she slipped past the group and through the front doors. *It's like he simply waits for me to appear.*

The building was mostly empty and she hurried toward the base of the stairwell leading to Headmaster Flynn's office at the top of the tower. When Professor Worley appeared around the corner, she almost ran into him.

"Miss Alby." The huge man smiled beneath his wild beard and brushed a few curls out of his eyes. "Where are you off to in such a hurry?"

"I have a few questions for Headmaster Flynn." She nodded toward the staircase.

"I see." Worley's frown darkened. "He's not there, though."

"What?" she sucked a piece of bread out of her teeth and glanced up the stairs again. "Where is he?"

"He is elsewhere, currently." The professor tried to smile again. "Maybe there's something I can help you with."

"Oh. Um...maybe." *Elsewhere? Where would Flynn go?* "I had questions about Leander being here. My—"

"Your familiar, yes. I'm aware. How's that pen working out for him?"

"He seems to like it. I wanted to ask the headmaster about getting Leander out of the pen. You know, to stretch his wings a little."

Professor Worley chuckled. "Off the ground, I assume."

Raven couldn't help but smile. "That's part of it."

"Well, I can't speak for the headmaster when it comes to a trained dragon familiar flying over school grounds, Miss Alby." He stroked his wild beard, tilted his head thoughtfully, and glanced toward the front of the building. "But I intended to suggest this tomorrow anyway. I think we'll hold my class out of the barn and in the open. I invite you and your familiar to join us. That should let him stretch a little more, at least."

"It definitely would." She nodded and grinned at the thought. *And we get to stretch what we can do together, too.*

"That is, as long as you feel confident that your familiar can handle being so close to everyone else and theirs."

"Absolutely. One hundred and fifty percent confident."

"That's hard to argue." Worley chuckled in a mild and somewhat distracted way. "Then bring your familiar out tomorrow before my class and we'll take the training to him."

"Thank you, Professor."

"That's why I'm here. Enjoy the rest of your evening." Professor Worley walked away and moved slowly through the dark stone hallway.

Raven turned around to call, "Do you have any idea when Headmaster Flynn will be available?"

"Tomorrow morning, at the very least." The man

vanished around another corner on his route to the front doors.

For a moment, Raven stood at the base of the curving staircase and stared at the walls, a little bewildered. *I thought Flynn lived in his office, too. I definitely saw a bed there yesterday.*

She glanced over her shoulder, but the halls were empty. *I would've done this if Worley hadn't stopped me.* With a quick nod, she sighed quietly and headed up the stairwell. "I'll make a quick check. I told Leander I'd find answers tonight."

Her footsteps echoed in the stairwell and she reached the top much faster than she expected. The large door to Headmaster Flynn's office was still closed. *It doesn't mean anything.* She drew a breath and knocked firmly but there was no response. Once she'd knocked again, she stepped down one step and pulled the door open using the iron ring.

"Headmaster Flynn? Do you have a minute to talk about—"

A low growl issued from beside the desk. Rider sat and bared his teeth in a warning snarl as she leaned through the open doorway.

"Headmaster?" The office was entirely empty as far as she could tell—other than the massive wolf who sent a very clear message. "Did he leave you here by yourself?"

Rider snarled again and took a few quick steps toward her, his ears flattened against his head.

"I'll come back." Raven stepped down the stairs and shoved the huge door closed with a decisive thud.

The snarls cut off abruptly and were replaced by the

click of hard nails across the wooden floor. *Point taken. That's one way to keep people out. So where's Flynn?*

With a frown, she descended the staircase and scowled as she chewed on the inside of her cheek. "I guess I'll have to track him down early tomorrow. That dragon needs to fly."

CHAPTER NINETEEN

Lying snugly in her bed across the dorm room from Elizabeth, Raven turned in her sleep with a little groan. *No way are those goats up this early.*

The noise of so many excited animals grew louder, and she dragged the covers over her head. *I still have another hour, at least—*

A mighty roar jolted her completely awake. She threw the covers off and sat, her heart thudding. *I'm not at the ranch.* "Leander."

She scrambled from her bed and immediately recognized the sounds of many animals in distress. The dragon's next thunderous cry made her breath catch in her throat. She forced herself to move and jammed her feet into her boots before she yanked her jacket off the chair behind her desk.

Elizabeth's bat familiar squeaked, and Raven turned as her roommate shuffled into a seated position in bed. "What's going on?"

"It woke you too, huh?" She thrust her arms through her jacket sleeves.

"Kind of, I've been reading, though. It's not that late." The girl brushed her bangs out of her eyes and glanced at the window. "I've never heard a dragon roar like that before."

"Me neither. Something's wrong." Without waiting for a reply, she jerked the door to their room open and raced down the hall. *Please, please, please. Let him be okay out there.* It didn't even occur to her that of all the animals kept beside the barn in the stables, Leander was the one least likely to be attacked.

Her footsteps pounded down the hall and she didn't care who heard or who else woke. *All the noise is gonna do that anyway.*

A few doors opened as she sprinted past, but she only had eyes for the staircase. In a few minutes, she darted across the common room, barreled through the front door of the dormitory, and surged toward the stone archway and into the field. Leander hadn't uttered another massive roar, but she could hear him snort amidst the other panicked whinnies, squeals, and squawks that issued from the stables.

Raven aimed her headlong run to the gate to his pen but stopped when two flashing golden rings caught her attention at the edge of the forest that bordered the back of the school grounds. She squinted into the darkness and identified the massive outline of a shape she knew too well. *What are vagreti panthers doing stalking around Fowler Academy?*

A loud, screeching grate of sharpened claws on metal tore her away from the panther, and it vanished quickly into the woods without a sound. With wide eyes, she whirled toward the pen and tugged the sleeve of her jacket up to expose the access rune on her arm. Orange light flared, the gate clicked open, and she hurtled inside.

Leander spun in a tight circle, his nostrils flaring as he emitted huge, steaming snorts of air. A huge forepaw dug divots into the ground and ripped dirt out. She didn't think twice before she ran to him, her arms outstretched to catch his attention.

"Woah, woah. Leander. Hey. Everything's all right."

He turned his glowing yellow eyes toward her and snorted again. After a moment, he settled a little more while she approached and his wings twitched out to half their span.

"You're okay." Raven settled her hands on his large, warm snout and nodded. "I'm so glad you're okay."

"Of course I am. Physically."

A few shouts rose from across the field. She ignored them. "You had me worried there for a second. That's quite a roar you have."

"That was anger."

"What?"

"Miss Alby." Headmaster Flynn didn't exactly shout her name but it was firm and commanding and caught her attention. The man appeared in the walkway that led to the pen's open entrance, his hands raised in front of him as he studied Leander. "A word with Miss Alby, if you don't mind."

She gaped in astonishment. *He's asking Leander's permission.*

When her dragon snorted and pawed at the ground, she leapt away from the massive talons she knew wouldn't have come down on her anyway. More voices rose from outside the pen and quickly grew louder. With that added to the uproar from all the panicked animals in the stables, there was suddenly too much noise all at once.

"Make them stop," Leander growled. He pulled his head away from her hands and turned in a tight circle toward the back of the pen.

"I'll do what I can," Flynn replied. "Thank you. Miss Alby?"

With a frown, Raven darted one last glance over her shoulder at the pacing red dragon before she slipped through the gate and began to close it behind her.

"Ah. Just one moment, please." The headmaster raised a finger and nodded toward the gate. "Perhaps it's best to leave that gate cracked, for now. I don't wish to make your familiar feel excluded from this conversation."

It's a little too late for that now. She peered around him at a small crowd of both professors and students that had formed closer to the noisy stables. Professor Worley's huge, dark form marched across the grass toward the entrance. The gate creaked when he stepped inside, and his low, murmuring voice rose wordlessly between the stalls.

"Would you care to explain what happened?" Headmaster Flynn asked.

"I don't know what happened." She ignored the onlookers but some of the students pushed forward for a better look at the dragon pen before Professor Gilliam tugged them back again. "But it wasn't Leander's fault. He didn't do anything."

"Except wake the entire school." The irritated comment came from a tall professor with a completely bald head who taught a class first-years weren't allowed to take. She had seen the man a few times on the grounds, but that was as much as she knew about him.

"And I'm sorry about that," she replied although she looked only at the headmaster. "But if Leander made so much noise, I know it was for a reason—"

"Trying to start trouble, I imagine. As dragons do," the bald professor added and moved toward them. Professor Gilliam pressed her lips together and shared a nervous, wide-eyed glance with Professor Fellows, who'd apparently tied his hair back for the night instead of leaving it down as he did during the day.

"He's not trying to start anything." Raven balled her hands into fists at her side. "He's not trouble, either."

"He's a dragon, child—"

"That's quite enough, Professor Dameron." Headmaster Flynn glanced briefly over his shoulder and raised a hand toward the other man. "I believe Miss Alby is quite capable of relating these events in her own words."

"Not if she's trying to protect the thing—"

A loud snort—not nearly as loud as Leander's—rose from the stables, followed by a sharp, swift kick against the stable wall and Professor Worley's muffled curse.

"See? I told you penning a dragon beside the stables was a fool's endeavor, Headmaster. Not to mention keeping a beast like that on the school grounds, in the first place."

169

"Thank you, Professor." Flynn's voice had lowered into a warning at this point.

"We'll be lucky if that thing didn't spook every other creature under Jeremy's care to the point of physically harming themselves," Dameron added. Another thump and a quick scuffle rose from within the stables and the man pointed at the outer wall. "Or him. If you ask me, that dragon—"

"That's the thing, Professor." Headmaster Flynn finally turned fully to face the disgruntled bald man who'd almost reached him and Raven. "I did not ask you. I am already painfully aware of your opinion on the matter, and if you'd like to discuss it further, we can arrange a more private setting for that purpose. Now, if you cannot contain yourself while we're all out here getting our robes wet in the grass, please take your opinion somewhere more appropriate."

Dameron blinked, scowled first at the headmaster, then at Raven, and whirled away to stride back toward the main buildings.

"This wasn't Leander's fault," Raven said as she took a step closer to Flynn and fought to not hold her breath. "He's not a beast—"

"Oh, on the contrary, Miss Alby. That dragon is certainly a beast. A fantastic, regal, exquisite beast I feel fortunate to have at this school." A small smile bloomed above his long gray beard. "I'm more inclined to listen to reason than fear, at any rate. Do continue with what you wished to tell me."

She swallowed. *At least I have the headmaster defending Leander on this one too. That'll help.* "Thank you. I'm not exactly sure what happened, but I saw…" She turned toward the forest and sighed, reluctant to voice it. *They're not gonna like this one.* "I saw a vagreti panther sneak into the woods. It turned to look at me. I don't know why it was here, but if anything spooked the animals in the stables, I'm willing to bet that was it."

A murmur of surprise rippled through the few students gathered with the other professors. Headmaster Flynn turned again to fix the small crowd with a commanding stare, and the voices fell silent. "Are you certain it was a vagreti panther and not another dark creature in the night?"

"I've seen one before with my own eyes," she said with a firm nod. "They're very recognizable."

"Yes. They are." He tugged his beard a few times and glanced at the slightly open gate to Leander's pen. "That may explain one piece of this, Miss Alby. At the same time, I have very little reason to believe that one vagreti panther would spook a dragon to this degree. I want to know what did."

"Nothing," Leander's low voice responded from inside the pen with a short, metallic echo. "And there were two."

"I'm sorry?" The man glanced at the open gate, then frowned at her. She shrugged.

"Unless you wish to speak with walls between us, mage, either step toward the gate or invite me through it."

The headmaster uttered a soft, tired chuckle and closed his eyes. He looked at Raven and gestured toward the gate. "With your permission?"

"Sure." *If Leander's willing to talk to him, my permission doesn't mean much.* "I'll come with you."

171

"Yes, I think that's the most cautious option."

Raven opened the gate barely wide enough for the headmaster to stand in the opening with a full view of the pen. She stepped all the way in herself and stopped between Leander and the entrance. *I trust him completely but I'm not sure I trust anyone else around him yet.*

"Thank you, Miss Alby." Headmaster Flynn took one step beyond the gate, then nodded at Leander. "And thank you for the invitation."

"To clear up false assumptions, mage. Nothing more."

"I understand." He lowered his hands at his sides and held the red dragon's glowing gaze. "Would you mind explaining your earlier statement?"

"Which one?" Leander paced the far end of the pen and raised his head on his long neck occasionally to sniff the air.

Raven bit her lip. *Exactly like this morning. Whatever it is, he feels it again.*

"Both, I suppose," the headmaster replied with a small shrug. "If you don't mind."

"Nothing spooked me. I tried to get those dumb animals to listen but they're impossible."

This time, the man pressed his lips together and tried not to laugh. "I understand your frustration."

"I wanted to sleep." The dragon paused his measured tread with another snort. "And I tried to tell those idiots in the stables that the beasts stalking across the grounds were as afraid as they are. Again, dumb animals."

"Ah, yes." Flynn nodded, his brow creased in confusion. "And the stalking beasts?"

"The large cats you call vagreti," Leander growled. "There were two of them."

Raven's eyes widened. "And they were afraid?"

"I could smell it." The red dragon raised his snout for another sniff. "So could the barnyard beasts. The difference between us is that I understand what it means and those idiots don't know enough to realize it wasn't their own fear they smelled."

Headmaster Flynn gave her a concerned glance. "We're very fortunate to have you here to interpret, Leander."

"Don't get used to it. I'm here for Raven Alby."

She ignored his expression—half amusement and half concern—and stepped toward her dragon. "So you became angry and that's what all the roaring was about?"

"Yes. That, and my own concerns. Those panthers weren't here to feed on the animals in this pen and they're smart enough to stay away from me."

"Then why were they here?"

Leander turned quickly to study Headmaster Flynn for a brief moment before he turned his gaze to Raven and lowered his head. "They were running away."

"Two vagreti panthers taking their chances on the grounds of this school and past a dragon." The headmaster tugged his beard again. "Yes, I may be as concerned as you are. Thank you, Leander."

The dragon rumbled again but said nothing more.

As Flynn turned away from the gate, Raven ran toward Leander and brushed her hand against his front leg. "Something's still bothering you, isn't it? Whatever made the panthers come out here. That's what you feel."

"Yes, Raven." His muscular tail thrashed the grass before it stilled. "If I knew what it was, I would tell you."

"I know. Thank you for talking to him and clearing this up."

"They're still afraid of me."

"They're only getting used to having a dragon around." She glanced at the open gate and grimaced at the sound of hushed whispers and a few gasps in the night. *At least the stables are quiet again.* "All that will settle too."

"It shouldn't. They are right to fear a dragon but that's not the most important fear."

"Yeah, there's definitely something going on. I'm working on finding out what that is."

"Work faster." Leander shifted his footing again, but he stilled when she patted his leg and uttered a small laugh.

"Yeah, I have the same issue with patience. Are you okay in here for the night?"

"I'm fine. If those brainless snacks in the stables start again, though, they might not be."

"The panthers are gone and it sounds like the animals are settled." *It sounded like Professor Worley might have a few bruises in the morning, though.* "I'll be back before classes tomorrow, okay?"

The dragon didn't respond but stepped away from her to turn a few circles in the grass before he curled in on himself and closed his eyes.

"Okay. Goodnight."

Raven reached the gate before the low rumble of his voice followed her. "Goodnight, Raven."

With a smile, she stepped out of the pen, closed the gate firmly behind her, and waited for the heavy click when the latch slid into place. She turned to locate Headmaster Flynn again, who now stood in front of the gathered students and what few professors had arrived to see what all the trouble was about. "No, Miss Reynolds. A few wild panthers making their way into the woods is not a cause for concern. They wanted nothing to do with this school, I assure you."

Great. We stopped one panic about a dragon only to start another over panthers. Maybe I can help.

CHAPTER TWENTY

R aven didn't have an opportunity to help Headmaster Flynn explain what had happened. The man ended the abrupt conversation when he simply told everyone to return to the dorms and get some sleep. "Your studies are still the priority here. And I expect each of you to focus on your training at this school far more than spreading false rumors to the others come morning. Is that understood?"

The students nodded but a few of them looked incredibly disappointed at not having witnessed a real spectacle they could brag about in the morning. Most of them, though, merely looked terrified. So did Professors Gilliam and Fellows, even when they ushered the students away from the stables and across the field toward the school's main buildings.

"Headmaster." She stepped behind Flynn and waited for him to turn. He did, but he stared after the retreating students with narrowed eyes. "I'm fairly sure the whole school will know about this tomorrow."

"Of course they will." He turned toward her with another tired smile and sighed with weary exasperation. "I know the futility of my request, Miss Alby, but if they feel entrusted with whatever they think they know instead of threatened into keeping a secret, there's a chance that only the facts will slip through. Or most of them, at any rate."

"I guess we'll see."

"Yes." The man glanced at the dragon pen and scratched above his eyebrow. "I want you to know that Leander is still welcome here, whether or not he appreciates the welcome."

"Thank you."

"How is he in there?"

She bit her lip. "He says he's comfortable and he likes the grass."

Flynn chuckled. "That's a start."

Raven couldn't bring herself to laugh with him. "He also says he feels something...not quite right."

The headmaster studied her for a moment and his smile faded a little. "Indeed. That's made itself quite clear after tonight's events. I'm inclined to agree with him."

"Do you know what it is?" The wind picked up and blew through her pajamas. She shivered and rubbed her arms through her jacket. "Whatever's off?"

"I wish I did, Miss Alby, but no. That doesn't mean I don't also feel something stirring." Another strong breeze pulled at his beard, and he gestured toward the wall around the main buildings. "It's chilly and quite late. If you need to finish with your familiar—"

"I already did for the night."

"Then I wouldn't mind a little company on the walk back."

Raven nodded and joined him on the return across the field. The night had fallen into its usual silence again, which made the opening and closing of the stable doors that much easier to hear. She glanced over her shoulder to where Professor Worley turned away from the building as he ran a hand through his thick hair. A dark shape appeared from the other side of the stables, and the man looked down to mutter something she couldn't hear. *Another familiar, I bet.*

"Headmaster?"

"Miss Alby."

"My grandfather gave me this orb a few years ago. When there's danger, when something's...well, not quite right, it turns—"

"From white to red. Yes, I've seen it myself once or twice." Flynn gave her another distracted smile, his hands clasped behind his back. "Do you have it with you?"

"It's in my room. I came to talk to you about it in your office after class today, but you...weren't there."

"Ah. That's why Rider was so ruffled."

"I didn't mean to upset him—"

"You didn't. My familiar can be somewhat territorial, especially of my personal space. I appreciate you not trying to confront him on your own."

Raven couldn't help but laugh at that. "That would've been almost as dumb as someone else trying to confront Leander."

"Hmm. Almost." Flynn smirked and glanced at the sky.

"That orb, though. It's almost completely red."

He stopped abruptly and turned to look directly at her. "When did that start?"

"A few months ago. The worst I'd seen it was when Leander and I won the dragon competition in Nadine."

"And tested out of the dragon trials. Yes." He resumed his walk so she pushed herself to fall in beside him again.

"I thought it was almost completely red then, but when I looked again today… Well, it turns out I didn't know how much it was still picking up on." She brushed her hair away from her face and wished she'd brought something to tie it back with.

"Has Connor seen it?"

She glanced at her boots that whispered rhythmically through the dew-covered grass. "Yes. Is that why he left?"

"It's possible, Miss Alby. I can't honestly say." They passed beneath the stone archway and into the courtyard of the main buildings.

Okay, it was a shot in the dark. "So how are we supposed to find out what that danger is, exactly?"

"That's an easy question to answer. At this point, the most we can do is wait for the danger to reveal itself. Yes, that's a bitter truth to swallow but for now, that's all the truth I can offer. It's not the most important question, though."

"What is?"

"How do we prepare to meet that danger when it does reveal itself? The answer to that question is what every skilled and powerful mage learns to discover, Miss Alby. The key is to be prepared, no matter what arises—even if we have no idea what's coming until it reaches our front door. Or gates, as it were." Headmaster Flynn chuckled and gestured toward the front gates of Fowler Academy before they turned toward the girls' dormitory.

That's what I need to do, then. Be prepared. Raven's fingers brushed against her mother's pin. *For anything.*

"I believe this is where we part ways." He gestured toward the entrance of the dormitory and lowered his head in a way that made it look more like a bow. "I very much appreciate your assistance tonight, Miss Alby. I've known for some time that having a dragon at one's side is a very useful way to prepare for the what and the when. I'm also very glad to see that I can still be surprised by everything a creature like your familiar has to offer."

"Thank you, Headmaster. And thanks for listening to him. He might not show it but I think he's much happier here. I might be too."

"Never expect a dragon to show all their cards. I'm sure you've already discovered this for yourself." The headmaster wrinkled his nose when he laughed again before a darker shadow of pain flashed across his brow.

It was there and gone in an instant, but Raven caught it. *He had his own dragon once too.* "I know Leander still has a few tricks up his sleeve. Hopefully, I'll be able to learn all of them."

"Ah. That is an admirable goal. If I may, I'd advise moving through every day as if you discovered your dragon's tricks again for the first time. It's merely one more way of being prepared, isn't it?"

"Right." She bit her lip and glanced at the door. "I'll keep that in mind."

"I'm sure you will." The man turned toward the great hall with another small, curt nod. "Goodnight, Miss Alby."

"Oh, one more thing."

He turned back with another chuckle and raised an eyebrow.

"I wanted to ask about flying with Leander."

"To my knowledge, you've already mastered that part of things."

"No, I mean I wanted to ask if that's all right. It's been a few days and I think he's getting a little antsy. That might be obvious. Is it okay if I take him out when he needs it? I know not everyone's happy about a dragon at Fowler and for some reason, I'd feel better knowing I won't make things tenser if I simply assume we're all good."

Headmaster Flynn laughed, shook his head, and lowered his chin toward his chest. "Yes. For some reason, it seems Connor Alby's granddaughter considers asking permission as often as he did. Which, to be clear, wasn't often."

Raven grinned. *Grandpa had a rebellious streak in him. It's only a little surprising for a retired dragon rider.*

"Don't worry about asking permission," he continued. "That dragon is your familiar and your responsibility. If taking him out to fly is part of you taking responsibility, then by all means. As long as it doesn't interfere with your classes or anyone else's and as long as you're not out after dark."

Now he sounds exactly like Grandpa. "Deal."

"Ha! Hardly a deal, Raven Alby. After all, you're the only one with a key. Now, if you'll excuse me, I need to find my bed before someone else finds me curled up here in the courtyard. Goodnight."

"Goodnight." With a grin, she watched the man who'd

gone from dragon rider to Headmaster of Fowler Academy as he disappeared through the front doors and into the main hall. She opened the door to the girls' dormitory and crossed the empty, dark common room.

We'll go flying tomorrow. If nothing else, it'll clear both our minds and give Leander a chance to work out that nervous energy. Then, we can focus on being prepared.

When she reached the third floor, most of the lights were on behind the other girls' closed doors. Her door was open, exactly the way she'd left it on her race to comfort Leander. A low buzz of conversation filtered beneath the other students' doors with the light, but she ignored it. *Everyone's bound to talk about it anyway. What they do is none of my business.*

Elizabeth was still awake, seated in her bed with her nose in a book again. Her bat familiar pounced and scrambled across the bed after the melon balls she had apparently stored somewhere for a late-night snack.

"I thought you'd be asleep." Raven shrugged out of her jacket and hung it over the back of the desk chair again.

"I thought you'd be gone longer." The girl closed her book and pushed her swooping bangs to the side before they fell over one eye again. "What was all that about?"

As she stepped out of her boots, she sighed and crouched in front of the oilskin bag she still hadn't unpacked. "Everyone's already talking about it. I bet if you stepped out into the hall, you'd hear all kinds of things."

With a snort, the other young mage raised her arms above her head for a long stretch. "I'm not even a little interested in gossip. Getting the story straight from you is different."

She relayed everything to her new roommate as she yanked clothes out of the bag and folded them before they found their new home in the provided dresser. Her timing was good and she reached the end of her retelling as she finished unpacking. "So get ready to hear every kind of twisted version of this from whoever feels like telling it tomorrow."

She expected Elizabeth to look worried or maybe at least a little surprised. Instead, her companion shrugged and lobbed the last piece of melon to Iggy. "Vagreti panthers, huh? Those things are so cool."

Raven laughed in surprise. "Yeah, until they're right up close and trying to steal one of your goats."

"It's a good thing I don't have any goats, then."

The girls shared a joking smile before she crouched in front of the oilskin bag and retrieved the two worn leather journals. With a sigh, she sat on the edge of her bed and ran a hand along the cracked, dust-engrained covers.

"What are those?"

"My grandpa's old journals. At least, I think they're his." She frowned. "He didn't exactly say who they belonged to, but they were in his old trunk, so—"

"Journals from a spent mage's old trunk, huh?" Elizabeth hissed a sigh and shook her head. "I wasn't sure I'd like having a roommate, but you keep surprising me."

"Thanks. I think." With a smirk, she opened the first page of the top journal and paused. *Everyone still thinks Connor Alby used all his magic. It's probably better to not correct that assumption.* She focused on the first page, which didn't have any inscription beyond the same seal of the dragon riders that was embroidered into her grandfather's old patch.

With a widening grin, she skimmed through the pages and waited for something to catch her attention first, just in case. *Why wait for the good stuff if I can find it first?* After a few minutes, she stopped at a page not quite in the middle of the journal with a written title at the top of one page in a much larger script than the rest and underlined twice. *Magic Meld.*

"Woah." Raven read through most of the spell, but her mind raced now with possibilities instead of focusing on the actual words that filled the old, yellowed page.

"Have you found some juicy secrets already?" Elizabeth asked with a raised eyebrow.

"Maybe…" She tilted her head and tried to focus. *This is the spell he used to heal my shoulder. And he said he'd never teach it to me. Did he forget it was in here?* "It's not a secret. Only something I didn't expect to find."

"That's usually how journals work, isn't it?"

She jerked her gaze toward the open door of her dorm room where Teresa stood, her arms folded as she leaned against the doorframe. *Damn. Bella's gonna hear about the journals and the panther issue now.*

"Something like that." Trying to play it cool, she closed the journal slowly and set both behind her on the bed. "Can I help you with something, Teresa?"

The girl shrugged and fixed her with a small, calculating smile. "I don't know yet. Is there anything you wanna tell me about what happened out there?" She nodded toward the window.

Who is she trying to be? Professor Gilliam? "Headmaster

Flynn asked people not to start spreading rumors. I agree with him."

"It's not spreading rumors if I get the real story from you." Her eyes widened when she said it and she glanced at Elizabeth briefly when the girl snorted.

"It was only a couple of spooked animals in the stables," Raven replied.

"And a spooked dragon?"

She shook her head with a small, knowing smile. "No. Leander was a little irritated by all the noise. He likes to sleep."

"That didn't sound a little irritated." Teresa's gaze darted toward the edge of the journal that poked out a little. She shrugged again. "There had to be something else going on. Come on, Raven. You can tell me."

You mean open up to one of Bella Chase's best friends and flunkies? Fat chance. "He's a dragon. Everything looks and sounds bigger with a dragon."

The girls stared at each other for a few seconds before Elizabeth looked up from her book and pierced Teresa with an expressionless gaze. "I'm going to bed now."

The intruder frowned. "Okay..."

"Since you're standing there, can you shut the door?" The girl's eye not covered by her dark, swooping bangs widened a little when she raised her eyebrow.

With a huff, their visitor grasped the door and actually did close it for them before she returned to her room. Raven's sound-dampening spell cut out all the noise of the other girls too excited by the night's events to go back to bed now, including the sound of Teresa slamming her door.

Raven chuckled. "That was nice of her."

"I honestly didn't think she'd do us such a meaningful favor." Her roommate turned slowly to look at her and the girls burst out laughing.

Elizabeth still chuckled quietly as she curled under her covers. Raven rescued the old journals from the bed and tucked them into the oilskin bag. When they were secured, she shoved it under her bed and climbed under the covers. *I'll find a better hiding place tomorrow.*

She pointed at the magically glowing lantern hanging from the ceiling and muttered, *"Nullen lucidis."* The light winked out and she tried to get some sleep.

CHAPTER TWENTY-ONE

Professor Bixby waddled to the front of the History of Magic class the next morning and her frizzed copper hair caught the sunlight through the window. The squat, incredibly round professor stepped precariously onto the raised platform behind her desk and clapped briskly. "Settle down, class. I expect everyone's full attention this morning as I do in every class. I think many of you will enjoy today's lesson."

Raven swiped loose red hair out of her eyes and tried to focus on the woman's high-pitched and slightly nasally voice. *I need to get more sleep. Consistently.*

She glanced at Murphy seated two desks away, who doodled something with her quill and looked entirely distracted. Henry sat a few rows behind her near the back and leaned toward Rory Davidian with wide eyes as he listened to the not so quietly whispered accounts of, "...the dragon fighting a whole den of vagreti panthers last night..."

I can't say that's completely unexpected. She rolled her eyes and shook her head at her desk. *But it doesn't help the situation.*

"Now, you all remember the blood spell we performed a few weeks ago to reveal your personal family trees, yes?" Professor Bixby leaned forward over her desk, peered at her students, and waited for a response. None was forthcoming. "Yes, that was quite interesting. Many of you discovered things about yourselves you simply may not have had the opportunity to otherwise know."

A few rows in front and on the right, Bella Chase turned slightly to look over her shoulder and catch Raven's glance. The girl tossed her hair over her shoulder and returned her attention to their tiny professor. *We have more in common than we thought, too.*

"Today, you'll learn about the magical lineage of everyday things. These are family trees as well, in a sense, but perhaps not in the way you might expect." Bixby tapped her wand on her desk, read whatever she'd written on the parchment paper in front of her, and cleared her throat. "Everything has an origin. A source we can trace all the way to the beginning. If you pick up an acorn, you hold thousands of generations in your hand. Your familiars also have a magical lineage, as do your quills and the parchment paper you write on, whether we like it or not. Let me remind you how important it is to respect the past and our history and where we come from because everything in this world is connected to its past. Today, you'll draw forth the lineage of individual inanimate objects in the same way you used the blood spell for your family trees."

Tessa raised her hand.

"Yes, Miss Hambridge."

"Why?"

Bixby squeaked a laugh. "Why? My dear, you cannot be expected to master spells or even your magic if you do not understand where they come from. If you forget one link in the historical chain, you may end up with a completely different result than you intended. Now, this isn't a spell we'll simply throw around willy-nilly. I sincerely hope none of you do that but let's not fool ourselves. You're first-years."

One of the boys in the back row muttered, "Isn't that giving us an excuse to mess around?"

A few others snickered, but Bixby either didn't hear or ignored them. "Now, come up here to retrieve another blank roll of parchment paper and a copy of the lineage spell. You worked with partners last time, but I think it's high time you branched out on your own. This is much simpler than the blood spell, although no less important. I expect each of you to produce something on that parchment paper."

Chairs and desks groaned and shifted as the students stood to shuffle toward her desk to gather their few supplies. Raven indulged a massive yawn before she stood, and Henry rapped his knuckles on her desk. "Did the panther fight keep you up last night, Alby?"

She looked at him with heavy eyelids and pushed to her feet. "I told you what happened before class."

"Oh, I know." He grinned and gestured for her to step in front of him in the line toward Bixby's desk. "Lemme tell ya, the stories everyone else throws around are much more exciting."

"Rumors are always more exciting than the truth, aren't

they?" She yawned again and tried to shake off her fatigue. "Besides, I never really pegged you for the gossiping type."

"Oh, no way. I'm merely a sucker for a good story."

They reached Bixby's desk to collect what they needed and followed the other students to return to their desks. Almost everyone looked more or less clueless.

Professor Bixby regarded them through her thick glasses and smiled pertly. "Now. Allow me to demonstrate how this works." She lifted her quill into the air and set it on the blank parchment paper. Then, with one finger on the corner of the parchment paper, she recited the spell—without having to read it, of course. *"Fateo ortus."*

No one could see the ink lines scrolling across the parchment paper on her desk, but when it was finished, the professor lifted it and turned it for the class to see. Thin, intricate lines stretched across the page in a surprisingly lifelike drawing of a goose.

"We already know where a feather quill comes from," Rory muttered. "What's the point?"

"Ah-ah." Bixby raised a finger with one hand and wiggled the parchment paper with the other. "This is only the first half, my dears. Observe." She cleared her throat, tapped the drawing of the goose, and almost shouted, *"Anima narratis."*

The parchment paper suspended between her fingers jerked once, then twice, and the goose drawing peeled itself away completely. Black lines materialized into a thick black bill and feathers in white, brown, and gray. The bird's webbed feet were the last to emerge, and the drawing-sized goose uttered a startled honk before it flapped its wings madly and took flight across the room. It landed on

Murphy's desk with a solid thud. The girl leaned back quickly against her chair and raised both hands, and Fritz hissed beside her feet.

"Excellent." Bixby clapped in excitement and nodded as she scanned her students' faces. "You will draw the lineage from whatever item you choose. It can be anything in the room or anything on your person. This is to practice for a much more important version for our next class, which will have significantly more meaning for all of you. Begin."

A flurry of excited voices rose from the class, which startled the miniature goose that had tried to make a nest for itself on Murphy's desk. The girl uttered a little shriek as Fritz leapt into her lap, swatted at the magicked creature, and hissed in fury. The goose honked and hissed in response, and its wings buffeted the air, Fritz, and Murphy with merciless outrage until it took off again toward Bixby's desk instead.

Raven leaned forward to meet Murphy's gaze. Her friend's hair was untidy, puffed out all over her head, and some fell over her eyes. "Are you okay, Murphy?"

"Yeah. I only...ew." Her friend sputtered and removed a miniature tail feather from her mouth, then flicked it away with a grimace. "Goose feathers."

"Hey, check it out," Mike called. "Murphy's making down comforters for everyone!"

A round of laughter rose at that, and the girl wrinkled her nose with a disgusted frown. As soon as she met Raven's gaze, they both laughed.

"This is still a classroom," Bixby called and clapped sharply again. "And you are all still here to learn. Get to learning."

A little reluctantly, everyone turned to their desks and parchment papers, ready to attempt the spell for themselves. Raven's eyes lit up when she realized which inanimate object she wanted to try reanimating—or at least find the origins of. She drew a textbook from her satchel and flipped through the pages to locate the tiny scrap of burned parchment paper she'd taken from her grandfather's dead fire at their house.

There's a chance, right? I might as well take it.

She studied the red seal with the crossed weapons and the tower in the background, set it on the parchment paper, and muttered the first half of the spell.

The spell itself worked perfectly and lines of ink etched themselves across the blank surface in only a few seconds. The resulting image, however, wasn't the letter Connor Alby had burned in their hearth before his unexplained flight from both the Alby Ranch and Brighton. Instead, a full tree stretched across the parchment paper from the longest, lowest-reaching root to the highest branch.

Raven sighed and her shoulders sagged a little. "Of course. The source, not the last form it took."

"Raven, did you get it?" Murphy asked and tapped her parchment paper before she muttered, *"Fateo ortus."* The ink she'd dripped onto it spread into the thick, dark lines of a pile of charcoal beside a drawing of potatoes. "Awesome. My prize is coal and zero flavor."

"Yeah, I got it." She pressed her lips together and stared at the drawing of a tree. "I kind of expected something else, but I guess I wasn't thinking."

"Anima naratis," Henry muttered. A loud, rumble issued from the back of the class. The drawing of what looked like

rocks on his parchment paper emerged from the ink, but the pile of rocks continued to grow on his desk. Loose chunks spilled onto the floor and into his lap. He pointed at them and whispered harshly, "Stop. *Stop.*"

"Are you having a little trouble, Mr. Derks?" Professor Bixby waddled down the center aisle of the classroom, her eyes huge behind the glasses. "Oh. Ha. I believe your pebble was sourced from a rock quarry in Ingeval."

"It won't stop!" he shouted and scooted his chair back to stand. The pile of rocks in his lap skittered onto the floor while the students seated around him either watched with amusement or ignored him to focus on their spells.

"*Satis animo.*" Bixby tapped his parchment paper and the rumbling mountain of stones ceased their endless flow from his desk. "Stones can be difficult to discern, Mr. Derks. I daresay you did a fine job with this one, despite the mess. Please pick that up."

With a little groan, he dropped to his knees and made another sloppy pile of rocks the size of his hand.

"Oh, Miss Murphy." Bixby stopped at the girl's desk and studied her parchment paper with a little frown. The woman's head rose only to Murphy's shoulder, and she had to look down at the professor to meet her gaze. "It's ingenious, really—trying to trace the lineage of ink. Carry on."

Murphy blinked in surprise and a grin bloomed on her face before she focused on the second half of her spell.

Raven tapped the edge of her parchment paper and whispered, "*Anima narratis.*" The tree drawn there by her spell lifted itself slowly and tiny branches and even tinier leaves rustled as the treetop peeled away in a fully formed miniature. Everything but the roots lifted away but remained tethered to the parchment paper by the tips of those roots that still clung to the page.

"Ah, Miss Alby. Well done." Bixby clapped in approval and nodded.

"It didn't come all the way, though." She slid the parchment paper from one side to the other on her desk, which made the miniature tree's branches sway again.

"The roots have nowhere to go." Professor Bixby uttered a high-pitched giggle and shook her head. "If you'd like to try again, you might add a speck of dirt to the spell. I imagine the entire tree would then be fully rooted and able to rise completely. But this is very well done. Yes, yes. What object did you use?"

Raven pressed her finger over the edge of her grandfather's burned letter and completely covered the seal before she slid it across her desk and into her lap. "It was another piece of parchment paper."

"Very well done. Yes."

A sticky, suctioning squish issued from the other side of the room, followed by a round of surprised disgust from the group of students at the surrounding desks.

"What the heck is that?"

"Dude, what did you put on that parchment paper? Snot?"

"I can't...ugh!"

Bixby toddled off toward the commotion and burst out laughing. "Mr. Jeder! Do tell me what in the world you chose for this."

"Um...leftover bread from breakfast." Mike grimaced at his parchment paper. "And Patsy tried to eat it, I think."

"Ah. You'll have to try again before the end of class. Hop to it."

"Way to stink up the whole room, Mike," someone else called.

"I didn't know he'd slobbered over it, okay?"

Raven passed her hand over the surreally lifelike tree that stood on her desk, the leaves soft and green beneath her fingers. She glanced toward Bella Chase's desk, where Professor Bixby had also stopped to inspect the other girl's spell. A lilac bush bursting with purple flowers covered most of the surface.

"Beautiful, Miss Chase. Quite extraordinary. I'll give you the same tip I gave Miss Alby. Adding soil to the spell would have enabled the roots to fully emerge. But very well done."

The girl waited for the professor to return to the front of the classroom before she turned to look at Raven's tree. One thin eyebrow raised, and she inclined her head in acknowledgment before she turned away to sniff at the blooming lilacs.

Was that condescension or approval?

Murphy raised her hands from her desk, which was covered now in a pile of coal, a mound of dirt, and a handful of thick brown potatoes. "I'm gonna have black all over me for days." She laughed and leaned toward Raven. "Bella didn't think of the dirt either, huh? Do you want some of mine?"

She laughed. "Where'd your dirt come from?"

"I don't know. Maybe a coal mine?"

"Huh."

At the end of class, Bixby clapped again and peered at

them from the platform behind her desk. "Now, before you all rush out of here like someone conjured fire under your backsides, listen up. You have an assignment to complete before our final class of the week. The day before the Spring Gala, we'll go over something a little different. I want each of you to find a personal item of your own to bring to class—something with meaning and magical significance. If you don't have anything you care about enough, get something from your parents or grandparents. The older, the better. Understood? Yes? Excellent. Goodbye."

The students rose from their seats in a hurry. Raven brushed her hand over the tree again and smiled. *Something with meaning and magical significance, huh? It's a good thing I have a lot to choose from.*

Murphy joined her as they headed out of the class and through the dark stone halls. "Do you have any idea what you'll bring next time?"

Raven tapped her fingers on her satchel and shrugged. "Not yet. I'm thinking about it, though. You?"

"I don't know. Maybe my mom's robes from when she graduated Fowler?" The girl wrinkled her nose. "As long as Bixby says the spell won't ruin them."

Reflexively, her fingers went to her mother's pin on her jacket. "I hope she wouldn't make us bring in something meaningful only to destroy it. That's a little harsh."

"Do you know what's harsh?" Henry limped a little as he joined them and stumbled with a false laugh when Thomas punched him in the shoulder and hurried away. "Getting your lap pelted by a never-ending supply of rocks.

I think I have bruises in places I don't even wanna think about."

The girls chuckled and Raven asked, "What did you use?"

"Some pebbles. Literally, that's it. You know, a boy's best projectile friend." He whipped his slingshot out of his pocket, pulled the sling back, and aimed over the heads in the hallway before Professor Gilliam glared sharply at him in passing. "Whoops." The slingshot disappeared into his pocket again.

"What are you bringing for the next class, Derks?"

"Hmm." He tapped his fingers on his lips and barked out a laugh. "Hey, Norman's hair would be a fun experiment. You know, to see where the gene pool got so shallow with him."

Raven snorted. "You'll end up making a golem of your brother."

"Uh…" Henry shivered and shook his head. "That is a good point. No one needs two Normans running around. One's already enough. I guess my parents didn't figure that out until they had me."

"Yep. There can only be one Henry Derks. No doubt about it." Raven bumped him with her shoulder.

"The one and only! Hey, do you think doing that spell with my hair would help me study for exams? I mean, a golem can study, right?"

Murphy leaned forward, her arms wrapped around her book, and stared at him with wide eyes. "You're not serious, are you?"

He shrugged. "Maybe."

"I don't think any of our professors are gonna be all

that forgiving of a miniature Derks golem seated with you at your desk and scratching away at the exams you didn't study for."

"But it's a nice image, huh? Hey, Bennett! Hold on. I gotta hear this story about…" Henry darted through the crowd of students making their way to their next classes.

The two girls shook their heads. "I hope he doesn't try it," Murphy muttered.

"He probably won't. I don't think he'd know what to do with himself if he…you know. Conjured himself. It's an interesting thought, though." *I wonder what else that lineage spell works on. Or if there's a way to change it to bring the rest of Grandpa's letter back.*

CHAPTER TWENTY-TWO

At the end of classes, after waving goodbye to Henry and Murphy as they started their walk toward Brighton's town center, Raven hurried to Leander's pen. She pushed herself to move faster and felt less exhausted now with a dragon to look forward to.

When she reached his pen, Leander didn't wait for her to open the gate. "I'm hungry."

She chuckled. "It looks like someone has their appetite back, huh? I'll be right back."

Rounding the long side of the stables, she hurried inside and retrieved another burlap sack of dragon feed and heaved it over her shoulder. There were only three more stacked in the pile, and she turned to search the rest of the feed supplies. *Either the school brings in new shipments, or Leander and I are gonna have to make a food run to Moss Ranch.*

The thought made her laugh, and she was still grinning when she stepped out of the stables and headed toward the pen.

"Hey, Raven."

The sack of feed almost fell over her shoulder when she spun toward the greeting. "Oh. Hi, Daniel."

"I thought I might find you out here."

"You did, huh?" With a smirk, she repositioned the dragon feed and continued toward Leander's pen. "What makes you think that?"

"Well…" He gave a nervous, breathy laugh and fell into step beside her. "I mean, everyone knows your dragon's out here. I thought…if I had a dragon on the grounds, I'd be here all the time. Are you not?"

She thumped the sack onto the grass outside the gate and turned to him with her hands on her hips. "I am. I was messing with you."

"Oh, okay. Yeah. Cool."

Cool. Here we go again.

He smiled and ran a hand through his hair but did nothing more than simply stare at her.

Raven smiled and raised her eyebrows. "I assume you came out here to find me for a reason, right?"

"Oh, yeah. Totally. I wanted to ask you again about—"

A loud bang rose from the closest pen wall, followed by a snort. Daniel jumped a little, and she pressed her lips together. *A second-year with no vocabulary and a seriously hungry dragon. That's a great combo.*

"Woah." He glanced at the pen with wide eyes. "He's really in there, isn't he?"

"Yep. He merely keeps a low profile." She glanced at the pen walls but didn't see a hint of the red dragon peeking up over the top. "Literally."

"Cool. That's so cool."

He grinned at the enclosure and nodded repeatedly, and she decided she couldn't wait any longer. "What did you want to ask me? I'm about to feed that hungry dragon, so..." She shrugged. "It's probably a good idea not to keep him waiting."

"Yeah. Right. Yeah." Daniel smiled at her again and stepped closer. She kept her hand on the top of the feed sack but stepped smoothly behind it to protect her personal space. "So you haven't given me an answer yet." He grinned and lowered his chin toward her.

Okay, he admittedly has cute dimples. He's not much of a conversationalist, though. "About what?'

"The dance, Raven. You said you'd think about going with me as my date. I came to see if you made your mind up yet."

"Oh..." She glanced at the pen where Leander uttered another snort and scraped his talons through the earth. "I don't know, Daniel—"

"If you keep putting me off, though, I'm gonna keep asking." He shrugged and chuckled at himself, apparently finding that witty.

Leander's tail thumped against the wall.

He's gonna break out of there if I keep him waiting. She eyed the gate warily. "Sure, Daniel. That's fine."

"That I keep asking, or that you'll be my date?"

"I'll go to the dance with you." She lugged the feed sack toward the gate and listened intently for signs of her dragon's growing impatience. "That works. No problem."

"Cool." He ran another hand through his hair.

Fighting to not roll her eyes, Raven laughed instead. "Yeah. Okay, so, I have to feed my dragon. This is a Raven-

Alby-only zone right now, and I don't think Leander's in the mood to meet new friends—"

A harsh, thick flap of beating wings came from the other side of the wall, followed by the translucent red tips of Leander's outstretched wings rising above the pen walls.

"Woah. Yeah…" Daniel stared at the ridged wingtips and the leathery membranes that glowed blood-red in the sunlight. "Hey, I heard all kinds of stuff this morning about what happened last night."

Oh, come on. She banged an aggravated fist against the pen gate, which was swiftly returned by a thump of the dragon's tail. "I wouldn't believe everything you hear, Daniel. Many people say weird things about everything."

"Did your dragon really fight off three vagreti panthers to save all the other animals in the stables? 'Cause that would be the coolest—"

"I didn't fight or save anything, you walking bag of hormones," Leander growled and his voicing echoed with a tinny ring within his enclosure. "Go away."

Raven bit her lower lip so hard in her effort to not laugh that she was surprised she hadn't drawn blood.

"Woah!" Daniel laughed and glanced from Raven to the pen and back again. "That's—"

"Cool. Yeah, I know. I gotta do this, so I'll see you later. At the dance if not somewhere else, okay? Bye." She shoved the feed sack a little closer to the gate and raised her forearm toward the latch. The orange lights glowed in tandem before the gate opened.

"That is so cool," Daniel muttered. "See ya, Raven. And Raven's dragon."

"His name's Lean—"

"Maybe I'll eat him instead, Raven." Leander snorted and the boy's smile vanished as he turned and walked quickly across the field.

"I'm coming." She pulled the gate open, lugged the sack inside, and made sure the latch was locked. "Sorry about that. He's gone now."

"I know." He paced on the opposite side of the pen and watched her drag the feed toward the trough. "Everything's so cool until there's something real to fear."

"Well, at least he's smart enough to be a little afraid. I had honestly begun to wonder." Raven took the dagger from her boot to open the top of the bag, then tipped the contents into the trough. She yanked the empty burlap away in time to prevent it from being gobbled with the red dragon's first starving bite. "Woah. You weren't kidding."

"Not about food." Hot breath from his nose blew a few pellets of feed out of the trough as he guzzled another huge mouthful.

"Not even when you're threatening to eat a mage in training, huh?"

"Adolescent boys taste too much like they smell." The feed crunched between the razor-sharp teeth in his massive jaws, and she bundled the burlap sack before she tossed it on the grass beside the gate.

"I choose to believe that was a joke and not based on your own experience."

The dragon made no response.

She stood in silence and watched him eat for another five minutes before the trough was completely empty again. Leander raised his head for the first time since he'd started and released a massive belch. She clapped a hand over her nose and turned away.

"More."

"More? I'm not sure that's a good idea."

"I'm getting restless, little girl. My appetite returned and if I can't stalk all these children telling ridiculous stories, at least let me get my satisfaction somewhere."

"No. I'm not about to let you start down the road toward emotional eating."

He reared away from the trough and stalked across the pen again, his wings twitching. He raised his head with another wary sniff and growled.

"Okay. You just ate, so we can scratch being hangry off the list. I know what you need."

"That is doubtful."

Raven considered going to him and trying to settle him with a little affection, but she decided the surprise would be better. "I'll be right back. Just hang tight."

"I'm not a bat, either."

Choking down another laugh, she slipped out of the gate, closed it a little firmer than necessary—just to be sure —and headed into the stables. When she returned and thumped Connor Alby's old dragon saddle and harness into the grass, the dragon froze. His yellow gaze settled on the tack and remained fixed on it.

"I told you this morning, didn't I? We have the all-clear to fly and right now, what you need is to get your head in the clouds and leave everything else down here behind you. So do I. Are you up for it?"

His great red head lowered almost to the ground before he turned away from the wall of the pen and took two steps toward her. He lowered his belly to the ground and snorted. "A long flight."

"A long flight. I just got out of class for the day so we have enough time."

"Then let's use it."

With a broad grin, she picked up the saddle and harness, brought it to him, and swung the saddle with expert skill after so many months of practice. The harness slid over his head and down his neck, and she slipped the straps quickly through the buckles beneath his underbelly when he stood.

She rushed toward the gate, pulled it wide, and gestured for him to follow her out. With a snort, Leander raced across the area and his lumbering footsteps made the ground tremble beneath them. With his head outstretched on his long neck and his wings tucked tightly against his back and twitching at the ends, he could have been a one-dragon stampede.

He's gonna crash through the pen. "Careful—" She darted aside as her streamlined dragon thrust through the open gate. He slowed immediately once he passed her and turned to snort at the horses that made wary, startled noises inside the stables. "That's one way to do it."

Raven shut the gate and moved quickly toward her dragon. "Leander, are you—" She laughed and stepped aside when his wings stretched with a heavy, thick blast of air. "Are you prancing?"

"I said restless. Get on or stay here."

"You don't have to tell me twice." Her smile had almost become a permanent fixture and she ran toward him and leapt into the saddle as he lowered himself to help her reach. Her boots slipped quickly into the stirrups before Leander broke into a run across the field. "Go, go, go!"

A laugh burst from her mouth but cut off when the dragon launched them into the air and the wind streamed down her throat and made her gasp. He climbed almost vertically, his wings beating mightily, but she squeezed her knees against his flanks and bent almost completely forward over the saddle to run both hands along his neck.

"You weren't kidding."

"Not about flying, either." He leveled out high above the treetops of the forest behind Fowler Academy, the barn and the field, and the tallest tower of the school's main buildings.

Somehow, everything looks so much smaller in the daylight. She spent only a few minutes studying her school and her new temporary home from a birds-eye view. A thin stream of students, so tiny below them, rushed through the stone archway and out onto the field to watch Raven Alby flying on her dragon familiar.

This time, when she laughed, it wasn't forced away by the wind. She blinked the wind-buffeted tears from the corner of her eyes and spread her arms at her sides. *Take the wheel, Leander. Wherever you want to go. Just fly.*

She didn't have to tell him. The dragon felt each of her movements as clearly as she felt her own. He dipped forward and the tips of his wings angled down until they dropped in a breathtaking dive. She whooped with joy and fought to catch her breath again, while her feet slipped from the stirrups.

Raven tightened her hold with her knees and watched

the ground rush up to meet them. *I don't even need stirrups. I'm on and I'm not coming off.*

Leander pulled up, banked left again, and climbed once more into the sky. The excited shouts of the students on the field were a thin, wordless hum from up there. She laughed and patted his neck in front of the saddle as he took them over the tops of Fowler Academy and off the grounds, heading north. "Now you feel like showing off, huh?"

He turned his head slightly toward her as his wings pumped through the sky. "No more rumors."

That looks like a smile to me. She grinned in return. "Yeah, that'll take all the guesswork out of it." She brushed the loose hair away from her face, her thick red braid streaming out behind her, and glanced at the harness leads wrapped loosely around the saddle horn. *I didn't use those, either. Maybe we really can ride without any of this.*

For now, she tilted her head back and let the sun warm her face as the spring air brushed over her. *We shouldn't have waited so long for this.*

CHAPTER TWENTY-THREE

L eander took them out toward the huge wall surrounding the kingdom, although they didn't cross it this time. Raven thought they might until the dragon snorted quickly and wheeled away from the top of the wall so far below them. "Is everything okay?"

"I changed my mind." His response didn't sound either enthusiastic or unconcerned.

Or he feels something's off over the wall. That's been coming for a while, hasn't it?

She turned to look over her shoulder at the wall again as they changed direction, but there wasn't much to see before he soared across the kingdom and deeper into the safety within those walls. *He knows my intentions and knows I'm curious. And he still turned away.*

Her thoughts turned quickly to her grandfather and the things she'd grown up hearing over and over. "The wall keeps us safe, granddaughter. But sometimes, a physical boundary is simply that. Don't assume that anything is truly safe. That's the best way to protect yourself and those around you."

The tears returned to her eyes and she sniffed, but they weren't from the wind brushing across her face and buffeting her clothes. *He knew something was coming even when I was small. Is that why he left?*

"What's wrong?" Leander turned his head toward her again as he caught another current and glided across open fields and ranches within the kingdom's allegedly secure borders. His broad, winged shadow was only a little bigger than one of the Alby dwarf goats as it moved across the grass below.

"I'm only..." Raven wiped at her eyes and shook her head. "I didn't know I missed my grandfather as much as I do. Until right now, that is."

"I understand." The dragon faced forward again and said nothing more.

He can feel it, can't he? Because he knows what it's like to miss someone close to him too.

"Okay, Leander." She leaned forward and patted the base of his long, majestic neck. "Let's make a stop at Moss Ranch."

For a few seconds, he didn't reply and he didn't alter the course of his route. Then, his low voice rumbled and she felt it vibrate through him beneath the saddle. "For you or for me?"

"Both of us, I think."

Leander banked sharply and moved to the southwest but skirted the town center of Brighton like they had on their flight to Fowler Academy. She nodded. *He doesn't want to scare anyone either.*

In only a few minutes, they passed over the outer fences of the Moss Ranch property and descended gently toward the dragon stables and the pen that no longer belonged to a headstrong red dragon who couldn't be trained. Leander's shadow rippled over the other dragons spending the fine spring day in the massive field and his feet touched lightly on the trodden dirt on the opposite side of the barn.

"Do you feel better?" She patted his neck again and he lowered himself to his belly so she could dismount.

"As much as I expected."

"Yeah, me too." *Not all the way better, though. We're about to fix that.* A plume of dust puffed beneath her boots, and Leander rose again before he took a few steps away from the barn. "Hey, where are you going?"

He pointed his muzzle fully toward the end of the building, where William stalked toward them with a grin. He ripped the broad-brimmed hat off his head, slapped it against his other hand, and laughed. "Did you miss me already, huh?" He spread his arms wide and forced himself to slow his approach to the young mage and her familiar. "It's only been a few days."

"It feels like much longer," she called in response and glanced at Leander. "I was about to take that saddle off. Unless you feel more comfortable wearing it for fun."

The dragon uttered a low rumble and stepped toward her. "I didn't expect this to be a long visit."

"Hey, you trust me, right?" He didn't move when she stepped toward him and stretched under his belly to undo the straps. The old saddle thumped into the dirt. "Good. You'll want this off anyway while we're here."

"I always want it off." He pawed the ground once and lowered his head slightly when William approached.

The dragon trainer maintained a respectable distance, grinned, and scratched the side of his face. "You two sure know how to make an entrance."

"Why, thank you." Raven patted Leander's side and walked toward her friend. "At least you're glad to see us."

"I always am, Raven. Are you kidding?" He smirked and folded his arms to regard her curiously. "How's dorm life?"

"It's convenient, mostly. Which I guess is the whole reason I'm there."

"And Leander likes the new pen, huh?"

"Mostly."

"Okay, now it sounds like you've left a few things out." He gestured toward the fence around the huge dragon enclosure. "Is everything okay at mage school?"

When they reached the section of the fence that continued behind the stables, Raven folded her arms on the top rung and sighed. "He says he feels like something's off."

"Huh. You know, if it were any other mage in training talking to me about any other dragon, I'd offer to help you find out what."

Raven chuckled. "Good luck finding another mage with a dragon familiar running around."

"Exactly. You know him better than I do and I know you. Whatever it is, you'll take care of it."

She nodded, her gaze fixed on the other dragons in the distance. They lounged in the sun, stamped around each other, jumped into low flight, or released short bursts of fire or ice. "We had a little incident last night, too."

"That's...not what I expected you to say."

Raven frowned at her friend. "Not with Leander. He merely woke everyone up." William snorted and shook his head. "I know. It sounds funny and it kind of is now. But it doesn't change the fact that two vagreti panthers ignored—or someone pushed through—Fowler Academy's wards to reach the forest on the grounds. They stalked across the field past Leander's pen and all the other animals."

"Vagreti?" Her companion rubbed his chin and closed one eye in a thoughtful squint. "They don't generally roam close to a group of people and especially not close to dragons."

"I know." She turned to look over her shoulder and caught a glimpse of Leander, who stretched his wings again before he settled into the dirt. *Our flight took the restlessness out of him, at least.* "Leander said they were running away."

"From what?"

She shrugged. "Whatever it is, I doubt it's good."

They leaned against the fence a little longer in silence, then William smacked a hand on the top rail and leaned back. "All right. There's no way everything that's happened to you living at that school is all worries and no fun. Otherwise, you would have come for a visit much sooner."

"I would have, huh?" Raven laughed. "You sound so sure."

"I like to think you enjoy the company." He gave her a crooked smile.

"Of course I do. Let's see." She grasped the top rail of the fence and bent away from it to stretch her back. "Spells are fun. Leander and I get to start training with Professor

Worley and the rest of the class tomorrow. You know, familiar training."

"They're gonna let Leander out of that pen to go to class with you." William raised an eyebrow.

"Not quite." Raven nudged him with her shoulder. "I'm fairly sure they're taking the class to him. Not in the pen but next to it. I think."

"Wow. That's some serious student-professor trust."

"We're finally convincing people that Leander and I trust each other enough to make it work." She straightened and tipped her head back to stretch her neck. "Hopefully, no one tries anything. We came close before we headed out to come here."

"Some kids tried to jump on the dragon pen to have a look at the beast inside it, huh?" With a low whistle, William shook his head and shoved his hat onto it. "It's one more reason why Moss Ranch isn't open to the public. Or near a school."

"Not exactly. You know, for the most part, I think everyone at Fowler knows enough about dragons to want to keep their distance. Except for this one guy today. Daniel Smith."

"Please tell me that big softy over there buffeted this Daniel Smith around a few times."

They both glanced at Leander, who'd now rolled halfway over in the dirt and squirmed on his side to enjoy a nice scratch.

Raven barked a laugh and watched the dragon enjoy himself for a little longer. "If the guy had gotten into the pen, it would've been more than a game of cat and mouse."

"Dragon and mage."

"Beast and boy."

They laughed and she rolled her eyes. "I hadn't even fed Leander yet, and this guy wouldn't take the hint that he needed to leave us alone and get out of the way. Maybe he's smart enough to stay away from a dragon, but I don't think he's capable of staying away from me."

"Oh…" William's eyebrows raised. "One of those problems."

"I guess. We have this spring gala coming up in a week. Daniel asked me to go with him and he wouldn't leave me alone about it. Anyway, I finally said yes to get him off my back." She wrinkled her nose and glanced at her friend. "I think I might be regretting it already."

"Raven Alby has a date." He said it jokingly enough but his smile faded.

That's a new look. William Moss doesn't normally wear disappointed. "Everyone calls it a date but it's more like showing up together. I'll probably end up walking away as soon as we get there."

He sucked a breath in through his teeth. "Harsh."

"No, not like that. Daniel Smith has girls fawning over him all the time. He'll be fine." She studied her friend's easy smile when he chuckled. *No, it's definitely not disappointment. Maybe he's as surprised about a magic-school dance as I was.*

"Well, if you have to let him down, let him down easy. Thanks, but no thanks. It's not you, it's me. That kinda thing."

Raven turned away from him and leaned sideways against the railing. "We're not dating. It's one dance and he only got a yes from me because Leander threatened to

eat him. It's not like the guy has any serious misconceptions."

William pursed his lips and shrugged. "Or he's too into
you to notice the serious misconceptions."

"William Moss." She leaned one arm on the fence rail,
rested her other hand on her hip, and regarded him with a
challenging look. "This is a ridiculous conversation. And
it's not why we came here."

"First, agreed. Moving on. Second, if you didn't come
here to gaze upon your friend's smiling face, tell me your
reasons." He slid another glance toward Leander and
laughed. "There's not enough dirt at Fowler Academy."

"He says he likes the grass better."

"Yeah, they all say that until they start rolling in the
dirt." He flashed her a wide grin and slapped the top fence
rail again. "Go on. Spit it out."

"We need to let Leander out there with the others. We
planned to the other day before I did all my packing and
messed up the schedule. Also, I want to do something that's
completely for him."

William released a long, slow breath through pursed
lips, rubbed his jaw, and gazed at the dragons gathered in
their clans on Moss Ranch. "I don't know, Raven. I haven't
prepared for any of that today. I didn't expect you. If the
other dragons aren't expecting him either, anything could
happen."

"Okay, forget the other dragons. Only his mother."

He lowered both hands to his sides and stepped away
from the fence. "You want to let him in there, on his own
and where you might not be able to get to him, so he can
see his mother."

"Exactly. He deserves this much, at the very least. He shouldn't have to in the first place, but Leander's earned it. You can't argue with me on that one, so don't even try."

"Oh, I know. There's nothing to argue." William's hand came down on the top of his hat and he patted it a few times in a distracted way. "There's not much we can do about it if the two of them decide to repeat his grand entrance again and break out on their own."

"That won't happen." Raven folded her arms. "I know it won't. He'd break my trust and turn away from everything we've done together. I trust him."

For a few seconds, her friend simply studied her with narrowed eyes. "You really do. Okay, so why the sudden trip to Moss Ranch for a dragon family reunion?"

She swallowed, turned toward the sunbathing dragons, and willed the tears to not form in when she thought of her grandfather. "I think I understand more about what he's going through. Right now, I think I'd give anything for a tight hug from Connor Alby and one of his old stories."

"There it is." She didn't expect to see him grin at her when she turned to look at him. "And way faster than I thought."

"What are you talking about?" The pain of missing her grandfather vanished when she laughed at the goofy way the dragon trainer tilted his head and examined her like she'd put a costume on.

"Your connection with Leander has been strong enough for him to feel what you're feeling—distress, fear, excitement. He's responded to your intentions for a while now. But this…" He slapped his hand down on his head and shoved the wide-brimmed hat askew. "This is you feeling your dragon, Raven Alby. You're taking it to a whole new level."

"Well, we were bound to get to that point anyway, weren't we?"

"Uh-uh." William pushed away from the fence and clapped briskly. "Most dragon trainers don't get anywhere near that far. Maybe they don't know it's possible or perhaps they don't want to feel their dragon's emotions. I've reached that point a few times with Teo, but it's only little glimpses and even those fade quickly."

"He's my familiar now too, you know. Not only my dragon."

"Yeah…you know, part of me thinks that has nothing to do with it. You go distract him for a while, okay? I'm gonna take care of a few things first."

"First?" Raven turned as her friend strode toward the barn.

He turned and his bootheels kicked dust up as he walked backward and spread his arms in an extravagant gesture. "And second, we'll have a Moss Ranch reunion."

She laughed as he disappeared into the barn and turned toward Leander, who still lay on his back in the dirt. "Did you hear that, Leander?"

His belly rose and fell in slow, contented breaths and he snorted. "I stopped listening when you said, 'Daniel.'"

With a grin, she watched her dragon enjoying himself in the sun and bit her lip. *He's gonna love this.*

CHAPTER TWENTY-FOUR

Way down the fence on the other side of the dragon enclosure, William whistled and waved at Raven. She waved back and turned to look into Leander's glowing yellow eyes. They seemed wider than usual and his nostrils flared with the occasional short burst of air. "Are you ready?"

"That's a pointless question."

"I only wanted to make sure." Raven patted his shoulder and rubbed his flank a few times. Thin trails of dust shivered from beneath his scales. "Let's go."

The huge red dragon didn't need to hear anything else. He moved quickly beside her and she grinned at the other red shape ahead of them. William said something she couldn't hear to the other dragon, but it didn't matter. She glanced at Leander again and maintained her pace. *Any minute now, he'll race toward her exactly like he did out of his pen.*

But the closer they got, the slower he walked.

Finally, he stopped altogether with a few quick, nervous snorts and thumped a huge paw into the dirt.

"Hey, what's going on?" Raven reached for him but he stepped away and his wings twitched out above their heads.

"I don't...know."

"What do you mean?" They'd made it halfway to William and the other red dragon at the far end of the enclosure. The trainer adjusted his hat and gestured as if to query the delay. "Leander, that's your mother over there. I know you miss her and I know you shouldn't have been kept away from her for as long as you were. I wanted to do this for you, and I..." She scratched her head in confusion. "Honestly, I thought you'd crash through the fence by now."

"It's been too long, Raven." His wings flapped again to stir more dust, then settled immediately. He snorted and stepped aside, away from her and the dragon enclosure.

"No, it hasn't. Hey. Come here."

A puff of thick smoke burst from his nostrils, although he wasn't nearly close enough to have the same burning, cough-inducing affect she knew all too well.

"You deserve this, Leander. You've always deserved it. I've heard you two screech to each other since the day you and I met. And look." She pointed down the fence to where the other red dragon stood with her wings partially spread and her long neck swaying from side to side. "Your mother's waiting for you. I think you've both waited long enough, don't you?"

"Get rid of the trainer." Leander turned away from the fence and lowered his head.

"William?"

"You can stay, but I don't want him there."

"Leander, he's the one who's making this possible right now—"

"No, he's the son of the one who made this necessary right now. No trainers, little girl. If she and I are to meet each other again, it won't be under a trainer's eye. Not under command and not under judgment. I want...I want her to feel as free as I do. That won't happen if he stands there waiting for something to go wrong."

"Wow." Raven shook her head quickly and rubbed her hands down her face. *Never say a dragon can't get emotional about his family.* "Okay. I'll go tell him. Do you wanna come with me, or—"

"When the trainer's gone, Raven, I will come."

"Right." She took a deep breath and turned toward William and Leander's mother.

He muttered something to the other red dragon, then hurried toward her on the opposite side of the fence. "What's wrong?"

"I think he doesn't believe this reunion is about to happen." She looked over her shoulder and shook his head. "He's nervous and a little scared. Probably embarrassed too and I didn't know that was even possible."

William cleared his throat. "Yeah, that happens some-times. He knows she's waiting for him, right?"

"He definitely knows—"

The red female dragon inside the enclosure uttered a piercing screech. Both Raven and William clamped their hands over their ears and the very same wailed call rose from Leander a second later. She lowered her hands.

"That's all they've been able to say to each other for how long?"

"A few years." He frowned. "It's not my favorite part of the job. I doubt any other trainer enjoys having to separate young dragons from their clan, but—"

"You were doing your job. And if Leander hadn't been too stubborn to cooperate his way out of that pen, I wouldn't have found him as easily—or maybe at all. That's the silver lining I choose to take away from this. That and the fact that this is something he's wanted for a long time."

"I know, Raven." William yanked his hat off his head, twisted it in both hands, and sighed heavily. "He wants it too much to let anything stand in the way at this point. Your dragon wants me to step aside, doesn't he?"

"You know, for a dragon trainer who had one hell of a time with Leander, you sure do know him well."

"Ha. You get to know anyone well enough when they throw you around a few times and are so stubborn, you start to lose sleep over it." He rubbed the back of his neck in indecision and stared at the dirt at his boots before he looked at her. "All right. I'll step aside."

"Just like that?" She couldn't quite let herself smile. *I must feel Leander's hesitation more than I realized.*

"Just like that, Raven." The dragon trainer braced himself with one hand on the top rail of the fence before he swung easily over it in one leap. He dusted his hand off and nodded toward Leander. "I know he doesn't particularly like me. I'd say the feeling is mutual, but that's only when I'm the one trying to make him understand what's in both our best interests. You're right, Raven. Leander deserves this and I don't want to stand in his way again. If you trust him enough to handle it, so do I."

She stared at him and her smile widened.

William glanced away, looked over his shoulder, and shrugged. "What?"

"You really do care about every single dragon that comes through here."

"Of course I do. Jeez, I hope I never gave you a different impression."

"No, no." Raven shook her head and set a hand on his shoulder. "That's not what I meant at all. I only… I always knew this was more than a job for you and I've seen you with Teo. But I imagine it's a little harder to care about a dragon who'd rather burn you to a crisp than do anything a trainer says."

A little awkward, he twisted his hat in his hands again and glanced quickly at her hand on his shoulder. "You caught me. It won't be for a while but eventually, Moss Ranch will be completely my responsibility. I started early with dragons. Beyond you and the few other hired hands we have around here, I'd say those stubborn, regal, scaly creatures are more friend to me than anything else."

"I understand. Thank you."

"For what? All I did was jump over a fence—"

Raven stepped toward him and wound her arms around his neck for a quick, tight hug. His hand moved lightly to the center of her back and when she pulled away, they both laughed.

"It means a lot to Leander. And to me. And we wouldn't have reached this point without you." She released him and stepped away, her smile still in place. "That's all."

"Maybe I should up my game if common courtesy and trusting a few friends gets me a reaction like that." He chuckled again through a confused-looking half-smile.

I think I embarrassed him, which wasn't what I intended. "No, you don't have to change anything. I'm gonna go get that stubborn, regal, scaly creature now if you don't mind."

"Go ahead." The dragon trainer stepped away from the fence and gestured toward Leander. He watched Raven hurry toward her red dragon familiar and bunched his hat in his hands as he deliberately put a fair distance between himself and the fence along the dragon enclosure. *Raven Alby, dragon rider and mage. What did I get myself into?*

Leander sidestepped again as she approached him, his wings tucked closely against his back.

"Okay. You're all good to go."

"He agreed? William agreed?"

"Yes, he did." She rubbed her hands together and turned to point at William Moss, who stood about a hundred yards away from the fence and nodded at them. "You see him over there, right? He trusts you. I trust you. So please, trust us for a little while longer. You'll forget all about us as soon as you step into that enclosure."

"I will." He gave as close to a determined nod as a dragon could and raced down the line of the fence.

Raven had to jog to keep up with him and laughed when his mother uttered another piercing screech echoed not a second later by her son. The mage in training pushed herself hard when she realized something. *The wards won't let him in without an open gate.*

She reached the gate at the far corner of the enclosure at the same time Leander did. Both red dragons moved swiftly to the fence and their heavy footsteps made the ground tremble. Her fingers fumbled with the latch when it slipped out of her hold, but she managed to open the gate. Leander stormed through it with his head held high.

"Go get her," she whispered and latched the gate closed again. Her dragon spread his wings to their full span, turned, and strutted away from his mother. "What is he doing?"

The other red dragon—not quite three-quarters his size —stretched her neck into the air and screeched again. He reared on his hind legs with a mighty flap of his wings before his forepaws pounded together onto the ground. Snorting and huffing, he turned and faced his mother and the two great beasts circled each other in their private section of the enclosure. A few of the other dragons paused what they were doing to watch but most of them weren't interested.

He's not still nervous, is he?

The female dragon thumped all four huge paws into the dirt, going nowhere, and almost marched in place. She lowered herself almost to the ground—as if William approached her with a saddle—and stretched her neck toward her son.

"I see you." Her voice was low, strong, and powerful. Massive wings extended to their full expanse to stir up thick clouds of dust, and her neck swayed from side to side again. "I see you."

Leander snorted and stepped slowly toward her. He paused once to look at the other dragons minding their own business—not their clan, not their problem—and approached the other red far more slowly than Raven expected.

William was right. Anyone who calls a dragon a dumb beast has no idea what they're talking about.

From his viewing position far from the fence, Raven, and the reuniting dragons, William shook his head in disbelief. "And I was surprised by how gentle he was with Raven. This is...wow."

The closer he got to his mother, the farther he lowered himself into a crouch like she had. When he finally stopped, they'd settled themselves in the dirt with their wings outstretched and long necks raised toward each other. A few snorts and sniffs were exchanged, and Raven couldn't tell if the low rumbling came from one dragon or both.

"You are bonded," Leander's mother said gently and moved her snout to the side of his face for another quick sniff.

"In a different way." Leander's head didn't move now as his mother inspected him.

"Yes. A better way, perhaps." The female nudged the side of her long snout against his, and a low rumble rose from his chest. "I feel it." She moved her head away and rose out of her crouch a little. He backed away and did the same, still holding the older but much smaller dragon's gaze.

Raven glanced from one to the other. "That's it? That can't be it. That was so—"

Leander tipped his head back to face the sky and released another piercing screech, although this one didn't hold any of the mournful tones. His mother repeated the cry and he launched himself into the sky.

Raven didn't have enough time to question it before the female surged after the larger red dragon. Her tail thumped against the dirt before it left the ground completely. A gust of wind blew dust and dirt and a few crushed weeds against the fence and Raven, but she could only laugh. She blinked and rubbed what was left of it out of her eyes and grinned at the two dragons as they wheeled through the air, dipped and dove after each other, and shared one joyful screech after another. They didn't venture too far above the others in their clans scattered across the enclosure, but they didn't stay in one place for very long either.

"Would you look at that!" She slapped her hand on the top rail of the fence and whooped loudly. First Leander and then his mother screeched, and the mage in training found tears in her eyes again. *It's almost like they answered me this time. Even if that's not it, this is the best thing I've ever seen.*

CHAPTER TWENTY-FIVE

R aven and William stood halfway between the enclosure fence and where the dragon trainer had stood to make Leander more comfortable. They'd watched the two red dragons soar over the enclosure, their red scales flashing in the sun against the glowing red membranes of their wings like flames through a frosted windowpane.

"This is incredible." She laughed as they dove toward each other and their wings barely brushed as they passed close to the ground before they wheeled up in a wide, glittering circle.

"Believe it or not, it's called dancing." He smirked, his arms folded and his wide-brimmed hat securely on his head again.

"Oh, I believe it. It's beautiful."

"I've only seen it one other time. The dragons form bonds of their own with each other too. Obviously, there are the clans. Some clans are closer than others, exactly like some dragons."

"They don't all do this?" She couldn't help but grin, even while she frowned at her friend.

"No. They don't." He laughed, the sound a little rough, then sniffed and rubbed under his nose.

She lowered her head to look under the brim of his hat. "Are you okay?"

"What? Of course I'm okay." He sniffed again, turned away from her, and swallowed quickly. "Spring allergies get me every year. You'd think someone would have come up with a spell for that by now."

"I bet an apothecary would have something."

"I don't need cream or potions or anything. Only the pollen out of my eyes."

You don't fool me, William Moss. You got a little emotional. Raven pressed her lips together to hide a smile and gazed at the mother dragon dancing with her child.

William turned toward her with a self-conscious smile and nodded at the dragons. "This was worth it, though—to see it again. I think I was seven the last time I saw it."

"The meaning of stuff sure changes when you're older, doesn't it?"

He chuckled and nodded quickly. "You can say that again."

A few minutes later and after what had to have been half an hour of nonstop flying across the dragon enclosure, Leander settled onto the dirt with another snort. His huge head shook vigorously and his wings rippled before he tucked them against his back again. The smaller red landed in the same way and her back came only to the tops of his muscular shoulders. Both dragons walked side by side toward the fence and the gate, their scaly hides occasionally brushing up against each other.

Raven watched them for a moment, then looked at William. "They're not...done, are they?"

"With the dancing part, yeah." He nodded and scratched the side of his face, his expression thoughtful. "It looks to me like they want something else. Judging by the way they're looking at us, Raven, I think the safe guess is they want you over there."

"What? Why me? I didn't—"

"Dragon rider!" Leander shouted and his voice cracked across the open ground of Moss Ranch. "Come."

William burst into a fit of laughter and smacked his hands on his thighs. "Your familiar calls, war mage."

"Stop. That isn't—" Despite her protest, she laughed anyway. "That's not funny."

"It's very funny. He's more focused on ordering you around right now instead of defying anyone else's orders. A dragon in his natural state."

"I don't order him around." She couldn't wipe the smirk off her lips. "Not anymore."

"Go on. You don't want to keep two red dragons waiting on you, Raven. It might be an unforgivable offense."

"Well, at least he's not waiting for me to show up. Or feed him."

He snorted and she slapped his arm with the back of her hand before she strode toward the fence.

By the time she reached the dragons, she was a little out of breath and squinted against the glare of the sunlight on their fiery-red scales. Leander's mother had taken a few paces back and now stood a half-dozen yards behind the much larger red. Despite the distance, she watched the young mage closely as she approached.

"Leander, that was incredible."

"Yes."

"I've never seen anything like that. I'm so glad you—"

"Raven Alby." He inclined his head and fixed her with his yellow, highly intelligent eyes. "Stop talking. Step through the gate."

"What?"

"I want you in here with us."

Puffing her cheeks out, Raven looked at William. *If he'd heard that, he'd be running over here right now to stop it.* "Are you sure?"

"Did I confuse my words?"

A surprised laugh burst out of her, and she shook her head. "No, you most definitely didn't. Okay. I'll come in."

She released the latch and opened the gate wide enough to slip inside quickly before she closed it again.

William clapped his hat tighter on his head and lurched forward. "What is she doing? Raven? Raven! What are you—"

"It's fine! I'm fine." She waved him off and turned to face her dragon familiar and his mother.

Shaking his head, William took a few halting steps forward. *No, Leander will have to deal with me being a little closer. This girl's gonna make me have a heart attack and I'm not even that much older than her.* He gritted his teeth and decreased the distance between him and the fence by half before he stopped. "Just…call if you need help—"

"I'm good." Raven nodded firmly and stared into Leander's yellow eyes. "We're good."

"I know. Come with me." With a snort, the huge red dragon turned away from her and lumbered toward his mother.

The smaller female watched them with an almost human-like curiosity and the scaled ridges over her yellow eyes raised as the girl approached. "This is the one."

Leander snorted but didn't say anything.

She stopped a few yards from the older dragon. *It's about respect and I'm literally in her house right now.* She lowered her head and tried to emulate the way she'd seen Headmaster Flynn do it, then stuck one foot out to keep herself from stumbling forward. The whole time, she held the female dragon's gaze. "It's very nice to meet you, um…"

A low rumble rose in the female's throat, although it wasn't nearly as intimidating as Leander's. *And I'm used to that already.*

"They named me Zora, young mage. You may call me the same."

"Zora. It is very nice to meet you."

"You are my son's mage, yes?"

Raven nodded again. "And he's my familiar. We kind of lumped it all together when he passed the dragon trials."

"Yes." Zora glanced briefly at Leander, who stepped closer to Raven and lowered his head.

William tugged on the collar of his work shirt, then wiped a beat of sweat from beneath the brim of his hat. *If I didn't know Raven, I'd say two dragons staring at a mage in training is the wrong combination. Please don't let me be wrong about that too.*

"My son has given me your name," the female continued and raised her head again to study the young witch from a different angle. "Raven Alby."

"That's me." She grinned.

"Hmm." Zora's wings twitched outward before she took a step toward her and sniffed the air. There were still a few feet between them, but she felt the dragon's warm breath on her anyway. "You look very much like your mother, Raven Alby."

She froze. *Did I hear that right?* "You knew my mom?"

Zora's eyes closed and opened again slowly. "We met once or twice. A fine thing it is to uphold Sarah Alby's legacy."

A dragon couldn't make this up, right? Raven's fingers brushed against her mother's pin on the collar of her jacket and she nodded. "I'm doing what I can—and making my own destiny along the way."

"With my son. His dragon rider. Hmm."

The conversation stopped there, and she tugged the bottom of her jacket down, mainly for something to do with her hands. *Grandpa won't talk much about Mom, even if he wasn't gone. Zora might.*

Another low rumble issued from Leander's throat, and he bumped the side of his head against her shoulder. With a chuckle, she stroked his muzzle. Within seconds, her cheeks ached from how much she'd smiled this afternoon. *I'll come back and ask about Mom later. This is Leander's moment.*

"Thanks for letting me be a part of this," she muttered to her familiar.

He wuffled a warm breath. "This is how I'm thanking you."

"I'll take it." It surprised her when Leander turned away from his mother and headed toward the gate. Raven gave Zora another smile and a nod, then followed her familiar.

"Raven Alby."

The mage in training glanced over her shoulder.

"Bring him again, if you can. Join us. I wouldn't mind getting to know the dragon rider as well as the dragon."

"I will. Thank you."

"Hmm." Without another word, Zora turned and stalked away across the dragon enclosure toward the other dragons who must have been part of her clan but didn't want any part of her reunion.

No, this was a personal thing. One I'm a part of now.

When she and Leander reached the gate, William hadn't moved any closer. His eyes were wide as he stared at Zora's retreating figure and he hissed out a laugh. "I can't believe it."

She opened the gate and stepped out of the dragon enclosure, Leander on her heels. "Which part?"

"Take your pick, Raven. Hell, all of it. Nothing about today has been normal around here. I shouldn't be surprised at this point, but…wow." He shook his head, folded his arms again, and grinned at her. "You keep surprising me."

"I'm starting to think that runs in the family too."

"Well, wherever you get it from, I'm happy to stand back and watch it."

Raven bit her lip when she shot him a sideways glance. "Except for when I stepped into the enclosure."

"Okay, maybe happy isn't the exact word I'm going for. Not to describe every single moment, at least. But you handled yourself very well. So did you, Leander."

The red dragon kept pace with his rider and walked so close to her, she could feel the warmth of his body and all the sun's heat rising off his scales. "If I cared about your good opinion of me, flyboy, I might thank you for it."

William laughed. "That's about as good a compliment as I'm gonna get, isn't it?"

"Hypothetically speaking." A rhythmic hiss escaped Leander's parted lips as he nudged her shoulder with the side of his head again. "Raven Alby deserves more than compliments."

"I didn't do anything." She stroked the top of his scaly snout and nudged his head playfully in return. "No compliments necessary."

"You can't know the meaning of what you gave me today, mage. I am…" Something like a purr and a high-pitched whine escaped the large dragon. "I'm happy."

She laughed. "Yeah, I can tell. Good. Being happy is a good thing."

"When it happens, yes. Usually, that comes from food and sun and flying."

"Well, you can add friendship to the list, Leander. That's why we came here."

"Indeed." The dragon lowered his head as they walked to the barn and he snuck a glance past Raven toward William who walked on the other side of her. "I won't say the trainer is my friend."

William chuckled and shook his head.

"He's my friend, though. So by association, it's almost the same thing."

Leander snorted. "If you're trying to convince me, little girl, that one needs more work."

CHAPTER TWENTY-SIX

When they took to the skies again after leaving Moss Ranch, Raven's mind floated through the clouds with her. *Going back to Fowler seems like so much work after the last few hours. And I still need to find something to bring to Bixby's next class.*

"Oh." She leaned slightly to the side as she scanned the ranches that passed quickly below them. "Leander?"

"I know." He dipped his wing and took them in a wide, sweeping curve slightly off course on their way back to the mage school.

She grinned and patted the scaly neck in front of the saddle. *I don't even have to ask. That's in the top three best parts of riding a dragon familiar, for sure.*

The air cooled significantly now that the sun had begun to set, but she hardly felt the cold beneath the exhilaration of flying. "It never gets old."

The wind whipped her voice away from her, but she heard Leander hum in agreement anyway.

His huge shadow crossed over the gate off the road and

MARTHA CARR & MICHAEL ANDERLE

the sign for Alby Ranch with the large embellished A branded into the wood. A few of the ranch hands looked up and shielded their eyes from the fading sun. Many of them forgot about their end-of-day work altogether and dropped rakes, hammers, and harvesters to watch the dragon glide low over the fields.

They landed on the far side of the ranch beyond Connor Alby's house. Leander settled on the grass just inside the property fence and hunkered down so Raven could dismount.

"I'll be back in only a few minutes, okay? I have to find something with meaning and magical significance."

"I hear sarcasm."

She laughed and headed toward the back of the cabin in which she no longer lived—for now. "I've always heard dragons have incredible hearing."

Leander snorted and turned in a few tight circles before he shifted into a more comfortable position in the grass at the top of the rise to wait for her return.

When she reached the cabin and rounded the corner to the front door, she noticed Deacon and Patrick running toward her.

"Raven! I know you have your schooling and all that familiar business to focus on right now, girl. But…" Deacon paused and bent over to prop his hands on his thighs and catch his breath. "Girl, what the hell kind of craziness possessed you to bring a dragon onto a goat ranch?"

Trying not to laugh, she turned partially and pointed up the small hill at Leander. "Probably that crazy dragon lying there minding his own business."

"Until he decides he'd rather mind a few dwarf goats," Patrick added and wiped a sheen of sweat from his brow.

"Really? Come on. I wouldn't have brought him here if I seriously thought he was dangerous. Do you know how much time I've spent taking care of those bleating bone-heads?" Right on cue, a few goats uttered warbled cries from inside the pen. She laughed. "I would not throw that all away so Leander could have a little snack. And by the way, I've never seen him eat anything but dragon feed."

"That don't mean he won't..." Patrick leaned sideways to peer around her and up the hill. "He might still."

"No, he won't. He ate maybe two hours ago. A lot."

Deacon laughed weakly and nudged the nervous ranch hand beside him. "All right, man. Quit mean-muggin' the dragon, huh? Have you ever known this girl to rush into something headfirst without knowing exactly what she's doing?"

Patrick glanced at her again, his expression openly skeptical. "You're not making a very good point, Deacon."

"Aw, no. I mean something serious. Come on. Raven has a good head on her shoulders. And do you hear that?" He cupped his hand around his ear and leaned toward the goat pen.

"Hear what?"

"Exactly." He slapped a hand on Ed Patrick's back and chuckled. "If those jabbering dwarf goats aren't making the tiniest noise with a dragon lying uphill and upwind, I'm gonna go with trusting Raven. If the goats aren't worried, I'm not worried."

Patrick stared at the other man for a few seconds, then turned slowly toward the goat pen to meet at least three pairs of wide eyes above three goat mouths that calmly and effortlessly chewed on the remains of the hay bale. "Well, the minute they start acting up—"

"We won't be here that long. I'm only picking something up for school. I forgot to pack everything." Raven turned toward the front door of Connor Alby's cabin. *It's not technically a lie.*

"All right, then. Ed, help me finish those last few slats on the barn roof, huh? We'll get this thing knocked out and I won't have to climb up this ladder again tomorrow."

The door to the front porch creaked and banged shut behind her before she stepped into the house again. A shiver ran down her spine, and she rubbed her arms beneath the jacket and tried to fight the goosebumps. "I had no idea it could get this cold in here with no one inside and no fire to warm it."

She scanned the few shelves along the walls of the living room. *Meaningful and magical, huh?* Her gaze fell on Connor's old metal trunk against the wall in the corner. *I already have their patches at school...no. There's gotta be something better in here.*

As she moved slowly through the cold house that was still her home—despite feeling emptier than she ever remembered it—she folded her arms and squinted. Her fingers brushed against her mom's pin. *Nope. I won't risk damaging this. What can I use?*

Once she'd cleared the living room, she walked down the hall and peered into her grandfather's bedroom. Her gaze fell on the large, off-white skull Connor had placed on the shelf after the first time he'd shown it to her. "Now that fills all the requirements."

With a grin, she almost skipped across the room to retrieve the huge, shadow-riddled skull of a Skiffling. "Not that Grandpa's wildly into war trophies, but this would definitely count as one. This was a Swarm general and that's gonna score me serious points with Bixby. Meaning, magical significance, and history."

With the skull balanced in one hand, she pointed at it with the other and muttered, "*Adtenuo.*"

The Swarm skull wobbled a little on her palm before it shrank quickly to the size of an apple. Raven grinned, tucked it into the outside pocket of her jacket, and gave it a little pat. *Shrinking inanimate objects is easy. Too bad I didn't have the time to find out how to do it right with the goats. It would've made herding them a heck of a lot easier.*

With another glance around the cold living room, the empty hearth, and the emptier hallway, she sighed and headed to the door. *Grandpa won't be gone that long. We'll both be back here soon enough.*

When she stepped outside, the sun now cast glowing gold and orange light across the ranch before it sank behind the tallest mountain peaks. Deacon and Patrick still stood where she left them. "So you decided not to finish the roof, huh?"

"What? Oh. That, uh…" Deacon nodded up the hill behind the cabin. "Does that dragon of yours always do that?"

"Do what?" Raven turned to see Leander crouched over his forepaws, his back legs tucked beneath him and his wings spread halfway. The thick, powerful tail lashed from side to side, and he seemed to stare intently at the two ranch hands. She laughed and covered her mouth. "I think he's messing with you."

"He looks like one of those panthers getting ready to pounce on a big fat sheep." Patrick licked his lips, his eyes wide and his gaze fixed on the dragon.

"I told you, he just ate." She chuckled again. "And I'm sure he's enjoying how confused you guys are right now." *At least, that's what it feels like. It's not something I'd find all that amusing on my own, is it?*

"Well, I won't turn my back on a dragon to climb onto a roof, that's for damn sure."

"Hey, in a few minutes, you can turn whichever way you want." Raven raised a hand and gave the men a brief wave. "We're heading back now."

Patrick folded his arms and squinted even more intently at Leander.

Deacon shook his head at the man, then headed toward her and looked only a little wary to also be walking toward a dragon. "Hey, how's that school treating you as a place to lay your head, girl?"

"Not bad, actually. I have no idea who puts it all out, but there's a huge table of breakfast in the dormitory every morning. And having Leander there with me all the time is the best part. It's probably the biggest reason Headmaster Flynn wanted me to move onto the grounds."

"And your grandfather too, I bet." He nodded.

"You're guessing about that, right? Because I can't get anyone to tell me anything about where he went or what he wanted. All he told me was that Flynn would know what to do. Who knows? Maybe the headmaster took a few wild guesses and hoped that having me on the grounds night and day would be better than letting me go home."

The man chuckled. "Would you agree with him, though? That it's better?"

"Yes." Raven smiled at him and shook her head. "I miss him, though. And I'd like to know that he's okay. Maybe even where he is."

"I know, Raven. But trust me. In all the years I've worked for Connor Alby, running deliveries and odd errands into town, I've learned a fair amount about the man. Three things come to mind above everything else." The ranch hand counted on his fingers and slowed a little as they approached the top of the hill and the dragon crouched on it. "He doesn't do anything without a good reason for it. Those good reasons are weighed against the alternative, over and over, until he's sure of it. And he would never put anyone in harm's way if there wasn't a way to pull them out again, including himself. And you, of course."

"Right. I appreciate the pep talk."

Deacon hissed a laugh and waved casually, the other hand thrust deep into the pocket of his trousers. "Uh-huh."

"I'm not worried about him, Deacon. Not really. I miss him already, which is weird because he's only been gone a few days."

"That's a long time when you've had a person greet you every morning before you head out and every evening when you come home. I understand."

"And I wish he'd given me more to go on. A little information isn't too much to ask for, is it?"

"No, Raven. It's not. Believe me, I'd love to know why

Connor Alby was so suddenly willing to pay his ranch hands a significantly higher wage after a decade and a half of being one of the most frugal men I know. But he likes to keep his business to himself and there's where I have to draw the line. The rest is out of my hands."

But not out of mine. Grandpa still should have told me something.

They stopped a few yards away from Leander, who remained utterly motionless now as he stared at the ranch hand who walked beside the mage in training. A slow, slightly nervous whistle petered out between Deacon's lips. "That is one gigantic creature you got there, girl."

Raven pressed her lips together so she wouldn't laugh. "He's not even standing up."

"Does, uh…" He licked his lips. "Does he get too nervous with people around?"

"Are you saying you want to meet my dragon familiar, Deacon? Up close?"

"Aw, now, I wouldn't go that far with it, necessarily—"

"Leander? This is my friend Deacon. He's worked with my grandfather for a long time and wants to come say hi. What do you think?"

The red dragon's tail whispered across the grass on the top of the hill. "As long as he doesn't try to pet me." The hardened ridges of Leander's lips parted to reveal glistening rows of razor-sharp teeth.

"Oh, now…" Deacon swallowed.

"Again, he's messing with you." Raven tugged on his elbow and gestured up the hill. "Come on. At the very least, it'll give you a story the other ranch hands won't grow tired of you telling for the next few weeks."

He frowned at her and looked completely startled. "Who's been bad-mouthing my stories?"

"What? No one. Not that I've heard, anyway. He's perfectly safe, Deacon. I promise."

"As long as I don't try to pet him."

"Well, yeah. Don't do that." *I'm not gonna make Leander promise not to bite if he doesn't want to be touched.* Raven waved the ranch hand along behind her until they stopped a few feet from where the red dragon crouched in the grass. "Deacon, meet Leander. Leander, Deacon."

"Uh...how...how do you do?" The man gasped and his mouth dropped open when the dragon chose that moment to raise his belly off the grass and stand to his full height. "Woah... It's a good thing I left Presley in her pen."

"Probably," Leander rumbled.

"Hey." Raven laughed, stepped toward her dragon, and extended her hand to stroke the top of his muscular shoulder. "Don't scare the man half to death, okay? He was brave enough to come all the way up here because he wanted to meet you."

"I'm not so sure I'd call it bravery at this point, girl." Deacon stared with wide eyes at Leander and didn't move a muscle.

"Normally, I wouldn't call it that, either." The dragon stretched his wings, tucked them again, and lowered his head. "But you asked permission and you're a friend of Raven's. I'd call that...refreshing." His lips peeled back again in an even wider grin to show almost all his teeth.

"Leander..."

"Ah. Now." Deacon nodded and reached for Raven like he tried to put his hand on her shoulder, but she stood too far away. He finally gave that up and snatched the wide-brimmed hat off his head before he held it in front of him with both hands. "I appreciate your time, Leander. And I think I'll return to work now."

"Enjoy your evening," Leander responded.

"Uh-huh. You...you too."

"Good to see you, Deacon." Raven waved cheerfully. "Have a good night."

"Raven." The man backed down the hill, unwilling to turn his back on the first dragon he'd met face to face—or seen up close in his entire life.

The dragon lowered himself again briefly so she could swing into the saddle, and the ranch hand laughed in surprise.

"Girl, you look exactly like your mother when she had the itch to take out one of her horses. Of course, I...I know this creature is not a horse."

"Not even close." Raven grinned as Leander stood fully again and spread his wings.

"And he lets you climb on up like that to go flying around?"

She leaned forward to stroke the dragon's neck and gave him a gentle pat. "You know, Leander and I are alike that way. No one really lets us do anything. It's merely a good connection that gets me up in this saddle."

"It's as simple as that," Leander added.

"Uh-huh." Deacon glanced over his shoulder to where Patrick stood beside Connor Alby's house with a gaping jaw. "Okay, Raven. You...fly safe."

With a laugh, she waved again. "See you soon. Bye, Ed."

The other ranch hand lifted a jerky hand in farewell, his fingers as stiff as if they'd been carved from wood.

Raven glanced at the sky streaked with orange, pink, and purple, and her dragon familiar beat his mighty wings as he sprang into the air to take them home. She allowed herself a loud whoop and pressed her hands against the ridges of Leander's back and slid her feet out of the stirrups to test her theory again. *That's a good thing to put on the list of familiar training later.*

CHAPTER TWENTY-SEVEN

On the Alby Ranch that night beneath the stars, the dwarf goats woke in their pen, bleated and jumped in sudden anxiety, and wobbled and milled in confusion. The ground rumbled beneath the center of the ranch, and a thin, snaking trail of upturned dirt cut a path through the fields toward the small cabin Connor Alby shared with his granddaughter.

A few goats screamed when the earth trembled beneath them and made the gates of the pen screech and groan under the shifting weight. The upturned earth paused for a moment before the trail resumed. It cut around the cabin and moved slowly, its senses probing the darkness ahead.

The Skiffling that tunneled beneath the surface moved around the house in search of the source that had called it there in the first place. Abruptly, it darted beneath the Alby cabin and a second later, the floorboards of the main room splintered upward and churned within the whirlpool of earth. A single, undulating tentacle thrust from below and flopped once against the floor. It straightened, waved like a banner, and opened the glistening pincer at the end. The cabin was silent, of course, but the pull of the Swarm's consciousness was stronger than silence, even when there was nothing in the house that would try to escape.

The wooden floors shivered and shattered again as the tentacle stretched even farther. It whipped toward the empty hearth in the wall and slapped against the wood until it bumped against Connor Alby's old metal trunk. Retracting only briefly, the snaking appendage slipped around the corner of the trunk and jerked it quickly away from the wall. It thumped the floor again, retreated, and slithered into the massive hole in the living room before it vanished completely.

What the Swarm wanted had been there but now, it was gone.

A lantern flared to life in the closest cabin—another hand had lived closer only a few months before, but the man had gone too far with his drinking and burned the whole place down. He lifted his lantern even higher as he stepped outside in the darkness. "Those damn goats. I took this job knowing full well it's a goat ranch, but I don't know what the hell I'm doing with a herd of noisy animals in the middle of the night."

Grumbling to himself, he stalked up the dirt road toward Connor Alby's cabin and the pen in front of it. Shadows danced along the posts of the enclosure and the roofed shelter where the animals slept. The bleating settled a little, but the animals still bucked and kicked in agitation. A few of them simply stood and trembled.

"Are you shittin' me right now? None of you made a peep with that damn dragon sittin' up on that hill earlier but now, you're bouncin' around like you've all lost your tiny goat minds." The sound of a voice they recognized quieted the animals even more until only a few soft, unsure cries rose from the back of the pen. Patrick laughed despite how much he didn't appreciate being woken up by this nonsense. "See? There's nothin' here, you tiny little—"

A loud creak rose from the front of Connor's cabin, followed by a bang and a loud crash of wood falling on wood.

"What the hell?" The ranch hand glanced at the goats again, then lifted his lantern a little higher and approached the house. The firelight flickered across the screened-in porch and illuminated the giant gap where the screen door usually was. Now, the entire thing lay half on the steps, fallen completely off its frame. Patrick looked up higher at the slanting angle of the roof, then down at the warped boards of the porch. "Huh. It's only an old cabin shifting. I wonder how we didn't catch that during the day?"

Weariness and irritation warred within and Patrick's mouth stretched in a wide yawn as he shrugged. *I'll get Samuel to help me line everything up again in the morning. If Connor gets back and his house is all off-kilter, there's no way in hell we'll see those raises he promised.*

The man turned—without further thought about stepping inside his employer's house to take a closer look—and headed down the narrow slope of the dirt road toward his cabin. A goat bleated in protest when he passed, and he moved the lantern to illuminate the pen briefly. "You know, I think you are dumber than you look. Huh. You're more scared of a door than a dragon."

Before he reached the few steps up to his porch—much

smaller than Mr. Alby's—a tremor passed through the ground. He stumbled forward and the lantern swung wildly in his hand, but he managed to catch himself on the porch railing. In the darkness, he thought he saw the dirt rise in a mound before it rippled across the road. In the next moment, it was gone and the tremor faded.

"Damn earthquakes. They make me see things." With a snort, he shook his head and trudged to bed to sleep the rest of the night uninterrupted.

CHAPTER TWENTY-EIGHT

The rest of the week had passed in a blur of classes and training and flying, and it now began to catch up to her. Raven had misjudged how much time she had left when she returned to the girls' dormitory the morning before the spring gala. She'd fed Leander before dawn and sat to talk to him for a while, then she'd hurried to her room to retrieve her satchel for the start of her school day as a mage in training. When she stepped into the common room of the girls' dormitory, only a few of the other girls were up. They all mumbled sleepily and yawned as they filled small plates with breakfast from the almost over-flowing banquet table along the left wall.

The weather's changing into spring, now. The light comes earlier but class times don't change. Raven eyed the table and the pile of steaming, freshly baked rolls. *It's better than being late.*

She stopped at the table and had to pull the sleeves of her jacket over her hands to keep from burning her fingers on the rolls. Rather than sit anywhere, she took them with her to her room on the third floor.

The door was already open. Elizabeth sat in her bed, her legs crossed beneath her and her eyes closed, but she'd already dressed for the day. She rocked forward a little, then jerked her head up. Her bat familiar lay sprawled in her lap.

"Are you tired?" Raven asked softly, not wanting to startle the girl.

"I stayed up too late," her roommate mumbled as her head jerked again. "I couldn't stop reading."

Chuckling, Raven knelt in front of her bed and pulled out the oilskin bag. "Did you turn the light on after I passed out?"

Her roommate's only response was a long, drawn-out groan.

"I'll take that as a yes. Breakfast is out, though. Or do you want one of my rolls? I've eaten these first thing in the morning since orientation."

Elizabeth swayed a little where she sat and held her hand out. "Yes, please."

She laughed, took two huge steps across the room, and placed a piping hot roll in her hand. "Careful, it's hot—"

The girl crammed the entire thing into her mouth with a deep breath and didn't react to the temperature. Her eyes fluttered open and she turned to look at Raven with drooping eyelids. "That helps."

"Good."

"I'll see you in…whatever class we have together." Elizabeth slid off her bed, swung her satchel over her shoulder, and scooped her familiar up with one arm. The bat squeaked and almost toppled onto the bed before it dug into her shirt with the hooked claws on his wings. Without another word, the young witch and her familiar shuffled out into the hall to make their way downstairs.

"And I thought I was bad without enough sleep." She chuckled again and shook her head before she returned her attention to Connor's oilskin bag on the floor. Quickly, she unbuckled the straps and opened it wide enough to stare at all the things she hadn't yet found a better hiding place for. Connor's two journals were stacked together beside the now completely red orb her grandfather had given her. She turned it a few times and frowned. *There isn't even a little streak of white now. I wish this thing came with a timeline for when danger strikes.*

She rolled it aside and picked up the black drawstring bag that used to hold the orb but now held her grandfather's shrunken Skiffling skull instead. "Bixby's gonna love this, though."

With the skull in hand, she pushed to her feet and moved to the window to look out at the field and the dragon pen on the other side of the stables. "It's all quiet with no angry dragon fire. He's still flying high after yesterday. Almost literally."

Laughing at herself, she eased the drawstring bag with the shrunken skull into her satchel, took the first journal out of the oilskin bag, and sat on the edge of the bed. *I still have time before classes. I might as well make the most of it.*

Raven opened the journal and flipped through it, looking for the Magic Meld spell again. *I should've marked the page.*

"Have you found anything good in there yet?"

She almost leapt to her feet when Bella Chase's voice filled her dorm room. She jerked her head up to where the girl stood in the open doorway, her arms folded. Her firedrake familiar sat on her shoulder, his long, thin tail curled around the back of her neck. "Yeah, actually. What are you doing here?"

"Well, I showed up a little early. You know, to get a quick head start on the day."

"I wouldn't call half an hour a little early." She closed the journal again slowly and tried not to draw too much attention to it. "I meant why are you standing outside my room?"

"Right." The girl raised and lowered her eyebrows and her gaze settled on the journal Raven inched casually across her lap. "Teresa told me about those journals." She didn't say anything else but bit her bottom lip and frowned a little at the source of her interest.

"I'm sure the library has what you're looking for."

"It doesn't." Bella swallowed and tossed her hair over the shoulder not currently occupied by her familiar. "I already checked."

Raven studied the girl who'd been her rival at Fowler Academy since day one and fought a scowl. *What did Teresa tell her about these journals?* "Okay…" She set the journal behind her on the bed and folded her hands in her lap. "Maybe if you tell me what you're looking for, I can help you find it."

"Actually, I—oh. Can I come in?"

For a moment, she simply stared, too surprised to answer. *Bella Chase politely asked for my permission. Maybe that's the danger Grandpa's orb is warning me about.* That thought brought a laugh bubbling up through her, but she squashed it hastily and cleared her throat. "Sure, Bella. Come on in."

Those are the weirdest two sentences I've said all year.

Bella inclined her head but didn't say thank you, then took a few slow, hesitant steps into the dorm room and looked around. "I guess it's kind of...cozy in here."

"It works. So, about what you're trying to find at the library."

Looking quickly at Raven again, she shook her head. "No...what I think I might find in that journal of yours."

The girls stared at each other. Wesley squeaked, the sound tense and high-pitched, and stretched his wings briefly. *This is so weird.*

"Okay, Raven. Can I be perfectly honest with you?"

"Sure." *I'll sit here and listen as long as she doesn't start badmouthing me in my room.*

"Remember that blood spell we did in Bixby's class?"

"Yeah. I remember it."

"Well, you and I had a few...similarities in our family trees which were kind of hard to ignore." Although the dark-haired mage in training tried to hide it, she didn't miss the little grimace that passed across Bella's face. It disappeared again as quickly, though. "You know what I'm talking about, right?"

"The fact that both of our moms were war mages. Yeah. It's kind of hard to ignore and even harder to forget."

"A little." Bella's familiar shifted his tiny clawed feet on his perch when she rolled her shoulders. "I don't normally guess, Raven, but I can only guess that that journal came from your grandfather."

She pays more attention than I realized. Absently, she moved her hand slowly to the top of the worn leather journal behind her on the bed and she drew a little more comfort from feeling it there. "It's a good guess."

"Thank you. I also guess that somewhere in there might be something about…" Bella took a deep breath, glanced at the ceiling, and sighed. "About your mom and probably about mine too given that we come from relatively similar backgrounds as far as war mages for moms go."

Despite her shock at this unexpected visit, Raven chuckled. "I'd say that's a little more than relatively similar, but I get where you're going with this."

"Good. I thought you might. And honestly, that last part was less of a guess and more of me hoping there'd be something in there that might, you know—"

"It's okay, Bella. I get it." Raven nodded with a small, sympathetic smile and picked the journal up again. *She won't come right out and say it but she doesn't have to. Neither of us had the chance to know our moms.* She set the journal in her lap and glanced at it. "You know, I've hoped the same thing, actually—that I might find something in here that tells me more about my mom than anyone's willing to say otherwise. Especially about her as a war mage."

"Yeah. That makes it more interesting."

They shared a tense, slightly uncomfortable laugh, and she looked up to meet the other girl's gaze before Bella glanced away. *Okay. Do it already.* "Look, Bella, I'm not really into reading between the lines or trying to work out what other people are thinking, so if you want to come to take a look at this journal with me before class—"

"Yes. Thank you." Bella moved quickly across the room, her eyes wide with anticipation as she stared at the journal.

Raven smirked and waited for the girl to sit beside her. Her visitor bit her bottom lip and stopped a few feet in front of the bed. "Can you read upside down?" she asked and tried not to laugh.

"What?"

"If you can't, it'll probably be hard to read anything from where you're standing." She patted the edge of the bed beside her and shrugged. "You might as well sit."

Bella studied the other young witch's face with a tiny, confused frown.

She thinks I'm kidding.

"Only until we have to get to the main hall before classes." The words tumbled out of the girl's mouth in a rush.

"Right. I don't have an excuse for being late since I live here. For now." Raven watched her one real competition at this school consider this mutual truce a little longer before Bella spun and plopped onto the mattress.

"I'm never late. So." The girl tilted her head and stared at the journal. "Are you gonna open it or what?"

"Uh-huh." She hissed a laugh, opened the journal, and flipped quickly through the first few pages. From the corner of her eye, she saw a tiny smile bloom on her companion's face as she leaned toward her for a better look. She shifted it closer to the center point between them and shrugged. "There's not anything very interesting in the first quarter of these pages."

"But you found something good?"

"Yeah, I think it's good." *I never thought I'd show Bella Chase a secret spell used by the best mages and dragon riders during the Great War. But here we are.* She flipped through the pages again, more slowly this time, and finally found the underlined title of the Magic Meld spell above the step-by-step instructions. "Have you ever seen this before?"

Frowning, the girl leaned a little closer and her eyes widened. "You're kidding."

"That wouldn't be very funny, would it?"

Forgetting their rivalry altogether, Bella snorted and scanned the spell. "I can't believe this. I've heard so many stories about the Magic Meld and how useful it was before the war. During the war too, probably. I began to think everyone had made it up."

Biting her lip, Raven gazed at the spell before them. *It doesn't sound like she knows about the last time the veterans used it.* "It's definitely real. I've…seen it used."

"Seriously?"

She nodded. For the next few minutes, the girls sat in silence while they read through one of the most powerful spells either of them had seen and committed the entire thing to memory. *If that's what I'm doing, there's no way Bella isn't memorizing it too.*

Finally, her visitor pointed at the page with an eager nod of her own. "I'm finished if you are. Have you read past this point?"

"Not yet."

"Then turn the page, Raven. Come on."

Raven glanced sidelong at the girl and smirked. *Knowledge. That's what she wants. Exactly like me.* Slowly, she separated the next page of aged, yellow parchment paper and turned it so they could keep reading.

"Woah." Bella's eyes widened. "Who wrote this?"

"You know, I'm starting to think it wasn't only one person. The handwriting's completely different on this page."

"Well, it had to be someone who fought in the Great War. I mean, look at this." The girl pointed at a footnote on the left-hand page. "Everything else is written like a historical account. Then there are pieces like this. Personal reactions."

Raven read through the footnote following the retelling of the moment the dragon riders used the Magic Meld on the Swarm—when it won the war and obliterated the creatures but backfired on the mages and their dragons at the same time. The footnote finished with a set of initials, and that was it. "Any idea who PR might be?"

"No. You?"

Shaking her head, she continued to read onto the right-hand page. "This is a little hard to follow. Some mages lost their dragons with the Magic Meld and some lost their lives. I knew there were survivors, but this talks about the war not being over after that. I thought that's what finished it."

Bella looked at her rival turned conspirator and frowned. "You've heard about this before."

"I'm not merely a goat-farmer, Bella. Neither is my grandfather."

The other girl fixed her with a startled look. "He talks to you about the war?"

"Only once, really. When he gave me these journals." Raven grimaced when she thought of them and Connor Alby in the same sentence. "Which, by the way, I promised I wouldn't take out of our house. No one's supposed to know I have these. So…I guess I have to trust you to keep this a secret and only between us. Can I do that?"

For a few seconds, her companion stared at the pages of the journal they'd already read, then she looked at her and shrugged. Wesley adjusted his footing on her shoulder and dragged some of her thick, dark hair with his razor-sharp talons. "I know how to keep a secret. And I know what it's like to have secrets kept from me."

"Yeah, tell me about it." *Grandpa told me more about the war then he might ever tell me about Mom.* "Promise me you won't tell anyone about these."

Bella scoffed. "You have my word, Raven. And the word of a Chase is not something we throw around whenever we feel like it."

She lowered her head in acknowledgment. "That's good enough for me."

"Besides, who am I gonna tell? None of the other students here are remotely interested in what's inside these journals. Not like we are. And if words get out that you have powerful historical documents on the grounds, I wouldn't put it past Professor Gilliam to storm into your room and confiscate them. Then where would we be?" Bella raised an eyebrow for emphasis, not worried at all about whether the two mages in training would be caught with something they weren't supposed to have.

It sounds like something I would say. This is getting weirder by the minute.

"That's a good point." She shrugged and glanced at the open door to her dorm room. "What about Teresa? She's the one who told you I have these."

"Don't worry about Teresa." The girl waved dismissively and shook her head. "She's trying so hard to be important. Which is not to say that she doesn't belong at Fowler. She's definitely talented. Not like us, but that can be said about anyone else at this school." She looked at Raven, surprised by her confession. "Teresa also told me what you had for breakfast yesterday and what kind of bag you packed your clothes in. I'll tell her the journals are yours. Like for writing in. And if I say it doesn't matter, she'll forget all about it."

"Okay." *It's kind of a big step for us, isn't it?* "I'm gonna hold you to that, Bella."

"You won't have to. It won't be a problem." The girl nodded at the journal again. "Turn the page. We have another ten minutes, at least. Let's make the most of it, right?"

"Uh-huh." Raven widened her eyes and turned the page. *I could get used to this. Conspiring with Bella Chase to keep a few secrets so we can both learn what they won't teach us.*

The girls skimmed the next page, which chronicled the actions of the war mages during the Great War. Someone had started a list of the war mages themselves, their names and ages, the year they graduated from Fowler Academy, and their weapon of choice on the battlefield. Among those names was Sarah Alby, and Raven slammed the journal shut without thinking.

"What are you doing?" Bella glanced briefly at her, then gestured at the journal again. "I wasn't finished."

"I am. We should get to class."

"We still have enough time, Raven. I was reading through that list. My mother was a war mage—"

"Yeah, I know. Mine too." She pulled the journal closer

in her lap and stared at the floor. "I'm not ready to see that yet." *Not with Bella reading over my shoulder and looking for her past.*

"Fine." The girl stood from the bed and brushed the front of her tunic. Her familiar spread his wings to keep his balance on her shoulder, then settled again. "I'm sure it goes without saying, but I assume that when you're ready, you'll let me know."

"Sure, Bella."

"And don't forget that I know about the journals now. I hope, for your sake, that you don't try to keep them from me."

Raven looked quickly at the girl and resisted another scowl. *It looks like our little bonding time is over.* "And I hope for your sake that wasn't a threat."

"No." Bella's smirk looked more like an irritated sneer. "Merely a friendly reminder."

"Well, consider me reminded. I'll see you in class."

Without another word, Bella turned on her heel and stormed out of the dorm room. Wesley released an aggravated shriek but it didn't slow their progress.

Raven sighed and stared at the closed journal in her lap. "We're right back where we started." *She's disappointed that she didn't get to find anything out about her mom. That's all it is. And I'm not ready to share anything that personal with Bella Chase.*

She stood from the bed and slipped it into Connor's oilskin bag with its twin and the fully red glass orb, then buckled it tightly and went to the dresser beside the desk. Once she'd shoved everything into the mostly empty bottom drawer, Raven glanced through the open door to be sure no one else stood in her doorway. *"Clausura."*

A dull orange light glowed around the drawer, and she double-checked by trying to open it. "That'll have to do for now," she muttered, satisfied when the drawer wouldn't budge.

Brushing her pants off, she stood, snatched her satchel, and headed out of her room to start another day at Fowler Academy. *Whatever's in those journals about Mom will have to wait a little longer. But I won't let it go.*

She closed the door firmly behind her and hurried down the hall.

CHAPTER TWENTY-NINE

The students who filtered into Professor Bixby's classroom carried more excited and nervous energy than Raven expected.

"Do you have a date for the gala tomorrow?"

"Of course I do. Aren't you on that planning committee?"

"I can't wait to see how they decorate this one."

"I'm going with Bryan Ranger. He's a second-year, and I heard Annie Callam expected him to ask her instead."

Henry rubbed his hair vigorously before he drew the strap of his shoulder bag over his head. He set it down with a sigh and gave Raven a wide-eyed glance. "Is everyone like this? Simply because of a dance?"

She shrugged, placed her satchel at the desk beside him, and slid into the seat. "I don't get the hype."

He snorted. "Of course you don't. You have a dragon for a familiar. It doesn't get much hypier than that. I only hope they put on a serious spread tomorrow night."

"It's not a real party if you can't eat, right, Derks?"

"You got it. I still can't believe you told Daniel Smith you'd be his date."

"Well, it was that or risk Leander breaking through his pen to give the guy a piece of his mind. I had to choose my poison." She gestured widely with her arms and grinned when he shook his head in disbelief.

He pulled Maxwell gently from his shoulder bag and set the toad on his desk before he retrieved a small, plain blue box with a blue satin bow pinned to the top.

"Who's the present for?" Raven asked.

"What present? Oh, this?" He jiggled the box a little. Maxwell watched the movement with his toady eyes but didn't budge. "Good work staying still, Maxwell. No, this is my meaningful object, I guess."

"The box or what's inside?"

Henry wrinkled his nose. "What's inside. My mom gave it to me when I asked. It wouldn't have been my first choice, but whatever."

"Huh." She took the black drawstring bag from her satchel and placed it on the desk. Through the thick fabric, she could feel the outline of the shrunken skull. *This is gonna be epic.*

"Morning." Murphy joined them, sat on the other side of Henry, and waited for him to acknowledge her. Instead, he rummaged through his shoulder bag, leaned far over his chair, and grew steadily more frustrated.

"Morning, Murphy," Raven said with a smile. The other girl returned it and nodded, then glanced quickly at Henry again when he grunted and hauled his entire bag into his lap.

"Here, Murph. Hold this for a second, will you?" He

slapped the blue box onto her desk, stuck Maxwell on his shoulder, and thumped his bag on the desk to give him better access.

Murphy froze for a moment before she opened the box slowly. When she saw the plain silver wedding ring inside, her eyes widened and she blushed furiously.

Raven bit her lip and pretended not to notice.

"Here it is!" Henry retrieved a huge quill from the bottom of his bag, the feathers mashed and mangled but the long, hollow quill itself still intact. "Someone needs to make bags with pockets." He stretched his hand toward Murphy and the box with a little laugh. "That was my grandma's. Hey, come on, Murphy. I asked you to hold it, not take it to keep."

Startled out of staring at the ring, she shoved the lid on and gave it to him. "Why do you have a ring?"

Completely oblivious, Henry gestured vaguely toward Bixby's desk at the front of the classroom. "Meaning and magical significance, right? I didn't even know where to start, so my mom shoved this box into my face and told me it would work. I guess we'll see." He shrugged and shifted in his chair before he lowered Maxwell to the desk again.

Murphy swallowed a few times, took a deep breath, then leaned forward to look past Henry at Raven. "What did you bring?"

She patted the drawstring bag in front of her and grinned. "It's a surprise."

"Yeah, you're full of those, aren't you, Alby?" He punched her shoulder playfully.

"I guess so."

The other students filtered in and took their places at

the closest desks. Bella moved toward the front of the room and took her usual place on the right. She glanced at Raven once, then eyed the black bag on her desk and turned her nose up before she drew out her item for their assignment.

So she's back to shooting me looks, huh? I guess being frenemies is a step in the right direction, anyway.

"Quiet down. Quiet down!" Professor Bixby shuffled through the chatting students toward the front of the room and clapped loudly to give fair warning of her approach. Her frizzed copper hair bounced as she walked between the rows of desks and she reached the front and climbed onto the platform behind her desk with a little grunt.

"Now, without even having to listen to all the gossip and the drama that is so prevalent this morning, I know you're all excited for the gala tomorrow. I am too." The short woman tittered and raised a hand to her hair that looked like she'd just woken up and rolled out of bed. "It's quite fun, and I know you'll all enjoy yourselves. But for the love of magic, students, pay attention in class. You might learn something, which is why you're here in the first place. Leave the gala for tomorrow night and focus. Understood?"

No one said anything, but the professor looked quite satisfied all the same.

"Very good. I'll start by asking who didn't manage to find a personal item to bring in today?" The students looked at each other, waiting for someone to raise their hand. When no one did, she responded with another high-pitched chuckle and clapped yet again. "This might be a record. Every mage in training followed the assignment.

Excellent. I'm flabbergasted by the few students with magic running in their family and their veins who can't think outside the box and find something worthwhile."

Henry jiggled the blue box on his desk and wiggled his eyebrows. "I'm thinking inside the box."

Raven snorted. "You're the only person I know who'd be proud of that."

"What can I say? I have my moments." He grinned and chuckled in surprise when his familiar leapt onto the box and stayed there. "And you have good taste too, Maxwell."

"So let's see what you came up with, shall we?" Bixby waved her tiny hand across the room and nodded. "Pull those items out. If it came wrapped, unwrap it. I'll move around the room to see what you've brought and I'll help each of you set an intention for drawing forth the magical history of what your item happens to be. It will be different for everyone, of course. That's why you were asked to bring them in."

The woman clomped down the steps and made her rounds from one desk to the next, humming and nodding and muttering a few suggestions to each student.

With a muted sigh, Murphy pulled a stack of folded green velvet from her satchel and placed it on the desk.

Henry narrowed his eyes and stared at her object. "Those aren't your mom's graduation robes, are they? 'Cause if that's what we have to wear when we're finished with this school, I might skip that part."

She gave him a small, self-conscious smile. "Not graduation robes. Only one of her dresses."

"It looks fancy."

"My mom wore it to the capitol after she graduated. I

think Fowler Academy sent her as a dignitary or something before the war. Or maybe after." She wrinkled her nose. "I should've asked."

Raven leaned forward and pointed at the green velvet dress. "That's a high honor, isn't it? A mage dignitary?"

"Yeah." The girl's face lit with pride, and she ran her fingers gently down the front of the gown. "It really was."

"Then how did your mom end up in Brighton again?" Henry frowned and his laugh sounded a little confused as if he tried to put the pieces together. "She's a seamstress now, right?"

Murphy's smile faded a little but that dreamy look returned to her face. "She met my dad at the capitol. They fell in love and he didn't want to hang around in the busy city to play politics. So she followed him here and they got married and...well, now I'm going to school here like she did."

"Woah. Some kinda falling in love." He scratched his head, his brow rumpled in thought. "My parents don't have a story like that. I think."

"What about yours, Raven?" The question was innocent enough, but it made him turn toward Raven with wide eyes.

She swallowed and pressed her lips together. *I can't blame her for asking. She doesn't know.* "I, uh...I don't know how my parents met, honestly."

"Really? I'm sure your grandpa has tons of stories. Have you asked him?"

Henry turned toward Murphy and shook his head slowly. She was too busy wondering how her friend could possibly not know these things to notice his warning.

"Yeah, I've asked him." Raven shrugged and tried to smile back at Murphy, but it felt too forced. "I'm still waiting to hear the stories."

"Oh. Does he... Okay, everyone knows Connor Alby keeps to himself and doesn't leave your ranch. I never even considered that it might be because—" Murphy clamped her mouth shut, then leaned over Henry's desk to whisper, "He hasn't forgotten, has he?"

"What?" Despite the fluttering in her stomach, Raven laughed wryly. "You mean like dementia? No, Murphy. My grandpa has all his lights on upstairs if that's what you mean. I know he remembers more than he's willing to say —or to tell me." She turned toward the black drawstring bag on her desk and nudged it with her fingers. *But he was starting to talk about the past. At least before he left.*

"Well. Here we go." Henry yanked the blue box's lid off, picked up the wedding band, and made an exaggerated show of setting it in front of him. "My special something. It's not much to look at, I guess."

"But it came from your family, Derks." Raven smirked at him. "That definitely has meaning."

"If you say so." He nodded at her black bag. "Is that what you brought? Something from your family?"

"Um...kind of." She widened her eyes at him and grinned. "Maybe even better."

"Oh, wait. It's a dragon scale."

"Nope."

"Dragon claw. Dragon tooth. Dragon patty?"

"Ew." Murphy laughed and shook her head.

"No, Derks." Raven loosened the drawstring. "It's not from a dragon at all." *It was brought down by a dragon, though.*

"Well pull it out, Alby!" Henry thumped a fist onto his desk and Maxwell didn't even flinch. "Don't keep us in suspense here, huh?"

"I'm working on it. Keep your head on."

"You know, I've had that mastered since the day I was born."

Murphy snorted and dropped her forehead into her hand.

Raven opened the top of the bag but paused when Professor Bixby clapped in excitement.

"Miss Chase, this is very good. What a phenomenal item for this assignment. And thank you for bringing in something I'm sure brings more personal attachment for you than you might have wanted to share."

Exchanging curious glances with her friends, Raven pushed up a little in her seat for a better look at the item. When Professor Bixby moved aside to the next student, she was finally successful. *It's a good thing I decided not to bring my mom's war mage patch. That's like wearing the same jacket.*

"I don't get it." Henry shook his head. "She brought a triangle with some stitching. What's the big deal?"

"It's a war mage's patch," Raven muttered. "Her mom's."

"Huh." He glanced at his grandmother's old ring, then at Murphy's mom's dress. "You have one of those too, Raven, don't you?"

"Yep." Her fingers went on their own to touch the silver and red pin on her jacket. "I brought something better, though."

"I guess you'll have to leave that to Judge Bixby to decide," the other girl muttered as their vertically challenged professor moved from desk to desk. "It looks like she was overly impressed by Bella's patch."

"I'm not worried about it." She opened the top of the black bag again and reached inside. "I have history right here. That's Bixby's weak spot, right?"

Henry licked his lips and stared at her bag as he nodded faster and faster. "The suspense is killing me, Alby. Just do it alre—woah."

She drew the miniaturized Swarm skull from the bag and set it gently beside it, lowered her hands into her lap, and grinned.

"What is that?" Murphy asked with wide eyes.

"It looks like a bird skull." Henry frowned. "What kind of bird doesn't have eyes?"

"Not a bird." Raven smiled at him and wiggled her eyebrows. "I had to shrink it to fit it in that bag. I couldn't shove it under my arm before riding a dragon to school. Watch." She cleared her throat and tapped the top of the fist-sized skull. "*Invorto adtenuum.*"

The faded, off-white skull shimmered. In the next moment, it ballooned to its normal size and took up the entirety of her desk and pushed the drawstring bag off.

"Holy crap!" Bennett shouted. "Look what Raven brought."

"Pulling more tricks out of a bag now, huh, Alby?"

"What the hell is that thing?"

"My brother came home with something like that. It was taken off a dark witch selling curses on the other side of the pass through the Mountains of Jared. His was much smaller, though."

"Yeah, that runs in your family, Perkins, doesn't it?"

A round of laughter rose around her desk, and the students closest to her continued their speculation while a few others at the front of the room turned to see what all the fuss was about.

"You really did it this time." Henry grinned and stretched a hand tentatively to touch the skull. His hand withdrew immediately. "You know what it is, right?"

Raven glanced at Bella, who'd turned in her desk and now stared at the skull with wide eyes. *That's right. You can't top this with a war mage patch.* "Of course I know what it is. My grandpa brought it back with him from—"

"Miss Alby!" Professor Bixby stood in the center of the room and pointed at the Swarm Skiffling skull, her face completely white. "*Adtenuo!*"

The skull shrank again to the same size that would fit in the bag, and Raven leaned back in her chair. "This is my item, Professor. It has meaning and magical significance."

Her disapproval carved into her features, Bixby stalked a path down the center aisle between the desks, her eyes wide and fixed intently on the skull.

"It's a part of history. Isn't that what you wanted us to —hey!"

Professor Bixby snatched the miniature skull off the desk, grimaced, and didn't even look at her when she pointed at the door out of the classroom. "Come with me, Miss Alby. Now."

The woman waddled toward the door and jerked it open. It struck the opposite wall with a loud bang. Confused, she stared at her now empty desk in shock. *What did I do?*

A soft chuckle came from the front of the room.

"Maybe you should've gone with those journals." Bella flashed her a wide, predatory grin. "And the Magic Meld too, huh?"

Raven's face burned hot and she clenched her fists in her lap. *She promised.* Before she could tell the girl off for breaking their little truce, Professor Bixby squeaked in indignation.

The woman spun in the doorway, her usually chipper expression replaced by a decided scowl. "You'll join us as well, Miss Chase. Let's go."

"What?"

"Don't make me come over there and pull you out of your seat by your ear. I said come with me." Bixby shuffled into the hall and left her class in stunned silence.

With a frustrated grunt, Bella packed her satchel and stormed across the classroom. She reached Raven as she slung her satchel over her shoulder and stood. "Look what you did, Raven Alby. Nice job."

"Hey, I'm not the one who broke a promise not even an hour after making it."

The girl stuck her nose up and stormed into the hall.

Raven glanced at Henry and Murphy with a shrug. "I'll see you guys later."

"Yeah, good luck."

"Thanks." *I'm gonna need it.*

CHAPTER THIRTY

Professor Bixby marched the two girls across the main hall and toward the other end of the building. Raven hurried a little to step beside her classmate, who'd earned and broken her trust in the same morning. "It looks to me like a Chase does throw their word around for no reason."

"You're only upset that Professor Bixby didn't praise your personal item as much as she praised mine." Bella tossed her hair over her shoulder but stared at their professor's back rather than look at her.

"You know what?" she whispered. "I have no problem admitting that part. But that's not your fault."

"Then why are you hissing at me?"

"Because you lied to me!" Her unintended shout made Professor Bixby turn and point another short, accusatory finger at them both.

"Silence. This isn't a field trip, girls. If you ask me, both of you crossed a line this morning, and I'm inclined to say that it's as far as this school should allow either of you to go. Headmaster Flynn has the final word on that, however.

So shut your mouths or I'll shut them for you and keep them shut." A yellow zap of light flickered from the tip of her wand. "Don't think I won't."

When the professor turned again, Bella rolled her eyes and hurried after her. Raven clenched her fists at her sides and fell in behind her. *It would feel good to shove her into the wall, but only for a second. Don't make this worse for yourself, Raven.*

They followed Bixby up the winding staircase to Headmaster Flynn's office, completely silent while their footsteps echoed against the stone. When the woman stopped on the second-to-last step, Bella almost ran into her. Raven snorted.

After a brisk knock on the huge wooden door, Bixby pulled it open by the iron handle and stepped inside. She stood at the door and pointed with the same angry finger toward the floor inside the doorway. Bella stepped in first and stared at the office, and Raven followed.

Professor Flynn stood slowly from behind his desk and regarded them calmly as he set a pair of reading glasses down beside the quill he'd been using. "Good morning, Professor Bixby."

"Headmaster." Bixby pulled the door shut behind her with a loud slam, grunted at the effort, then turned and shook her finger at the girls. "I'm sorry to have to interrupt your morning with something so unbecoming from two of our brightest students—that was not meant as a compliment, Miss Chase."

Bella's smile faded at that and she raised an eyebrow.

"These girls have… Well, they disrupted my class in the most unseemly—"

"Professor?' Flynn pursed his lips, his eyebrows rising in concern. "What happened?"

"This happened!" The professor wobbled across the office toward the headmaster's desk and set the shrunken skull in front of him. A little shiver ran through her body, which made her frizzy copper hair tremble on her head. She wiped her hand on her long robes and shook it again. "The assignment was to bring in a personal item with magical significance. We're working on historical lineages, Headmaster."

"Yes, I'm well aware of that."

"And Miss Alby thought it would be a wonderful idea to bring this…this thing into my classroom, never mind onto the school grounds. And Miss Chase! She began to talk about Magic Meld, Headmaster, and threw it around like it was a common levitation spell." Flynn's eyes settled on Bella for a moment before he glanced at Raven. Bixby didn't notice, however. "I tell you what. There's certainly something going on here, and I have half a mind to—"

"Thank you, Professor Bixby. That will be all."

"These students are perfectly equipped to know the difference between appropriate magic and endangering everyone around them by engaging in this useless—"

"Professor." Headmaster Flynn extended a hand toward the woman as he stepped around his desk. When he reached her, he bent at the waist and took one of her hands in both of his. "I understand your concerns and I assure you, they will not go unaddressed. I agree with you and I will handle this. Thank you for bringing Miss Alby and Miss Chase to me so I may do exactly that. Now, if I'm not mistaken, I believe you have an entire classroom of students with no professor to instruct them and no idea how to proceed."

"Oh. Oh, yes." The woman nodded furiously, patted the back of Flynn's hand, and withdrew hers from his grasp to turn away. "Thank you, Headmaster." On her way out, she stabbed a finger at Bella and then at Raven, still furious although she barely reached to the middle of either girl's torso. "You two should be ashamed of yourselves." She opened the door enough to slip through and vanished down the stairwell. The door shut behind her with a much softer thud.

Headmaster Flynn studied his students with a small, grim smile. "I believe I've spent enough time trying to correct Professor Bixby's choice of words this morning. It seems she was too rattled to realize my intention. I do hope that the two of you are more clearheaded as of this moment. So first, let me say that her parting words were undoubtedly spoken in haste and fear. I don't expect either of you to be ashamed of yourselves, nor should you be. Is that understood?"

The two girls nodded and Raven stepped forward and gestured toward the skull on the headmaster's desk. "I don't know why that made her so upset, Headmaster. It's a relic and it's something to be proud of. The Swarm was defeated and that's what ended the war. Why is it suddenly such a big deal to talk about it? Professor Bixby said to bring something with meaning. That's exactly what I did."

Bella scoffed, but she ignored her.

Headmaster Flynn set a few fingers on the edge of his desk and tilted his head slightly, his expression calm. "Is there anything else, Miss Alby?"

"What? No. I guess that's it." Her cheeks flushed a little. *I have no reason to be embarrassed.*

Slowly, the headmaster turned his attention to the shrunken skull of one of the Swarm and tapped it with a finger. It grew to its natural size again on his desk, and his office fell completely silent. When he turned toward his students, Flynn's face had gone a little pale around his graying beard.

He wasn't afraid of Leander. Why is he afraid of an old bone?

"As I understand it, you two discovered a rather similar thread within the histories of your families. Recently, yes?"

The girls nodded.

"We both come from a family line of powerful mages," Bella said.

Raven glanced at her, received no response, and added, "And our moms were war mages."

"Indeed they were." The man shook his head slowly and gave the giant skull a final glance before he stepped toward his students. "I had the honor of meeting each of your mothers at one point in time. They were fine women, incredibly skilled war mages, and fierce warriors who put everything on the line to do their part in protecting this kingdom. You would do well to remember this, even when attending your classes and presenting items of significance to your professors."

"I don't think either one of us can forget that, Headmaster." Raven raised her chin and held Flynn's gaze, even though she felt Bella turn to look at her in surprise.

"That's very likely the case, Miss Alby. In any event, Swarm relics are not toys or trinkets or appropriate ingredients for spells of any kind—including the Magic Meld. And yes, I'm now speaking to you, Miss Chase."

Bella responded with a surprised grunt and tried to argue. "Raven has that spell. I barely even saw it—"

Raven turned toward the girl and her belly clenched in anger. "You're pulling out all the stops today, aren't you? You gave me your word and now, you're trying to throw me under the wagon so you don't get in trouble. Which wouldn't have happened if you hadn't broken your promise."

"I'm not the one who brought a Swarm skull to school—"

"Enough!"

Both girls turned quickly to look at Headmaster Flynn, who hadn't moved, his fingers still pressed on the edge of his desk. The amusement that had constantly flickered behind his eyes was gone.

"Let me assure you, Miss Alby and Miss Chase, this isn't a game. What you two are dabbling in belongs to the history of Brighton, yes—the history of this kingdom, as well as your ancestry. And it spans so much more than that. Good war mages and dragon riders lost their lives in that war. Countless soldiers too. They gave their lives to defeat the Swarm, to reduce it to nothing more than so many skulls exactly like these." He pointed to the huge, eyeless hunk of bone that almost covered his desk. "To play around with such things out of spite or a viable yet highly irritating rivalry is direct disrespect to those who made our freedom and our safety possible by forfeiting their own. I don't want to hear any more talk about the Swarm or that particular spell. Especially now. Is that understood?"

"Yes, Headmaster," Bella muttered and chewed on the inside of her cheek.

"Miss Alby?"

"I didn't mean to disrespect anyone." Raven glanced at the skull again and shook her head. "I'm proud of that and the fact that my grandfather helped to destroy one of the swarm's biggest creatures and brought that skull home after. It wasn't supposed to be an insult."

"I understand, Miss Alby. Be that as it may, the majority of people are far less likely to fully realize your intentions with something like this. Now is simply not the right time to even attempt to enlighten them."

"What does that mean?" Bella stepped forward beside Raven now and shook her head. "What's going on right now?"

"Miss Chase, your attention and focus are much better placed on your studies—"

"You're talking about all the abandoned satellite ranches, aren't you?" Bella glanced at Raven, widened her eyes a little, and fixed the headmaster with a steady gaze. "All the families picking up and moving inside the walls."

I can't believe we're having this conversation. But better now than never. Raven looked at Headmaster Flynn, who removed his hand slowly from the desk and raised his chin. "I know a few ranches outside Brighton that were destroyed or had missing dogs and livestock. The Alby Ranch lost one worker who simply disappeared, but I don't buy that. Or the story about the other guy who got so drunk that he burned his cabin down himself."

The Headmaster of Fowler Academy frowned deeply and gave himself a few more long seconds to gather his thoughts. *They are exactly like their mothers. Sarah Alby and Vanessa Chase wouldn't have let me off the hook so easily, either.* He cleared his throat. "This is what I can tell you. Something is definitely not quite right, as your familiar can attest, Miss Alby. Myself and a few others have suspected this much for a few months now, but nothing's been confirmed."

"What do you think it is?" Bella asked. "Will there be another war?"

"You've missed a few crucial steps along the way, Miss Chase. We don't fully know what's happening. But this is not something we take lightly, either. Until we discover what's really in progress now—and Connor Alby left Brighton to do that—I don't want either of you to breathe a word of this to anyone." He folded his hands together and held them in front of his robes. "I need your assurances on this, girls. From both of you."

"Not a word," Raven said quickly, nodded at him, and took a deep breath.

Bella's firedrake familiar fluttered off her shoulder and landed on the floor beside her, stretched his wings, and sniffed at something on the dusty, scuffed wood. "Not a word." She looked at Raven and shrugged. "I'm sorry I said anything. It won't happen again."

Woah. Her eyes widened at the unexpected apology, and her mouth opened before she could think of anything to say. "Okay."

"Excellent. That is how we keep this kingdom safe. Trusting each other, acknowledging our own mistakes, forgiving, and moving on." Headmaster Flynn put a finger to his lips and squinted at them. "And keep important secret knowledge to ourselves, hmm?"

The two girls nodded.

"Thank you." He pointed quickly at his office door, which opened all on its own. "I believe you both still have a full schedule of classes ahead of you for the day. I appreciate your time."

Bella moved quickly to the door and Raven almost followed her but stopped after a few steps. "Headmaster? I have one more question. About a…seal I've seen on different documents."

He glanced at his office door before he stepped around his desk and picked his reading glasses up again. "Is it a crucial question at this exact moment, Miss Alby?"

"I don't know."

"If it can wait until after the spring gala, please come and see me again at that time." He lowered himself into his chair and nodded at her. "I appreciate the opportunity to have had this conversation with you both, but at the same time, I'm quite behind on my to-do list."

"Okay. I guess it can wait."

"Then I'll expect another visit from you when classes resume next week." He nodded and returned his attention to the parchment paper and quill on his desk.

Raven glanced down the stairwell. Bella wasn't exactly waiting for her and Wesley hopped down the winding stairs one at a time, but she wasn't going as fast as she could have either. With Headmaster Flynn once again preoccupied with his important business, she stepped through the doorway and turned to close the door behind her. The curving stairwell fell into semi-darkness, although it took only a few seconds for her eyes to adjust to the dim light.

The other girl continued slowly down the stairs but turned partially to mutter, "I didn't know your grandfather left."

"Well, Bella, you never asked."

"I thought he never left your family's ranch."

"So did I."

Their footsteps echoed eerily as they always did, then Bella added, "Personally, I think it's either the Swarm again or raiders."

"What?"

"Why everyone's leaving the satellite ranches and abandoning good work. I've seen many people go missing. It's not like the start of the war, but the capitol's starting to send warnings to the towns closest to the wall. So it's more of the Swarm or raiders."

"That's only a guess." Raven shook her head. "There's no real proof." *Except for the overturned sinkholes I saw when Leander and I were flying. And the lines of upturned dirt beyond the wall.*

"Well, if you have any better theories, let's hear 'em."

"I don't have any better theories, Bella. I have the same theories."

The girl's eyebrows raised when she glanced up the staircase again. A tiny smile flickered at the corner of her mouth. "I always knew you were smart but I might have underestimated you."

She chuckled. "I think the feeling's mutual."

They reached the bottom of the staircase and the firedrake familiar fluttered onto Bella's shoulder again before she darted her companion a quick glance. "Don't let it go to your head, Raven."

With that, she hurried down the hall through the main building. Raven took a deep breath and continued in the same direction toward her next class, which they happened to have together too. *That's good advice. I hope she applies it to herself.*

CHAPTER THIRTY-ONE

R aven walked across the field about fifteen minutes before her History of Magic class finished. She went directly to Leander's pen, thoroughly looking forward to a few minutes with him before their familiar training with Professor Worley began.

The field and the barns, as far as she could tell, were empty. *Wherever Bella went first, I'm really glad she didn't show up here early too.*

The dragon snorted as she approached the gate. "What happened?"

She shook her head and answered him through the walls as she pushed the sleeve of her jacket up to reveal the rune on her forearm. "I'm not sure, exactly. I'm a little..."

"Confused." The dragon wasn't asking.

"It comes off me that strongly, huh?" Her rune flashed orange, the gate did the same, and the deadbolt slid away from the wall to open the gate with a dull click.

"It doesn't matter how strong, Raven. I feel it all the same."

"Fair enough. I wish I knew how to explain what—"

"Miss Alby," Professor Worley called as he moved quickly toward her from around the far end of the stables. "Do you have a moment?"

She glanced at the slightly open gate. "Yeah."

"Thank you." He closed the stable doors and almost jogged down the long line of the building toward her. "Are the first classes letting out early today?"

"Oh. No. Mine was interrupted."

"Nothing serious, I hope." The giant bearded professor raised his eyebrows and chuckled.

Raven tilted her head from side to side. "I guess that depends on who you ask."

"It always does." He folded his arms, nodded, and glanced at the open gate. "This is good timing, though. It gives us a chance to go over a few guidelines before the class without being interrupted. Do you mind?"

"No. Leander and I are totally ready for this." She leaned toward the crack in the gate and added, "Aren't we?"

"I can neither confirm nor deny that statement." A low rumble echoed from within the pen.

Raven turned toward Professor Worley and wrinkled her nose. "He's trying to be funny."

"And succeeding, as far as I'm concerned." The man laughed and stepped away from the pen. "Leander, you're welcome to join us for this conversation, if you like."

"Not particularly." The dragon snorted at the open gate and blew a puff of hot breath, dirt, and a few blades of grass into the field.

Raven held a finger up toward her professor in a gesture for him to wait. She stepped in front of the gate and opened it enough to stare directly into one of Leander's large yellow eyes. "This'll be good for us. Professor Worley knows what he's doing as far as familiars are concerned."

"Not as far as dragons are concerned."

Worley laughed again. "You have a point there, Leander."

"Still." She smiled and spread her arms. "The more you and I can learn about how to improve, the better, right? Unless you'd rather stay in your pen through the whole class and listen to everyone else working with their familiars."

Leander stepped away from the gate and stretched his wings. "That's not why I came here."

"Oh, I know it's not. Still, it's your choice."

The dragon snorted again and stretched his neck to nudge the gate open with his snout.

She grinned and stepped aside as the huge red dragon moved slowly and calmly out of his pen and into the open fields beside the stables and the barn. "Thanks, Leander. And hey, if we don't learn anything useful today, we'll keep training on our own."

"That's quite the shoes to fill, Miss Alby." Worley stood his ground as Leander walked toward him, although his eyes widened and he unfolded his arms. "But I'll do what I can to offer something useful to you both. To the best of my ability, at least."

Leander stopped a few feet away from the man and stood perfectly still. "An ability that doesn't include working with dragons."

"Well, not yet." He nodded. "Ah, Miss Alby?"

"Yeah?" Raven walked alongside Leander and trailed her hand along his scales.

"Again, I've not had much experience, but don't most dragons use a lead or some kind of rope...or something?"

"Yep. Most dragons." She laughed and patted her familiar's muscular shoulder. "Not this one. That was one of the first deals we made and I don't see us going back on it anytime soon. Will that be a problem?"

"No, no." Professor Worley stroked his dark, bushy beard and his smile widened. "I can see you two know what you're doing as a mage and her familiar. I don't like to make a habit of expecting problems before they exist." Finally, he looked away from Leander's yellow eyes and grinned at her. "If you trust your dragon, Miss Alby, so do I. And as long as the other students and their familiars can pull themselves together enough to trust your connection, I think we'll be fine. I wonder, though, if you and Leander wouldn't mind waiting on the other side of his pen until everyone joins us here and class begins. Not inside it, of course. Merely around the back."

Raven looked at her dragon, whose only response was to raise his head into the air and take a few deep sniffs. "You don't want anyone else to see him first?"

"Not quite." He drew his hand over his mouth and chuckled again before he folded his arms. "It's one thing to see a fully grown dragon led out of his pen by a student with no lead and none of the usual training techniques. I think, for the other students, it might make an even greater impression to see that the two of you were out here in an open field the whole time and were able to remain both silent and unseen until the right moment. That is, of course, if you're both willing to play along for a little while."

"Leander?" She craned her neck to look at him and folded her arms. "I'm fine with it if you are."

The great red dragon lowered his head, turned away from both his mage and Professor Worley, and ambled toward the other side of the pen. "I'll play along. If that's his idea of fun, though, I'm sure I'll be incredibly bored today."

The professor responded with a loud, rumbling laugh and thumped a fist into his open hand. "That's good. Real good. I had no idea dragons were so funny."

Raven tried to frown at him but his laughter was too infectious. "It's a certain kind of wry humor, for sure. Most people don't pick up on it."

"Well, I've been around enough predatory animals to know when they're acting on instinct and when they're at least trying to be playful."

"Predatory animals?"

"Hmm? Oh, yes." The man looked away from the retreating dragon and shrugged. "That's more of a story for another time. But remind me to tell you more when we're not about to play dragon-in-the-box with your peers, yeah?"

"This sounds more like your version of a practical joke, Professor."

"Maybe." Worley wiggled his eyebrows, then turned to face the stone archway across the field. The growing noise of students' voices grew louder by the second. "I think that's our cue. I'll ask you to step forward when it's time. Feel free to make as much of an entrance as you like."

Raven laughed and slipped her satchel off her shoulders to set it beside the wall of the pen. "Do you have any other pointers for having familiar training out beside a dragon pen today?"

"Hmm. Make sure he doesn't eat anyone."

"I make no promises," Leander rumbled and his long neck and head poked out from around the side of the pen.

"Ha. Then the rest is up to you, Miss Alby, isn't it?" Professor Worley released another thunderous laugh and headed toward the stables. "I have to set a few things up first. Then we'll kick this class off in a way I haven't yet tried. I'm very much looking forward to it."

Laughing too, Raven followed the large curve of the pen until she reached Leander and they both retreated around the other side to be sure they were completely hidden. "I know it's kind of a big step for you, playing along with another trainer. I know Professor Worley appreciates it. And you know I do too."

"Yes." He lowered his belly onto the grass and closed his eyes beneath the sunshine. "That man trains familiars, not dragons. As long as he doesn't try to saddle me or pull me around like a pack animal, I'm interested to see what he thinks he can offer us."

"Fair enough." She sat on the grass and leaned against his side. "I'm sure he's thinking the same thing right now."

They waited for the other first-year students to appear at the stables for their familiar training. The field filled with excited voices, many of them commenting in one way or another on the giant, brand-new pen built at the end of the stables that hadn't been there the previous week.

Raven straightened and tossed her thick red braid over

her shoulder. "They have to know by now that this is where you stay, right? I mean, people have seen you."

"Some people see a thing and still aren't smart enough to believe their own eyes." Leander turned his head on his long neck to look directly at her.

She fought back a laugh. "I think this is the first time I've heard you whisper."

"I'm playing along. You should try it."

Trying to hold back the spontaneous laughter almost made her choke. She buried her face in her hands, and a low, stuttering hiss escaped the dragon beside her.

"Hey, Worley said we could make whatever kind of entrance we wanted, right? I have an idea."

"Oh, joy." Leander lowered his head to the grass and heaved a surprisingly gentle sigh.

"No, really. I think you'll like it."

"Look at this," Professor Worley announced, spread his arms in front of his class, and gazed at the sky. "I know some of you don't consider training with your familiar to be an actual class at this highly accredited school for mages. And perhaps that's because most of the time, we're in the barn. But what a day, huh? Spring is on the way!"

A few students laughed at that and turned their faces to the sun. Henry glanced around the gathered class and frowned. *We're all out here for Raven and her dragon. Where is she?*

CHAPTER THIRTY-TWO

Henry caught sight of Bella Chase with her crafty firedrake perched on her shoulder. Cupping Maxwell tightly in both hands, he shouldered his way through the other students. Most of them only partially listened to Professor Worley's opening statement. Most of their attention was on speculating about the dragon pen and Raven Alby's familiar allegedly living in it.

"Hey, Chase." Henry sidled up beside her and held Maxwell out to the side a little and away from the fire-drake. "Where's Raven?"

She gave him an unamused grimace. "I'm not her babysitter. And it's not my fault if you can't keep track of your friends."

He snorted. "That would be a good point if you weren't the last person to see her."

"We parted ways before History of Magic was even over, okay? Wherever she went, it's none of my business."

"Well, she's not here." He scowled at her and they both looked at Professor Worley as he began to talk again. "I'm sorry for not trusting you explicitly or anything. I heard her say something about a promise."

"It's none of your business, Mr. Derks. Stop asking me." Bella folded her arms and stared intently at their familiar-training professor.

"Okay. But if someone finds Raven Alby tied up in a closet or...I dunno, cursed into nonstop puking for two days, you'd better believe I'll be the first person to point the finger." He leaned toward her as far as he dared and nodded. "I mean at you, by the way."

Slowly, she turned her and her gaze settled on Maxwell's head where it was visible between his mage's fingers. "You might want to reconsider how easy it is to be threatening when you're holding a toad."

"Oh, yeah? Maxwell can be threatening." Henry shrugged and stepped away from her. "You haven't seen everything he can do."

She shook her head and stared at their professor again. "And I'm perfectly okay with that."

"Yeah, I bet you are. Whatever." Swallowing, Henry put a few more students between them and turned again, looking for Raven.

"And as you can see," Worley continued, "we're not only out here to enjoy the unseasonably enjoyable weather. We're out here because one of your fellow students had a few kinks in her schedule to work out before she was able to bring her familiar to Fowler Academy with her. If you ask me, the whole group of you should count yourselves lucky for not having had to jump through the same kind of hoops, as it were."

"Yeah, we get it," Thomas Sinclair shouted. "You're talking about Raven Alby."

"Your powers of observation are truly inspiring, Mr. Sinclair." Professor Worley clasped his hands together and shook them a little in Thomas' general direction.

"So where's the dragon?" Erin Barnaby asked.

"Hmm. That is the question of the hour, isn't it?" The man stared at his students and grinned through the wild tangles of his dark beard.

The field beside the stables went completely quiet as everyone waited for their professor to speak. When he didn't, a few confused whispers traveled through the class.

From the other side of the new pen came a loud snort and a muffled laugh.

"Woah!"

The students closest to the end of the pen backed away a little, bumped into those behind them, and tried not to look nervous. The red dragon's scaly snout was the first thing around the corner of the pen, followed by his long neck and two massive paws as he moved slowly out into the field.

"Did it break out of its pen?"

"Where's Raven?"

"It ate her! I bet it ate her."

"Professor? Should we still be here right now?"

Worley chuckled but said nothing as Leander moved slowly toward the gathered class, his wings tucked against his back but not entirely as far down as they would go.

Henry pushed his way through the other students and stood to the side. Grinning, he shook his head. "What are you doing, Alby?"

Leander increased speed a little. One of the girls closest to Professor Worley uttered a small shriek and leapt back. When the dragon accelerated to a slightly unnerving pace, both wings snapped out to either side with a burst of wind and a whoosh that startled them all. Raven Alby stood on his bare back, one foot set squarely in front of the other and her arms spread wide.

Henry gave a loud whoop and almost tossed Maxwell into the air. "Now that's what I call an entrance. Way to kill it with the crowd, Alby!"

Professor Worley burst out laughing again and threw his head back as his whole body shook. It took the other students a few more seconds to realize what they were seeing before the class exploded with shouts and cheers. Some of the other students hadn't managed to find their voices again or darted each other nervous glances.

Leander moved even faster out into the field and almost trotted in a wide circle with his wings at their full span. He snorted, lowered himself to the ground, and folded his wings again as Raven leapt off his back and landed on her feet with a thud.

Henry ran toward them, laughing with real delight. "Hey, nice trick, Alby! You couldn't help being a giant showoff, huh? Woah!" He stopped when Leander's yellow eyes fixed on his face. Then, he gulped and took a few steps back. "I'm gonna stay over here. Yep."

"That's probably a good idea." Raven laughed and turned to wink at her dragon. "I literally couldn't help myself with that one. Was it too much?"

"Oh, yeah. Exactly the right amount of too much." Her

friend nodded vigorously, his eyes wide. "Aren't you supposed to have a saddle on him?"

"Only for flying and maybe not even then. I don't know. We'll work on it."

"Thank you for that unexpectedly entertaining performance, Miss Alby." Professor Worley clapped a few times and stepped briskly through the uncertain students toward Raven and her dragon. "And Leander, of course." He stopped beside Henry and clapped a huge hand on the boy's shoulder. Henry grunted and staggered sideways as Worley regarded the dragon with a broad grin. "I see you decided to play along after all. Well done."

Leander turned his head away from the man and the students who stepped hesitantly after their professor. "I had hoped a few more people would run."

Raven rolled her eyes and shook her head at Worley. "That is also another joke."

"Oh, I know." The professor turned and gestured extravagantly. "This is where we'll train with your familiars today. I want everyone to spread out. Give yourselves enough space to spin in a circle with your arms outstretched. Feel free to take as much as you need. There's a fair amount of it out here and very few walls." He laughed again and stepped away from Leander and Raven. "Give Miss Alby and her familiar their space too. I'll wait."

The students scattered slowly across the field as they talked to each other and no longer bothered to whisper their amazement at seeing a dragon at Fowler Academy.

Raven returned to Leander's side and folded her arms. "You have to admit that was great."

"I'll settle for how much you enjoyed yourself. You did seem comfortable standing on me."

She smirked. "Of course I was comfortable. I trust you. It's not like you were gonna try to buck me off or start flying around."

"No. But I considered it." He turned his huge head to fix her with one eye. "So have you."

"Flying without a saddle? Yeah." She grinned at him and nudged his snout aside playfully when he snorted in her face. "Maybe we'll practice with that too if you're up for it."

"It's an excellent idea."

"You know, I had a feeling you'd say that."

Professor Worley made them practice giving their familiars non-verbal commands, exactly as Raven had been required to do with Leander during their impromptu familiar test in the barn almost two weeks before. A number of students had connected with their familiars enough to be mostly successful, but the hard part seemed to be getting their familiars to obey a complicated command all the way to the end.

Raven and Leander didn't have that problem. When she'd stood beside Professor Worley and thought about Leander leaping into the air for a quick lap around the stables, that was exactly what he did.

Worley leaned toward her and muttered, "I take it he's not usually prone to circling large buildings for fun."

Wrinkling her nose, Raven cast her professor a sidelong glance. "Not really, no."

"You two are demonstrating your connection exactly as I thought you would. You should be very proud, Miss Alby."

"Oh, I am. I'm always proud of that dragon."

The man hummed and inclined his head toward her, although he still watched the agile beast covered in fiery-red scales gliding across the grass toward them. "That's obvious. But I was talking about you. Don't let him take all the credit, huh? You're in this together." With a nod at Leander who landed a few yards away, the professor moved to the next student who was ready to show him what he could do with his raccoon familiar.

She watched the giant man walk off in bemusement. *I didn't expect that.*

Leander stepped beside her and nudged the back of her shoulder with his snout. "I take it that was exactly what we were supposed to do."

She turned toward him and grinned. "It was. You did a great job."

"Compliments tend to fall a little flat when they're given for something so easy, little girl." A few short hisses burst between his lips. "This is magic school?"

"Yeah, okay. I get it. You wouldn't find it so funny if you had to sit behind a desk and start casting spells with various professors breathing down your neck. Out of all of them, I'd say Worley's the most…laid back."

"He's not afraid of me, either. I appreciate it."

"Me too."

They watched the other students and their familiars for the rest of the class. Henry and Maxwell passed with flying colors judging by the way he pumped his fist in the air with a loud, "Yes!" and scooped his toad off the grass before he actually kissed his familiar.

Murphy didn't seem to have any trouble with Fritz,

either, at least until Tessa's butterfly familiar became a little too curious and moved too close. At that point, the barn cat abandoned Murphy's instructions in lieu of swatting at it. Tessa shrieked and tried to chase Fritz away, while Murphy tried to defend her cat by blaming it on the butterfly.

Familiars darted in every direction, either at their mage's command or completely against them. Leander rumbled softly and his tail teased the grass behind them as it curled around his hind legs. "We made a spectacle of ourselves, Raven. Still, it was much better than this."

She burst out laughing and covered her mouth when Julia, on the other side of her, jumped in surprise. Her wombat raced away from her and she hurried after the animal with a frustrated groan.

"We're much better now, yeah." She tried to keep a straight face when she added, "But I remember this one dragon who constantly crashed into a wall instead of flying over it. Too many times to count, I think."

"And I remember a mage in training who didn't know the difference between ordering a dragon to do something and asking if he wanted to in the first place."

"Touché."

A golden streak darted through the sky above them, followed by a piercing little shriek. They both looked at Bella's firedrake, who spiraled in a wide circle above them.

Raven scanned the students scattered across the field and finally found Bella. The girl stood with her arms folded and her weight shifted onto one hip. She glared at Raven and Leander but said nothing.

"She's been watching us for a while," Leander said.

"You noticed, huh?"

"Yes. She was watching you when I circled the stables."

Narrowing her eyes, she drew her gaze away from the girl and looked at Wesley, who still wheeled above them. "I honestly can't decide what she wants, Leander. This morning, she was actually...well, I wouldn't say nice but bearable. She didn't insult me or try to rub my nose in anything. And just like that, she goes back to giving me the death stare."

"She envies you, Raven."

"Yeah, I don't know why. She's as skilled with her magic as I am with mine. Maybe even a little better with a few spells. I don't know what her deal is."

"Envy. That's the deal."

Laughing, she turned toward the red dragon and peered at him. His long shadow fell over her and blocked the sun. "You sound sure about that. But you can't feel Bella Chase's emotions."

"No." He snorted and turned his head to look at the girl. "I can smell them."

"Huh."

Bella blinked and unfolded her arms when she noticed Leander looking at her as well. Her firedrake darted in front of the red dragon and his mage and uttered another shriek before he vanished again as a flash of gold in the sunlight.

"Thanks for clearing that up." Raven patted Leander's scaly shoulder and nodded. "I'm still not sure what to do with—"

Another piercing shriek cut her statement short. Bella's

familiar darted toward Raven, who stepped out of the way before the firedrake pulled up at the last second.

"Now what's she trying to do?" Meeting Bella's gaze, she spread her arms in a wordless question. The girl simply stared at her.

Only a few feet above Leander's head, Wesley shrieked again and released a quick stream of fire. Raven ducked, although it wouldn't have hit her anyway. The firedrake had obviously aimed for Leander's head and the small stream of flames found its target. Leander snorted as the flames brushed across the scaled ridges above his eyes, and his wings twitched along his back.

"Hey, that's not cool. Are you okay?"

"It's like being struck by a human infant's hand. Honestly, it's not painful." He lowered his head toward her, although his yellow eyes were trained on Bella's firedrake where it fluttered over their heads. "I don't think he likes me."

She scoffed. "He can not like you all he wants. Bella needs to call him off. And we both know she can."

"I'll handle it."

Despite the nervous flutter rising in her belly at how deadly he made those words sound, she laughed. "Don't hurt him, Leander."

"I don't intend to." The dragon's head moved a few centimeters from one side to the other as he watched the shrieking, fire-breathing Wesley.

Raven glared at Bella and shook her head. "Don't do anything stupid, Bella." *She can't hear me, but still.*

Wesley shrieked again and dove toward Leander, darted around the dragon's massive head, and batted at the red-scaled face. The firedrake opened his mouth, which glowed a bright red as he prepared to unleash more flames. With incredible speed, Leander's head lurched forward on his long neck like a striking snake. He snapped his jaws together and the many razor-sharp teeth clacked ominously less than an inch from Wesley's open mouth. The firedrake hiccupped and emitted a puff of smoke when the fire in his throat went out completely. He shrieked and flapped unsteadily in front of the massive snout.

The red dragon spewed a thick cloud of hot, acrid smoke at Bella's familiar. It hurled the terrified creature into a sequence of airborne somersaults, and he fought to gain control of his wings before he thumped against Professor Worley's back and from there, into the grass with a thud.

"What's this?" The man turned, coughed, and waved the smoke out of his face.

Wesley screeched again, darted away from the professor's boots, and launched himself to streak back to Bella.

"Is everything okay over there?" the professor called and gestured toward Raven and Leander.

With a wide grin, she gave the man two thumbs-up. "All good."

Beside her, Leander's lips parted to reveal almost all his teeth in a dragon's grin that was much less reassuring.

With a snort of laughter, he turned to look at Bella and her familiar—who didn't offer anything other than another screech—while the girl glowered.

"She knows better than that," Raven muttered. "Telling me to mind my own familiar."

A rumble rose from Leander's throat and he lowered

his scaly lips around his teeth again. "Does her face often turn that shade of red?"

"No, this is a first. Does it still smell like envy?"

The red dragon snorted. "With undertones of rage."

She nodded and folded her arms. "That's what I thought."

CHAPTER THIRTY-THREE

On the day of Fowler Academy's spring gala, there were no classes. Raven half-expected Bella to appear at her dorm room and demand another look at Connor Alby's old journals. Fortunately, the girl apparently had better things to do that morning.

Raven took a few rolls from the steaming pile on the banquet table as she moved through the common room. She ate them as she ran across the school's center courtyard, under the archway, and out into the field. Leander greeted her from his pen with a snort and a puff of steam in the chilly morning air.

"I know." She wolfed the last roll and unlocked the gate with her access rune. "I'm a little later today than I have been since we moved in. I hope you weren't too worried."

When she jerked the heavy metal gate open and stepped into the pen, he lay curled in a tight ball on the cool grass. He raised his head, turned it toward her, and set it down again. "I don't worry in my sleep."

She laughed. "You slept in too, huh?"

"We were both up late last night, as I remember it."

"Because someone kept wanting to test the riding without a saddle trick."

"That was you, little girl."

"Hey, don't try to tell me now that you didn't have as much fun as I did. We're getting better at it. You'll be flying with a mage and without a saddle in no time." With a dismissive wave, she checked his trough, which was still half full from the night before. "Were you too tired to eat before you fell asleep?"

"I'm not hungry."

Frowning, she walked slowly to her dragon and studied him with a concerned expression. "Do you feel like something's wrong again?"

"Not again, Raven. It's always there but it's a little stronger today. And I had...bad dreams."

She snorted, then covered her mouth and shook her head. "Sorry. I'm not laughing at you and I know what bad dreams are like, trust me. I'm merely surprised that dragons even have dreams."

Leander's head raised from the grass and a little shudder rippled down the scales on his neck and down his back before it shivered out into his wings. "Of course dragons dream. I'd go so far as to say they mean more than human dreams."

"Huh." She stepped close to him and slid her hand over the hard ridges of his snout and between his eyes. "You're probably right about that, honestly. Do you wanna talk about it?'

"The superiority of a dragon's imagination even in sleep?"

Raven chuckled and nudged his face away. "I meant your dream. The bad one."

"I prefer not to."

"Okay. If you change your mind, I'm here to listen—"

"The earth split open." His tail, still curled tightly around his body, thumped on the grass.

"Oh." She sat in front of him and crossed her legs. "Like an earthquake?"

"Like a black maw. You fell into it."

"Wow. Yeah, I think I'd call that a nightmare."

Leander snorted again and his hot breath brushed against her bent knees. "I felt you but I couldn't find you, no matter where I looked or how fast I flew. Then the gaping mouth rose from the ground and ate the rest of the world."

She waited a few seconds longer for him to finish, but that was apparently the end. "Did anything else happen after that?"

"I heard you running and woke up."

"Well, it sounds like perfect timing." She leaned forward and caught his gaze before she shook her head. "Just so you know, I'm not going anywhere."

"I know that." He looked sleepily at her through half-closed lids. "It was a dream, Raven."

My dragon's sending me seriously mixed messages. "I'm glad we covered that. How do you feel now?"

"I'm still not hungry. You're feeling nervous."

"I…" With a sigh, she pushed to her feet. "Okay, maybe a little nervous. That gala or dance or whatever is tonight."

"You're not nervous about having fun."

"No. I'm nervous about not having fun. I think." Raven

rolled her eyes and dragged her hair back to tie it into a loose ponytail. "I'm starting to regret telling Daniel I'd be his date. I don't even know the guy and I didn't say yes because I wanted to."

"You made a necessary sacrifice and I appreciate it." Leander pushed slowly to his feet and his wings stretched wide before he curled them again.

"Yeah, well, I'm fairly sure that sacrifice is gonna bite me in the ass tonight. So yeah, I'm a little nervous."

The dragon paced slowly along the far end of the pen. "There's a very simple cure for that, you know." His wings stretched again.

"Do you want to eat first?"

"Maybe after. I'm ready to go now."

"Okay, okay." She grinned as she strode to the gate and pushed it open. "I'll be right back."

"We could try it without a saddle."

"I'm tempted. Really, I am. Let's take a raincheck on that, though. I don't know if me being nervous about a silly dance and you thinking about your bad dream makes either one of us a hundred percent on our game. We could fly without a saddle. I'm sure we could. But we still have to be careful."

Leander swung his head from side to side and his tail thunked against the pen wall. "You're still standing there."

Laughing, she slipped through the gate, closed it behind her, and went to the stables for her grandpa's old dragon saddle and harness. *Maybe for the last time if we're as coordinated as we think we are. We're almost there.*

Taking flight on a dragon's back at this time of the morning was indescribably more exciting than her regularly scheduled classes. The chilly wind nipped at her face and brought the same hot tears she'd experienced before to her eyes before they were swept away from her. *This is what we need. And we can take our time.*

She slipped her boots out of the stirrups and spread her arms. The reins remained loosely tied around the saddle horn and she hadn't touched them once they became airborne. Leander wheeled through the sky and pushed himself faster and faster until it felt like he was trying to chase the sunrise.

Raven shouted with joy and freedom, her arms still spread to either side. The dragon banked, turned again, and descended a little. Her hands dropped instinctively to his neck as the air rushed down her throat and she fought for breath. When he leveled out again, her laughter finally made a sound.

"And I thought playing with fire was good for clearing the mind." She clapped and laughed again. "Nothing's better than this!"

He made another sharp turn before he aimed them toward the sky and climbed even higher.

Feeling on top of the world like this? Yeah, I'd say that's a good time to try.

As soon as she thought it, the dragon sensed her intention and leveled off as they flew high above the top of the forest that backed the school grounds. She patted his neck and reveled in the feel of his wings beating and all his muscles coiling and tensing beneath her.

He turned his head to look at her. "Do it."

She laughed again. "I didn't say anything."

"You don't have to, dragon rider. Do it."

Raven wiped her hands on her trousers and shook them. Blowing out a long, steady breath, she nodded. *Trust the dragon. That's all I need, even for this.*

She braced both hands on the front of the saddle below the pommel and lifted her left foot slowly from Leander's flank. Focused, she leaned forward and brought her boot up quickly onto the saddle and crouched there with one leg dangling over the dragon's other side. *I won't fall. Even if I tried, he wouldn't let me.*

With a final lurch, she straightened her leg with her boot on the saddle and stood. Her other foot settled on the dragon's scaly hide in front of the saddle horn, and with her hands outstretched to either side, Raven Alby stood to her full height on the back of a flying dragon.

"Ha!" She wobbled a little as she adjusted to the different way the wind buffeted against her, from head to toe now. After a moment, she steadied her footing and released another joyous laugh. "Yes! Whoo!"

Leander responded with a piercing screech. Raven startled and leaned forward to correct her balance. Her left foot slipped off the saddle, and she somehow thumped down where she'd been seated. She jerked her right foot down again to squeeze his back between her thighs but kept her hands away from the saddle horn or the reins.

"Woah." Despite how fast her heart hammered in her chest, the mage in training could only grin. *My foot slipped off the saddle, not his back. There's more traction with dragon scales than a piece of leather worn smooth over the last fifty years.*

"That was it," Leander added and glanced at her with wide yellow eyes. "It's a start."

"You're telling me!" Shaking her head, Raven caught her breath and leaned to pat his neck again. "We'll get there."

She straightened, spread her arms again, and let her dragon familiar fly wherever he wanted to. *We have all the time in the world today.*

They flew for a few hours before he returned to the stables and his pen. The minute she leapt off his back and had the saddle unbuckled beneath his belly, the dragon all but barreled toward the gate.

"Wow. I didn't think I'd ever see you so excited about getting into a pen."

"I'm hungry now."

"Oh, okay." Laughing, she opened the gate with her rune and barely had it pushed all the way before he raced inside and headed to the trough. "I'll go get you some more. Are you good in here?"

His only reply came in the form of munching away at the dragon feed, his tail resting on the grass.

"I'll take that as a yes." Raven closed the gate again and took her grandfather's old dragon saddle back into the stables to stow it with the other tack. When she returned with another full bag of feed, the trough was empty and the dragon hovered over it, waiting impatiently. "It looks like you needed that ride as much as I did."

He snorted and barely waited for her to dump the feed in before he was at it again. He stamped a few times as he ate and his back legs shuffled from side to side in eagerness.

She sat with her back against the wall of the pen and watched him eat. *I stood on a flying dragon. Whatever else happens today can't make a dent in that feeling.*

It took him about ten minutes to fully empty the trough, but he spent another minute sniffing for more until he was convinced he'd eaten everything. With a long, satisfied rumble, he turned away and spun in a few tight circles before he lowered onto the grass, tipped over onto his side and wiggled a little, and belched.

"Is there anything that would make you happier than this right now?"

"No pen. A fresh carcass in my belly instead of carcass-flavored kibble."

Raven laughed. "Have you ever eaten a live animal?"

"Once. I pretend that's what I'm eating at every meal." Leander's hind legs stretched in the grass and his claws twitched open and closed again in contentment.

"Huh. Whatever gets you through the day, right?"

"For the time being, I'd say I'm relatively happy."

She took that opportunity to cross the pen toward him and squatted in front of his great head that rested upside down in the sun. The underside of his chin twitched when she scratched it. "That was incredible, by the way. Thanks for the ride."

"Thank you for not falling off in complete silence."

"Well, you can keep thanking me for that, Leander. I don't plan to ever let that happen. And I know you don't, either."

One large yellow eye opened to regard her with silent approval.

"I'm gonna go try to get ready for this dance, I think. I'll come to say goodnight after it's over. I probably won't even be out there for the whole thing, only long enough to make an appearance and have dinner, I think."

"If Mr. Cool gives you any trouble, you know where to find me."

She laughed and pushed to her feet. "Yes, I do. So does he. I can handle it."

When his eye closed again, she took it as her cue to leave. "Enjoy the sun. It looks like nap time."

The dragon said nothing and didn't move again. She closed the gate firmly behind her and headed across the field, most of her previous anxiety effectively pushed aside.

CHAPTER THIRTY-FOUR

After she snagged a few pieces of fruit left from lunch in the common room, Raven went to her dorm room on the third floor. Elizabeth once again sat on her bed with her legs crossed and her head lowered over another book in her lap. "Did you have a nice flight?"

"Yeah, actually." *She has no idea.* She paused once she'd shut the door and regarded the girl curiously. "I didn't tell you I was going out for a ride."

"Nope. But we have a decent view of the landing strip." Her roommate gestured toward the window without looking up from her reading. "You were gone so long, I almost thought you weren't coming back."

"No, I have to come back. I want to." She crossed the room toward the dresser beside her desk and opened the drawers to dig around in her clothes. "Although staying out on the back of a dragon long enough to miss this dance completely sounds like a good excuse. Why didn't I think of that?"

"For some reason, I have the impression that you're not

excited for the gala." Elizabeth clapped her book shut with both hands and waited for her to turn again before she smirked.

"Thank you, Mistress of the Obvious." Raven gave her an exaggerated little bow and they both laughed. "It's not that I'm not excited for the gala specifically. I kinda sorta told Daniel Smith that I'd be his date."

Elizabeth coughed and tossed her bangs out of her eyes. They fell back almost immediately. "That was weird. I thought I heard you say Daniel Smith is your date tonight."

"There's nothing wrong with your hearing." She wrinkled her nose. "It was a reaction. He kept me between a bag of feed and a ravenous dragon and I simply said, 'Okay. Now leave me alone.'"

With a little snort, the girl shook her head. "That can be interpreted in so many ways."

"You know what I mean." She turned to the drawers again and tossed her clothes aside in each one. "This is basically a joke. I don't have anything to wear. Seriously, who grows up on a goat ranch with their grandfather and has a wardrobe of formal clothes from which to choose for a surprise party?"

"Oh, I don't know. Maybe the same person who has a dragon familiar. Who she goes flying with for hours at a time." Elizabeth chuckled and tickled her bat familiar's belly. Iggy emitted a happy little squeak and rolled to sniff his mage's hand. "Or we could change it around a little and say that the mage in training who grew up on a goat ranch but rides dragons has the best roommate ever, and that's how she gets something to wear to Fowler Academy's spring gala."

The way the other girl rolled her eyes and adopted Professor Gilliam's nasally voice of extreme etiquette made Raven burst out laughing. "That's really good."

"I do many impressions, actually."

"For real?"

Her roommate shrugged and bit her lip. "I'm proud of my Bixby. 'Now, students.'" She clapped sharply and straightened where she sat while her head wobbled in perfect mimicry. "'It is imperative that you understand the historical significance of the very underwear you keep tucked beneath your britches. With one wrong step, you might miss the restroom altogether.'"

"Wow." Raven tried to hold back another laugh and failed. "Do you spend time practicing those? Because that's dead-on. Other than the fact that she'd probably stammer uncontrollably if she heard anyone mention their underwear."

With a secretive smile, Elizabeth uncrossed her legs and slid off the bed. "I spent time practicing before you showed up and I got myself a roomie. I'm sure the other girls on this floor think I'm insane."

"Either that or they thought you were holding meetings in your room with all the professors." The thought made her laugh again.

The other girl shrugged, went to her dresser, and pulled out a few of her drawers. "They can think what they want. I don't give a damn as long as people leave me alone."

"Somehow, I'm friends with the girl who only wants to be left alone."

"Yeah, well, you don't butt into my business and you're

not trying to figure me out. Plus, you haven't said a word about how much I read, so. Respect."

"Fair enough."

"Oh, yeah. Here we go." Elizabeth turned to her and wiggled her eyebrows. "I found it."

"You were serious about letting me borrow something for tonight."

"No. I wanted to see the look on your face when you realized I let you down hardcore." She laughed and pointed at her roommate. "Yeah, that face. I'm kidding, by the way. Here." She withdrew a long, flowing piece of black fabric and let it tumble toward the floor.

"Wow. That's really pretty." With a grin, Raven stepped across the room and studied the full-length dress. "What are you gonna wear?"

"I dunno. Not this." Elizabeth made a face at the garment and handed it over. "My mom made me pack all kinds of things I knew I'd never need. I guess neither of us considered the fact that someone else might need to borrow something."

She took the dress and held it in front of her. "I don't think I've seen anything like this before. What's it made of?"

The girl shrugged again, returned to her bed, and crossed her legs beneath her again. "Something fancy."

With a snort, she nodded and laid the dress on her bed. "That's a good guess. Way fancier than anything I've put on. Ever."

"It'll look great with your hair. And you look like my size. If it doesn't work, toss it back in the drawer."

"Thanks, Elizabeth."

"No problem. I bet Daniel Smith will like it. Wait. Did you want him to like what you're wearing? 'Cause if not, we could definitely throw something else together that would make him run away screaming instead."

"Uh...I'm not sure that's what I'm going for. But I'll keep it in mind." Raven sat on the bed beside the dress and stared at it.

Elizabeth shrugged again and picked her book up without another word.

A few hours later, before the students were supposed to gather in the open area on the other side of the school's main buildings opposite the barn and stables, Raven glanced at herself in the borrowed dress and shook her head.

"Who am I kidding? I don't even know how to move in something like this. You can't...run in a dress." She hiked the flowing hem of the black dress up and took a long step forward to test how far she could extend her leg.

The other girl tossed her bangs out of her eyes and snickered. "Are you planning to run away screaming?"

"I don't know!" She released the dress again, twisted awkwardly to peer over her shoulder, and tried to look at the way it fell at the back. "I think I'm one of those people who end up having to run somewhere for something anyway. Okay, I get it. Dresses were invented to slow people down."

"Not all people." Laughing, the other girl slipped on her dark-purple jacket with draped sleeves, pulled the silk shirt down over the top of a long purple skirt, and shrugged. "I don't know. It kinda helps with the heat, right?"

"The heat of what?" Raven gave her roommate a playful

MARTHA CARR & MICHAEL ANDERLE

frown. "Yeah, it's been getting warmer but it's not the middle of summer."

"Dancing, Raven. You know. Moving around, limbs flailing, sweat flying, people knocking each other over."

"I don't think this is that kind of dance."

Elizabeth exaggerated a disappointed pout that made them both laugh. "Well, neither of us have to wear this for too long if we don't want to. I'll probably end up calling it a night after I stuff my face with party food."

Raven responded with a pert smile. "I like you more and more every day."

"Yeah, same here. Are you ready?" Her teammate scooped her bat familiar up and waited for him to hook his claws into the lapel of her purple jacket.

"Not really." She glanced at her boots where they peeked out beneath the hem of the fancy dress and chuckled. "Let's go."

As soon as she opened the door, it sounded like every girl in the school had gathered on the third floor of the girls' dormitory to head to the dance together. Raven winced against the noise, and Elizabeth scrunched her face. "That sound-dampening spell of yours is almost too good."

"I know. Jeez, look at this."

Girls hurried down the hallway as they fixed each other's hair, giggled, and squealed in excitement, while others ran down the stairs. The two girls exchanged a confused glance. Elizabeth patted her familiar and frowned at the mass exodus of girls in their finest formal attire.

"Okay, there's another reason I'm cool with you as my roommate," she muttered as Raven closed their door.

"Oh, yeah?"

"You don't squeal like that."

Raven laughed as they headed down the hall toward the stairs. "Not that you've heard."

"Yeah, nice try. I don't buy it."

"I wouldn't either."

When they reached the bottom of the stairs and the common room, the place was almost empty. Three girls stood in the corner. Two of them tried to console a third, who sobbed uncontrollably with her face buried in her hands. "Is she okay?" Raven asked.

"She's only a little nervous." One girl patted her friend's shoulder and nodded at Raven. "We got it covered. Thanks, though."

"Sure." She slowed to watch the distraught girl, but there was no sign that the sobbing would slow anytime soon. *I thought I was nervous. I feel like a pro compared to that.*

They left the girls, crossed the common room, and pulled the front door open to step out into the evening air. Raven took a deep breath and closed her eyes. "This helps."

"Uh…" Elizabeth nudged her shoulder and whispered, "Accidental date at ten o'clock."

"What?"

"Hey, Raven."

She looked up quickly and took a reactive step back when she realized that Daniel Smith stood almost directly in front of her. Her back bumped against the closed door into the dormitory, and she forced herself to smile. "Hi…" *He seriously doesn't understand what most people call personal space.*

"That's my cue. See you out there, Raven. Or not." Elizabeth shrugged and stepped around Daniel to stroll to the back of the main buildings and the gate leading to the event.

Daniel ignored the other girl completely and grinned at Raven. "You look great. That dress is…"

"Cool, right?"

He laughed and wrinkled his nose. "Yeah. How did you know I was gonna say that?"

"It was a lucky guess." *It is so hard to keep a straight face right now.*

"Well, anyway, I like it."

"Thanks. You look good too." When he glanced at the slightly darker version of what he wore virtually every day—plus a vest with a few shiny silver buttons—she clenched her eyes shut. *Try not to say anything stupid, Raven. That was strike one.*

"Do you think so?" He patted the vest and shrugged. "Naw. It's only something I threw together. I bet you spent a long time getting ready, huh?"

Telling him fifteen minutes would probably be strike two. She shrugged instead and hung onto her smile. "I guess."

"I can tell. So, Raven Alby. Do you care to join me for the gala?" He offered her his arm and straightened as if it was some kind of momentous occasion.

"I already…oh. You mean to walk out there together. Yep. I'm ready." She linked her arm through his and pretended to nod at some of the other students who wandered in the same direction so he wouldn't see her widen her eyes in disbelief. *If this is normal for being someone's date, I seriously suck at it.*

"Do you like dancing?"

When she looked at him, he'd leaned his head so close

to her face that she jerked back in surprise. A laugh escaped her as she gave him sidelong glances and waited for him to pull away a little. "Sure. One of the ranch hands who did seasonal work during the harvest when I was little used to bring a banjo. I did much more dancing back then."

Daniel grinned and his eyes crinkled at the corners. "That's cute."

"Thanks." She wrinkled her nose and finally had to laugh at herself. *Stop worrying about what you're supposed to do. It's not like you're the best at following the rules, whatever the rules for this are.* "What about you? Do you dance a lot?"

He shrugged and led her through the open gate onto the field the students rarely used. "Yeah, I got moves."

A sharp laugh escaped her, and he grinned even wider. "Good for you, Daniel."

"You think I'm kidding. Just wait. You'll see."

"Okay."

He shook his head and looked at the twinkling silver and green lights with spells cast to keep them floating in draped strands above the gala. Raven turned her head a little to look at his profile. *He's cute when he's not trying so hard to be cool. Maybe this won't be so bad.*

A few of the professors put the last finishing touches on the lights while Professor Worley lifted a hay bale onto the top of a stack and brushed his hands off. He pointed at the hay, muttered a spell, and every stacked bale flashed with a green light before it was completely covered in brightly colored flowers. On the other side of the particularly large dancefloor, someone started with a fiddle.

"What?" Raven leaned forward and tried to get a better

look at the man who struck up a lively tune. "Fellows plays the fiddle?"

"Right before he starts wielding that bow as a weapon." Daniel smirked. "It sounds good."

"It does. Is he gonna stand there and play all night?"

"Does it matter?" He lowered his head and smiled at her, his dimples stained green and silver from the lights that hovered above them.

"Probably not."

"What about food, then? I'm starving."

Okay, that's a sentiment I can relate to. "Sure. Food first, then dancing. It sounds like the perfect way to get a good stomach cramp."

"Not if you do it right. Come on." He nodded toward the long tables on the far side of the makeshift pavilion and guided her in that direction, her arm still hooked through his.

Raven didn't even notice the food at first. She was too busy smiling at all the first-year girls—and even a few second-years—who darted dreamy gazes at her date and less dreamy glares at her. One second-year leaned toward her friend and whispered something before they both looked at her boots beneath her borrowed dress.

"Yeah, but let's see you try to run in heels," she muttered.

"What?" Daniel's smile looked a little clueless.

"Nothing. Only a bunch of nothing." *Not like getting stared at or whispered about is anything new, anyway.*

They reached the banquet tables, and her mouth dropped open. "Wow. This is insane."

"Right? They pull out all the stops for these galas. Hell,

I'd move into the dorm to eat like this every day, but I hear the grub isn't nearly as good."

"It's not bad but it's definitely not this."

He handed her a thin tin plate and gestured for her to go ahead of him.

She eyed the fruit and too many pastries to count, sliced ham, four different blocks of crumbling cheese, what looked like either a chicken or a duck covered in sauce with more fruit, plates piled high with tiny bite-sized desserts, and huge glass bowls of a drink that smelled strongly of strawberries. She chose only a few things and had barely covered half her plate by the time she reached the end.

"They have chocolate." She stretched to take one of the intricately decorated pieces of fudge with a few zigzag lines of green frosting along the top.

"Wait, wait. Don't take one of those." Daniel hurried toward her at the end of the tables, shaking his head. "Everything else is safe. Not the green squiggly lines."

"And why's that, exactly?"

"One of the guys ate a whole plateful of these last year, and Fellows had to literally wrap his arms around this kid to get him to stop dancing."

Raven laughed. "That doesn't make sense. It's a dance."

"Yeah, this happened two hours after it ended, though." He chuckled and nodded toward the off-limits deserts. "I don't know what's in there or how much you have to eat to get to that level of dance-off, but I stay away from them completely."

"That's good to know. Thanks for the warning." *And who's spiking the fudge?* Shaking her head, she selected other tiny deserts with less chocolate and more strawberry flavor.

"Hey, Alby! Get a load of this, huh?" Henry almost ran down the other side of the table, shoved an entire slice of ham into his mouth, and gestured enthusiastically. "P'uddy fantashtic, uh?"

"You know, Derks, I'm surprised there's anything left, honestly. Did you get held up?"

He gulped his huge mouthful and flashed her a crooked smile. "Something like that. I was waiting for Jenny." He nodded across the dancefloor, then muttered, "No, Raven, don't turn and look."

"You did ask her to be your date." With a grin, she turned anyway and waved. Jenny gave her a self-conscious smile and waved in return. "No tutoring tonight, though, huh?"

"Whatever. Hey, nice dress. I don't think I've ever seen you wear one."

"Well, thanks. It's not mine but I guess it works."

"I like it," Daniel added and leaned way too close for comfort once again.

Henry squinted at her date, who hadn't even acknowledged him across the table. "Uh-huh. Oh, hey! These look great." Before Raven could share the warning, Henry snatched a tiny square of chocolate with green zigzag frosting and popped it into his mouth. "Oh, yeah. It's on, now. Have fun, Alby!"

"Wait, Henry—"

But he'd already snagged two more of the allegedly spiked chocolates before he darted away from the banquet table. He gave Raven a goofy salute, smiled around a mouthful of fudge, and returned to Jenny.

"Great. This is gonna be an interesting night." She brushed a few stray hairs out of her eyes and picked at a few strawberries she'd put on her plate.

Daniel stepped closer. His hand settled gently on the small of her back and made her freeze. "It's gonna be amazing. You'll see."

CHAPTER THIRTY-FIVE

R aven nibbled as much as she could of her food before she set the tin plate in the wooden crate at the end of the table. Daniel wiped his mouth with the back of his hand and grinned. "It was seriously good stuff, that. I wish they threw more galas."

"That's not the right word for it, though, is it?" Raven wrinkled her nose and studied the lights, the flower-covered hay bales, and the dancefloor. "It's more like a barn party or something."

"Yeah. Without the barn." Daniel laughed and lurched forward like he thought he was hilarious.

He doesn't have the best sense of humor but at least he's trying. Raven laughed with him, more out of sympathy than anything else.

A second later, Professor Fellows' single fiddle was joined by four other string instruments and some kind of weird drum that looked like another crate. The next song started with an incredibly loud opening, and Raven jumped before she spun to stare at the one-man band that had suddenly become six musicians. "Who is that?"

Her date laughed and pulled her away from the banquet table toward the dancefloor. "I think they pay other people to be Fellows' backup."

"They appeared out of nowhere!"

"You know, Raven, for a girl who rides dragons, you're much jumpier than I expected."

She looked at him and his consistently winning smile as they moved between a few other students who paired off into dancing couples. "That's because I know exactly what to expect from my dragon. Which doesn't include an insta-band." *We'll skip over the part where I didn't know how to interact with a dragon in the first place, let alone train him.*

"Still." He caught her hand and twirled her on the dancefloor. The black dress fanned around her despite the current song not being conducive to much twirling at all. "I bet being out here for this dance doesn't even make it on the list of cool things Raven Alby does."

Cool, cool, cool—stop it. "I don't know about that. But yes, training and riding a dragon is way cooler than a school dance."

"You know, I'm not even a little offended by that."

Raven laughed. "It's good that I wasn't trying to offend you, then."

"Yeah, I appreciate it." They began to dance a little to the upbeat tempo of Professor Fellow's impromptu band, although she hadn't entirely loosened up yet. A moment or two later, Daniel slipped his arm around her lower back and pulled her closer. She leaned away on instinct but looked up to meet his gaze. "I think everything you do is amazing, Raven. Have I told you that yet?"

She startled and tried to look across the dancefloor but couldn't quite pull it off. "Uh…maybe in not so many words." *Is he being serious or trying to butter me up?* "But thanks, either way."

"I'm serious. I don't know…I'm not normally at a loss for something to say. Not around girls. But…well, your dragon almost ate me the other day, and hoping you know how much I like you is still a hell of a lot scarier than a dragon calling me a walking bag of hormones."

The laughter escaped before she could stop it and she covered her eyes with her hand. "He did call you that."

"It was a fairly witty insult, if you take out all the threats and how close he came to knocking that pen down."

"He didn't come close. Trust me, his bark's much worse than his bite."

"He barks too?" His eyebrows raised quickly and his mouth dropped open a little.

He has to be the most gullible person in Brighton. "No, Daniel. My dragon doesn't bark."

"Whew. Okay. I thought my brain was about to explode."

Raven laughed and tried not to look too surprised by his reaction. *He's smart enough and skilled enough to make it to Fowler Academy. I guess the testing for common sense isn't nearly as strict.* They continued to dance as more students moved through their own awkward phases of navigating a gala and a date. Daniel bit his bottom lip and did a weird little shimmy with hips and shoulders. *We're all trying to make it, right?*

She caught sight of Henry and Jenny on the other side of the dancefloor. He jumped around like some kind of monkey and occasionally spun in tight circles, and Jenny merely laughed. Murphy danced with a boy whose name Raven couldn't remember. The girl looked a little put out and turned to look at Henry before she tried to convince her dance partner that she paid attention to only him.

Beside one of the stacks of flower-encrusted hay bales, Elizabeth stood alone. Her dark bangs swooped over one eye, and her dancing only extended to bobbing her head to the music while she watched everyone else.

Daniel spun her in a tight circle again and made her laugh. *Maybe this whole school dance thing isn't so bad after all.*

The second she thought it, a loud, piercing screech shattered the night. A few students jumped, some of the professors ducked, and Professor Fellows' band wavered in the middle of their song before they resumed playing.

Raven yanked herself out of Daniel's arms and turned toward the school's main buildings and the stables on the other side. "Leander…"

"Is everything okay?" He frowned and touched her elbow gently.

"I don't know. I—"

Another screech made her tense again and someone shouted, "You'd better see what your dragon wants, Alby!"

A few people laughed but most of them simply stared at her as she raised a hand between her and Daniel and shook her head. "I'm sorry. I have to see what's going on."

"Sure. Yeah. I'll be here when you get back."

"Okay. Thanks." She turned and raced across the dancefloor.

Students moved out of her way even before she reached them, and once she pushed through the crowd at the spring gala, she hiked the bottom of Elizabeth's dress up and fled around the back of the school's buildings toward the barn and stables on the other side.

Leander's shrieks and growls continued and grew louder and more frequent the closer she got to his pen. Before she had even reached the barn, the dragon began to pound against the metal walls, clawed at the dirt and grass, and thumped his tail against whatever stood in its way.

He's gonna break the pen or seriously hurt himself. Or both.

"Leander!" she shouted. "Hey, it's okay. I'm coming!"

A low growl came in response before it rose to another furious roar. She whirled to scan the open fields and the tree line at the edge of the school grounds. *There are no vagreti panthers and no terrified animals in the stables. What's going on?*

Raven skidded to a stop in front of the gate and flashed the rune on her forearm against the gate's magic before the lock clicked and the gate opened. "I'm here. I heard you. Leander, I'm here."

The great red dragon snorted and shook his massive head as his wings flicked out and curled in again in agitation, over and over. When she slipped through the gate, she froze. The grass was all but ripped from the earth and large trenches had been dug into the ground with the way he'd pawed at it. Both the trough and the basin of water were overturned. Somehow, he had even lashed out at the few feet of the stables' roof that extended over that side of the pen. Pieces of shattered wood were scattered on the ground, and the end of the roof itself was damaged in the middle and the rest of it bent at a violent angle.

Leander raised his head and screeched again before he drove his tail against the metal wall beside him. Raven surged into action and stepped toward him, both arms outstretched. "Hey, it's okay. Woah, woah, woah. Everything's all right, Leander. Take a breath."

Snorting again, he swiveled his head toward her on his long neck, his yellow eyes huge with fear and concern. He paced against the far wall of the pen, and Raven moved quickly.

"Come here. It's okay."

His head reared away when she approached him but he stopped pacing. The scales at the top of his chest and shoulder quivered when she touched them, his wings still outstretched. Finally, a low rumble rose in his throat and he settled. A forepaw stamped the upturned earth twice more, then he turned away from her and snorted a hot burst of steam and a little smoke into the night sky.

"There you go. See? Everything's okay—"

"Everything is not okay, Raven." The dragon's next rumble sounded much more like a warning growl. "Something's very wrong. I felt you, and then I felt...wrongness."

Well, yeah, I was nervous about the dance, too. That went away quickly though. "Wrongness from me? Because I'm having a good time tonight, Leander. I promise. It's a little weird, but I'm safe. I didn't mean to worry to you."

"I'm not talking about you."

Shit. I should've made a Plan B. "Okay. Can you tell me any more than simply 'wrongness?' I want to help you find this...whatever's going on. Let's talk it through—"

"Someone's coming." Leander raised his head again and his forelegs lifted off the ground a little as he tried to see over the wall of the pen.

Raven heard the pounding of hooves galloping down the road toward the school. She patted his shoulder again and nodded. "I'll be right back. I'll go see who it is."

He snorted but didn't try to stop her.

She slipped through the gate again and left it cracked slightly to save time.

"I have a message for Headmaster Flynn!" The shout came from the front of the school. "I need to speak to the headmaster!"

No one can hear him over all the music and dancing.

"Hey!" Raven waved her arms and darted across the field. With a grunt of frustration, she hiked up the bottom of her dress again in one hand and waved with the other. "Over here!"

The small form of the rider atop the horse turned toward her, then he dug his heels into his mount's sides and raced across the grass. They met halfway across the field, and she caught her breath as the horse reared and she saw the rider.

"It's you." She looked at the hostler boy she'd met in Brighton the day after orientation. "Quinn, right?"

"Yeah, hey." The boy ran a hand through his hair and dropped the reins from one hand to give his horse's neck a reassuring pat. "Raven Alby."

"You have a good memory. I see you don't have any water to throw on me this time." Her smile faded when he glanced across the field with a worried frown.

"Not tonight. I came with a message, Raven." His horse

stamped a few times, and he reined the animal in and glanced quickly at the empty courtyard of Fowler Academy. "Jamie MacMillan sent me to warn the school. There's trouble at the wall."

"What? What kind of trouble?"

Quinn shook his head. "Just trouble. I don't know anything else. Where is everyone?"

"Behind the school on the other side. I'll get Headmaster Flynn. He'll want to hear it from you."

Behind her, Leander uttered another piercing screech. Quinn's horse snorted and backed away a few steps, but the boy had enough control of his mount to stop it. He leaned down and offered Raven his hand. "This is faster."

"Yep." She hiked the long dress up again as he slipped his foot out of the stirrup. Her boot slid into it instead, and he hauled her up as she swung her other leg over the horse to sit behind him in the saddle.

The boy clicked his tongue and turned the horse toward the back of the school. They surged into a gallop across the grass and veered around the buildings until they reached the other side and the lights, music, and laughter of the spring gala.

"Stop right here," Raven said and slid out of the saddle again when he complied. She nodded toward the dance as Quinn looked with wide eyes from her to the party. "I'll be right back. He'll want to talk to you and I think that should be private."

"Yeah, okay." He swallowed and remained where she left him with the horse.

She scanned the faces on and around the dancefloor. Fortunately, Headmaster Flynn stood on this side of the gathering beside a stack of flowering hay bales, talking to Professor Worley and grinning with a drink in his hand. She hurried toward him, the long black dress bunched in both hands.

"Excuse me, Headmaster Flynn?"

He turned toward her and Professor Worley stepped back so she could join them. Both men grinned at her, but their cheerful expressions vanished quickly. "What is it, Miss Alby?"

"A messenger came from the wall." She turned partially to nod at the nervous-looking Quinn. "He's looking for you and said something about trouble at the wall."

The headmaster set his cup down on the hay bale and strode swiftly toward the messenger. He reached Quinn in seconds. Professor Worley and Raven watched them as the rest of the students and staff at Fowler Academy danced and enjoyed themselves, completely oblivious.

"Do you know what's happening, Raven?" Worley muttered and leaned toward her while his gaze remained focused on the headmaster.

"Quinn didn't tell me anything else. I only know we can't ignore it." She looked at him and frowned. "Leander felt it too. Something's wrong."

Flynn nodded at Quinn. "Thank you, young man. I suggest you head back now. We'll need a messenger with a clear head and a swift horse if anything else comes up."

"Headmaster." The boy darted another hasty glance at Raven before he turned his mount and pushed it into a run toward the road to Brighton's town center.

The headmaster moved briskly toward Raven and Professor Worley, his normally calm features contorted in a grim frown. "Miss Alby, I appreciate your foresight in bringing the rider to my attention and not the entire school's."

"What now?"

"We wait and hope we're prepared for whatever trouble arises." He cast her a sideways glance and said nothing else.

Another earsplitting screech erupted from Leander across the field, and Raven turned. "Whatever it is, I don't know if Leander can wait. He feels it too. Shouldn't we do something? Send someone out to look or at least—"

"No, Miss Alby. If we hear word again of some other—"

The dragon's next warning shriek ended in a thunderous roar. The musicians playing with Professor Fellows wavered a little at the sound but managed to pick their rhythm up again.

"I have to go to him, Headmaster. If he knows something else, anything...he needs me." She didn't wait for an answer but raced toward the pen, the dress hitched unglamorously once again. *It's definitely not made for running.*

"Raven, wait!" Headmaster Flynn lurched after her and moved swiftly around the back of the school.

She ignored him. *Leander's all that matters. If he doesn't calm soon, we might have a bigger problem.* She had reached the far end of the school's buildings when a massive, earth-shattering crack hurt her ears. Two more of the same followed quickly and echoed into an ominous rumble. She stopped in surprise and glanced at the ground, which trembled beneath her feet.

The music cut off abruptly. All the laughter and conversation and dancing froze, and the silence made the last massive crack and rumble in the distance even louder.

Leander roared and thumped against the pen. *Someone has to find out what's going on.*

Raven jerked the dagger from her boot and sliced a long slit in the side of Elizabeth's fancy black dress. She stowed the blade and sprinted across the field.

"Raven Alby!" Headmaster Flynn continued his approach, his eyes wide. He slowed on the grass and shook his head. *She's not wrong. I would have done the same if it were Asher in that pen.* "Use your head, girl," he muttered and stared at the young mage who raced across the grass while the ripped dress whipped around her legs.

CHAPTER THIRTY-SIX

Raven pushed herself as fast as she could go toward Leander's enclosure. The dragon uttered another shrill, screeching cry.

"Leander!"

The unlocked gate burst open when he shoved it aside with his head and the red dragon stormed out of the pen and into the field. His wings stretched wide as he turned and headed toward her.

When they reached each other, he turned and lowered himself to the ground enough for her to leap onto the thickest part of his tail. Her boots held steady against his scales like she knew they would, and she ran up her dragon's back to the place at the base of his neck. His wings cut through the air as she sat astride, squeezed with her thighs, and leaned forward against him as he launched them skyward.

"The wall!" she shouted, her chest heaving from the run and the wind that caught her throat.

"I know."

That was all they had to say before Leander turned to the south and the source of the awful sound they'd heard all the way out there on the school grounds. They flew directly over Brighton now without care for who saw the young mage and her dragon familiar overhead. As they soared over fields and ranches, she leaned down to get a better look at the Alby ranch on their right. Something about her grandfather's house felt off. *I can't tell what it is from up here.*

As if reading her mind, the dragon descended and made another sweep, close enough for the moonlight to offer some illumination. She squinted at her home and finally saw the thin lines of upturned dirt that snaked across the field, stopped at her cabin, and turned toward the wall again. *This is bad.*

Leander pumped his wings faster, climbing high to get a better view.

"There it is," Raven shouted and pointed at the high stone wall that encompassed the entire kingdom to keep them safe. "Oh, no…"

A huge hole gaped in the barrier from the ground to the top and massive chunks of stone and rubble spilled into the kingdom like a trail. *Whatever broke through came from the other side.*

Leander banked and turned left, following the angle of the fallen rubble.

Where are the guards?

The earth rumbled as mage and dragon wheeled in a wide arc. "Leander, do you see anything?"

"The ground is moving."

"What?" She leaned down on his other side and saw it.

Thick trails of earth were dislodged by an unseen force that moved directly below the surface at an incredible speed. *That has to be the Swarm. Nothing else moves like that. We need to get ahead of it.*

Feeling her intention, Leander stretched his neck and sliced forward to gain speed against the upturned ruts that sliced across fields, past stables and barns, and moved around houses. "They aren't stopping. Grandpa said the Swarm acts on mindless hunger. This isn't...why are they avoiding everything?"

They headed toward Brighton's town center again while the trails pushed forward below them. A bell tolled at the center of town, followed by shouts to raise the alarm and the clash of armor and weapons being drawn. The soldiers looked incredibly small from where Leander and Raven glided across the town, but they gathered quickly and efficiently at the south end of town where the road snaked toward the outer ranches and the breach in the wall beyond.

They don't know.

Raven glanced over her shoulder when they passed Brighton, and Leander responded perfectly. He banked sharply to the left and brought them down toward the fountain in the center of town. Shouts of alarm and fear greeted them as he descended gently and beat his powerful wings to keep them off the ground. Dust, grass, and leaves kicked up along the cobblestones, but the soldiers stood their ground and stared at the dragon and his rider.

"They already broke through the wall!" Raven shouted and pointed in the other direction. In that moment, she knew where the Swarm was headed. "We passed over them. The Swarm is on the way to the school. Fowler Academy!"

A decorated general with bushy gray eyebrows stepped forward from the ranks of wide-eyed soldiers. "That's a big claim to make, girl."

"Maybe from someone else." Raven clenched her fists. *They have to believe me.* "But I'm a mage on a dragon making this claim, and I saw them myself. The Swarm's back, they're headed to the school, and we'll need all the help we can get. This is what Brighton's best have trained for, right?"

The general narrowed his eyes. "Does Headmaster Flynn know?"

"He will as soon as we get back." None of the soldiers moved, and the general stared at her. Leander uttered a low growl, which startled Brighton's military into action. "Trust me. We need your help. And if this isn't enough to convince you, think about what'll happen if you don't come. This is happening now!"

Without waiting for a reply to her challenge, the dragon turned swiftly and launched skyward. The general yelled orders she couldn't hear over the wind that rushed past her face. *I wish we had more time to explain. Here's hoping Brighton's army really is ready for anything.*

They hurtled through the sky again and soon caught up with the dark streaks that plowed across the earth toward Fowler Academy. Leander descended a little lower and sniffed the air.

The earth beneath them erupted in a spray of dirt, pebbles, and grass only a few yards in front of them. It churned into a swirling whirlpool and from its center shot two thick, undulating tentacles with deadly pincers that snapped together at the ends. Two more dark appendages sprouted from the ruptured soil, and the earth bucked as something dark-green and nightmarish pushed itself from below.

A Skiffling.

There wasn't enough time to think, but neither of them needed it. Leander unleashed a massive ball of flame as they rushed toward one of the Swarm's eyeless, mindless monsters.

"*Sequantur flamma!*" Raven extended both hands and felt her spell tug on the dragon's fire. She jerked it down and launched the flaming fireball the size of her grandfather's cabin into the churning earth and the flailing tendrils. One whipped toward the dragon before the creature ignited with an agonized screech.

Leander darted sideways and turned ninety degrees to avoid the snapping pincers. She cried out and squeezed her thighs against his back with so much force that they shook as she flattened herself against the back of his neck. When they leveled off, she turned to look over her shoulder at the burning, flipping tentacles that gradually lost their strength before they flopped motionless for everyone who came after to see.

If that doesn't convince them, nothing will.

The red dragon's wings cut through the sky as he pushed himself to go faster. The other thick trails of tunneling Swarm nightmares swerved around the flaming Skiffling but didn't stop or slow down. More earth exploded behind them in a wide arc, and from the massive hole in the ground, hundreds of giant, glistening Swarm beetles surged to the surface. Their clicks and squeaks as they scuttled away from the piles of upturned soil sent a shiver down her spine.

We have to warn the school.

The cold, whipping air made it almost impossible to catch her breath when her dragon rocketed forward with a renewed burst of speed. She blinked more tears away and stared in awe as the ground rushed past them. "Is this as fast as you can go?"

"Almost. I think." His words were hard to hear and she tucked her face against her shoulder to take another breath.

The headlong flight took them over the countryside and finally, the grounds of Fowler Academy. Headmaster Flynn stood in the center of the field in front of the barn with Professors Worley, Fellows, Gilliam, and Dameron. The dragon pulled up, beat his wings quickly to stop short, and lowered quickly to the ground.

"My word," Professor Gilliam muttered.

Headmaster Flynn stared pointedly at the lack of saddle and harness on the red dragon's back, his lips pressed firmly together. "What did you see?"

"It's the Swarm." Raven leapt from Leander's back before he'd completely lowered himself. He straightened and stepped away from the professors with a snort. "We saw them, Headmaster. They broke through the wall and ignored everything else. And they're headed directly toward the school."

"Impossible!" Dameron shouted, shook his fists, and glared at Leander. "The Swarm is gone. Eradicated. The Great War ended such a vile mass of—"

"Thank you, Professor Dameron." Flynn's voice cracked sharply to silence the man. "Miss Alby, I need you to tell me exactly what you saw."

"We don't have time for that, Headmaster—"

"We have time to get it right." He nodded firmly at her. "What did you see?"

"A hole in the wall and moving streaks under the ground—like drawing a line in the dirt but from below instead. But they're above ground now. A Skiffling with all the tentacles. Green...arms, I think."

"A barbequed Skiffling, now," Leander added and stamped a little behind her as he lowered his head.

The professors stared at him.

"And hundreds of beetles. They're awful." Raven grimaced quickly and shook her head. "Each of them was the size of a horse. And they're coming here, I'm telling you."

"Why would they do that? Even if the Swarm did still exist in part, they have no way to tell a ranch from a magical school." Professor Dameron shook his head. "These are fantasies. You spend too much time with your head in the clouds, Miss Alby."

"Brighton's army doesn't seem to think so." Her nostrils flared and she turned to Headmaster Flynn. "They rang the alarm bell and are headed this way right now. They know what's coming." *I hope.*

"Headmaster?" Professor Fellows turned toward Flynn and raised his chin. "It's your call."

"You can't seriously be considering this," Dameron retorted acidly.

Leander snorted and raked the ground with a forepaw.

"You'll consider your own death soon enough if you don't. I know that smell beneath the earth."

Raven turned toward him and frowned. "What?"

"The same as that tiny skull you carried in that bag." The dragon's wings twitched outward and in the distance, a sound rose like thousands of horses and crumbling stone and the clack of hard, shimmering carapaces.

Headmaster Flynn's eyes widened, and he turned toward Professor Gilliam with surprising calm. "Eleanor, call the gala off. Take the students to the main hall and wait for my instructions. Tell any other professor you see that those who wish to fight—for the first time or again—should join me in the barn."

"Aiden, have you lost your mind?" Dameron shouted.

"Quickly," Flynn told her again. She nodded and hurried toward the dance on the other side of the school.

"You plan to fight a threat that doesn't even exist and you're sowing panic for no reason!" The man turned on the headmaster, spittle flying from his mouth. "I'll have no part of this. That child has a taste for being the center of attention, and I will not enable her outrageous fantasies."

"Miss Alby is a mage," the headmaster said coolly. "And a dragon rider. I fought beside more than one person in her family, Dameron. Both Raven and her familiar have my complete trust. Now, if you will not take a stand with us here, feel free to wait the threat out with the other young people in the main hall." The headmaster turned away from the bald, fuming professor and nodded at Raven. "You've done this kingdom and this school an incredible service, Raven. Both of you. I can't tell you to lock that dragon away knowing full well what's knocking at our gates. But I want you to join the other students with Professor Gilliam."

Raven shook her head and stepped forward. "Headmaster, we can help. We destroyed one of those Skifflings already—"

"It's too dangerous. I'm not in the habit of allowing my students to endanger themselves, no matter how far-reaching their abilities are. My job is to keep you safe."

"Leander and I can fight!"

"Now, Miss Alby!" He strode away from her and headed toward the barn. The other professors gave her grim looks before they followed the headmaster.

I can't sit back and let them fight the Swarm when I know we can help.

"Go on." Professor Worley nodded at her, then glanced at Leander. "We'll handle this, Raven."

"I can handle it."

"You heard Headmaster Flynn. Our job is to make sure you're safe. Go on." He turned and followed the others into the barn and even a grumbling, sputtering Professor Dameron trailed after them. The door closed with a bang.

She stared at the structures. The noises from the other side of the grounds and the spring gala had stopped and were now replaced by the shouts of professors who ushered students into the main building of the school. Louder than that were the confused and curious voices of her peers.

Her mind made up, she turned toward Leander and shook her head. "I won't go to the main hall."

"I know."

The cacophony of the Swarm's approach grew steadily

louder. Her heart pounded in her chest. "Can you make a little noise while we go past your pen? I won't lock you in there, but—"

"They'll never know the difference." he turned and shambled toward his enclosure, his wings twitching out as he snorted and made a show of being led to where everyone else thought he belonged.

Maybe he can't read my mind but he sure does come close.

Raven exhaled slowly and hurried to his side. When they reached it, he smacked his tail against the outside and snorted. He caught her gaze with yellow eyes and lowered his head. "I don't like this."

I never thought I'd stage a conversation with a dragon.

"I don't either. But this is how we all stay safe, right? Headmaster Flynn knows how to fight the Swarm. And Brighton's army should be here any minute. Just…don't worry about breaking out of the pen if the fighting gets too close. I'll find you."

A soft hiss escaped her dragon, which he cut off abruptly as he stood beside her. Raven shut the gate a little harder than she had to and paused. *I gotta make it sound real.*

Without delay, she stormed from the pen and toward the school's main buildings. Leander uttered another wailing screech behind her. She turned to glance over her shoulder and fought a smile as he snorted and thumped the outer wall with his tail again. As soon as she saw him tuck his wings and stalk around the other side of the pen in complete silence, she broke into a run. *Now, I have to be as quiet as a dragon to pull this off.*

CHAPTER THIRTY-SEVEN

R aven stopped less than halfway across the field, doubled back, and followed the tree line of the forest to avoid being seen or heard by the professors gathered in the barn. A bright, steady light spilled onto the grass between the wooden slats, and the professors' voices were muted but still audible in the quiet.

"If the army's really on their way, we have to face this."

"Without war mages? Without dragon riders? It's impossible."

"We have to try. And we're not alone."

Progress was a little slower than she wanted as she had to take care to stay out of the light, but she finally darted past the last few trees and reached the other side of the stables. Leander crouched in front of her, perfectly still as he listened intently.

"They're almost here," he whispered and nudged his snout against her ear.

"I know. Flynn will forget about us disobeying him when they see what you can do. I hope."

"What he forgets means nothing."

"Shh. Who's that?"

Two dark forms stalked toward the barn and muttered in low voices. She couldn't see the professors' faces in the darkness between the narrow slats, and the barn door was on the other side. A shout and the sound of horses' hooves from the road distracted her for a moment.

The barn door banged open, and Headmaster Flynn strode toward the general and his army of Brighton's finest where they marched across the grounds. "The Swarm," the general shouted. "Be ready to fight, Headmaster. I'm sorry either of us has to live through this a second time."

"So am I, General Merson. So am I."

Horses, soldiers, and weapons flashing under the moonlight spread across the field beside the front gates of Fowler Academy. "This is where we'll take a stand! Be ready, soldiers. This is your duty."

The rumbling of the Swarm grew louder and made the horses whinny and snort in unease. A screech split the air, echoed by a second. Leander crouched lower beside her and they both looked up at two dragons that wheeled across the sky.

He growled. "Those dragons have no idea what they're doing."

"That's all they brought," Raven whispered. "Two dragons and Brighton's army. And a group of mages with more practice teaching than fighting."

The air filled with the scuttling rumble of too many sharp, insectoid legs on a destructive path toward the school. The ground moved in the distance and flashed here and then under the moonlight. Raven's mouth dropped open. *Not the ground. It's the Razorbacks.*

Headmaster Flynn clapped his hands together and dragged them apart to create a shimmering wall of bright light between his palms. "Hold, mages!"

The other professors beside him readied their spells as the massive black beetles scurried toward them and the earth trembled. One of the dragons swooped over the first line of beetles and unleashed a column of fire. Most of it missed completely, but a few giant beetles screeched shrilly and flailed as they were consumed quickly by the flames.

"And dragons that can't aim." Raven clenched her fists and stood from her crouch behind the end of the stables. "They need us—"

"Stop."

She was jerked back when a hand clutched the back of her dress. "What—" She spun furiously. "Bella! What are you doing here?"

Bella Chase offered her a small, determined smile and shrugged. Behind her, the firedrake darted through the air. "I couldn't let you have all the fun in a fight neither of us was invited to."

The soldiers beside the mages bellowed a resounding battle cry in hundreds of voices and in a moment, the Swarm had reached them. The massive black creatures with spikes along their shells scuttled blindly into swords, shields, and spells. The dragons overhead shrieked and unleashed more flames. Soldiers shouted and yelled while Headmaster Flynn called commands to anyone who would listen.

Raven shook her head and stood. "Leander, let's go."

"Raven, you can't go out there."

"Yes, I can. They need all the help they can get and there's hardly anyone here to fight."

Both girls flinched and crouched when the ground erupted somewhere in the battle and sprayed earth and stones everywhere. A handful of soldiers screamed before the cries were cut off. "We're wasting time!"

"I came to help you, Raven. Look!" Bella fumbled with a drawstring bag tied at her hip and her fingers working feverishly to get it open.

She stared at the shrunken Skiffling skull inside. "How did you get that?"

"I snuck into Flynn's office and took it." Bella scoffed. "It seems fairly obvious to me."

"How is that supposed to help us, huh? Throw it at the Swarm and hope it hurts?"

"No. Just listen." Bella set the skull on the ground and muttered, *"Invorto adtenuum."* It grew instantly to its natural size and a gurgling, hissing wail that could only belong to one of the Swarm issued from somewhere far beyond the first line of combat.

Leander snorted and stepped away from the skull. "They feel it."

"What?"

More screams rose from the fighting soldiers.

"Oh, wait!" Raven stared at the girl. "History of Magic."

The other girl nodded grimly and pointed at the skull. "Magical lineage, right?"

"The Swarm...they came to the school because of this skull?" She shook her head. "That doesn't make sense. They're only a mindless...swarm."

"But everything's connected. It's the only thing that makes sense, Raven. I overheard Gilliam telling Bixby what you saw. If the Swarm ignored everything else in the kingdom to get here, it means those giant bugs are looking for something—intentionally. What else is here?"

"Bixby didn't freak out because I brought the skull." Her eyes widened and she stepped back to stare at the eyeless Swarm relic on the ground. "She didn't want me to cast a spell that would draw that skull's history up in her class."

Bella gave her another determined smile. "It's worth a try, right?"

"Yeah, at least."

The clash of Swarm Razorbacks against the soldiers and mages on the other side of the barn continued. The defenders shouted warnings and commands at one another and horses reared and whinnied. Another spray of earth erupted and pelted the stables.

Fire can kill them. This skull had better burn.

Raven looked at Leander and nodded. He'd obviously waited for her go-ahead, and the red dragon drew his head back like a snake coiling to strike and unleashed a massive column of fire at the skull.

The two girls stepped hastily away from the blaze. Another bellow wailed from beyond the fighting beetles, and it was much closer.

"What the hell was that?" a soldier shouted.

"Hold, men! Hold!"

When the flames faded, her stomach sank. "It's not working."

"Try again."

Leander didn't need another prompting and responded

365

with another fiery exhalation. Bella's firedrake swooped to land at the girl's feet before he added his round of flames to the blaze. When they finished, she clenched her fists.

"I don't get it! That would have melted the whole dragon pen. Why is this skull still here?" She kicked it in frustration, but it barely moved. A trace of smoke curled from the toe of her boot. "How are we supposed to destroy this?"

"The same way the war mages and dragon riders destroyed it the first time," Bella said and gazed at the unharmed skull. "No one could do it on their own."

Raven sucked in a sharp breath. "The Magic Meld."

The girls looked at each other with wide eyes. "I know you rememorized it," Bella said.

"Yeah. But many mages didn't make it after casting that spell, Bella."

"Well, we're only two mages casting it on a skull. What's the worst that could happen?"

She gestured in vague surrender and fixed her companion with a resigned look. "Famous last words." *If this doesn't work, I guess it won't matter how angry anyone is at me.* "Okay, let's do it."

Leander snorted and stepped closer to her. "A familiar strengthens your magic, Raven."

"Well, get ready for a massive power-up, then." She reached for Bella's hand and gritted her teeth. "I'm ready when you are."

The girl slapped her hand into hers without a second's hesitation, and they tightened their grasp. Together, they raised their other hands toward the skull and recited the lengthy, complicated spell Connor Alby never wanted his granddaughter to learn.

A jolt of warm energy pulsed from their clasped hands. The buzz tingled up Raven's arms toward her shoulder, through her chest, and down into her other hand. Leander reared and filled his belly with fire before he unleashed it on the skull. The column of flames was ten times hotter, which made both young mages take a few steps back. Neither of them faltered in the spell.

Come on...

Above them, one of the wheeling dragons uttered a piercing shriek. It cut off abruptly and was followed moments later by a wet crunch. The other dragon rider cried out in horror.

The flames rushed from Leander's mouth and were joined by Wesley's, who now hovered beside Bella. The girls' clasped hands felt like they were on fire too, but they tightened their hold on one another. The colors of the red and orange dragon fire shifted and the blazing glow melted into a deep, dark-blue and grew steadily lighter and brighter, now streaked with white.

Raven could no longer feel Bella's hand or the heat of the flames.

When the dragon's fire faded and petered into a burst of thick smoke from her dragon's mouth, she thought for a second that she'd lost her hearing, too.

The field was entirely silent. The sounds of scuttling beetle legs and large Swarm monstrosities thrusting from the ground were gone. She released a shaky sigh and turned to look at Bella. The other girl's face was completely white, but a tiny smile lifted the corner of her mouth. "It worked."

The skull was gone, reduced to a pile of black, smoking ash.

Her fingers slipped out of her companion's hand, and she couldn't hold herself up any longer. *Why is it so quiet out there? Were we too late?*

CHAPTER THIRTY-EIGHT

The stunned soldiers and mages still standing on the school grounds gazed around in amazement. The field was covered in massive Swarm carcasses as if they'd dropped from the sky. The last one near the front toppled onto its side like the others and didn't even twitch.

"Are they..." A soldier stepped forward bravely and hacked at the closest beetle with his sword with no alarming response.

"They dropped. Just like that." Professor Worley's eyebrows lifted and disappeared under the shaggy hair that fell over his eyes. He ran his hand over his hair and turned toward Headmaster Flynn.

The man running Fowler Academy swept his gaze over the horde of dead and fallen Swarm monsters he'd hoped never to see again in his life. His eyes twitched as he searched for movement among the unnatural bodies. *They're not smart enough to play dead. Nothing stops them like this.*

"Headmaster?"

A startling bellow rose from the other side of the stables. The surviving army that had hastily joined Fowler Academy's professors turned quickly toward the sound. Leander bellowed again and barreled around the side of his pen. "Help her!"

Flynn launched into action and sprinted toward the distressed dragon, followed quickly by Worley and Fellows. Brighton's soldiers erupted in cheers. They laughed at their unexpected victory by default and raised swords, bows, and shields toward the night sky. The remaining dragon landed in front of the dead horde of the Swarm and snorted smoke as she and her rider mourned their fallen companion.

When the headmaster reached Leander, the dragon growled but stepped aside. "Over there."

"Raven!" Aiden Flynn rushed toward the young mage who sprawled in the grass. Her red braid caught enough starlight to be recognizable. "And Bella Chase. You…" He turned to look at Leander. "What happened?"

"They saved your lives," he rumbled.

Startled, the headmaster looked around and his gaze settled on the smoking pile of ash, the empty drawstring bag in the grass beside Bella, and the girls' hands outstretched toward each other as if they'd been clasped together. "In all my days… They did it." He turned to Worley and Fellows and gestured them forward. "Get these young mages out of here and into the infirmary. Quickly."

When Professor Worley stooped to pick Bella up in his arms, her firedrake familiar jumped onto his mage's chest and curled in her lap. The man nodded and turned away as

Professor Fellows scooped Raven up and hurried after the others.

Headmaster Flynn stood and turned to face the great red dragon who stared after Raven. The army across the field still celebrated their victory and none of them paid any attention to the two professors who carried unconscious teenage girls to the main buildings of Fowler Academy.

"Leander." He inclined his head toward the dragon, who looked away from the open field to meet his gaze. "She deliberately disobeyed my instruction."

"Yes."

"You helped her."

"Always." The massive wings twitched out but settled quickly against his back. He stretched his neck to look around the headmaster again, then gave up and fixed Flynn with his wide, cautious yellow eyes.

"And she almost got herself and Bella Chase killed with magic I told them both to forget."

Leander snorted. "You're worse at saying thank you than I am, dragon rider."

The headmaster stared in surprise before he uttered a quick, sharp laugh. "I suppose that's because I'm rather out of practice in this type of situation. But I will say I've missed a dragon's honesty. It's been a long time."

"Not so long that you've forgotten her," Leander said and narrowed his eyes.

Flynn took a breath and held it. "No. I could live forever and not forget my dragon. We're quite fortunate that you two found each other, Leander."

"Will she be all right?"

"In a few days, I think. But yes. Your mage will be up and running around with you again in no time. And, I daresay, telling the story of tonight far more times than she wants to. Well done."

With a snort, Leander lowered himself and settled his massive head on his forepaws. His large yellow eyes remained narrowed, but he said nothing more.

Headmaster Flynn nodded at the dragon before he turned and walked around the stables toward the stunned and relieved army of Brighton's finest. *They've proven themselves enough. That dragon doesn't need to be in a pen any more than Raven Alby does.*

Raven woke in the infirmary with a pounding headache. *Why?* She sat up quickly and groaned at the sharply increased pain. She closed her eyes briefly against the bright light, then turned to look at Bella who lay in the bed beside her.

"It's about time you woke up," the girl muttered and closed her eyes with a sigh. "If you tell me everything hurts, I'll know I'm supposed to feel this awful."

With a grimace, she rubbed her head and tried to focus. "Wait. Did we do it? Did it work?"

"Don't yell." Her companion groaned. "What's wrong with you?"

"We did it, right? The spell and the skull." A tiny smile grew on her lips before her head pounded with another wave of pain. "Of course we did. There wouldn't be an infirmary if we hadn't succeeded. There wouldn't even be a school."

"Raven, stop talking—"

The door opened swiftly, and both girls scrunched their eyes against the loud noise and the rush of people who entered the room.

"Look who's returned," Professor Fellows said with a chuckle.

Bella groaned again and shut her eyes. "Everyone has to be so loud, don't they?"

Raven bit her bottom lip and glanced at the professors who had filed into the infirmary, all of them smiling in varying degrees—even Headmaster Flynn, who tugged on his graying beard and studied her in amusement. "What happened with the Swarm?" she asked.

"They were wiped out, Miss Alby." The headmaster nodded. "You and Miss Chase succeeded in accomplishing something very few mages attempt in their entire lives and something many mages died trying to perform. But your theory was exactly right."

"It killed them all?" Bella asked, her eyes open now although she stared at the ceiling.

"All of them," Professor Gilliam added.

"This wouldn't have been possible with merely any two mages." When Professor Bixby clapped, Bella grimaced again and swallowed through the pain. "Two young mages from two extraordinarily powerful bloodlines worked together with their familiars. And one spell. Your pasts caught up with you both the other night, and I daresay that was the only thing that would have accomplished what you girls did."

"None of us saw this coming, Miss Alby." Flynn nodded. "Not truly. We weren't ready for a second siege by the Swarm because, in my opinion, this kingdom wanted nothing more than to forget the past that led us to this point in time. I can only speak for myself when I say I wanted to forget. Thank you both for reminding us that avoiding what we do not wish to see is never an option."

"Only if you don't mind dying," Bella muttered. "Or feeling like you're dying."

"It's a small price to pay, Miss Chase, I'm sure."

"That's easy for you to say."

His smile widened at the girls as he looked slowly from one to the other. "A small price now, yes. Especially for saving this school and your fellow students and who knows how many others who were threatened the other night. You took it upon yourselves to ignore your professors and put yourselves in life-threatening danger—which is why you'll also be given detention for the next week."

"What?" Bella bolted upright and grunted, her fists clenched around the blanket over her legs. "We wiped out the rest of the Swarm and you're punishing us?"

"Every decision has its consequence, Miss Chase. It's nothing you can't handle. And maybe you'll think twice about taking matters into your own hands next time. Good day." Headmaster Flynn nodded, turned on his heel, and strode across the infirmary before he vanished into the hall.

Bixby chuckled and clapped again. Worley, Fellows, and Gilliam darted the girls sly glances of approval and gratitude and followed the headmaster out without a word.

"Detention." Bella's eyelids fluttered before she turned slowly to glare at Raven. "Thanks a lot."

"Oh, that's right. I'm the only one who broke the rules." Raven rolled her eyes but smiled anyway. "And I couldn't have done it without you."

"I can't believe this is happening right now." The other girl eased gingerly onto her pillow and shook her head. "Don't expect me to appear every time you need help breaking the rules, Raven. That's not how I do things."

"Got it." Raven rubbed her pounding forehead and sighed. "Thanks for making an exception."

"You're welcome. I guess."

A few hours later, Henry poked his head through the infirmary door with a grin. "Hey, I'm looking for a war mage who single-handedly brought down the Swarm…this time."

"Not single-handedly, Derks." Raven pushed to a seated position as Bella rolled her eyes, turned over, and drew another pillow over her ears. "I had help. We both did." She nodded at her companion, and Henry tiptoed across the room.

"I'll be quiet, then."

"Not quiet enough," the other girl muttered.

"How are you feeling, Alby? You sure look like you almost died."

"How sweet of you."

He laughed. "Man, I wish I'd been there to see it! The Swarm. The army. Headmaster Flynn leading the mages." He settled into a chair beside her bed and leaned forward with a grin. "That must've been something."

"Yeah, that's one way to put it. But everyone's okay, right?" *Minus the people who didn't make it.*

"Oh, yeah. Sure. People keep talking and talking about what they think happened. Flynn had a little gathering to explain the situation. I don't think he gets it that telling us the story doesn't keep people from, you know…improving it a little."

"More rumors, huh?" She rolled her shoulders and tried to stretch. "Ow. Yeah, I feel like I almost died."

"But you didn't." Henry nudged her shoulder with his fist. "And they're not rumors, per se. More like imaginative retellings. Some people took a little more creative liberty than others."

Laughing, Raven shook her head. "Like what?"

"Like you and Leander shooting fire at every single beetle lying out there to kill them one at a time. And I think there was something about a flaming sword…I don't know the details, though."

"Oh, jeez. It's gonna take a ton of work to set the record straight."

Henry winked at her. "Enjoy it while you can, Alby. Honestly, I'm a little hurt that none of the other stories I've heard mention me even once. Can you believe that? Your best friend was tossed right out of the picture."

"You should be glad you weren't there, Henry. It wasn't as awesome as it sounds."

"That's easy for you to say, war mage." He smiled at her, leaned back in the chair, and looked out the window. "You know, when I heard that they'd brought you to the infirmary, Maxwell and I tried to sneak in. A toad has an affinity for healing, right? Man, Professor Gilliam runs a tight ship around here. She caught us and kicked us out. Twice."

Raven chuckled. "Well, even if she doesn't, I appreciate the fact that you tried."

"It's the thought that counts, I guess, huh? Hey, I saw Professor Worley dragging one of those dead beetles into the barn this morning. I think he's gonna try to take it apart and study it. Or make us study it." With a little shiver, he shook his head and shrugged. "Either way, I'm proud of you, Raven. And yeah, I guess Bella with an H gets a little credit."

The girl snorted, her back still turned toward them. "There's no H in my name."

He shrugged and the two friends shared a knowing smile. "Yeah, maybe not. My bad."

Bella mumbled something about being at this school without knowing how to spell, and Henry choked down another laugh.

"Does William know about what happened?"

"I'm reasonably sure all of Brighton and the three closest towns know by now. But yeah. William came by to take a look at that other dragon. The one that...made it. And you were still knocked out when he was here, so he said he'd wait until you and Leander made it to the ranch." He frowned. "It's kinda weird the way he said it. Like he knew you'd be coming back anyway. Hey, it must be a dragon-riding thing, huh?"

"I guess so." Raven took a deep breath. *We need to visit William and Teo at the first chance we get.* "Hey, how's Leander doing?" She frowned at her friend. "It's been a few days, right? He's been fed and everything?"

"Yeah, Worley's got that covered."

"Good. It's not like anyone could forget he's there. But does he seem okay?"

"Leander?" Henry scratched his head. "He's been a little tired and grumpy. I tried to say hi to him yesterday. You know, to let him know that you're okay. He told me to go play with my toad. So I guess he's fine."

She chuckled. "That sounds about right."

"Don't take my word for it, though. He's your dragon."

With a grin, she nodded at her best friend and took a deep breath. "He sure is." *And I think he might actually be able to read my mind after the other night.* She frowned when a thought occurred to her. "Wait, how did Worley get into Leander's pen to feed him?"

His eyed widened and he grinned. "He didn't. Fowler Academy has its very own resident dragon simply hanging out by the barns. No pen. No lead."

"No saddle…" Raven smiled at the memory of it. *We did it. There's no way Leander will let me put that on him again after that.*

"Yeah, you know, I heard about that," Henry said. "People are gonna start thinking you have a death wish."

"Nope. Only a dragon familiar."

CHAPTER THIRTY-NINE

The old mage veteran Peter slipped quietly along the perimeter of the soldiers stationed at the wall. *And they think this many men in armor can keep out what's coming for us.* He snorted and cast a wary glance toward the troops before he looked at the starry sky overhead. *The Swarm was only the end of the beginning. No one's paying attention to the real danger.*

Hidden by the darkness, his cloak, and the wide-brimmed hat, Peter paused now and then when those guarding the wall turned toward him. As usual, they didn't see him. *No one ever sees the crazy old veteran who spouts useless crap about the end of the world. Not until it's too late.*

Finally, he reached the massive hole in the great wall surrounding the kingdom of Lomberdoon. "I watched them build this useless thing," he whispered. "And now I get to watch it fail. It's too much for one life, old man." Shaking his head, he climbed over the rubble that hadn't yet been cleared. "Too much."

Finding a relatively comfortable section of broken stone to lean against, he took a deep breath and pulled up what little magic he had left. "Save it until you need it, isn't that right? *Visus abstemia.*"

A shimmering circle of light appeared in his hand, and he curled his fingers around it like a telescope before he raised it to his eye. The spell allowed him to see farther than anyone else in the kingdom—across valleys and hills, past the abandoned satellite ranches, and through forests. He panned slowly from side to side, searching, then stopped.

With a little hiss, Peter grimaced and forced himself to watch. "Raiders. Oh, sure, they're camped now, but in the morning, they'll know exactly where to go to find an easy way beyond this wall. Thanks to the giant hole right —oh, no."

He adjusted the spell and looked again as he swept his magical telescope to capture every detail. Finally, he forced himself to look farther, beyond the first encampment, and his old heart raced. He clutched his chest and dragged in a sharp breath. "All of them. Every tribe, every war family— they're all together. And you know they'll clamber over these boulders in a few days. The next thing you know, they'll sail in across the sea from Malenspire and the Grimshale Isles—"

"Hey, Melrose. Did you hear something?"

"Nothing but your severely off-tune whistling. Is there anything left in the gruel pot? I haven't eaten yet."

Peter hunched his shoulders, canceled his spell, and turned to verify that the soldiers on patrol still hadn't seen him. *It won't matter soon anyway. But I can't do what I came to do if they stop me first.*

The men passed without even pausing to look through the gaping hole in the kingdom's alleged protection. The old wizard pressed his lips together and glanced out across the open fields beyond the wall again. *It's time to send the signal. You knew this was coming, old man, and no one wanted to listen. Well, we'll give them something they can't ignore, won't we?*

Slowly, he clambered over the boulders, moved through the shadows, and stopped beside the wall with enough open space for his next—and maybe last—act of service to the kingdom. With his eyes closed, he took a deep breath and conjured the spell every mage in his order had been taught for times such as these.

He pushed his hands together and felt them grow warm. The tingling rushed up his arms as he muttered the spell and focused. After a few moments, he squatted with a grunt and pressed both hands against the cold earth beneath him.

The force of his spell knocked him onto his backside when it burst from the earth. A column of brilliant green light erupted into the sky, flashed vividly, and illuminated the entire encampment only a few yards away. The air filled with a rumble like thunder and the searing green light lit up the old veteran's eyes as he stared at the mages' signal.

Soldiers shouted in surprise, and one of them caught sight of the crazy spent wizard sprawled on the ground. "Hey, piss off, old man. Go on. It's not safe out here." The man sneered at him and couldn't decide whether to chase the beggar off or stay well away from the pillar of green magic that streaked into the sky.

Peter scrambled to his feet and backed away from the light. *You can't ignore what's almost upon us. I only hope the others out there are watching too. If they get my message, we might have a chance.*

CHAPTER FORTY

Two days later, the two girls were cleared to leave the infirmary and return to their everyday lives of classes, studying, and being teenage mages in training.

"That's a relief." Raven brushed her hair out of her eyes and slipped her feet into her boots.

"Don't get too comfortable with that relief," Bella muttered and shrugged into her jacket. "It's not gonna be as easy as you think trying to get ahead in classes now. Not with everyone talking about the Swarm and your dragon and whatever else they think is so important."

"It's not that bad, Bella." She smiled at the girl, who merely rolled her eyes.

"I have actual studying to do. It's been a real blast sharing a room with you for four days. But now, we can finally put it behind us."

Biting her lip, she tried not to laugh as she followed her companion to the door. *She's only trying to save face. I give her a week before she appears at my dorm room to ask about those journals again.*

Before the girl could step out into the hall, Headmaster Flynn appeared in the doorway and looked very pleased with himself. "Excellent. You're both looking quite well and ready to get out of here, I see."

"Who wouldn't be?" Bella stared at the headmaster, then glanced behind him into the hall, hesitant to ask him to move.

"What's going on?" Raven asked.

Flynn raised his eyebrows. "There's been a slight change in your schedules today, young mages. Follow me." He turned and led them out into the hall.

Bella scoffed and glanced over her shoulder to glare at her. "Now what did you do?"

"What?" She laughed. "I've been in a bed next to you for days. I didn't do anything."

"Hurry, please," the man called.

They followed him through the stone halls of the school's main building until they passed through the great hall and out the front doors. The headmaster walked so quickly that Raven almost had to jog to keep up. "Head-master Flynn," she called. "I didn't have a chance to ask you about—"

"There's been no word from your grandfather, Miss Alby, if that's what you're wondering. Though I'm certain he's caught wind of the events from several nights ago." The man didn't even turn to look at her.

Okay, it's a little creepy that he knew exactly what I was about to ask.

The girls shared a confused glance when he led them under the stone archway and out into the fields. "Wait."

Bella hurried to catch up with him. "Headmaster, shouldn't we get to class? We've missed enough days already and I don't want to fall behind any more than I already am. What are we doing out here?"

"I believe I mentioned both of you receiving detention for a week, did I not?"

"What?" She stopped short and glared at Raven when she caught up. "Great. Now I get to miss even more classes because of you."

"Hey, I didn't hold a knife to your throat and tell you to steal a skull from his office and cast a dangerous spell with me to stop the Swarm. You make your own choices, Bella. Exactly like I made mine."

"And look where they got us."

Still, the girls had no choice but to follow the head-master past the barn and toward the open door into the stables. They paused when he opened the doors and stepped inside, and he waved them forward without turning. "Don't just stand there. Detention won't suffer itself."

Raven sighed. *Great. We saved the school and we get thanked for it by having to muck out the stalls every day. And miss more classes.*

Headmaster Flynn stopped in the center of the stables and finally turned to face them. "This is the consequence for not doing as you're told. Every day at this time, both of you are expected to be right here. As for your missed classes, I have no doubt about your ability to make up the rest of your classes on your own time. Speak with your professors. Make up the lessons and assignments. But do not for one moment think that I will tolerate either of you trying to skip this. You are talented mages. It's time to take some responsibility for that talent. Excuse me."

The man brushed past them again, his hands clasped behind his back, and he left without another word.

"What the hell are we supposed to do here?" Bella spread her arms and turned full circle as she glanced at the stalls and the supply crates of feed against the far wall beside the tack. "He didn't even give us a starting point."

"Maybe that's the point," Raven suggested. "We're supposed to figure it out?"

A shadow fell across the open doorway, and the girls turned as a tall, thin woman stopped in the aperture. Her gray hair was twisted into a neat bun on the top of her head, and she wore the same kind of military uniform Raven had seen on Brighton's general. She stood with her hands clasped behind her back and raised an eyebrow at the mages in training. "Follow me, please."

The woman turned and left like the headmaster had, and Raven wrinkled her nose. "Have you ever seen her before?"

"Nope." Bella brushed past her to step out of the stables. *What the hell is going on?*

When they joined the woman, she nodded at them and didn't bother to smile. "My name is Alessandra Barnasis. You may call me ma'am. In light of recent events, I've been ordered to come all the way out here to the outskirts of Brighton for the two of you."

The girls glanced at each other. Bella swallowed. "For punishment?"

Alessandra inclined her head. "If that's how you want to think of it, fine."

Leander walked calmly from around the other side of the pen and approached the woman. Raven grinned and he snorted in greeting. Alessandra jumped a little and twisted to look over her shoulder at the huge red dragon who walked up behind her. She smiled and seemed to recognize him, then turned toward the young mages and cleared her throat.

She's not even a little worried to see him that close.

Bella leaned toward her and whispered, "Look at her shoulder."

With a frown, she complied and froze in surprise. *She's wearing a war mage patch.*

"Since you two are so insistent upon sticking your noses into what two young mages in training have no business doing, we're setting up something different for you here at Fowler." Alessandra eyed Leander as he moved around her toward Raven but didn't react more than that. "And I'll be your instructor for your new class."

Bella folded her arms and tilted her head. "You mean detention."

"No, Miss Chase. I mean training for you and Miss Alby both. As war mages."

The End

Raven Alby has been sent to represent Fowler Academy and learn diplomacy, explore a new city in a distant part of the kingdom. But will the marauding raiders find them?

Will Raven, mage in training, and her frenemy Bella be enough to protect their temporary home? Find out in *WarMage: Uncontrolled*!

Get sneak peeks, exclusive giveaways, behind the scenes content, and more.
PLUS you'll be notified of special **one day only fan pricing** on new releases.

Sign up today to get free stories.

CLICK HERE

or visit: https://marthacarr.com/read-free-stories/

Have you started the Goth Drow series from Martha and Michael? Book one is Once Upon A Midnight Drow and it's available now through Amazon and Kindle Unlimited.

I'm not Goth to hide my Drow heritage, I'm Goth because I'm not a quitter.

My name is Cheyenne Summerlin, remember that name. Somebody should…

The world can't know I'm a Drow halfling. Not yet. I

barely have these powers under my control, but time's up. I'm about to take magic for a test drive. Want to come along?

The black ops government group believe they can run my life... But I have plans of my own.

Watch out magical evil doers – I'm about to crash your party.

But will my training be enough?

Grab your copy today from Amazon or Kindle Unlimited.

AUTHOR NOTES - MARTHA CARR

MARCH 22, 2020

Author notes from the time of the Corona virus. From inside the bunker – also known as my dream house. Things could be worse. I've actually been in some kind of isolation for weeks before everyone else because I had pneumonia. Weird timing, but there's a lot about this year that's weird.

I've been trying to make sure there's enough of things, just in case. Not get to hoarder levels and not let things run out and create an unnecessary crisis for myself, or someone else.

The easiest way to take care of things is to look to online sources. For myself, I turned to Hungry Root. It's a healthy choice that can accommodate special needs and they have some pretty tasty things. For the good dog, Lois Lane and the sweet pittie, Leela I ordered from Chewy.com.

Fun fact, when you order from Chewy, everything comes in a much larger size. Okay, okay, I didn't read the fine print. Frankly, I was in the middle of a hacking coughing spell and it was late at night and I was more interested in seeing when it would all come.

Five days later, two huge boxes arrived... What is this? One of the boxes I had to do that crouched over, teeter totter just to get it inside. So much for trying not to touch outside things. I had to do the full body wrap to pick it up. Fortunately, I'm freakishly strong and whipped that box inside before the dogs had a chance to make a run for it. They're unaware of social distancing and would still like to meet everyone.

Inside was a forty-pound bag of dog food. Bigger than I've ever seen in the grocery stores. And the treats I ordered – enough for two weeks, just in case – were also super-sized. Is this the cosmos telling me it's gonna be more like a month?

Things are going reasonably well here on my small frontline. The neighbors all post on our FB group when they have something they can share or when they need something. I have a few projects to play with that I can now get to and feel like I emerged with something done. And I'm reading chapters from some of my new books every day at 1 pm CST from my Facebook author page. Plus, like a lot of other people I've set up regular Zoom get togethers and I take long, slow walks, crossing the street when I approach someone else. It all helps and some of it is very weird.

It's cool to see how much everyone is offering up their talents to share with others both locally and nationally. I hope that continues after we are all set loose again. And I cannot WAIT to hug so many of you this November in Vegas on Fan Day. I will be loaded down with troll paraphernalia (pins, stickers) and some Bernie stuff too. Until then, everyone please stay safe, be kind to yourself and others and reach out often. We'll get through this one day at a time – together. Love you all. More adventures to follow.

THANK YOU for reading our story! We have a few of these planned, but we don't know if we should continue writing and publishing without your input. Options include leaving a review, reaching out on Facebook to let us know, and smoke signals.

Frankly, smoke signals might get misconstrued as low hanging clouds, so you might want to nix that idea.

Of course, if you ARE in the land of the Warmage, I imagine smoke signals would be at least a little appropriate.

Personally, I'm waiting for the awesome VR graphics that allow me to enjoy walking around a fantasy land, where we see a flight of dragons way up in the sky.

Damn, that would be so cool...

Diary week of March 22 to March 28th, 2020

I live on the Strip in Las Vegas, and it is presently one week since I got back from London and five days since most of the hotel-casinos on the Strip shut down due to the efforts to constrain Covid-19.

I live next to the Aria, beside the Cosmopolitan and across the street (and a block or two down) from the MGM Grand and New York New York casinos.

The Aria and New York New York are important because the restaurants I frequent are inside them. You know, inside where I can't get to them for take-out anymore?

Presently, it is 1:30 in the afternoon, and traffic on Las Vegas Blvd (always a mess on Friday nights and Saturday afternoons) *is not a mess.*

In fact, the whole Strip is about 95% shut down. There are a few restaurants open including Giordano's (we are helping them stay open to help pay a few workers), McDonald's, (a hot dog place in front of Bally's, I can't remember the name, but I purchase a Mexican Coke every time I am over there), and also Wahlburgers, plus any CVS or Walgreens, which seem to occur every few blocks near my place.

I have a theory about why we have any traffic on the main Strip.

Theory: People from outside the Strip here in Las Vegas (think Henderson or Red Rock area) are taking a drive to see the closed Strip. The expectation of no cars traveling up and down the Strip is not a thing because of sightseers driving in to see the absence of cars, and since they are now here, there are cars.

Well, it's a theory.

This morning, I went up and down the Strip, buying a little from each of the stores, trying to give everyone a bit of business. Cleaning hands wherever I went as I walked through the stores looking for TP or anything we might be able to use that didn't require refrigeration until I got *sold* on buying frozen dinners.

So, how did that happen? I'm glad you asked.

I purchased this food from a Walgreens across the street because the manager personally showed me the Walgreens app and the items in the freezer on sale. I tried to show her what I was *already* carrying, which was a few bags. I explained I was walking back and couldn't carry very much more.

She told me to take the little shopping cart on wheels and just return it.

I stared at her, she stared back at me. *That was the final straw. She broke me.* I had to buy from her at that point. Who else gets to take the carts out of the store and bring them back?

I bought more than I technically needed at that store, and I WILL be going back. Not just to return the cart (it's so damned cute!), but also to support them and their efforts to stay open when the Strip is closed for business.

I wish I had a larger freezer to help them out.

However, I hit two CVS stores and two Walgreens, plus a Target, and I scored one roll of tissue paper among all five of them. That's not a package containing 4, 12, 16, or 24 rolls. No, it was *a single roll* from all five stores.

They had about thirty single rolls on the shelf, so I took my one and felt like I had just been hunting and downed a 14-point buck at 200 yards through trees so thick it looked like a fence.

(Is fourteen points a good-sized deer rack? I really don't

know as I don't hunt. If you were nodding your head with my story and thinking, *that's a hell of a deer!* remember, I am *paid* to lie for a living. It's a good life.)

If you live here in Las Vegas, remember that the little (*expensive*) stores on the Strip have way fewer shoppers. One of our people inside LMBPN mentioned that no one remembers that truck stops often have toilet paper. I tried that.

They didn't have any.

(*Editor's Note: We did too, same results*)

I suppose it is possible there is a different side of the store than the one I went into to find the elusive TP. Where I looked, it was a seriously small shelf space that was empty. *Hmmm.*

I should have called Stephen Russell (Author S.R. Russell), who was a truck driver for a few decades to ask him before I left there empty-handed the other day. Well, *not* empty-handed. They had buy 1 get 1 free on M&M's.

I figured, why the hell not? We might need protein (peanuts), emotional healing (chocolate), and calories (sugar) in order to survive the next few weeks.

There, if you needed an excuse to buy Peanut M&Ms, you're welcome. If you don't, I applaud your lack of concern when purchasing junk food. I had to give myself a reason to load up on them.

I've used that damned 'sugar is calories' excuse a LOT in the last seven days.

Take, for example, the following 'food' I purchased using the "sugar is calories" excuse.

It has *Mike* in the name. How can I not support *THAT???*

For now, we here in the Cave in the Sky™ are doing fine.

Neither the wife or I have tried to suffocate each other yet, nor have we tried to toss each other out of the windows. Fortunately, I purchased a mattress topper a month ago to put on my couch in the office for naps. If I need to, I can hang out here if the wife starts to moan...

BRAIINNNZZZZ.

All joking aside, this is a new time in our world. The challenges we have encountered will be overcome, and the new society that comes out the other side will be interesting. It's time for those who can to help those who need it.

For those who need help, raise a hand when your neighbors ask.

I am grateful to you, our readers, who consume our books.

Ad Aeternitatem,

Michael Anderle

BOOKS BY MARTHA CARR

Series in the Oriceran Universe:

SCHOOL OF NECESSARY MAGIC
SCHOOL OF NECESSARY MAGIC: RAINE CAMPBELL
ALISON BROWNSTONE
THE DANIEL CODEX SERIES
THE LEIRA CHRONICLES
I FEAR NO EVIL
FEDERAL AGENTS OF MAGIC
SCIONS OF MAGIC
THE UNBELIEVABLE MR. BROWNSTONE
REWRITING JUSTICE
THE KACY CHRONICLES
MIDWEST MAGIC CHRONICLES
SOUL STONE MAGE
THE FAIRHAVEN CHRONICLES

Series in The Terranavis Universe:

The Adventures of Maggie Parker Series
The Adventures of Finnegan Dragonbender
The Witches of Pressler Street

OTHER BOOKS BY JUDITH BERENS

OTHER BOOKS BY MARTHA CARR

JOIN THE ORICERAN UNIVERSE FAN GROUP ON FACEBOOK!

BOOKS BY MICHAEL ANDERLE

For a complete list of books by Michael Anderle, please visit:

www.lmbpn.com/ma-books/

All LMBPN Audiobooks are Available at Audible.com and iTunes

To see all LMBPN audiobooks, including those written by
Michael Anderle please visit:

www.lmbpn.com/audible